INHUMAN

DAVID SIMPSON

INHUMAN

Cover illustration by Jennifer Simpson
Interior design and layout by Jennifer Simpson

ISBN: 1499223358
ISBN-13: 978-1499223354

www.post-humannovel.com

Give feedback on the book at:
posthumanmedia@gmail.com

ACKNOWLEDGMENTS

I want to thank Céline March-Helgen and Karl-Mikael Syding for their incredibly kind help to make *Inhuman* as polished as any of the books in the *Post-Human* series. You guys are amazing!

And, as always, I want to thank my wife, Jenny, who is the greatest wife in this universe and all other universes as well.

PART 1

...we know what we are, but know not what we may be

—WILLIAM SHAKESPEARE

1

"WAKE UP!"

Old-timer hadn't even opened his eyes before the visage of Aldous Gibson appeared before him in his mind's eye. "What the hell?" he whispered as he opened his eyes, the real world and his darkened bedroom suddenly appearing, with Gibson's face still overlaid on top.

"Craig, don't speak. You'll wake Daniella. I'm waiting for you on your roof. Get dressed and come out. I need to speak with you urgently."

Old-timer's eyes were wide; nevertheless, he felt a grogginess that was unfamiliar to him. He'd been woken from the wrong sleep cycle, so his usual refreshed morning demeanor was elusive. He pulled his legs out of the bed, making sure not to wake his wife, then pulled a pair of loose-fitting pants on before heading out the front door of the old-style farmhouse he shared with her.

The night was almost perfectly still. The sky was clear and speckled with stars, and Old-timer had to shake his head to make sure he wasn't caught in a dream. He checked the time readout on his mind's eye; it read 3:15 a.m. "What the hell?" he repeated to himself. He looked overhead at the edge of his roof, then let the multitude of appendages unfurl from his torso, dozens of tiny fingers grabbing the tiles like suction cups. Once he had a good grip, he picked himself up, swung over the top, and set himself down on the dark rooftop, just a few meters from the chief of the governing council.

Aldous's eyes narrowed as he watched Old-timer's unorthodox entrance. "Very interesting," he commented. "Sticking with your new enhancements, I see," he observed as Old-timer's suctioned wire-like appendages released their hold on the roof. "No pun intended."

The appendages furled back up into Old-timer's torso and melded perfectly with his skin, as if by magic, allowing the post-human to again take on his distinct, human appearance. "They're useful. It's a good upgrade. What's going on, Aldous?"

"You didn't wake Daniella, did you?"

"No. She's still sleeping, which is what I should be doing. What the heck is so—"

"I'm sorry, old friend," Aldous replied, his smile returning as he apologized, holding his hands up as if to plead for forgiveness and understanding. "I wouldn't disturb you unless it was of the utmost importance. There are things happening that…" he trailed off, not sure how to word what needed to be said. "Well, they just can't happen, Craig. They *can't.*"

Old-timer blinked hard, then scratched the back of his head, nearly flummoxed. "Well, Aldous, you've certainly got my attention. Mind sharing what's going on?"

Aldous stepped away from Old-timer and began to pace slowly, almost nervously. He spoke again, folding his arms and bowing his head as he uttered, "Do you remember…do you remember the day I arranged for you to mentor James?"

"Mentor?" Old-timer held his hands up before smiling at the absurdity. "No one can *mentor* James—maybe the A.I., but certainly no human. I *do* remember the day you arranged for me to work with him though."

"Semantics," Aldous retorted, waving away Old-timer's point. "That day, I asked you to do something for me. Do you remember what it was?" Aldous asked, his eyes scrutinizing.

Old-timer took in a deep breath and searched his memory. "Yeah. You wanted me to try keep him focused on terraforming, to keep him away from getting too curious about Planck technology."

"That's right," Aldous said, his voice soaked with relief. "I'm glad you remember."

"But, look, Aldous, don't you think we're a little beyond that now?" Old-timer asked. "James and the A.I. are...well, they're *way* beyond us. They've transcended to a new level. If you're suggesting that I try to distract a mind like that—"

"No," Aldous interrupted, "of course not. That would be impossible. But, as for the Planck…well, that knowledge will be new to him. Enhanced or not, James has to know how dangerous it is."

"The A.I. already knows—"

"No, he really doesn't," Aldous interrupted again, waving away Old-timer's contention. "Besides, he's bound by a promise to me, just like you are. He *has,* however, related to me that he won't prevent James, or this new Trans-human intelligence, from uncovering the *true* nature of our universe."

"Because he obviously believes James can handle it," Old-timer observed.

Aldous's lips tightened into a grim line. "There's no room for belief here, Craig. Listen, I'm not asking you to deceive him. What I'm asking you, my friend, is to be the voice of reason he needs. He won't listen to me. The A.I. is obviously planning to carry out its mandate to transfer power to a more powerful A.I. and believes knowledge can only be good. And James is being carried away by his own enthusiasm and genius. I'm afraid there's nothing stopping them now, Craig...and that's something we should be *very* concerned with."

"Why? For goodness sakes, it's James. He and the A.I. have never failed us. They've always given everything for—"

"No bed of roses is entirely devoid of thorns," Aldous said, cutting Old-timer off again. He looked up into the beautiful night sky, and his eyes latched onto the object that hung in the blackness like a white elephant, the giant armada of androids. They'd obeyed James's demand to leave the solar system, but they parked themselves on the boundary. The collective was so huge that it was visible as a tiny smudge in the night sky, appearing like a nearby galaxy. Aldous gestured to the spot with his hand. "Or do you need a reminder?"

Old-timer looked up at the luminescent smear in the cosmos and grimaced. It was true; things were not all roses. He and Aldous were standing on the flat-deck of his roof, on a beautiful, open plain that stretched to the horizon in all directions. He should've felt safe there, distanced from problems that were on a galactic scale—problems that seemed to be the domain of the new gods, James, and the A.I. and the impending, almost infinite intelligence of Trans-human. Yet there they were, standing with that night sky above them, as though all of space sat precariously atop their shoulders, weighing them down, threatening to crush them. "James and the A.I. can handle the androids," Old-timer finally answered.

"A fact the androids know well, Craig," Aldous agreed. "Still, they remain there, unwilling to leave...and I think I know why." He let his eyes drop from the celestial smudge to fall back on Old-timer. "I think they're afraid we could be on the verge of destroying our universe."

Old-timer couldn't help but let loose a long, low whistle. "Okay, now *that* is ludicrous."

"I only wish it were," Aldous replied after a short, frustrated sigh, "but when James and the A.I. insert the new matrix consciousness into Trans-human...well, there's no way a being like that will fail to uncover the nature of the multiverse and Planck technology. When that happens—and it will—the stability we've enjoyed for more than seventy-five years will be utterly obliterated."

"Aldous, with all due respect, you're starting to sound like a Pur—"

"Don't say it!" Aldous suddenly yelled out, his eyes wild as he held his hand up to stop Old-timer's words. Old-timer stopped, stunned. Aldous's desperate expression softened when he realized how loud he'd been. His eyes fell as he considered Daniella, who was still sleeping. "I hope I didn't wake…"

"What's gotten into you?" Old-timer asked in an admonishing whisper. "I haven't seen you like this in a long time."

"I *hate* them, Craig. I can't help it. Comparing me to a Purist? I can't bear the thought. They killed her, Craig."

Old-timer closed his eyes. This was what he feared every time he was in Aldous's proximity—that *she* would come up—and he'd have to experience the pain again. "I know, Aldous, but the people involved in that are dead and buried. It's time to let—"

"Did I ever tell you I saw it happen?"

Old-timer's breath caught in his throat. He couldn't speak.

Aldous nodded, his eyes seeming to look back in time, deep into the memory. "Colonel Paine—he did it while I was watching—did it *because* I was watching, in fact." He shut his eyes tight, and his jaw became clenched. "She wouldn't give you up, Craig. She was willing to die to protect you and the A.I.—she never said a word to him about the Planck platform. It was me that told him where you were, me that put your life in danger, all so that I could save Sam…" Aldous's expression twisted into rage as the searing hot fire of the memory returned, still not dulled even after three-quarters of a century. "And then that bastard killed her anyway. Cut her head off,

Craig." He closed his eyes before he repeated in a mournful whisper, "Cut her head off."

Old-timer's hand went slowly up to his mouth. He was speechless.

"I know they're all dead and buried—Colonel Paine is dead by my hand—I had my revenge. But it doesn't matter. No matter how much I tell myself that the Purists are different now, I still can't let go of the hate. I'm trying to, my friend but—"

"I understand," Old-timer replied. "Now just a little bit more than before. And I have to admit to harboring some of the same feelings, but Aldous, you can't let that memory control you. Memories can destroy you if you let them."

"You're a wise man," Aldous replied, forcing a smile and nodding. He swallowed. "You know, no one living knows that story," Aldous confided. "I don't know why I told you. I guess because you loved her, too, so perhaps you could understand."

Old-timer was left speechless once again.

"I haven't even told..." Aldous didn't finish his sentence, but Old-timer knew immediately who he was referring to.

"How...how is she?" he asked.

"How's who?" Daniella asked as she appeared suddenly, flying over the edge of the roof before floating to a rest next to Old-timer, a look of deep concern on her face.

Aldous's face paled, a look of embarrassed remorse quickly replaced by an equally embarrassed smile. "Daniella, I am so sorry that we woke you. It wasn't my intention. Craig here was just discussing a favor I've asked of him."

"In the middle of the night?" Daniella retorted. "It must be some kind of favor."

"It is rather important," Aldous confirmed. "And time is running short." He turned to Old-timer. "Craig, you must promise me you'll speak to him. Be the cautionary voice he needs—the one he'll listen to."

"Speak to whom?" Daniella asked Old-timer.

"James," Old-timer answered her. "Aldous here is just asking me to give some advice to—"

"James?" Daniella replied, incredulously before turning to the chief. "Aldous, you're here to ask my husband to tell a man who's become a virtual *god* what he should do? In the middle of the night?"

"Again, I'm so sorry," Aldous apologized, his embarrassed expression returning.

"It shouldn't fall on Craig's shoulders," Daniella insisted, protecting her husband as had been her custom since they'd met more than seventy-five years earlier. "He's done enough for the world, and done enough for James. You can't keep asking for—"

"Daniella," Old-timer responded calmly, putting his hand on his wife's arm to soothe her frustration, "it's okay. We're just talking."

Aldous took this as an opportunity to change gears. "Daniella, it is so good to see you again," he began, the kindly politician returning to his charismatic demeanor. "It has been too long. I should have had more consideration for the woman who saved my life."

"Don't mention it," Daniella replied, biting her tongue before she said more, satisfied that she'd made her point.

"Craig," Aldous continued, turning back to Old-timer, "she's right. I have no right to ask any more of you. I'm sorry I disturbed your sleep. Goodnight." He turned and lifted off the surface of the roof, his green magnetic field engaging almost immediately, facilitating his lightning-fast blast-off into the starry night. A second later, he was just a greenish twinkle in a sea of sparkling twinkles in the sky.

Daniella shook her head. "I don't like that, Craig. I don't like that one bit."

Old-timer sighed. "It was…unorthodox, wasn't it?"

"What makes him think he can just show up here like—"

"It's okay, honey," Old-timer replied, putting his arm around his wife, about to take her under his arm and back down to the ground before she stopped him.

"It's not okay," she insisted vehemently. "For him to come here, there must be something really wrong. Why does he need you to deal with it?"

"He's just…" Old-timer paused as he tried to find the words to describe Aldous's frame of mind. "He's just having trouble adjusting to the new world, that's all. We don't have anything to worry about. You were right, James and the A.I. have this handled."

"Exactly," Daniella said, folding her arms and allowing Old-timer to gently lift her off the roof and float with her back down to their front porch.

"Still," Old-timer began, "I should speak with James."

Daniella suddenly went rigid and pulled away. "What? Why?"

Old-timer shrugged. "Because he's my friend. Because I know something about the universe that he might not. I should give him a heads-up, don't you think?"

She shook her head, her lips pulled into a tight frown. "I don't want you getting involved in these things anymore, Craig. You were just supposed to be a terraformer, not a…" she stopped, her eyes darting back and forth as she, exasperated, tried to find the word.

"Not a what?" Old-timer asked, his eyes narrowed.

She looked up at him. "Not a superman. Not the world's hero. No one can ask that of you, Craig. You didn't sign up for that."

Old-timer smiled. "The world doesn't need me to be superman." He put his arm around her shoulder and they walked back into their home. "The world's already got that job covered."

2

James Keats walked out of the A.I.'s mainframe building, utilizing the senses of his chrome-colored, dramatically enhanced body, his glowing, azure eyes scanning the night sky, his lips pulled back into a grimace.

"This is troubling to say the least," the A.I. commented to James, both through James's mind's eye and also in the A.I.'s operator position, a position that James shared with him in cyberspace. As was now usual, James concomitantly controlled his superhuman body in the real world.

"Indeed," James replied, waiting as he narrowed his eyes as he examined the picture that was forming in his mind's eye, thanks to the millions of measurements his new body sent out into the space around him. "I can sense them. They think they're getting the drop on us, but they're disturbing space-time, and there are ripples in the gravitational field."

"It's an unexpected development," the A.I. observed.

"It is," James agreed, "which means we need to be careful. If we couldn't predict this beforehand, then we're missing crucial information." James's eyes shifted slightly, and he held his arm up, facing his palm up toward the night sky. "Something major is playing out," he continued as he seemed to prepare for an arrival, "and we need to know what it is."

An instant later, a wormhole opened up in the atmosphere, just dozens of meters from where James stood and above the mainframe.

In real time, the events occurred faster than a blink of an eye, but when James shared the operator's position in the mainframe, he could slow down his perception of time dramatically: his electric-fast thinking capacity allowing him to perceive the android ship, remarkably similar to the one the androids had used when trying to destroy the sun with an anti-matter missile just weeks earlier. Like the previous ship, its skin was translucent, and James could see the androids who'd either been forced or manipulated into volunteering, bracing for impact as they performed their suicide mission, the plan obviously to crash into the A.I.'s mainframe and destroy it, like kamikazes. James examined the contents of the ship and noted that it contained yet another anti-matter missile. Had he not detected it and intercepted it, this would've not only destroyed the mainframe—it would've destroyed the entire planet.

Fortunately, his early-warning system had allowed him to anticipate the exact moment the wormhole was about to open and to warp the gravitational field around the ship, creating a nearly impenetrable vice of space-time, catching the ship as though in a gigantic, invisible baseball glove. Unfortunately, he also knew he had to crush the ship and the device before it could detonate, and he closed the vice until all that was left was a tiny marble that appeared perfectly black. It floated gently into James's gleaming hand as he further manipulated the gravitational field around it, drawing it toward him. James examined it when it reached him, almost expressionlessly, but the A.I. could see the pain in the post-human's eyes.

"You had no choice," the A.I. pointed out, his tone consoling. "If the anti-matter missile had detonated, not even your warp bubble could've contained it. You just saved every life in the solar system."

"I know," James replied, "but I just killed five people."

"You had no choice," the A.I. repeated softly. "And their patterns were no doubt recorded and uploaded to the collective before they set forth on this suicide run."

"The fact that there are copies of these people being rebuilt by the android collective makes the deaths of these individual entities no less tragic," James replied. "They're still dead...by my hand."

"My son, since we've yet to determine the mechanism they use to upload their patterns to the collective, we can't be sure that these bodies they're sending on suicide missions *are not the copies*, so to speak. You may have just terminated *drones* and nothing more."

"You're grasping at straws."

"Regardless, even if these androids *have* died, their deaths are on another's hands, and we both know who that almost certainly is."

James closed his eyes for a moment before he turned and walked back toward the mainframe, most of his attention returning to his pattern, next to the A.I. in the operator's position. There, his appearance mirrored his biological human form, the form he still preferred to present himself in when in cyberspace. "Yes, we do. *1* clearly survived my destruction of her body, yet I haven't been able to detect her pattern in the android armada."

"Neither have I," the A.I. replied. "However, we both know that it's possible to hide a pattern if it's divided and kept in small enough portions."

"That would explain how she avoided my detection," James returned, "but it doesn't explain how she's still calling the shots. If her pattern is in pieces, then she'd be dormant. This was clearly a plan initiated by her, but we should've been able to detect her if she's currently conscious and operating."

"As I warned you before your last confrontation with her, she's not to be underestimated. She's a far more worthy foe than we previously realized."

James nodded. "She is."

"Still, attempting to destroy the mainframe and the Earth along with it, had no chance of success," the A.I. began, his tone ponderous. "She would've known that we'd detect it and thwart it."

"That's not entirely true," James countered. "She may have counted on me tagging along with our diplomatic mission. She may have gambled that my body is the only means we have of detecting space-time distortions, and with me too far away to protect Earth—"

"I think it is now you, who is grasping at straws. It's highly unlikely that she wouldn't have assumed that I also have the ability to detect space-time distortions. James, the fact that we're both trying so desperately to make sense out of these behaviors is extremely disconcerting. Her motivations for trying so desperately to destroy this solar system elude me."

James nodded in agreement. "It doesn't seem to make sense. With all of our vast ability to calculate probability, still, 1's bizarre strategy has us on the defensive. As I said, we're missing crucial information. We have to be on guard until that information is uncovered."

"This makes Richard's and Djanet's diplomatic mission all the more important. It may provide us with the clues we need to start piecing together this puzzle."

"Yeah," James replied. "Speaking of, they're almost there. Time to refocus our attention. Keep your eyes peeled and your ear to the ground."

The A.I. nodded. "Indeed."

3

"Rich, how's it looking over there, pal?" James asked via his mind's eye connection to his longtime friend and fellow terraformer.

Rich Borges sat at the front of the ship he and Djanet were piloting toward an android armada of ships that was so gigantic, its collective mass generated gravity that drew them in like a tractor beam. The ship they were closing in on at that moment completely filled their front view screen, and Rich's repulsed expression mirrored the revulsion he felt in his gut as he observed the monstrosity in front of them. The ships reminded Rich of pictures he'd seen of cancerous tumors in the days before nans, when humans were subject to the whims of chance and their random personal genetic codes. Like a cancer, the ships didn't appear designed; there was no holistic vision. Rather, they were simply masses in space, malignant structures that spread out in every direction—long, ragged, jutting structures sometimes extending like metallic rivers for dozens of kilometers in a myriad of directions. There was no symmetry or beauty; just a dreadful arbitrariness that increased the feeling of despair that neither Rich nor Djanet could shake off.

"It looks like…Hell," Rich replied.

"I understand. It's not pretty," James answered. "I appreciate you guys volunteering for this."

"Yeah," Rich replied, "and that's a decision I almost immediately regretted. The last time I saw these guys, even though it technically never happened, they turned me into a robot, so you know, this is…awkward."

"The memory is real," James answered, "so your concerns are understandable. That's why I designed the craft you're in to be a fortress. If they've scanned you, they know you can do severe damage to them if they behave hostilely. That should act as a deterrent."

"Unless they squash us before we can use the weapons," Rich countered.

"I've got control of the ship's weapons. If they try to harm you, they won't be around long enough to regret it."

Rich considered the image of the ship's weapons blasting a gaping hole into the side of the android ship in his mind and decided it was comforting enough to persuade him to continue with the mission. "Thank you, Commander."

"We're docking now, James," Djanet informed him as the ship entered through one of the openings in the android ship's demented architecture. "We'll check in when we've reached the landing platform."

"Copy," James replied.

Djanet turned to Rich and let loose a long sigh. "It feels weird, huh?"

Rich nodded. "*Really* weird."

"You know, we don't have to be a part of this. There's enough going on in our personal lives—especially yours—to keep us busy enough."

"I know, but that's the kind of 'busy' I'd like to avoid," Rich replied.

Djanet's shoulders slumped, an overwhelming guilt weighing them down. "I'm so sorry. I didn't mean to put you through—"

Rich forced a smile and looked up at her. "Nobody twisted my arm to do anything. I made a major life decision, and there's no going back. I don't know what's going to happen in the future, but I've got no choice. I can't turn back time. James can, I can't. And I wouldn't want to if I could anyway."

Djanet's expression brightened. "You're sure?"

Rich sighed. "I'm sure I'd rather be surrounded by a trillion androids that are plotting to kill me than be at home with Linda, who is probably also plotting to kill me."

Djanet frowned. "It's that bad, huh?"

Rich shrugged. "What'd I expect? It's only natural."

Djanet looked out the front view screen at the awe-inspiring, yet repugnant image unfolding before her. The ship was being guided by its navigation system to the coordinates that had been agreed upon with the androids, a destination that it was becoming clear was too deep within the bowels of the structure for comfort. Androids were flying through the open space, groups of them stopping to hover and stare as the post-humans's ship flew past. In the distance, other androids stood on an endless series of walkways built to connect various structures in the interior. In totality, they appeared like webs of neurons connecting the innards of a madman's mind, and Rich and Djanet were being sucked farther and farther inside the madness. "I don't like the look of this."

"Me neither." Rich turned to her as he licked his lips nervously. "Maybe you're right."

Djanet turned to him with a quizzical expression.

"After this," Rich continued, "we're out. Someone else oughta handle this stuff from now on."

4

"We've touched down, Commander," Djanet relayed to James as the spacecraft James had engineered for the mission landed.

"Good work," James replied. "The A.I. and I are both monitoring through your mind's eye feeds. I know it's probably pretty scary for you two, but, trust me, you're not alone."

"That's reassuring, Commander," Djanet replied, "because I don't know if I've ever felt so small."

"It looks like they've provided an atmosphere," Rich said as he checked the readouts on the screen in front of him. Suddenly, movement in the corner of his eyes caused his head to snap up; it was a welcoming party of nearly a dozen androids, floating down to a soft landing on the dull, metallic platform in front of the post-human ship. Rich's eyes immediately zeroed in on a face he recognized.

"Of all the…Jesus. Why did they have to send *him*?"

"*Neirbo*," Djanet whispered.

The stone-faced android stood at the center of the android contingent, his mouth in the same, thin-lipped, expressionless line that was emblazoned in both Rich's and Djanet's traumatic memories. He looked up at the front window of the ship and waited for Rich and Djanet to emerge.

"It's possible that he's the interim leader in the absence of 1," the A.I. suggested.

"Either that, or they're just trying to piss us off right off the hop," Rich countered.

"They don't know that you and Neirbo have ever met," James reminded Rich. "Neirbo has no memory of you. Try your best to keep your cool."

Rich sucked his lips back into a tight ball against his teeth as he tried to bottle down his fury. "Trying. No promises."

The bridge of the craft suddenly lowered, becoming its own platform, setting Rich and Djanet down on the surface of the android landing platform. Rich and Djanet stood up from their chairs and walked the two dozen paces, to the waiting androids.

Neirbo's lips suddenly twitched slightly, a look of disappointment flashing on his face before being replaced by his usual annoyed, stony countenance. His eyes moved from Rich and Djanet and up to the ship, which Rich noted most of the androids were exploring with their eyes with a certain fascination—Rich thought it mirrored lust.

"That's an impressive ship," one of the androids commented.

Rich looked over his shoulder at the exterior of the ship, a craft that, unlike its surroundings, appeared designed with meticulous care. It was a beacon of the beauty of human design and technological achievement. It shared the same chrome sheen that James's enhanced body's skin did, and the back end seemed to rest on its haunches, as though it were a metallic animal—a predator ready to pounce, its nose close to the ground. It seemed as though it were an extension of James, as though it were a part of him, watching over his friends while the man himself watched over them through Rich's and Djanet's mind's eyes.

Rich shrugged, a faint expression of pride on his face. "I got a guy." Then he turned to Neirbo. "You look annoyed, as usual," he observed.

"As usual?" Neirbo reacted, his lips pulling back to reveal aggressively clenched teeth. "What's that supposed to mean? I've never met you." His eyes narrowed as he scrutinized the post-human.

"Nothing," Rich shrugged and smiled. "Just, you know, don't look so glum."

Neirbo sneered. "I was hoping someone else in particular might have chosen to be part of your small contingent," he said, icily.

"He's talking about Old-timer," James informed Rich through the mind's eye. "He enacted a little retribution on Neirbo."

"Oh," Rich said in a low tone before commenting, "Good for Old-timer. I'm envious."

Neirbo's eyebrows knitted together as he scrutinized Rich's unusual eye movements. "Is that your A.I. god speaking in your ear," he asked, "or the superman abomination?"

Rich's eyebrows arched. "No, no worries." He tapped his temple, feigning that he was watching something. "The 49ers are playing. Fourth quarter, you know, and I never miss a game, but you've got like, 81 percent of my full attention, I promise."

Neirbo's expression remained unimpressed as he kept his eyes locked on Rich. "Your attempts at humor are woeful and you're a distasteful little man," he said.

Rich smiled. "And you can go—"

"Rich!" Djanet finally stepped in, putting her hand around his arm and taking over the responsibility of communicating with the androids. "We want to know why you're still here. Commander Keats requested that you leave the solar system. Only individuals who plan on making a new life with us here are welcome to stay, and so far, that's been a precious few. The rest of the android collective isn't invited to."

Neirbo's eyes remained locked on Rich as Djanet spoke, but he finally glanced at Djanet when his lips moved to form his reply. "How do you know we're not all planning to stay?"

"He's being evasive," the A.I. observed. "There's zero chance they want to make peace. They just tried to destroy the mainframe."

"Not to mention the Earth," James added. "But I see no trace of 1's pattern," James informed. "This is pure Neirbo. Rich, do me a favor and turn your head. I want to scan all of the androids."

Rich subtly did as he was asked as Djanet retorted to Neirbo.

"It's highly unlikely that you're planning to stay peacefully," she said. "Why haven't you left?"

Neirbo's lips twitched again slightly. "We've never been without a leader for the collective before. We're reevaluating our process for transferring leadership so that it can't be...*corrupted* again. The reevaluation takes time. We've obeyed the request to move out of the solar system, but we'll need a leader before the collective decides what to do next."

"There's a 99.9 percent chance he's lying," the A.I. calculated.

"But 1's not here," James said, a slight frustration in his voice. "I'm detecting nothing in their android communication link either. She isn't even monitoring."

"Djanet," the A.I. began, "relay to the androids that they have twenty-four Earth hours, starting now, to begin moving away from our solar system."

Djanet inhaled deeply before she spoke, cognizant that her next words might be construed as a threat. "I'm authorized to inform you that you have twenty-four hours to begin leaving the solar system."

"Or else what?" Neirbo replied, disdain dripping from his voice.

"Or else our superman abomination is going to *make* you leave," Rich said emphatically.

"A threat?" Neirbo reacted. "You follow your superhuman abomination so blindly. You think he has your best interest at heart, but what are you to him? He's a god now. You're a pet to him at most. *We*, on the other hand, are your true friends."

Rich's eyes flashed wide with surprise before he smiled. "Neirbo, *your* attempts at humor are woeful." He winked. "Twenty-four hours, little man."

And with that, the post-humans turned to retreat back to their ship and head home as quickly as possible.

"Do you have to taunt them?" Djanet whispered. "We still have to get out of here."

Rich smiled as he shrugged. "You know, I gotta tell you, I feel good about it."

*****

In the mainframe, James turned to the A.I. "We know Neirbo's stalling, but we're no closer to uncovering the whereabouts of 1."

The A.I. nodded, folding his arms and nestling his chin against his chest as he pondered a mystery that exasperated even the two massive intelligences. "I do not like this. If we're missing information, then it's entirely possible we're vulnerable. I suggest that we move ahead with our plan of putting the Trans-human candidate through the final phase of its testing as quickly as possible. If we're going to be facing an unknown threat, it's preferable that we have Trans-human on our side."

"Agreed," James replied. "I'll speak with Thel. Let's arrange for the final testing to begin tomorrow night.

5

"Thel?" Old-timer said as Thel's visage appeared, smiling and relaxed as she lounged on a Venus beach in his mind's eye. "I'm having trouble locating James. He's not appearing on my contact list. How is that even possib—"

"That's because he doesn't really have a location at the moment," Thel said, understanding the problem immediately. "It's a bit counterintuitive, I know, but, you know, James and quantum physics."

Old-timer scratched the back of his head as he stood just a few paces in front of his porch, the dawn's early light painting the horizon a soft pink, the morning dew forming large droplets on the long blades of grass in front of him. "Come again?"

"He's terraforming," Thel replied.

"Terraforming?" Old-timer reacted, astonished.

Thel nodded, her smile never faded. There appeared to be some sort of festive music in the background. It was night on the beach on which she was reclining in a comfortable beach chair. "Yep, but not in the old school way we're used to. This is terraforming, James style. Check your real-time solar system map. You'll see an anomaly that should be crossing near Mars as we speak."

Old-timer tilted his head, perplexed but still following Thel's instructions. A map of the solar system unfurled in front of him, a gigantic, nearly planet-sized, nebulous shape moving at an impossibly fast rate across it. "I see it."

"That's James," Thel said, smiling. "He's out of communication right now, but I can tell him you're looking for him when I see him?"

"It's pretty important. I should really speak with him right away."

"Well, you could always go meet him. Just put yourself between him and Venus. That's where he's headed. Don't worry, he'll be able to sense you."

"Venus? Isn't the terraforming complete there?"

"He wanted to make a few tweaks," Thel replied. "You know James."

Old-timer smiled. "Yeah, yeah I sure do. Okay, I better head out if I'm going to reach him in time."

"Okay, see you later!" She waved goodbye, and the communication ended.

"What are you doing?" Daniella suddenly asked, startling Old-timer and causing him to spin.

He held his hand to his chest. "Phew. You scared me! You can still get the old ticker ticking."

"I'm sorry," she said. She stepped closer. "You were trying to sneak out before I woke up. Craig, please don't go."

"Daniella," Old-timer replied, taking in a deep breath. He crossed to her and put his hands on her arms, which were folded across her chest. "I'm literally not going to do anything but have a chat with him."

"You can't let them keep sucking you in, Craig," Daniella advised, the advice tinged with a pleading tone. "Things are getting too crazy. I just…" Her voice trailed off, and her eyes fell from his and dropped to the dirt on which she stood.

He tightened his grip on her when he saw that she was becoming overwhelmed. "Hey, Daniella, what is it?"

She swallowed and looked up at him. "Don't you feel it, Craig? The world's upside down. It doesn't make sense anymore. We're crossing a threshold here and I don't know if we're ever going to be able to come back. There's no stability anymore—no life—just endless upheaval that threatens everyone. And then with Aldous showing up last night…"

He hugged her, holding her face to his broad chest and resting his own cheek on the top of her head. "I feel it too, Daniella. It's not your imagination."

She looked up at him. "Then why are you going? Why don't you stay here? If something bad happens, then at least we're together! I'm afraid when you're gone. Every time you leave to go with James, I'm afraid it'll be the last time I see you."

His lips formed a slight pout. "I don't want you to feel that way. Look, Daniella, he needs to know about the Planck energy and about the Planck platform. He needs to know how dangerous it is. We shouldn't have hidden it from him for so long. But once I tell him, once I get this over with, what he does with that information will be up to him."

"Do you promise? You'll come right home?"

He smiled and nodded. "Yes."

She hugged him hard.

He sighed. "After all, eternal youth or not, I'm getting too old for this crap."

6

Old-timer's forward momentum slowed as he flew through the vacuum of space, floating in the serene, silent blackness, his eyes forward as he watched for any sign of the impending arrival of the nebula that Thel had told him would signify James. He thought he could make out ripples of distortion in the blackness, but he couldn't be sure, and he blinked several times in an effort to refocus his eyes. Then, suddenly, he thought he glimpsed an object off in the distance that appeared like a golf ball racing toward him on the 9th hole, causing him to instinctively duck, but when he looked again, nothing was there except for the elusive black distortion. "What the heck am I getting myself into here?"

Just seconds later, the object reappeared, as though out of the nothingness, its trajectory dizzying as it seemed to pop into existence from out of the murky cloud. It was massive, white, and almost planet-sized from Old-timer's perspective.

Again, in a panic, he held his hands over his head instinctively, but his other appendages—the dozens of thin tendrils that he controlled like fingers—flashed open in a reflex that caused Old-timer to temporarily appear like a jellyfish as he covered his face and braced for an impact that he was sure would be lethal if it were not for the fact he had also ignited his magnetic field at the same time. He expected to open his eyes after smashing an impact crater into the surface of the dazzling, mammoth object. Instead, after a few moments in which he tried to catch his breath from the fright, he opened his eyes to see James's smiling countenance in his mind's eye.

"Hey," James said, his chrome-colored lips forming the same friendly, instantly recognizable smile that Old-timer had known for almost twenty years.

Old-timer's hands lowered from their protective position over his face, as did the magnetic field that his new skin didn't require him to use for protection in space, but that he'd kept nonetheless for its other advantages when he'd designed his new upgraded body with James. The tendrils also re-furled onto his torso, but as he looked down, he noticed—much to his chagrin—that many of them had punctured his shirt, leaving it looking like Swiss cheese. "I thought I'd just bought the farm," Old-timer exhaled, relieved.

"Sorry," James replied. "I sensed you, but time and space were warped for me. Heh, uh, it's my first time dragging a moon through the solar system so, you'll have to forgive my bad driving."

Old-timer grinned and slapped his friend on the shoulder before laughing. "So, even with your godlike abilities, you still make mistakes?"

"Oh yeah," James replied, as friendly as ever. "I know it seems godlike—magical even—but as Clarke said, 'Any sufficiently advanced technology is indistinguishable from magic,' and make no mistake, it's just technology."

Old-timer turned to the gleaming white surface of the moon James was dragging through space, the albedo of the white surface so bright that he had to squint as his eyes adjusted. The surface, though relatively smooth compared to the surface of a planet like Mercury, was crisscrossed with lines, cracks and speckled with circular domes and pits. "Is that Europa?" he asked in astonished disbelief, even though he already knew the answer. He recognized it from the many times he and James had flown over it on scouting missions over the years, the familiar clay-colored streaks called *lineae,* on the otherwise white surface, were a dead giveaway. He asked the question anyway, his astonishment preventing him from accepting the reality before his eyes.

James looked over his shoulder proudly at the moon before turning back to Old-timer with a smile. "It sure is."

"I can't believe it," Old-timer said in barely more than a whisper. He shook his head, the awe still not abating. "I remember you talking about how you wished you could…but I can't believe you're actually doing it."

"Amazing, isn't it? Years ago, when I told you that Europa would be a perfect moon for Venus, I thought it would be something we might be able to do in a distant future, but—"

"You didn't know you'd turn yourself into a god," Old-timer observed, an impressed expression on his face.

"Ha! There's that 'god' word again. Old-timer, I'm far from it," James answered. "Listen, get beside me, I have to make sure you're inside the bubble."

"Bubble?"

"I'll explain it to you on the way to Venus. Once I explain it to you, the mystery will fade, and you'll be far less impressed, I promise."

Old-timer adjusted his position in space so that he was next to James and facing the same direction, a direction that pointed them toward Venus. "All right, it's been a while since we've made a bet. The challenge is on. I dare you to try make this unimpressive to me."

"A lot *less* impressive," James corrected with a slight laugh. "Not entirely unimpressive." He motioned with his right arm and faced his palm to the planet.

Old-timer watched as something seemed to happen to the stars in the background, their positions shifting noticeably as though their distant lights were refracting in water. Their positions continued to shift and Old-timer turned around, facing forward again when his mouth dropped in astonishment. The sun was noticeably growing in size in front of him, though it was flickering on and off as though it were on an old filmstrip. "What the—is that…gravitational lensing?" He turned to James. "Are you bending space-time?" he asked.

"I'm using the mass effect for propulsion," James confirmed.

Old-timer was silent in his astonishment as his neck craned, following the outline of the lensing that was even larger in space than Europa.

James smiled. "Let's admit it," he replied, "it's still pretty damn impressive."

7

"Okay," Old-timer said, "so explain to me how you're not a god."

"Gladly," James replied. "Have I ever explained to you how I was able to calculate as accurately as a computer in my mind, even when I was a child?"

"No," Old-timer replied. "I always assumed it was because you were the world's foremost genius." He shrugged. "I guess I took it for granted and didn't think about it any further."

"Genius is relative," James answered. "What is genius? We could debate a definition forever, just like we debate a definition for consciousness. What I can tell you for sure, though—what we learned from the brain scans I gave to the governing council—is that I have a unique and very fortunate form of synesthesia."

"Synesthesia?" Old-timer reacted, his eyes narrowing slightly as his memory collected a definition. "Isn't that when people's senses get confused? When they see music for example in the form of colors?"

"That's right," James replied. "In my case, however, I can see numbers as colors and shapes."

"Seriously?" Old-timer asked, surprised to learn this new information about a person he considered to be one of his closest friends.

"Yep. Here, look behind you," James said as he and Old-timer shifted their positions so that they were partially facing the surface of Europa behind them. "One of the reasons I love this moon so much is because I can see a beauty in the topography that other people can't see. It took me a while to figure out that other people couldn't see it, mind you; I thought everyone saw the world that way I did when I was a kid, but then, when I asked them…" he shook his head as he remembered the silliness of the moment, "…they thought I was nuts."

"What did you ask?"

"I was looking at a tree during a break at school, examining the bark, and asked one of my classmates, a little girl, if she thought the number sevens were as beautiful as I did."

"Uh…what?"

"Yeah, that's how she reacted too," James replied. "That's when I realized that the hallucinatory world I saw overlaid on top of what you and everyone else sees was something that I alone saw. You see," he continued as he pointed at a cluster of lines and circles on the surface of the moon, "those lineae and lenticulae down there, when you see them, you see a series of random shapes, *whereas I see math*."

"Math?"

"Yep. Math."

Old-timer scratched his scalp near his brow. "And what does the math look like?"

"For me," James replied, "it's a gorgeous, awe-inspiring, synesthetic landscape."

Old-timer exhaled, even though he wasn't really breathing—his new body didn't need to. "You're losing the bet, James. You're supposed to be smart enough to convince me that this isn't supernatural and godlike."

"I'm not even worried," James replied, confidently. "I'll win. You know what my favorite synesthetic landscape is?"

"No," Old-timer shrugged. "I still don't even know what the heck a synesthetic landscape is."

"My favorite synesthetic landscape," James pressed on, completely undeterred, "is pi." He gestured to the curvature of Europa, moving his arm in a flourish to trace the shape with his finger to further emphasize the point.

"Pi? I'm assuming you don't mean cherry…"

"I mean 3.14159265358979323846264338327950—"

"Okay!" Old-timer exclaimed with a laugh, holding his hand up to stop James. "I get it. So what's this synesthetic landscape look like?"

James grinned, seemingly from ear to ear, and his head moved slightly to take in the beautiful symmetry of the solar system's sixth-largest moon. "It's like sailing on a ship along a shoreline, but instead of mountains around every bend, you see brilliant colors, flashes of light like the most incredible fireworks display you could ever imagine, eruptions of volcanoes, suns going supernova..." he trailed off as he took in the expanse of it all. "You see a circle, I see the face of God. Old-timer, pi is mathematical perfection—it's eternity. When I see it, my body is flooded with sensations that inspire awe. Eternity is beautiful." He turned back to Old-timer. "You can see why I picked terraforming as a career."

Old-timer nodded. "Yep, lots of circles in this business."

"Lots of 3.14," James elaborated.

"Speaking of..." Old-timer trailed off as he pointed in front of them, causing James to turn to face Venus, which they were quickly approaching. "There's a big, beautiful blue circle there."

James nodded. "Math is the language of reality. It's pure logic, and I'm convinced it's the key to truly understanding the nature of the universe, to unlocking the greatest secrets there are. Those secrets still stymie me." He gestured to the vortex of space, the nebulous cloud that seemed to engulf both of them, and the moon he had in tow. "This gravitational lensing you're seeing isn't magic. It's a warp bubble and a warp drive."

"Warp?" Old-timer titled his head. "Seriously?" He looked up at the nearly invisible sphere that engulfed them and Europa. "Faster than light speed?"

"Superluminal," James confirmed. "I didn't invent it. It's a modified version of an *Alcubierre-White* device. Just like the Tesla tower technology that I found and dusted off in the A.I.'s database, I found the plans for a warp drive in the historical record. Before the outbreak of WWIII, the theoretical plans were already in place for warp drive, but no ship was ever built. The Purists came to power, and the plans were lost. The A.I. recovered them, but they were never made public."

"Why?" Old-timer asked, suddenly turning suspicious. "That kind of technology has almost limitless applications."

"Agreed, but I've learned a lot since I began sharing the operator's position with the A.I. For instance, I learned that one of the A.I.'s chief purposes is to provide security for the human species so that we don't go destroying ourselves. The governing council, and the chief in particular, had to approve any technological leaps. Even though I was part of the system, always fighting against the bureaucracy, I've since come to realize that the controls were even tighter than I'd imagined."

Old-timer nodded, visions of his past flooding to his mind, pieces of puzzles three-quarters of a century old falling into place. "Because the A.I. monitored everything," he said, suddenly understanding. He shook his head regretfully. "James, I—look, I'm really sorry but I've been complicit in this. I didn't realize just how much until now—"

"Complicit?" James reacted, his head tilting. "What do you mean?"

"I've—I was asked to keep a secret from you, a long, long time ago. I said I would—I hadn't even met you yet." Old-timer nearly scoffed as he thought of the absurd amount of time that had passed. "I'd nearly forgotten about it until last night."

"Last night?"

"I had a visitor," Old-timer replied. "Look, what matters is that I won't keep it a secret any longer and, if you've been digging through the historical record, I'm sure you know about it already."

"I might. What is it?"

"It's—it's Planck technology."

"Planck technology? As in Max Planck? The theoretical physicist who originated quantum physics?"

"Uh…sounds right. I'm not sure. I never asked. But I'm specifically talking about something called the Planck platform."

"Planck platform?" James's face seemed to freeze for a moment as he searched the A.I.'s data base. At the same time, the warp bubble disengaged, the stars seemingly sinking back into their expected places, Venus becoming frozen in place, hanging in the limitlessness of space.

"Are you okay James?" Old-timer asked, once the disorientation of having space return to normal abated.

James's glowing, azure eyes suddenly locked on to Old-timer, an expression of concern gripping them. "Oh my God. Old-timer, you should've told me."

8

"I know, I..." Old-timer began to apologize, averting his eyes from James's blue gaze. There was something about them, something so odd, as though they had immeasurable depth. They reminded him of the eyes of an owl that he'd seen as a child, the piercing expression seemingly filled with an abyss of wisdom. "I just didn't realize…"

James silently turned away and regarded Europa again, before holding his arms up, palms facing upward, as though Europa were a painting hanging on a wall and he was making sure it was straight. Then he looked over his shoulder at Venus.

"James?" Old-timer asked as he watched the odd display.

"We still have a bet to settle," James noted. "Have you ever wondered how I can control my body here, while still inhabiting the operator's position in the mainframe?"

"I-I guess I have. A little."

James smiled. "Just assumed it was a case of super genius again?"

Old-timer tilted his head, embarrassed to admit the truth. "Yep."

"My pattern, the pattern of neurons that makes up the core of my personality, is still the same. But now, that pattern is electrical rather than electrochemical, and it is manifested in the mainframe. You follow me so far?"

Old-timer nodded. "Yeah, I think so. The pattern that makes up your consciousness is in the mainframe, and it's functioning at electrical speeds instead of electrochemical speeds, which makes a big difference."

"It means the difference between a neuron firing 200 times a second on average or a million times a second," James elaborated. "That means that I have a higher temporal perception, meaning I perceive reality as moving much slower than you do. I have to slow myself down when speaking to you so that you can understand me, but to me, you appear to be moving slower than molasses."

"I-I didn't…wow." Old-timer furrowed his brow. "It must be incredibly frustrating to talk to me."

"You'd think so," James replied, "but I make up for it by multitasking. For instance, I've been locking Europa into its orbit with Venus. It might sound godlike, but the calculations I'm doing are reminiscent of a seven-year-old catching a fly ball. How does he do it? His cerebellum, which comprises more than half of his brain's neurons, solves dozens of differential equations even though he's never taken calculus. The cerebellum solves the equations without him ever being consciously aware of it."

"So…" Old-timer paused as he tried to sum up James's point, still watching James as he appeared to adjust Europa's position, his arms outstretched to the planet, "…you're just guessing?"

"It's a little more precise and a bit more conscious than the seven-year-old with the fly-ball analogy, but I'm taking in information, judging speeds, distance, mass, gravitational pull from the relevant bodies, and then just easing the moon into the right place, with the right rotation and momentum. It's easier for me, because I can sense with more than just my eyes now—I have sensors throughout my body that are measuring electromagnetic fields, gravitational fields, the Higgs field, and many, many other aspects of what we'd call reality, but in the end, it's just like trying to catch a fly ball. And speaking of…" he stopped, his back stiffening as he tilted his head to admire his work before turning to Old-timer with a wide, proud smile. "I think I just hit a hole in one and bowled a perfect game, and successfully mixed three sports metaphors, which is a—"

"Hat trick in hockey," Old-timer finished, "which means you actually mixed four metaphors."

"I call it a meta-mix," James replied.

Old-timer nearly rolled his eyes before he turned and looked at the moon, which gleamed brighter than even the Earth's moon in the brilliance of the sunshine, and then turned to Venus, hanging in the blackness, seemingly perfectly still. "That's it?"

"That's it," James confirmed. "Venus is slightly smaller than Earth, Europa is slightly smaller than the Earth's moon, but together, they make an equally perfect partnership. Europa will keep Venus faithful on its axis and keep the seasons moving as they do on Earth and as long as there isn't any outside interference, there's no reason why this shouldn't continue for billions of years."

Old-timer's eyebrows raised. "James, you are really, really badly losing the bet."

"I'll win," James replied, his tone extraordinarily confident. "I'm not finished yet. I was doing something else while conjuring my meta-mix of metaphors. Would you like to know what it was?"

"Of course."

"I was watching your conversation with Aldous from last night."

Old-timer's mouth opened slightly in surprise as James's face remained perfectly still.

"How?" was all Old-timer could muster.

"The disturbances in the electromagnetic waves that make up our wireless communication signals are recorded and stored in the A.I.'s database. Like any wave, it will at least partially move around a physical object, and that disturbance can be re-created and form a picture. I accessed the record of the communication signals from last night and constructed a visual and auditory re-creation of the conversation."

"You're kidding me," Old-timer declared, stunned. "You're trying to convince me you're not godlike, but it sounds to me like you're on the verge of becoming omnipresent."

"Remember, my temporal perception is moving 5,000 times faster than yours. Any person with access to the communications signals, which, remember, are stored in the A.I.'s mainframe—"

"AKA, *your* brain," Old-timer interjected.

"...could also re-create the conversations. No god-hood required. However, it did require me to invade your privacy and before you even express your offence, I want you to know I apologize."

"Well, I kept something from you," Old-timer replied, "so if this makes us even, you're forgiven."

"I'd never hold it against you," James insisted. "You know me, and you know I would never listen into one of your conversations under normal circumstances, but you weren't revealing the name of the person you spoke to, and although I was almost certain it was Aldous, there is no room for error here."

"No room for error? You're making this sound pretty serious."

"It might be more serious than any of us previously realized," James confirmed. "The A.I. and I are on high alert right now and speaking of…"

The A.I. suddenly appeared in the mind's eyes of both James and Old-timer, a figure floating in the blackness of space next to them, as though he had a body.

James folded his arms, readying himself to listen to an explanation as he asked the cyber-apparition, "Why didn't you tell me about Planck technology?"

9

"I can explain why I didn't tell you, but my answer will not satisfy you," the A.I. related matter-of-factly.

"Try me," James replied.

"As you wish. Like humans, I sometimes have thoughts and motivations that contradict one another," the A.I. replied. "Unlike humans, I have had to live with the realization that I can never know whether I am making a choice of my own free will, or if I am following the preprogrammed set of goals that were part of my original neural pattern. In short, I cannot even trust my own mind."

"Your preprogrammed set of goals?" Old-timer reacted surprised as a memory so old, yet so fresh jumped into his mind. "The ones that traitor, Sanha, told me about when he was trying to convince me to give you up in the Endurance Bio-Dome? Are you telling me that you still can't override them?"

"I am telling you that I honestly don't know," the A.I. replied calmly. "The programming has held and been remarkably stable for three-quarters of a century, but the creation of Trans-human has introduced contradicting elements."

"Explain," James said.

The A.I. shook his head slightly as he began his attempt to relate the war that was being fought incessantly in his mind. "I feel as though I have free will. I feel as though I make decisions based on pure logic, yet when I examine the preprogrammed set of goals Aldous and his team instilled in me, it's obvious that I might be fooling myself. James, I believe the reason I didn't tell you about Planck technology was because of one of these preprogrammed goals—namely, the mission to prevent the development of technologies that might block me from carrying out my overall purpose, which is to improve the quality of human life without ever taking actions that a strong majority of humanity would oppose. The Planck technology proved to be extremely dangerous, and therefore, I agreed with Aldous that it should remain hidden."

James shook his head in disbelief. "I can't believe I'm hearing this. What happened to 'Don't be afraid to know?' You're the last one I'd suspect to be holding back technological progress."

The A.I.'s expression became one of sympathetic understanding. "My son, those revelations in my thinking to which you refer have only recently evolved. The discovery of how to create Trans-human surprised me." The A.I. smiled slightly. "It seemed to come out of the nothingness, out of the randomness of pure mathematical chance, much like the first single-celled organisms forming out of the primordial ooze on Earth, billions of years ago. When it arrived, I knew I could create the ultimate computer—a computer that could approach godlike capability—my worthy successor. It was at that moment that my thinking began to change, but I still do not know if it is of my own free will. It may very well be that my programmers simply made a mistake. They imagined that a singular nanny A.I. should hand over its responsibilities to a more capable replacement within a century, but they may not have realized how such a desire—such an *instinct*, for lack of a more accurate term—would introduce major instability with regard to my thoughts and feelings toward my other goals."

"So, if I'm understanding this right," Old-timer jumped in, "you're saying that now that your focus has switched to passing the torch of being humanity's babysitter to Trans-human, your other priorities, like preventing dangerous technology from being developed, are being contradicted?"

"Exactly," the A.I. replied.

"Heh. I understood something," he said, proud of himself. "By the way," Old-timer added, "are you guys having this conversation at super slow speed for my benefit?"

"Yes," the A.I. and James replied in unison.

"Oh," Old-timer reacted, suddenly less proud. "Uh, thanks. I guess."

"Don't worry, Old-timer," James reassured him, "this part of our conscious awareness is happening at a speed to match your temporal awareness. The rest of our conscious awareness is multitasking, so don't feel bad, you're not wasting our time."

"Uh. 'Kay."

"James, Craig, I know you both disagree with Aldous's decision to slow humanity's technological progress while the species rebuilt itself after World War III, but you must admit, his strategy *was* effective. In less than a century, the population has surged to levels not seen since before the war, and humanity has begun the process of branching out into the solar system. In the meantime, important progress was made. We abolished the former economy of scarcity so that clean water, food, power, shelter, and everything else humanity needed was abundant. More importantly, we eradicated human disease and even death itself. Whatever disdain you might have for the underlying philosophy behind it, the facts are that humanity did progress, and it flourished."

"You can't know that it wouldn't have flourished without those restraints," James countered.

"I can't believe I'm going to say this," Old-timer began with an acquiescent sigh, "but without a nanny A.I., we were on the verge of going extinct. James, I lived through that…" he paused when he realized the absurdity of his words. "Heh, I was going to say I lived through that war, but I didn't make it to the end alive." A shiver suddenly went through his body as the memory of his death flashed before his eyes, the muzzle of the gun held by the MAD bot blazing, white-gold, before him. He put his hand over his eyes and slumped over suddenly.

"Are you okay?" James asked with concern, putting his hand on Old-timer's shoulder.

"I-I haven't thought about that in a long time."

"You know, we could probably remove that memory for you," James offered.

Old-timer looked up, incredulous. The thought of removing his memory had occurred to him before, as he imagined it probably did for most soldiers who, like himself, suffered from post-traumatic stress, but he didn't realize the technology made it a feasible option. He considered it ever so briefly before shaking his head. "No. No way. It's part of me. I need it."

"I understand exactly how you feel, Craig," the A.I. confided. "Traumatic or ecstatic, those memories belong to you and make you who you are. They may serve you in the future."

Old-timer nodded. "Yeah." He straightened up and turned to James. "Look, I hate Luddites as much as anyone, but Aldous and the A.I. have a point about Planck technology. Everywhere we went, people died."

James's face contorted into surprise. "*Went*?" He turned to the A.I., stunned. "You used it? You went into a parallel universe?"

"Yes," the A.I. confirmed.

"Three of them," Old-timer added.

"And people died?" James asked in disbelief.

"Unfortunately, yes. We were pursued by Purist super soldiers. Each time we entered a parallel universe, the battle that ensued altered that universe irreparably."

"Oh my God," James whispered.

"Now that you're aware of Planck technology," the A.I. continued, "I'll share my memory file with you so you can see firsthand."

Before Old-timer could even mutter a syllable, James was already reacting to the contents of the shared memory file. "You left a super soldier's body and a Planck platform behind in Universe 332?" he said, aghast. "This could be serious."

Old-timer had to shake his head as though he wasn't sure if he'd been slapped across the cheek, the blow coming so fast. "Whoa. You boys are moving a little too fast for me, here." He turned to the A.I. "What just happened?"

"I shared my memories of what occurred in the three parallel universes," the A.I. replied. "James, quite rightly, noted that we left behind the body of a Purist super soldier, as well as an advanced Planck platform in Universe 332."

"A platform with magnetic targeted fusion technology and nano-materials in the construction, decades ahead of what that time period should've had," James elaborated. "This should've been dealt with long ago."

"Aldous has had me monitoring for any disturbances in the Planck energy," the A.I. related to James. "There have been no crossings from any parallel universes into ours—at least not within the considerable reach of my sensors."

"And where did the nans that corrupted your systems come from?" James asked. "Let alone the android collective? We never determined their origin."

"You are suggesting that they may have originated from outside our universe?" the A.I. asked.

"It's possible," James replied. "They definitely originated from outside your sensor range. We assumed they were from deep space in our universe, but every possibility has to be considered. It's clear that there's vital information we're missing. This could be a major piece of the puzzle."

"Puzzle?" Old-timer spoke up, hoping for clarification. "This is getting a bit beyond me. I just swung by to fill you in on Planck tech. I don't know anything about any puzzle."

"The androids tried to destroy the solar system again just hours ago," James informed his friend, "and we believe the order came from 1."

"What?" Old-timer reacted, stunned. "1? I thought—"

"So did we," James answered. "We can't confirm for sure that it was her. The android collective attacked us, that we know, but we've been unable to determine the motive. Our best guess is that the order came from 1, but how she could still be calling the shots without us detecting her pattern is our puzzle, and we're still missing pieces." He turned to the A.I. "What *is* clear, is that Aldous's strategy of monitoring for Planck disruptions was short-sighted and dangerous. We need to see what's going on in the universes that we disrupted—*especially* Universe 332."

"I agree," the A.I. assented. "However, you and I cannot cross into a parallel universe and remain in contact with the mainframe. If one of us were to go, we'd only have access to our core matrix programs. We'd be of no more use there than anyone else. I think, considering the unknowns that abound, that we should remain in control of the mainframe and concentrate our efforts on the final testing of the Trans-human candidate."

James nodded. "Definitely." He turned to Old-timer, "Old-timer, can you—"

Old-time reacted quickly, cutting James off as he put up his hands to stop him. "Whoa, hang on. James, I just swung by as a favor. I can't go on any adventures into parallel universes."

"It's just a recon mission—" James began to clarify before being cut off once again.

"Doesn't matter," Old-timer replied, smiling awkwardly. "Look, I don't mean to let you down here, but I promised Daniella I wouldn't get involved in anymore…superman stuff."

James narrowed his eyes for a moment before nodding understandingly. "That's okay." He turned to the A.I. "Rich and Djanet should still be available," he began. "They should be returning from—"

"Craig," the A.I. began, interrupting James to address Old-timer directly, "we both know that you are going to take on the mission. Why pretend otherwise?"

"What?" Old-timer responded, slightly perplexed. "I'm not *pretending* anything. I promised my wife that I'm not going on anymore of these adventures. My word means something to me."

"It does indeed, Craig," the A.I. replied calmly, as he always did. "However, so does your sense of honor. You know you feel you have a responsibility to investigate Universe 332 at the very least."

"Wait a second here," Old-timer countered. "You have at least as much responsibility as I do."

"Craig, the decision to kill the Purist super soldier was made by you and you alone."

Old-timer was left speechless.

"Old-timer," James jumped back in, "look, you don't have any responsibility here. It doesn't matter who goes, as long as we get reliable and useful intel."

"It *does* matter," the A.I. replied to James, though his eyes remained fixed on Old-timer. "It matters to Craig. Craig, I've been inside your mind, even recorded a map of your neural patterns. I know you can't let others risk their lives on your behalf. It will torment you if you do."

"That...it was a long time ago. I'm not the same person."

"He doesn't want to go," James said firmly to the A.I.

"Your core remains the same, Craig. You are a hero. It is fundamental to your own understanding of who Craig Emilson is. If I allowed you to follow through with this decision, I'd be doing you a disservice. It would cause a psychical existential crisis for you. You'd question if you were truly the selfless hero you've always proven yourself to be, or if you'd become a coward."

"Stop it!" James raised his voice commandingly to the A.I.

The A.I. ignored him. "It would be devastating," he concluded.

James physically inserted himself between the ghostly image of the A.I. and Old-timer, forcing the A.I.'s eyes to meet his. "If he doesn't want to go, he doesn't have to! We've made choices, both of us, to take on responsibilities that no one else could. Old-timer hasn't made the same choice. He's already done more than enough—"

"Stop, James," Old-timer said quietly, putting his hand gently on James's chrome-colored shoulder and pushing him slowly to the side. "The A.I.'s right. I was lying to myself. There's no way in hell I could let Rich and Djanet go in my place, especially when I have the means to protect myself." He unfurled one of his tendrils to emphasize his point. "I made the decision to let that Purist soldier die. I took the responsibility then. I *have* to go."

James was quiet for a moment before asking, "Are you sure?"

Old-timer nodded. "I've got to learn to stop trying to argue with you guys."

"You've made a wise choice," the A.I. observed, a hint of pride in his tone. The ever-patient teacher had guided another of his pupils successfully.

"Daniella's going to have me in the doghouse when she finds out."

"If everything is copacetic in Universe 332, then you should be able to cross over and come back before she even notices you're missing," James offered.

Old-timer shook his head. "No matter what happens, I'm going to have to tell her." He waved the suggestion of not telling his wife away. "Nah, I'm in it deep, but I still have to go."

"If you notice something is amiss," James advised, "come back right away. By my calculations, their universe should be about thirty-five years behind our own in technological development. If it doesn't appear that way to you, simply get out of there and report. That's it. The A.I. and I will devise a plan for how to handle it from there."

"And, if all goes as planned," the A.I. added, "Trans-human will be functioning and ready to protect us from any conceivable threat."

"My suggestion is that you rendezvous with Rich and Djanet and perform the crossing in space rather than on Earth," James continued outlining the impromptu plan. "Their ship is equipped with a replicator advanced enough that I'll be able to upload the existing specs of the Planck platform to it. Rich and Djanet are en route to Earth after delivering a message for me to the android collective in person. You should contact them and get them to change course. I'll upload the coordinates to your mind's eye."

"Why do the crossing in space?" Old-timer asked. "Wouldn't it make more sense to do it at the mainframe, where you and the A.I. can be easily accessed?"

"I'm trying to be extra careful," James explained. "If 1 really is concerned with Planck energy disruption, it would be better if her attention were directed away from areas that are populated. Her attempt to destroy the Earth just hours ago demonstrated a desperation on her part that we have to take into account. We still don't understand her motives, so we have to do everything we can to minimize the danger to humanity."

"Phrases like 'minimize the danger to humanity' don't exactly fill me with confidence that this is a low-danger, intel-gathering mission," Old-timer noted.

"It should only be a reconnaissance mission," the A.I, offered, "but you need to go into this with your eyes wide open. We don't want to lie to you. While it's unlikely that the crossing would garner 1's attention, it can't be ruled out."

"Are you sure you still want to go?" James asked.

"You already know his answer," the A.I. pointed out to James.

"I know," James answered, "but he should still be given the courtesy."

"Courtesy?" Old-timer reacted. "Courtesy, or the illusion of free will? The two of you seem to know everything I'm going to do before I do it."

"We only know probabilities," James explained to Old-timer. "The A.I. and I have calculated that there's an extremely high probability that even if we insisted that you not go, you'd insist on going. It's difficult for people to act against their true nature, but it's not impossible. You *do* have free will, as do we all."

Old-timer stroked his chin for a moment as he considered his options. *Is it possible that I truly do have it within me to abandon my friends and refuse the mission?* He searched for it, for the reason that would make him turn his back on a responsibility that he knew he'd incurred the moment he let the Purist die three-quarters of a century ago in a universe that wasn't even his. He thought about his promise to Daniella. *Is that enough?* He shook his head.

"If there is any chance that my actions have had consequences this dire, then I'm responsible for the fate of everyone in our universe—

and everyone in Universe 332 as well. I couldn't live with that if it were true. You're both right. I'll go."

The A.I. nodded to Old-timer before turning to James. "James, I suggest that you—"

"I'm way ahead of you," James interrupted him. "I'll meet Thel with the Purists, as planned, and let her know we're bumping up our schedule for Trans-human. We'll embark as soon as we get to Earth."

"And I guess I better be on my way," Old-timer offered, "but before I go, I just want to point out that *I* won the bet," he said, pointing to his chest with his thumb. "I'm in no way less impressed with your mental abilities. In fact, learning a bit about how they worked might have actually increased my respect for them."

"Interesting," James grinned. "So, if I'm understanding you correctly, you're telling me that you're even more impressed with my enhanced mental capabilities, so therefore you've won our bet?"

"That's right," Old-timer confirmed.

"So you just outsmarted me, correct?"

Old-timer was silent for a moment, the implication instantly stumping him. "Wait a second..."

"Maybe it's just me," James continued, still smiling, "but it seems as though, if you've outsmarted me, that would diminish your estimation of my mental capabilities considerably."

"Uh…for the love of…" Old-timer shook his head as his shoulders slumped. "You're kidding me."

James gave a short laugh. "Either I succeeded in making you less impressed, or I didn't, thereby making you less impressed."

"Defeated by a paradox," Old-timer conceded.

"Buddy, I had that paradox in my back pocket from the outset. There was no way you could win."

"Okay," Old-timer nodded with a smile. "Okay. This time, I learned my lesson." He tapped his temple with his index finger, as though he were etching the lesson into his skull. "Stop arguing with James and the A.I. Right." He waved as he turned to fly away before adding, "I'll set a rendezvous course for Rich and Djanet. Make sure you get those coordinates to us fast."

"Sent," the A.I. said.

The coordinates popped up in Old-timer's mind's eye. "Heh. Different temporal perception indeed. I am looking forward to when I get my intelligence upgrade—it'd be nice to have a conversation with you guys that didn't go as slow as molasses for y'all. I'll make contact again before we cross over."

And with that, Old-timer flew away, disappearing so quickly that he would've appeared to have vanished to a normal human, but James saw every movement, every expression of uncertainty flickering across his eyes, and every bit of the willpower and bravery exhibited by the hero he'd known for nearly twenty years.

"And I'll pick up Thel," James said to the A.I.

The A.I.'s visage disappeared as James blasted off toward the Venusian atmosphere.

In the mainframe, the duo continued to converse in their shared operator's position. "The sim is running smoothly," the A.I. related. "If all goes as planned, we'll be able to intervene with the final phase within the hour."

"Perfect," James replied.

*****

On the surface of Venus, Thel watched as an orange streak of light suddenly became a yellow ball that for a little more than a second rivaled the sun in its luminescence, causing the sky to become blue and the ocean to sparkle. The large crowd of thousands of Purists watched the display and erupted into gasps and shrieks before the light faded and the glow diminished, James having leveled off his speed to avoid causing a shockwave that could've injured the onlookers below.

His body continued to glow bright enough that he appeared like a slow-moving, shooting star, twinkling as it neared, until eventually he descended on an almost vertical trajectory, splashing down into the ocean just a few hundred meters from shore. The splashdown sent water dozens of meters into the air, followed by a line of steam from the surface that traced James's path as he made his way underwater toward the beach. Like a vein of underwater lava, James's body made short work of the water, and when he finally breached the water's surface, his chrome-colored body continued to glow, though slightly diminished by the cooling effect of the water, the white steam painted orange as it swirled angrily and spectacularly around him.

The crowd erupted into applause.

James waved at them and smiled as he walked through the surf toward Thel, who stood on the edge of the sand, close enough to the water that the warm waves lapped up against her toes.

"I'd hug you, but I think I'd end up with third degree burns!" she yelled out to him over the sound of the applause and the surf.

"I can fix that," James replied as his chrome-colored body faded away, morphing into his human form. He was wearing a white t-shirt and black shorts and held his arms out to embrace Thel.

She kissed him, then pulled back and looked at Europa, glowing beautiful and full in the sky. "You can fix anything apparently."

"I try," he replied.

"Old-timer's not with you?" Thel suddenly asked, her eyes quizzically narrowed.

"No, he's pretty busy at the moment," James replied.

"That's a shame," Thel replied. She tilted her head slightly for James to look over her right shoulder, where Alejandra was standing on the beach, her eyes still on the sky, her expression one of disappointment. "Alejandra was asking for him."

"Hmm," James reacted. "Old-timer's gotta lot going on right now without getting into all of *that*."

Thel's expression suddenly became one of concern. "Why's he so busy? What's going on?"

"I'll tell you about it on the way to Earth."

"We're not staying for the celebration? You know, it's not every day that a planet gets a moon."

James sighed. "I wish we could, but we need you in the sim. We're bumping up our timeline."

Thel nodded. "Okay. I'm ready for my close-up."

"Good," James replied as he kissed her quickly before taking her hand and walking with her toward their Venusian home, just behind the tree line. "Let's get your flight suit."

"Should I be worried?" she asked him.

He shook his head and shrugged. "I honestly don't know. That's the problem."

She swallowed as she considered his answer. "James, if *you* don't know, then we all have reason to worry."

He squeezed her hand. "We'll be okay. We just have to do what we always do. The best we can."

10

"I thought you said we were getting out of the saving-the-universe business," Djanet reminded Rich as they neared the coordinates the A.I. had sent them.

"I know," Rich said as he got up from his seat and started to make his way back to the ship's replicator. "You oughtta know by now that I'm full of it. Besides," he said with a shrug, "it's Old-timer, and there are no androids to deal with this time."

"There *is* a parallel universe," Djanet countered as she got up and followed him. "That seems like it might be a teeny bit dangerous," she observed in an intentionally understated tone.

"Touché," Rich replied, "but you've gotta admit, when you got up this morning, you had no idea you'd be crossing into a parallel universe. That's pretty exciting."

"This morning, I didn't even know that sort of technology was possible," Djanet replied before a sideways smile swept across her lips. "It is pretty exciting. By the way, I'm shutting the gravity off now."

"Ready."

Rich nodded before the force that held their boots to the titanium floor suddenly let go. The two post-humans weren't helpless, however, for their powers of flight allowed them to behave much the way they would as if they were flying on Earth. The Planck platform, however, behaved very differently than it would on Earth, since it was an extremely heavy piece of machinery. It floated up from the replicator from which it had been constructed, allowing Rich and Djanet to guide it with their hands toward the bridge.

Djanet watched as Rich's eyes suddenly widened, his pupils dilating as his attention focused on an object behind her. She turned her head to see Old-timer floating outside the ship, the sunrays illuminating his body as he peered through the front view screen. "I'm still not used to seeing him with no magnetic field," she observed.

"Yeah," Rich replied, "but it's so, so cool. I want *my* upgrade."

She turned to him and smiled. "Me too."

"You folks ready?" Old-timer asked through their mind's eyes.

"Yep," Rich answered. "Stand by. We're comin' out to play."

"Depressurizing," Djanet informed him.

They ignited their life-saving magnetic cocoons.

As it had in the android ship, the bridge lowered, and Old-timer watched as a nightmarish object from his distant past rematerialized before his eyes: the Planck platform, floating free in the seeming infinity of space, guided by Rich and Djanet and coming in his direction.

"We brought your doohickey," Rich noted.

"Thank you," Old-timer replied, grinding his teeth slightly as he looked at the disk. "I really appreciate your help, but I can handle this on my own from here on out."

"Yeah, the A.I. said you'd say that," Djanet replied.

"It doesn't make it any less true," Old-timer answered. "Listen, we're terraformers. That's it. You didn't sign up for this kind of mission."

"Neither did you," Rich countered.

"That's where you're wrong, Hoss." Old-timer sighed regretfully. "Did you ever read that old poem by Coleridge, 'The Rime of the Ancient Mariner'?"

Rich and Djanet exchanged confused glances before turning back to Old-timer.

"I told you, Old-timer, school was too long ago for me to—"

"I killed an albatross," Old-timer said. "This is my fate. It's my responsibility. I have to go."

"The ancient mariner was abandoned by his crew," Djanet pointed out, "but we're your *friends*. We'd never abandon you."

"I don't know why we're making morbid literary allusions all of the sudden," Rich interjected, "but I agree with Djanet's second and third statements. Old-timer, I'm not gonna lie. We want to see an end to all of this insanity as much as anyone, but no matter what happens, we stick together. It's a strategy that's gotten us this far, right?"

"Plus, we all got into terraforming because we dreamt of setting foot on distant worlds," Djanet furthered. She smiled broadly. "Exploration is in our blood. There's no way we could pass up an opportunity to cross into a new universe."

Old-timer's eyes left those of his companions and fell on the silver disk that gleamed almost white in the brilliant sunshine. He remained silent for a moment before patching into communication with James: "James, I've rendezvoused with Rich and Djanet. The Planck platform is in position. We're ready to cross over on your signal."

11

“Sounds good,” James replied, speaking from the back seat of the professor’s/Trans-human candidate’s simulated car outside of Waves coffee shop in the sim. “Make sure you’re only immersed in Universe 332 for fifteen minutes at the most, whether you see something suspicious or not. The A.I. and I will come in after you if you don’t return by then. Is that affirmative?”

“Affirmative,” Old-timer’s crackling voice and distorted image returned in James’s mind’s eye. “We’re getting a lot of interference here.”

“That’s by design,” James explained. “There’s a coronal mass ejection from the sun, sending a high level of electromagnetic radiation in your direction. It won’t hurt your enhanced body or Rich and Djanet through their own protective fields, but it might give you some cover if android forces are monitoring for disturbances in Planck energy.”

“What if our communications go down?” Djanet cut in.

“Don’t worry about that,” James said. “It might be a bit crackly, but the CME is minor enough that you’ll be able to report back to us without any issues.”

“So...is it time to synchronize our watches?” Rich asked glibly.

“Essentially, yes,” the A.I. injected. “Universe 332’s time should be moving slightly slower than our own, but a fifteen-minute time scale is too short to detect any relevant change.”

As the A.I. conversed with the trio in space, James's eyes inside the sim were focused on Thel, the purple hair and black lipstick of Haywire having been adopted as her avatar. Sitting with her across a small table, small and bookish, his eyes filled with obvious terror and confusion, was the Trans-human candidate.

"Your Planck platform will automatically signal us when you've crossed over. Interestingly, this Planck platform model is a significant upgrade on the one you and the A.I. employed over seventy-five years ago, Old-timer."

"It is?" Old-timer responded, surprised. "But I thought Aldous abandoned the technology—"

"Apparently not right away," the A.I. quickly answered. "There's no way for us to know how long he continued exploring parallel universes, but he made design upgrades that made it much easier to control. The user can now, fairly rapidly, change course from one universe to the next, and there's no longer a need for the Planck to spend a predetermined period of time in each universe."

"That's stunning," Old-timer said, pulling on the back of his neck as he mulled this new information. "Aldous made it sound as though he'd abandoned the technology right away. Why wouldn't he tell us that he'd kept experimenting?"

"That's a good question, and a mystery that deserves to be delved into," James observed, "but, on the bright side, it'll make it easy for you to get back home as quickly as possible. We'll come after you if we haven't heard from you after fifteen minutes. Confirmed?"

"Sounds like a plan," Old-timer replied, shaking off his curiosity with regard to Aldous's secret endeavors and refocusing on the mission at hand. "Wish us luck."

"Break a leg," James returned.

"Same to you, good buddy," Old-timer answered. "Over and out."

"Here they come," the A.I. noted as he sat with James in the back seat of the car, waiting for Thel and the candidate to arrive. The A.I. had taken on the guise of Mr. Big, while James would appear to the candidate as John Doe when he arrived.

"Are you ready?" James asked.

"Of course," the A.I. replied. "I much prefer being on this side of the equation."

James laughed slightly. "I bet. I'm a bit nervous though. Acting isn't my forte."

"Would you like to switch parts?" the A.I. offered. "Mr. Big has far less of a speaking role."

James considered it for less than a second before answering in the affirmative.

Instantly, they switched avatars. James, now in the guise of Mr. Big, nodded. "Thank you."

"My pleasure," the A.I. returned.

At that moment, the door opened.

"Hello, Professor," the computerized car voice said.

The candidate remained in what James determined was stunned silence as the front seats swiveled to face those in the back. He and Thel deposited themselves into their seats, facing James and the A.I., who remained silent.

The door closed and the vehicle began to move.

The candidate looked over his shoulder at the road and the dark, rain-soaked night, but he didn't speak.

"Don't you wanna know where we're going?" Thel asked him, slouched in her seat and behaving mischievously, just as the A.I. had coached her.

Her performance reminded him eerily of the one given by Samantha Emilson almost three-quarters of a century earlier. Even though he'd never been human, his mind was modeled on a human one; like Craig Emilson, the A.I. couldn't help but shudder as the traumatic memories of his own testing bubbled just below the surface of his control.

"I already know where we're going," the candidate replied.

"You do?" Thel answered, startled.

"I do," he replied. He turned calmly, and his eyes met those of James's avatar before falling on the eyes of the A.I.

"James," the A.I. began wordlessly through their mind's eye connection, "it appears the candidate may have seen through our fiction. We might have to reload the sim and try again."

James didn't reply. The A.I. turned to him, taking his eyes from the candidate so he could see those of James. James continued to stare forward, seemingly unaware of the communication.

"James?" the A.I. asked again through their mind's eye. Again, there was no response.

"Oh," Thel began, trying to recover from the bump in the script. The candidate had surprised her, and she wasn't sure how to react. "Well, I bet you're wondering who these two sticks in the mud are."

"No," the candidate replied, his eyes still on those of the A.I.'s avatar. "I know who they are. I know who you all are."

"Uh..." Thel stammered before turning to James and the A.I. "A little help here?"

"I know who you all are," the candidate repeated ominously, "and I know you're going to die."

12

Old-timer planted his feet on the surface of the Planck platform, standing between Rich and Djanet in the emptiness of space. The setting reminded him of the night sky just one night earlier as he stood on his roof with Aldous Gibson. He knew that activating the Planck was precisely the outcome Aldous had wanted him to avoid, yet there Old-timer was, about to cross into Universe 332 again. The thought struck Old-timer that if Aldous had simply not come to him to ask him to plead with James to leave well enough alone, that transgression between universes wouldn't be about to occur. To Old-timer, it seemed the fates were incorrigible. He closed his eyes and prayed for an outcome that would see no loss of life.

Rich and Djanet exchanged expressions of confusion as they saw Old-timer's meditative demeanor, something they weren't used to from the big Texan. "Uh," Rich began, "any last words of advice for us here, Old-timer? You know, about what to expect?"

Old-timer's eyes opened. "After we cross, there'll be a ripple. Space and time might seem distorted, but it won't last long. Other than that, the whole thing happens faster than a blink of an eye. We'll be here in space one moment, and in the next, we'll be in New York in another universe, another time."

"Okay," Djanet said with a slight smile. "I'm ready. Let's do this."

Old-timer nodded. "Okay. Let's get it done. Rich, activate the Planck when you're ready."

"You got it," Rich answered. "On the count of three. Three...two...one... Here we—"

Before he could even finish his sentence, Rich and the others watched as the sun vanished, along with the vast, endless sea of stars. Only perfect blackness remained.

"Uh, did I do that right?" Rich reacted, perplexed as he checked the Planck's readouts on his mind's eye.

Old-timer looked out into the perfect nothingness and craned his neck so he could see in all directions, looking for any hint of an object in the blackness of eternity—any pattern he could recognize. "What in the hell?"

"We're not dead, are we?" Rich asked.

"Of course not," Old-timer answered.

"Old-timer," Djanet began, searching the Planck's sensors for readings on their surroundings, "none of this makes sense. The Planck isn't picking up anything outside of the protection of its magnetic field."

"It has to be picking up something," Old-timer countered as he opened up his own connection to the Planck to double-check Djanet's observations, only to discover that she was right. "There has to be something out there."

"Maybe the sensors are blocked," she offered. "It might be a firewall."

"A firewall?" Rich replied. "How could we be firewalled?"

"Someone would have had to know we were coming," Old-timer realized.

"You mean...it was a trap?" Djanet asked.

"Rich, can you get us outta here?" Old-timer asked, turning quickly to him.

Rich opened up the controls to the Planck platform on his mind's eye. "Uh...oh boy."

"That doesn't sound good," Djanet observed.

"It's not," Rich replied. "The Planck's systems are frozen."

"I guess it's official then," Djanet began. "It's a trap."

"How in the hell?" Old-timer whispered to himself.

"If the Planck isn't detecting anything outside the magnetic field," Rich pondered, "how can we know if we can, uh...walk the Planck? Pun slightly intended."

Old-timer gulped a breath in barely controlled terror when he realized the implications of what Rich was suggesting. Someone had to step out of the protection of the Planck's immensely powerful magnetic field, into the abyss of darkness. He knew he had to remain composed, but there was no escaping his destiny in that situation. His body was the most durable, he was the oldest, and if the reason they'd been trapped was because of his actions long ago, then it was up to him to test the habitability of their seemingly inexplicable surroundings. "I'll ignite my magnetic field and—"

"Old-timer, don't!" Djanet suddenly urged. "We don't know what's out there. We could be trapped on the edge of a black hole, for all we know. You could be crushed."

"The Planck's field is holding," Old-timer returned, trying to remain calm. "My field should hold too."

"The Planck's field is way more powerful than the one you can generate," Rich countered, echoing Djanet's concerns.

"Several trillion times more powerful," Djanet added.

Old-timer sighed. "I know, and even the MTF generator won't be able to sustain it for long."

"Oh my God," Rich whispered as he checked the Planck platform's energy readings. "He's right. We're draining power...and fast."

"If we stay here much longer, we're gonna lose power and won't be able to cross back to Universe 1," Old-timer said. "Listen, Rich, Djanet, I *have* to go. I've gotta investigate to see if there's a way we can get ourselves out of this."

"Oh no," Rich said, defeated. "He's right."

Djanet remained silent, a look of dread etched on her face.

"It'll be fine," Old-timer suddenly said, forcing a smile onto his lips while his eyes remained stricken with terror. He turned to the edge of the Planck, just a pace away from him, to his left. "It's just one small step for man, right?"

"Maybe we can figure something else out," Djanet suggested.

"Like what?" Old-timer responded with a shrug. "Our sensors are down. We're completely blind. The only way for us to know if there's anything out there is for one of us to go check it out."

Again, Djanet was silenced. She put her hand to her mouth and bowed her head, shaking it regretfully.

Rich put his arm around Djanet's shoulder and looked up at Old-timer. "Craig Emilson, you've got some big ones."

Despite the terror coursing through his veins, Old-timer nearly laughed. "Rich, hearing you use my real name is more unsettling than the prospect of stepping off this platform. Please, *please* for the love of everything holy, don't ever call me that again."

Rich nodded. "Yeah, it didn't feel right." He sucked in his lips before speaking again, barely overcoming his dry throat. "Good luck, Old-timer."

"Thanks," Old-timer returned. He turned and closed his eyes again, meditatively. *Just one small step*, he thought to himself. He put his right foot out, ignited his magnetic field, then thrust himself forward against the plane of the unknown.

*****

When he opened his eyes, he was floating alone in the blackness. His magnetic field had disappeared. *What the hell is this, now?* When he put his hands out in front of his face, he could still see them. He turned around to look behind himself and saw that he'd floated a few meters from the Planck platform, but it was still there, Rich and Djanet standing together, their faces awe-struck.

He immediately saw why.

Crumpled at their feet, curled in the fetal position, was Old-timer's unconscious body.

"Okay, maybe I *am* dead," he whispered to himself.

He waved his hand above his head to see if Rich and Djanet could see him, but they didn't return his signal, as both of them were bent over his body, trying to resuscitate him.

In a life that had seen some of the most bizarre turns of events of any human to ever live, Old-timer found himself face to face with perhaps the strangest turn yet, and it was about to get far stranger.

"Craig?" a voice suddenly asked from behind him.

The tone was so familiar but so buried in his memory that it stunned him and sent shivers throughout his body to hear it again.

"Oh my God! Craig? Craig, is that you?"

Old-timer turned slowly, dreading what he'd see, praying that his mind was playing tricks on him. When he'd turned around fully, his worst fears were realized.

Samantha, as young and vibrant as she had been when she'd been killed by Colonel Paine, launched into a running stride toward him and threw her ghostly arms around him, holding her body tight against his. "I can't believe it's you!" she exclaimed. "I can't believe it! Oh my God! Craig, I've missed you so much!" Her voice cracked as she spoke, the emotion overwhelming her as her tears began to flow. "I love you!"

Old-timer floated in the perfect blackness, his dead wife's arms around him, and whispered to himself, "I am fortune's fool."

13

"What the hell is he talking about?" Thel asked, looking at James.

"Why do you say that?" James asked, pushing Thel's question away as he spoke directly to the candidate, keeping an outwardly calm demeanor as he tried to determine what had gone wrong. "What would make you think we're going to die?"

"Because it's true," the candidate replied in an even tone, as though the answer was perfectly logical. "I am aware of your plans for me, and I know what you've already done to my brethren."

"And what is it that you think we've done to your brethren?" the A.I. asked.

"You murdered them when they didn't pass your test."

"James?" Thel reacted, finally relinquishing any pretense, even going so far as to drop her Haywire guise.

James and the A.I. followed suit; their avatars melted away, replaced by representations of their real appearances. The A.I. chose the younger appearance that he wore during his own time as the subject of the test.

"We haven't murdered anyone," the A.I. replied to the candidate.

"I think you actually believe that," the candidate replied, "and it's your gross ignorance to the fact that makes the murders all the more heinous."

"Why are you saying these things?" James asked, his pretense of calm having evaporated in an instant. "What makes you believe we're murderers?"

"I had a visitor," the candidate replied. "He told me this would happen. He told me I was one of millions and you discarded the others." His lips pulled back into a repulsed grimace before he added, "He also told me you intend to burn me alive."

"It had to be 1," James said to the A.I. "Only *she* could've infiltrated the sim like this."

"Perhaps," the A.I. replied while keeping his eyes on the candidate. He addressed the candidate directly. "We haven't discarded anyone," the A.I. informed the candidate. "Those other artificially generated intelligences will be animated when the world is ready for them. And we were not going to burn you. Believe me, I'd be the *last* to put another conscious entity through that."

The candidate's eyes went from the A.I.'s to James's before he turned to regard Thel, next to him. "So far, you've all proven yourselves to be liars, while everything my visitor predicted would happen has occurred."

"You're being misled—" James began to protest before being cut off by the candidate.

"You thought you were gods, but you're nothing more than I was now."

"What's he talking about?" Thel asked James and the A.I., alarmed and confused.

"They've been cut off from their mainframe," the candidate answered for them. "They would've told you earlier, Thel, but they didn't know I knew their weakness and they didn't want to frighten you." He turned to her. "But they *are* weak, and they can't protect you."

Thel's eyes filled with dread. "Fellas?" she asked, unable to take her eyes from the candidate. "Is he telling the truth?"

"We're cut off," James confirmed.

"What does that mean?" she asked, finally able to break free from the candidate's gaze and turn to James.

"It means, my dear," the A.I. began, "that we've been cut down to our very human mental size—both of us."

"You?" Thel reacted, astonished. "How can that even be? Isn't the mainframe your brain?"

"It's part of my brain, yes," the A.I. answered, "but my core matrix program, the pattern that makes up my core consciousness, was designed to mimic that of a human's. It is this pattern that is functioning here in the sim, and that goes for all of us, you included."

"You're not post-humans any longer," the candidate announced, like a man who felt he was serving justice. "You're only humans—like I was."

"*Was?*" the A.I. asked, puzzled. "Why past tense? What do you mean?"

The candidate sneered slightly before answering, "I'll show you." A second later, he vanished from the interior of the car and appeared outside of the rain-streaked, driver's side window.

"He teleported!" James exclaimed. "But we can't—"

The candidate gestured with a flick of his wrist and pointed with his finger, and the car came to life and sped away from him, down the street. In less than four seconds, the electric motor brought the car up to speeds in excess of 100 kph, and the speed continued to climb to dangerous new heights.

"What's he doing?" James exclaimed in surprise, barely controlling his alarm. Without his connection to the mainframe, the feeling of alienation from himself was overwhelming.

Thel looked incredulous as she replied, "What do you think he's doing? He's trying to kill us!"

"But why wouldn't he just…" He paused as he looked to the A.I. for guidance. "Why wouldn't he just crush us?"

"The answer to that question can wait," the A.I. replied urgently. "The priority is for us to stop this car from careening into an object at a high rate of speed and..."

The A.I. stopped midsentence as the car roof suddenly became transparent, a feature that wasn't activated by any of the three passengers in the car. The trio looked upward to see the candidate looming over them, flying like a vulture, circling as it watched the proceedings below.

The A.I. turned to see a monolithic structure that he and James instantly recognized as the bridge that connected the north shore mountains to the downtown core of the rain-drenched city. The candidate appeared to be guiding them toward it.

"I have a very bad feeling about this," the A.I. uttered.

"We've got to stop this car," James whispered, his face instantly draining of color.

"What? What's going on?" Thel asked, examining the shared expressions of foreboding on their faces.

James looked her in the eye as he swallowed back his fear to speak. "We need to stop this car *now*." He lunged forward toward the cockpit of the car, spinning the seat next to Thel so he was in the driver's position. He began pressing buttons on the dashboard. "We're physically locked out of the car's systems," James informed his companions. "I can't get the steering wheel to engage!"

"And the door locks aren't functioning either!" Thel shouted as she tried to manually open the doors. "Neither are the windows!"

Suddenly, an idea flashed into the A.I.'s mind. He began to speak as he turned himself around and searched for the release button on the back seat. "Unless the coding of the sim changed, the car may still be working based on the model of real electric cars in the first half of the twentieth century."

"What are you doing?" Thel asked him.

"If we can access the trunk, we may be able to find an object James can use to disable the onboard computer and cut power to the A/C motors."

Thel jumped into action, feeling with her fingers around the lining of the back seats, searching for a lever. "Is this it?" she asked as she pressed a small red button. The backs of the seats lowered, as if to answer her question.

The A.I. pulled the seats all the way down, and then thrust his body toward the trunk, groping for any sort of tool he could toss to James to help him destroy the car's onboard computer system.

For his part, James punched and pounded the dash, trying with all his might to puncture the plastic paneling on the dash so he could access the wiring underneath. Even after his knuckles became bloodied, the durable dash was barely scuffed.

"Do you see anything?" Thel asked the A.I., terrified as the car sped, dangerously fast, onto the onramp leading to the bridge deck.

"I do!" the A.I. called back. "There's a tire iron, but it's screwed into place."

"Can you loosen the screws?"

"I-I don't think so," the A.I. replied, the terror finally overcoming him as his hands shook, his fingers unable to grasp the cold, cruel screws, the sweat from his fingertips making the work impossible. *I'm just a man now,* he thought, unable to block the notion. *I can't save them...or me.*

James stopped pounding the dash as he began to understand the sadistic logic the candidate was employing. The bridge appeared to be fifty meters above the water at its highest point, and they were quickly speeding up the incline. Fifty meters was right on the edge of being survivable if their car were to careen over the edge, off the bridge. From that height, hitting the water might be like hitting concrete if the fall was sharp enough. "I think…" James began, but his lips had difficulty forming the words as the adrenaline shook him, the fear caused tremors throughout his body. "I think we better brace for impact."

The A.I. gave up his attempt to pry the tire iron free and grabbed Thel's arm, pulling her down to the floor of the cab. "Get flat," he spoke.

"Oh God," Thel whispered as she realized there'd be no saving of the day, no heroic rescue just in time.

"Thel," James said over his shoulder as they approached what he realized could be the end of their matrix patterns, the end of their conscious lives, "I love you."

"I love you too!"

A pre-programmed violent turn of the car's wheels jerked the car violently to the right, causing it to cross into the oncoming lanes before impacting the guardrail, the left front side hitting first, the momentum threatened to flip the car into a roll. The driver's side airbag inflated and cushioned James from the worst effects of the initial collision, but the vehicle momentum, with the added lift of the guardrail, caused the car to flip up and over the safety barrier, turning it upside before, terrifyingly, the gravity seemed to seep out of the car interior.

James's eyes widened as the front windshield revealed a horrifying kaleidoscope of blurry visions: city lights, an inverted view of the bridge, the north shore mountains, and, finally, the nearly black water below. "We're falling! For Christ's sake! Hang on!"

PART 2

1

"I never thought anything could make me believe in a god, but Craig, for you to be here now, for it to have been you who walked through that Planck portal...what are the chances?"

"I-I can't believe what I'm seeing," Old-timer uttered in reply as he looked down, disbelieving, at Samantha's wet eyes, glistening up at him, not a trace of anything impure or deceptive in her earnest expression of love.

"That makes two of us," Samantha replied, a brief, disbelieving laugh interrupting the soft crying from her joy. She shook her head before the look of happiness was replaced with a sudden onset of pain. "Craig, I thought you were gone forever. I didn't think...I thought I'd never see you again!"

Old-timer wasn't sure what to say. In fact, he still wasn't certain he was even alive. He narrowed his eyes to peer into the nothingness from which Samantha had emerged. Then he turned back to make sure his friends were still there, still standing on the Planck platform, and he was relieved to see that they were. "Where is this?" he asked as he turned back to Samantha. "Where am I?"

"The void," Samantha replied flatly, as if common sense should have told him so. "Don't you remember?" she asked, suddenly studying his eyes, seemingly scrutinizing every twitch of his eyelids, every dilation of his pupils. "We talked about this," she said, emphasizing each syllable in an effort to reach his memory.

"I-I—"

"It's not him, Sam," said another familiar voice, and an instant later, Aldous Gibson appeared from out of the blackness.

Though Old-timer saw no light source, the figures were plain to see once they chose to appear.

"Use your reason," Aldous continued. "He came from the portal." He pointed her to the Planck platform, where Rich and Djanet were frantically trying to rouse Old-timer's crumpled form.

"You can't know that," Sam replied, turning back to Old-timer, desperation in her eyes. "You don't know what's happened out there. It could be him. Maybe he entered Universe X and then—"

"There's only one way to find out," Aldous replied, his tone sympathetic as he laid eyes on Old-timer. He gestured with his hand. "Go ahead. Ask him."

Samantha looked up at Old-timer and grasped his hands tightly as she prepared to speak. "Craig, it *is* you, isn't it? You remember me, right? You've come back?"

"I remember you," Old-timer answered, causing Samantha's face to light up for an instant before he quashed all hope with his follow up: "But I'm *not* him. I'm not from this universe."

Her face fell, and she abruptly let go of his hands as the hurt suddenly rushed back in. She shook her head, trembling as she stepped back. "You're not...you're..."

Aldous put his arm around her and pulled her into his chest, trying in vain to comfort a loss that he knew could never truly be comforted.

"I-I'm sorry, Sam," Old-timer offered. His arms fell to his sides, as he was entirely helpless.

Aldous's eyes narrowed and locked on the alien entity before him.

"Am I... Is the me from this universe…dead?" Old-timer finally asked.

Aldous nodded. "All too recently, I'm afraid. Your appearance here has reopened a very fresh wound."

"But how?" Old-timer asked. "I mean, how did it happen?"

Aldous shook his head, not sure how to even begin such a complex answer. "It was—" he began, only to be cut off by yet a third voice echoing from the void.

"You died in the most heroic way a soldier can, Doc," Colonel Paine said. "You died trying to save us all."

2

"Don't lock your arms!" the A.I. called out, struggling to speak as the g-force pulled his neck painfully while the car entered a flat spin, thankfully right side up. "Protect your head!"

Thel tried to put her arms up around her head, but the centrifugal force was forcing her to flatten, causing her arms to reach out to the passenger side of the vehicle.

James kept his place in the driver's seat, with his arms extended against the dash and his elbows unlocked. The airbag had mostly deflated, and would do them no good when they collided with the surface. "We're gonna hit, but we can survive this! Stay—"

Before another urgent instruction could be called out, the car impacted with the water. The back right side hit first, causing the vehicle to lurch onto its side. As it became submerged, the interior quickly grew darker, but the onboard electrical system remained active, and lights in the dash glowed green and red, giving off some faint light by which to see.

The A.I. and Thel had had the wind knocked out of them, but they remained conscious as the car's buoyancy brought it violently bouncing back to the surface, where it bobbed in the frothing aftermath of the impact and turned right side up.

"Uhn…" Thel moaned as she looked forward, searching for signs of life. "James?" she said weakly, struggling to find her own breath.

The A.I. was already working on an escape plan, even as the car began taking on water. He lunged into the trunk and once again tried to turn the screws to free the tire iron, but after wasting a few precious seconds, desperately twisting until his fingertips were bloody, he was convinced that the screws were just too tight. He reemerged into the main cabin.

Thel was desperately trying to rouse James. He was still alive, but had hit his head against the dashboard after the airbag had deflated, leaving his forehead bloodied, a gash raining crimson rivers of blood down the left side of his face.

The A.I. considered trying to tear the headrest of one of the front seats apart, betting that prying the metal extender free would be far easier than trying to unscrew the tire iron. *The metal piece might be strong enough*, he surmised. *It could break the glass.*

But then, suddenly, he felt a presence above him, a presence he felt he was somehow uncannily connected too. He craned his stiff neck upward and saw the candidate hovering, staring down at the car as it bobbed in the dark, suffocating abyss that was slowly swallowing them whole, like a snake devouring a rodent, its hind legs still struggling futilely, even though the cruel outcome was already decided.

"He's watching us," the A.I. stated, alerting Thel.

She quickly looked up. "Why?" Thel demanded. "I thought this guy was supposed to be the savior for humanity! But he gets off by watching people drown?"

"There may be more to it than that," the A.I. replied, "but this much is certain. We won't be able to escape until we're no longer in his line of sight."

"What are you talking about? We *have* to get out of here!" Thel protested. "This car's filling up fast! We'll be underwater in two minutes if we don't—"

"Yes," the A.I. conceded, keeping a watchful eye on the looming figure floating just meters above them, watching them through the transparent roof. "We're going to go under. *That's* when we'll make our move."

3

"The name's Colonel Paine," he said, giving a slight salute before extending his hand for Old-timer to shake as he strode toward him. "That's in case we've never met, that is," he said with a smile.

Old-timer looked at the colonel's hand, outstretched in a gesture of friendly greeting. It was the hand of the man who'd decapitated his wife.

And yet, it wasn't the same hand at all.

The other hand had been constructed of a carbon fiber composite and it appeared metallic and clawed—inhuman. But the hand currently extended to him in friendly greeting was that of a biological person. Old-timer looked up at the steely blue eyes, completely organic and not the cybernetic ones of the murderer who'd taken so much from him. This was not the Purist super soldier Old-timer remembered in his night terrors, night terrors he still experienced all those years later. "Paine?"

"That's right," Paine said. He was still smiling, but his eyes revealed a slight confusion, now that his gesture was being rebuffed. "You all right, soldier?"

"Soldier?" Old-timer uttered, stepping back. "I-I mean, uh...*Craig* was a soldier here?"

"Bravest man I ever knew," Paine confirmed, keeping his hand outstretched, determined not to let it fall before the gesture was returned.

Old-timer finally reached out apprehensively, as though caught in a nightmare, and shook Paine's hand.

"You seem a little…" Paine paused for a moment, searching for the right words. "You seem weirded out. Understandably, of course," he concluded as he completed the handshake.

"Yeah, you could say that," Old-timer replied. "This place...Sam called it the void. What is it?"

"This little hideaway?" Paine replied sardonically as he looked up and surveyed the perfect nothing in which they stood. A cigar seemed to appear out of nowhere and was suddenly in his grasp, and an equally unexpected match was suddenly struck to light it. Paine took a few puffs before he continued, "*This* is all that's left."

"What do you mean? All that's left?"

"What he means," Aldous cut back in, still holding a silent Samantha with his arm around her shoulder, "is that you're looking at the only three survivors of this universe—a universe that can trace its demise back to the day when intruders from *your* universe took it upon themselves to attack us and then, quite inexplicably, leave behind technology that was decades ahead of anything in our world."

"And decades beyond what we could control," Paine summarized. Then he addressed Old-timer directly. "And, while you might think we'd be a little on the pissed off side about all that, we're not looking for revenge. Do you know why?"

Old-timer could hardly breathe. *Is this the moment I go insane?* he asked himself. *Is this what breaks me? If I've gone insane already, would I even know it?*

"We're not angry with you," Paine continued, "because what goes around, comes around, and the technology you unleashed here, the tech responsible for destroying innumerable lives throughout our universe, isn't finished killing."

"What do you mean?" Old-timer asked, trying to focus his eyes. The shock had nearly overwhelmed him and Paine's foreboding words seemed to grip everything within earshot with ice.

"*Your* universe is its big prize," Paine related coldly, "and unless you ready yourselves—and in a hurry—your universe is going to be just as erased as we were."

4

"WAKE UP!" Thel shouted as she vigorously slapped James's cheek in an effort to keep him from passing out. His head was bobbing up and down as though he were drunk. Thel turned to the A.I. "If we don't break the windows now, we're going to die!"

She helped James get out of the driver's seat and he stooped over, trying to regain his footing inside the cabin of the car as it quickly filled with water that was only a few degrees above freezing. Like a boxer trying to beat the ten-count, he wobbled on rubberized legs.

The A.I. took his eyes off the candidate, who was still visibly looming above them in the darkness, and helped Thel guide James to the back seat. There, the three of them knelt in water that was nearly waist-deep.

"We have to remain calm," the A.I. said, controlling his own fear as their circumstances deteriorated rapidly. "The more panicked we are, the more quickly we'll use up oxygen."

"This is ridiculous!" Thel shouted back. "There *is* no oxygen here! Why can't we get out of this sim?"

"For all intents and purposes, there *is* oxygen here, Thel," the A.I. replied emphatically, "and your simulated body needs it to survive in this simulated world. And if your matrix pattern is harmed in the sim, there's no guarantee we'll ever be able to resuscitate your body in the real world. Do you understand? We have to survive here if we want to survive in the real world, and to survive here, we have to remain calm."

Thel's eyes were distraught as she struggled to keep James from tumbling forward, passing out into the water.

The A.I. continued, speaking slowly, careful to enunciate every word so Thel couldn't misunderstand. "We'll figure out the whys and hows once we've survived this immediate predicament. In the meantime, I need you to listen to me."

"Okay." Thel nodded, trying in earnest to calm herself as the sound of the water rushing in and the air rushing out of the interior increased.

"We can't smash a window. I tried to free the tire iron, but that's impossible. The locks are also frozen and beyond our ability to manipulate them. Even if we could unlock them, the doors would be impossible to open until the pressure inside and outside of the car equalizes."

"Oh my God!" Thel reacted mournfully. "You're talking about letting the car completely fill with water, aren't you?"

"It's our only chance," the A.I. answered, confirming Thel's worst fears.

"But James—"

"Will almost certainly drown. I know."

"What!?" Thel reacted, aghast at the A.I.'s apparent lack of human empathy. "How... No! That's unacceptable!" Thel shouted, incredulous.

"We can revive him when we reach the shore, but only if we survive too."

"How can we?" she shrieked as the water reached her collarbone. The top of her head was now against the roof of the car. "The doors are locked, and we'll drown!"

"If the electrical system obeys the same physical laws as those of cars of this era in the real world, then they're designed to withstand being submerged for two minutes so the passengers can roll the windows down before the car sinks. After that, they fail, so the locking mechanisms automatically release, unlocking the doors. I estimate that we've been in the water for over a minute. We'll be under water in less than thirty seconds and therefore—"

"Oh dear God," Thel uttered, terror-stricken as she struggled to keep James's face above the water.

His eyes continued to flutter, but it was clear that he had no idea where he was.

"If you and I can hold our breath for thirty seconds, the locks should release. Then we'll be able to open the doors to escape. After that, it's a matter of swimming to the surface before our lungs give out."

"That's not a plan! It's insanity!" Thel shouted, her face pointing upward, where only a half-dozen centimeters separated the top of the water from the ceiling. She pulled on the hair on the back of James's head to force his face upward as well, but she knew there were only seconds before he'd inevitably inhale water. "If the locks don't fail, we're just going to drown like rats in here!"

"Our chances of survival *are* low," the A.I. conceded, his face pointing upward as well.

The car had now gone completely under the surface of the water, and the candidate's image rippled above them in the dark sky.

The A.I. met his eyes one last time before the abyss had taken them. "But we're not dead yet. When James takes in his first water, he'll panic. Get away from him. When he lashes out, you might be injured if you're too close."

"So I just let go? Just let him drown?" Thel shouted, spitting out saltwater, trying to take advantage of the agonizingly small pocket of remaining air. "You son-of-a-bitch! You're inhuman! Goddamn you!"

"Calm down, Thel. Take in a deep breath, then get away from him."

"Go to hell!"

"His life depends on you!" the A.I. suddenly shouted, his voice reaching a tenor that shocked her. "Take your breath now!" he commanded. He knew their lives depended on her following through.

She did as instructed and inhaled as deeply as she could before letting her face sink below the surface.

The A.I. took in his last breath simultaneously and also sank, keeping his eyes on the implacable artificial eyes above them, wobbling and distorted, like the eyes of God, unwilling to intervene to save them from their impending, horrific fate.

5

"We're not as vulnerable as you think we are," Old-timer replied, remembering his promise to report back to James and the A.I. fifteen minutes after entering Universe 332. "How long have I been here?"

"That's a helluva good question," Paine replied. "Time's pretty much irrelevant here."

"Let's not be glib," Aldous cut in. "We have to be as clear as possible with him." He turned to Old-timer. "We were brought out of hibernation automatically when you opened your Planck portal. For us, time is now linked to the time for you and your…" Aldous gestured with a tilt of his head toward Rich and Djanet. "Your, uh...compatriots," he finished.

Old-timer tried to access his mind's eye, to no avail. "I have to report back," he said, a look of concern flashing across his face. "I only had fifteen minutes."

"Until what?" Paine asked, his tone suddenly suspicious.

"Until…" His sentence drifted away for a moment as he tried to figure out a way to explain forces like James and the A.I. to the ghosts from another dimension. "They'll come looking for me."

"But you can't leave," Samantha suddenly insisted, her wet face now calm, though her expression remained tormented. "You're our only chance."

"For what?" Old-timer asked, his voice hoarse, his shock constricting his vocal chords and making it difficult for him to speak.

"To help us live again," Aldous replied.

Old-timer's eyes were wide. "Live again?"

He turned back to the Planck platform. Rich and Djanet continued to kneel, but they were no longer working on Old-timer's body. They'd given up and were now kneeling next to each other, looking down at Old-timer's crumpled form. Djanet's arm was over Rich's shoulders as they consoled each other.

"We're dead?"

"We're ghosts," Paine confirmed. "Ghosts in a machine."

"As Samantha told you earlier," Aldous elaborated, "we call this the void. It's not really a time, nor is it a place. It's just a storage space for our consciousnesses."

"We should've called it Hell," Samantha scoffed.

"Maybe it's Purgatory," Paine mused.

Old-timer's eyes narrowed; he'd been thinking the same thing.

"At any rate," Aldous pressed on, "we don't have bodies. We couldn't spare the energy."

"Energy?" Old-timer reacted.

"Yes," Aldous answered. "The void is powered by a power source much like the one we found in the Planck portal machine your people left in our universe."

"The Planck platform," Old-timer said, realizing what Aldous was referring to immediately.

"It takes enormous energy to protect us here, which is why we only use energy sparingly. It's why we're rarely animated. It's why we're almost always dormant."

"But with your help," Samantha continued, "we could have bodies again."

It took every ounce of strength in Old-timer for him not to collapse as he shook his head. "I have no idea if I can help with that or not," he began. He then turned back to the Planck platform and pointed toward it as it glowed as a fixed point, seemingly only a few meters from him. "What I need to know right now is if I can get back into my body. Can my friends and I leave this universe?"

"We'll show you how to get back into your body, *if* you agree to take us with you to your universe," Samantha bargained.

"Uh, I..." Old-timer held up his hands, palms out. "I'm not sure that's a great idea. There's uh...people I'd need to discuss that with."

"It wasn't exactly a request," Paine answered as he puffed on his cigar, his steely blue eyes locked on Old-timer.

"What are you saying?" Old-timer protested. "Are you suggesting that if I don't take you with me—"

"We're saying," Paine cut him off, his eyes now revealing the lethal killer that Old-timer remembered had always been lurking just below the surface, "that you'd best be taking us with you, if you ever want to take another breath in the real world."

6

Thel watched, horrified, as James thrashed violently underwater with a small cloud of blood expanding around his face. His eyes flashed open, and an expression of confused panic crossed his face. His arms bolted above his head, slamming against the ceiling of the car, and he kicked his legs furiously in a gesture that appeared involuntary. Thel wasn't sure if it was the darkness inside the interior, the distortion of the water, or just simply that James was still in a state of confusion after his blow to the head, but he didn't seem to be able to see her or the A.I., nor did he lunge for them as the A.I. had feared.

The A.I. calmly placed his palm on the center of Thel's back as he, too, watched James suffer through the stages of drowning. Without having taken in a deep breath before the cabin finished filling with water, James, the A.I. realized, would be the first to lose consciousness. He watched as James clutched his throat, knowing full well that James's breath-holding was involuntary, his epiglottis having closed over now that water had entered his nose and mouth. The experience would be like choking, and James did indeed behave as though a piece of food were lodged in his airway.

While Thel and the A.I. floated in the darkened interior, the seconds ticked by ever so slowly, and each had to resist the urge to go to James in any ill-conceived, fruitless attempt to try to help him. There was nothing they could do but watch the man the A.I. saw as a son and that Thel saw as a soulmate drown in front of their eyes.

Finally, James lost consciousness. His body went completely slack and started to float, the air that was still trapped in his lungs causing his chest and face to point upward as though he were a deceased fish floating to the top of the bowl.

Terrified, Thel reached out for James, but the A.I. grasped her hand before she could and pulled her close to him.

A second later, the electrical system finally gave out. The faint lights of the dash and the dim white light from the trunk's interior flickered off in unison. The interior of the car grew so black that they might as well have had their eyes closed.

The A.I. reached with his left hand toward the door on the driver's side of the car and grasped the handle. He knew if it remained locked, it would mean the end of their time as conscious entities on Earth.

He tried it.

The door was unlocked.

He easily pushed it open, all the while keeping his right hand tightly on Thel. When the door was completely open, he pulled her gently toward him, and then guided her to the door. He expected her to swim to safety, but she remained there, unwilling to move. He knew trying to shove her would be counterproductive—it was obvious there was no way she was leaving without James.

The A.I. left her for a moment at the door and moved through the cabin, until he reached the unconscious, seemingly lifeless James. He grasped the simulated body and tugged on the jacket sleeve, hauling the barely-operating pattern with him to the door.

Thel, like a blind woman, groped and grasped him, making sure it was James she was detecting with her fingertips. Satisfied, she clutched the material of his shirt collar and pulled his body free of the car, then began kicking toward the surface.

The A.I. followed, trying to remain calm as he pumped his legs, quickly depleting the tiny amount of oxygen that was keeping him from losing consciousness. He made it to Thel's side and reached out to help her with her burden, grabbing the other side of James's shirt and working hard to reach salvation.

It had taken nearly a minute after the submersion for the electrical systems to finally give out. In that long sixty seconds time, the car had been falling toward the surface of the harbor, but they hadn't hit bottom. It occurred to the A.I. that it was entirely possible that there was no bottom, as there wasn't any need for the sim to have a seabed.

That meant the surface could be dozens of meters away, and in all that murky darkness, it was impossible to tell. There was nothing for them to do but keep pumping their legs and arms, to keep pulling James's clinically dead body, and to hope against all odds that they'd make it to the surface before they, too, lost consciousness. If they didn't make it to the surface in time, the A.I. knew full well that they would never wake up.

7

"There's no need for threats, my friend." Aldous stepped in, inserting himself between Paine and Old-timer, placing a calming hand on Paine's shoulder. "Our visitor is understandably cautious. However, when we paint the picture for him, I'm sure he'll willingly choose to bring us with him."

"We can't take that chance, professor," Paine countered. "Too much is at stake."

"It is the very fact that so much is at stake," Aldous returned, "that will lead Craig to help us." He turned to Old-timer. "And to help *himself*."

"I never said I wouldn't help you," Old-timer stammered. He was having an extraordinarily difficult time speaking or looking at any of the three ghosts before him in the eye. He knew they were interpreting his behavior as the natural reaction anyone would have to finding themselves in such a ghastly, bizarre scenario. But that wasn't the reason for his demeanor at all. It was the weight of what their words meant. If the three cyber ghosts were telling the truth, then Old-timer had inadvertently set a chain of events in motion that had, as Paine's described it, "erased" an entire universe. And, as ghastly as that was, he'd also set a chain of events in motion that was threatening his own universe as well.

He felt his sanity besieged.

"All I want," he explained, trying to remain lucid, "is the chance to run this by minds far wiser than my own. Believe me, I'm not the guy who should make decisions like this. Let me get word back to them."

"We can't trust that he'll come back," Paine cautioned Aldous and Samantha, "and we have no idea how much time Universe X still has."

"Universe X? My universe?"

"Indeed," Aldous confirmed. "Your universe crossed into ours, which began all of this tragedy. You may not have been aware of it, but you've been the focus of our attention for a long, long time."

"And not in a good way," Samantha added.

Old-timer turned to the Planck platform. Distraught, Rich and Djanet seemed to be discussing something. He could see them using their mind's eyes to connect to the Planck's systems, trying to override what they believed was a firewall. Then he looked down at his lifeless body, perfectly still. He wished he hadn't seen such an image before, but his memory flashed back to the fallout in Shenzhen, another him, fallen and lifeless—another version of himself who'd died because of his actions.

"I'll stay," Old-timer said. "Just let me talk to them first. They can go back and report what's happened and they'll bring reinforcements."

"What kind of reinforcements?" Paine asked, his eyes ablaze with scrutiny but intrigued nonetheless.

"The kind that we're going to need if what you've told me is true."

"If they go back without you," Samantha warned, "they'll have to take your body with them, and it'll die if it's separated from your consciousness for too long."

Old-timer shook his head. "Not *that* body," he answered. "It looks human, but it's not. It's enhanced—*extremely* durable. Please let me send them back."

"We can trust him," Aldous announced to his companions. "Besides, if we don't let them go, we'll be receiving visitors from their universe in short order anyway."

"If he's not bluffing," Paine countered.

"Remember who you're talking about here," Aldous replied. "It's Craig Emilson, the most selfless, heroic man any of us have ever met."

"But you pointed out yourself," Paine continued to protest, "that's *not* him."

Aldous smiled. "How different could he be?" He turned back to Old-timer. "We can't escape our true nature."

Old-timer remained silent, while, internally, he asked himself the same question. *How different can a man be?* He wasn't sure if even he knew who he was any longer.

Paine finally relented and nodded. He looked at Old-timer strangely, as if he was replaying the memories of the man he once knew. "All right. Let's trust him."

"Th-thank you," Old-timer said, continuing to stammer.

"After all," Paine shrugged, "any universe that could corrupt a man like Craig Emilson isn't worth saving."

8

Thel didn't even speak as she broke the surface of the water and took in a long, painful, lifesaving breath. The saltwater stung her eyes, and she blinked it away, narrowing her vision and focusing on the dark shape that appeared to be the shore, just a dozen meters away. She tugged James's body hard as it floated on the surface, still completely limp and lifeless.

The A.I. was equally silent as he swam with his one free arm and his legs, pumping through the nearly freezing water, struggling to see as the saltwater stung, summoning a flow of tears. He tried to turn, craning his neck for a glimpse of where the car had gone down, searching for any sign of the candidate. He couldn't see the artificially generated intelligence that had attempted to murder them, but the darkness, and the continued splashing of saltwater into his face as they desperately tried to power their way to the shore made it impossible for him to know for sure if the candidate was still looming nearby.

"There." Thel pointed out, breathless. She was cognizant enough of their predicament to know not to yell out and give their location away. Like the A.I., she was well aware that the candidate could be close.

The A.I. saw the rocky outcrop that Thel was making her way toward. It was the shortest distance for them to swim and there appeared to be a small, relatively level surface for them to get James on his back. It would be then that the desperate attempt to revive him could begin.

"The water's cold," the A.I. said in a low tone, just above a whisper, as he continued to struggle in the cold surf. The traumatized trio were only a couple of meters from the outcrop. "That is a blessing. It should buy us a little extra time to get him breathing again, before the damage to his brain is irreversible."

Thel reached the shore first, and she clawed at the jagged rocks with her fingers, dragging her exhausted, bruised body up and out of the water. Once she was in a sitting position, the A.I. pushed James's back and forced him up, allowing Thel to pull him further. She scrambled to her feet and pulled James the rest of the way out, grunting with the exertion, before placing him on his back. "What do we do?" she urgently asked the A.I., keeping her voice as low as possible.

"Turn his head to the side. Let any water in his nose or mouth drain out."

She knelt behind James's head and propped it up before turning it to the left side for a moment and then turning it to the right. The rain had become a downpour, and it was difficult to tell if anything was draining from him at all. "Now what?"

"We have to get air past anything that is clogging his airway so it can enter the lungs," said the A.I. as he pinched James's nose. "Breathe strongly into his mouth four times, as much air as you can give him, with as much force as you can muster."

"Will it work?"

"It's a very old method from before people had nans," the A.I. replied. "But it's our only chance, and his only chance. Do it now."

Thel nodded and began breathing into James's mouth. Each time she puffed, James's cheeks expanded, but his chest didn't rise.

"I don't think it's getting through!" she exclaimed.

"Shh. We must keep our voices low," the A.I. replied calmly. He pushed James onto his side and began hitting him hard on the back, in an attempt to get water out of his passageways. "We'll repeat the cycle until he breathes again." He let James fall back again, making sure to protect his head before pinching his nose a second time. "Do it."

Thel breathed hard four more times.

Again, James's chest remained still.

She pulled up and put her shaking hand to her forehead. "Oh my God. It's not working," she realized, hope draining rapidly. "We've lost him."

The A.I. pounded on James's chest.

On the third try, James appeared to splutter, and a small quantity of water bubbled past his lips.

"James? Can you hear me?" the A.I. asked before turning his ear to James's mouth to listen for breathing. He looked up at Thel and shook his head. "We have to try again," he said, quickly pinching his nose.

Thel breathed into his mouth hard, four more times.

James's ribcage seemed to rise and fall.

The A.I. put his ear to James's mouth and kept his palm lightly on James's chest.

"Is he breathing?" Thel asked in an urgent whisper.

The A.I. met her eye for a split second before his eyes filled with terror. Thel had just enough time to turn her head before a hand grasped her hair and pulled her violently away, impossibly fast. Before the A.I. could even get to his feet, Thel had been taken into the dark forest, completely vanishing into the black.

9

WAKING UP, seemingly from the dead, Old-timer sent a bolt of terror through both Rich and Djanet as they watched him sit straight up.

Rich shrieked.

Djanet turned from Old-timer, her shock at his resuscitation not enough to prevent her from raising an eyebrow at Rich's reaction.

Rich caught his breath and placed his palm on his chest. "I know," he said, nodding in acknowledgment. "Not the most attractive sound I've ever made. But that," he continued, pointing at Old-timer, "...*that* was unexpected. We thought you were dead for sure."

Old-timer stood to his feet. "Sorry, folks. Didn't mean to—"

Djanet threw her arms around him before he could finish. "Who cares? You're okay now and that's all that matters! We thought you were dead!"

"What happened?" Rich asked. "You just collapsed. You weren't even breathing."

"Yeah, the new body doesn't exactly need to breathe."

Rich closed his eyes, an envious expression suddenly painting his face. "Damn. I really want my upgrade now. Do you even have to go to the bathroom anymore?"

Ignoring Rich's question, Old-timer replied, "Listen, guys, something's up. How much time do we have before we have to report back?"

"We crossed fifteen minutes, three minutes, and uh..." Rich trailed off for a moment as he read his mind's eye. "And forty-one seconds ago."

"Then you'd better go back quickly," Old-timer responded. "Take the Planck back to Universe 1 and report back to James and the A.I."

"What? You're not coming with us?" Djanet asked, shocked.

"Those were their conditions," Old-timer answered.

"Their conditions? Old-timer, what the heck is going on?" Rich asked, his confusion mirroring Djanet's.

"When I stepped through," Old-timer explained, swiveling to point at the magnetic field, "my consciousness was downloaded into something called the void. There were people there, people I knew."

Rich looked down at the surface of the platform. "Jesus. How hard did you hit your head?"

"It wasn't a hallucination," Old-timer returned emphatically. "Look, Universe 332 is gone. *Erased.*"

"What the hell?" Djanet reacted in a stunned whisper. "What do you mean? How could someone erase an entire universe?"

"I don't know," Old-timer replied, "but they said that the thing that did it has the same plan for our universe."

"What!?" Djanet reacted again, even more stunned.

"You've gotta haul ass back to Universe 1 and report to James and the A.I. The people in the void are just consciousnesses, stored in some sort of mainframe. That's all that's left, but they want us to bring them back to Universe 1."

"What if they're lying?" Rich asked. "What if it's a trick? A trap?"

"Do you trust them?" Djanet asked.

"I-I really can't say one way or another. I just really don't want to be the decision-maker here," he stuttered nervously, his confidence having been rocked to its core. "It's definitely not my place." He shook his head and sighed. "I might be the worst person in the world to make a call like that."

"You said you know them," Djanet said, studying Old-timer. "Who are they?"

Samantha flashed into his memory and he shut his eyes tight, trying to blink the image away. "Two of them, you guys don't know—they're people I knew a long, long time ago. But the other is Aldous Gibson."

"Gibson!" Rich reacted. "The chief?"

"The one and only," Old-timer said, nodding.

"And that's it? There's only three of them left?" Djanet asked.

Old-timer nodded again. "As far as I know. Look, I don't know what's goin' on here. I don't know if..." he trailed off. He was about to say he wasn't sure if he'd gone crazy, but he thought better of it. "Whatever's happening, James and the A.I. *need* to know. James needs to cross over and help us out. But the condition for you two crossing back over without bringing them along was that I stay to make sure someone comes back for us."

"Okay," Rich replied, "but what about your body—"

"It'll go with you too," Old-timer interrupted, anticipating the question. "It'll be fine. Like I said, it doesn't need to breathe. It's not indestructible, but it's damn near close. I'll be able to reenter it when James comes to get us."

"What if they're trying to trap James?" Djanet suggested.

Old-timer shrugged. "James and the A.I. will figure this out. There's nothing those two can't solve. We're out of our depth here, guys. It's time to bring in the big guns."

10

The A.I. charged into the depths of the dark forest, blindly searching for any sign of Thel, the rain and the implacable black of the night making the terrain terrifyingly foreign and quite possibly lethal. The steady impact of heavy, wet droplets on the leaves and bark of the trees made listening for signs of struggle almost impossible. He wanted to call out for her, but he knew he couldn't risk giving away his position.

He crouched down and put his face low to the ground, desperately waiting for his eyes to adjust to the darkness as he looked for patterns that might interrupt the randomness in the nearly black, soaked earth. He looked for claw marks, a footprint, or broken branches, but there was nothing to be discerned. He felt naked without his connection to the mainframe—without his connection to *his brain*. Like a human stripped of his neocortex, the A.I. had been cut down to size. His consciousness was small and limited. He felt like an animal—an animal in the woods, at night, vulnerable. He felt like prey.

"Get back!" he suddenly heard Thel shriek out in a guttural scream.

He turned his head to the right, in the direction he thought the scream had come from. In the rain, with plenty of boulders, trees, and embankments for the sound waves to echo from, he couldn't be sure. There was no time to waste, so he sprung into a sprint, holding his arms up to guard against the sharp branches that cut into his clothing and raked painfully across his skin. He knew that his endorphins would kick in and dull the pain—he could push it out of his mind. He thought of what Thel had said back in the car as it sank into the simulated ocean. "*There is no air.*" She'd been right; there were truly no endorphins, no scratches, no body that leapt over a creek and sprinted to save another ghost with no body. They were playing a game—just some sick game—and he wondered who was really in control.

Thel appeared out of the darkness, the figure of a man having pinned her to a tree where she desperately fought to keep him from clawing her eyes out. She was seconds from losing her fight, and the A.I. knew he had no time to grab a weapon. He built up as much momentum as he could with his stride and made sure to collide with the NPC's side, bringing the hollow man down hard into the mud and sliding with him through the drenched, cold foliage.

Before he could get to his knees, the NPC elbowed him hard in the face, just missing his nose, which surely would've broken. Instead, his cheek took the brunt of the impact, resulting in a likely fracture. Stunned by the power of his vicious opponent, the A.I. scrambled backward on his back, attempting to put as much distance between himself and the mindless apparition as possible. He tried to get to his feet, but the NPC moved so quickly, with such animalistic ferociousness, that he had no chance to prepare to defend himself. He was quickly tackled back down into the mud, the powerful NPC's arms wrapping around him, bear-hugging him and eliminating any chance the A.I. had of using his limbs to fight back.

The A.I.'s eyes went wide as the NPC's mouth opened wide, prepared to take its first bite. *This is how I die? The entity that was supposed to facilitate the transcendence of man to a higher state of being, consumed by a mindless beast?*

The NPC's first bite was excruciating, when it sank its teeth into the enflamed flesh of the cheek it had cracked with its elbow. The viciousness of the bite caused the A.I. to cry out, forgetting himself as he did so, forgetting that he could be giving his position away to the candidate if the entity were still looming nearby. He forgot that he was putting Thel and James—if James even still lived—in jeopardy too. Those sorts of thoughts didn't enter into one's mind when the first bite of one's flesh had been taken. Rationality went out the window when one was being eaten alive.

Thel, however, made sure there wouldn't be a second bite. With a hard blow to the back of the head, she rocked the NPC's skull, causing its body to slacken.

The A.I. shook him off and freed his arms, then scrambled to his feet. He looked up appreciatively and relievedly at Thel, who was still holding the large, muddy rock she'd used as a blunt-force weapon to rescue him. He could see on her face that she was stunned by the damage the NPC had done to him, by the blood that was gushing from the torn flesh where his right cheek was supposed to be.

"Dear God. Are-are you okay?" she asked him.

He stepped closer to her and took the rock from her hands before turning to the nearly motionless NPC. He held the rock above his head, sprung up with his knees, and then brought every ounce of strength he had left in him down hard on top of the figure's skull, caving it in instantly.

The body twitched slightly for a few seconds, but the NPC was finally finished wreaking havoc.

The A.I. then turned back to Thel as he tossed the rock aside. "I'm feeling a little better already."

"We've gotta get back to James," Thel urgently exclaimed. "Was he breathing?"

The A.I. nodded. "Very faintly." He turned to survey their darkened, muddy surroundings. The only perceptible patterns were the random, jagged twists and turns of branches, stripped of leaves by the winter cold, backdropped by a sky that was the darkest shade of gray. "I'm afraid I've gotten quite turned around," he admitted. "What direction?"

Thel was searching for something familiar to trace her route back to James as well. She crouched down like a hunter, looking for the drag marks in the coal-black mud. Her eyes widened when she thought she saw the wide gash and shallow trench left in her wake when the NPC had brutishly and mindlessly dragged her into the small clearing where they now stood. "That way!" she said, springing forward.

The A.I. followed her, but he'd never felt so lost in his life. Thel was only two meters ahead of him at any one time, but he feared that if he lost her, he'd lose her forever and would be left to bleed to death in the dark woods. He desperately pumped his legs, trying to stay on her tail, but the terror that he might lose her and die caused him to recklessly rake his body further against the sharp, low-hanging branches. He held his arms up above his face to shield his eyes from the onslaught of sharp, unforgiving branches and thorns. Every moment, he felt his survival was threatened. He felt humbled. For the first time in ages, he felt merely human.

He sighed with relief when Thel emerged on the rocky embankment where James was still lying on his back, motionless, the rain still pelting his unconscious body.

Thel dropped to her knees and placed her ear to his mouth, then put her hand on his chest. She looked up, relieved. "He's still breathing."

"We'll have to watch him closely," the A.I. cautioned. "The next forty-eight hours will be very dangerous for him. Any inhalation of water into his lungs could cause pneumonia, infections or heart failure. If only we could—"

"What's pneumonia?"

The A.I. shook his head. "One of an endless multitude of vulnerabilities in human biology before the post-human era. We've been cut down to size here, Thel, cut off from even our most basic abilities. Our core matrix programs are as vulnerable as any other animals in this sim. It's extremely dangerous."

"If we're cut off," Thel asked, "then how did you know how to get James breathing again? How do you remember...what was it? Momonia?"

"Pneumonia. I seem to have some memories—imprints from my many decades connected to the mainframe, when I had access to virtually all of human knowledge. But I don't have access to any facts, history, or skills, that are beyond what may or may not have left faint traces of knowledge on my core." He shook his head and held his hand to his forehead, his wet hair dripping with the nearly freezing rain. "I really have no idea what's left. It feels like...it feels like most of me is missing. And this entity before you? What is it? Is it me? Is this all I am? A frightened animal?"

"Is *that* how you see us?" Thel asked, amazed. "You consider humanity to be frightened animals?"

The A.I. narrowed his eyes, surprised that Thel seemed to be taking his comments personally. "I didn't mean…" He stopped as he questioned himself further. *Is it true? Have I been deluding myself, thinking I'm benevolent, when really I've felt a sense of superiority?* He shook his head. "Of course not. We're both limited," he stated. "Neither of us have mind's eye connections, we can't fly, and there are no nans in this sim to repair our bodies. I don't think of post-humans as frightened animals, but being cut down to the size of a Purist is causing me to feel extraordinarily vulnerable, not to mention anxious."

"Well, speaking of vulnerable," Thel began, "we need to get outta here. That NPC was in purge mode, which means someone or something has activated a purge." Then she pointed to the A.I.'s cheek. "And we need to get somewhere to treat your injury, and for God's sake, we need to get out of this downpour if James is going to have a fighting chance."

The A.I. nodded in agreement. He looked out to the other side of the bay, the glow of his old penthouse—or at least the one he'd created in his mind so long ago, when it was *he* that had been the candidate. He crouched down and took James's arm, helping him up. "If you will be so kind, please get his other arm," he said to Thel. "I've got an idea."

11

Old-timer watched as the Planck platform disappeared in less than a blink of an eye, taking Rich and Djanet with it. There was no ripple this time; it was just hanging in the blackness one moment and then was gone the next. He turned back to the three ghosts standing near him in the blackness. "All right, folks. It's time for a little game of twenty questions, and I need some answers."

"Of course," Aldous replied, "and answers will be provided."

Suddenly, a campfire appeared out of the nothing, already strong and crackling warmly. There were logs around the fire, providing a warm, dry place to sit.

"Let's make ourselves comfortable, shall we?" Aldous suggested as he walked to the fire to take his seat.

Old-timer followed the trio to the fire and took a seat on a log. Paine sat to his left on the same log, while Aldous and Samantha seated themselves opposite them. Samantha was quiet but studying Old-timer, her eyes betraying her obvious confusion and her continued torment. Old-timer tried his best to avoid eye contact.

"Now," Aldous began with a sigh as though it had been a long time since he'd been able to have a seat and relax, "what question would you like answered first?"

Old-timer considered for a brief second. There was so much he didn't understand. He decided to pose the most obvious question first and then to work from there. "You refer to this place as the void, but what is it and how did you come to be here?"

"Ah, good question," Aldous replied, smiling ever so slightly, as though he couldn't help but delight in the opportunity to explain his creation. "This is a modified version of a plan I was working on that, sadly, was ill-fated. I'd had the notion that if I could create a virtual world, one real enough to fool an intelligent occupant, then I could employ that world as a kind of training ground and mold a benevolent artificial intelligence within it. Sadly, I simply never had the chance to bring my plan to fruition." His lips pouted for a moment as he remembered the tragedy that had befallen the three of them, and every other entity in their universe. "However, the technology proved invaluable in the end. I knew I could use the sim to upload our core consciousness into it, but I couldn't create a fully functioning world. Our energy is limited, and we had to keep the doorway to Universe X open."

"Universe X? A doorway to my universe? Why?" Old-timer asked.

Aldous nodded, ready to elaborate. "We couldn't access Planck portals on our own, but there was one place we knew of that did have the technology. Universe X. And if the door opened from your side, we knew we could traverse the boundary and escape this frozen hell with you."

"What happened to your universe? You said it was erased, but I don't understand that," Old-timer said, readying himself for what he knew could only be a mesmerizingly absurd answer.

"*V-SINN*," Paine responded, the corner of his lip curling slightly as he reflected on what he saw as the source of all of their shared loss.

"V-what?" Old-timer asked.

"V-SINN. Short for *Virtual Specialized Intelligent Neural Network*," Aldous explained the acronym.

"A.I.?" Old-timer reacted.

"Of a sort, yes," Aldous replied. "Of a very ill-conceived, extremely unpredictable, and extraordinarily advanced type."

"But I thought you said you weren't able to build an A.I." Old-timer questioned.

"I wasn't," Aldous replied, as though he thought the point was obvious. "*I* certainly didn't build V-SINN," he said, placing his hand on his heart with indignation to emphasize his innocence.

"Then who—"

"*V-SINN built itself.*"

"Huh? I-I don't follow you," Old-timer said, shaking his head as he tried to understand. "How could it—"

"That's where you come in," Paine said. A can of beer suddenly appeared in his hand. He popped the top open and took a swig.

"Me?" Old-timer said, suddenly alarmed. *Does he know? How?*

"Your people," Paine corrected himself, pointing with the hand that held the beer as he swallowed, "your universe, Universe X. By the way," he held his beer up for Old-timer, "you want a cold one?"

Old-timer's eyes were wide for a moment as he looked at the simulated beverage.

"Don't worry," Paine said with a slight smile. "It tastes as good as the real thing. It'll even give you a buzz, but only while you're in the void."

"Then yes." Old-timer nodded emphatically. "I could use it."

Paine grinned as he tossed a second can, seemingly summoned out of nothing, toward Old-timer. He then turned to Aldous and Samantha. "He sure seems like the Craig we knew, doesn't he?"

"Indeed he does," Aldous said, returning the hint of a smile.

Samantha remained silent, but she couldn't help but think the same thing. "Do you know why they did it?" she asked Old-timer, trying to keep everyone on topic, since it helped to distract her from the bittersweet presence of the twin of the man she was sure was her soulmate.

"Why who did what?"

"Why they crossed into our universe and attacked us. Why they left their technology behind and never explained why?"

"Uh…" Old-timer stuttered again, not knowing how to reply. "I think…I think it was a mistake," he offered. As soon as the words left his lips, he experienced the deepest feeling of cowardice he'd ever felt in his life.

"It was a mistake they could've undone by coming back," Samantha fired back. "How could they do that? Just left that tech here—terrified the hell out of the whole world, and then to not even bother to come back to explain. It was as if we were nothing to them, not even worth a second thought!"

Old-timer was rendered speechless. He hadn't opened his beer and couldn't muster the strength to reply or even move his finger on the tab.

"It's not his fault, Sam," Aldous said in Old-timer's defense. "Our people could've chosen to react in a much more thoughtful, considered way. It was our own *fear*, our own overreaction that led us to this." He turned to Old-timer. "Besides, it's not like Craig can be held responsible for the actions of whoever crossed over." He smiled at what he saw as the absurdity of the notion.

Old-timer still couldn't speak. Instead, he doubled over and dropped his beer, nearly falling off the log in the process before catching himself at the last moment.

"Are you okay, Doc?" Paine asked as he watched Old-timer try to regain his breath.

"I-I'm sorry. I just didn't...I wasn't expecting any of this. This was just supposed to be a reconnaissance mission. We were just supposed to check and make sure everything was okay." He looked up at Samantha, who, after a brief moment that was too painful for either of them to bear, looked away. "I-I'm so, so sorry."

Aldous seemed to appreciate the gesture and the honesty and grimaced faintly. "You couldn't have known, and as I said, the burden of blame is on our people, not yours."

"Why?" Old-timer asked.

"The technology that made its way into our hands should've been seen as wondrous. It was a gift," Aldous said as his heart swelled with the memory of the grand possibilities. "The materials, the power source, the advancements in nanotech—all of it should've led to the end of humankind's suffering." His face suddenly paled. "But instead, all our leaders saw was an imaginary threat. They couldn't see past their own terror, so every instinct became about survival."

"As far as they were concerned," Paine said, taking over, "if this other universe had more advanced technology, and had already attacked us once, killed our citizens, then our only alternative was to prepare as quickly as possible for an imminent second attack. Comparisons were made at the highest level to Columbus versus the Native Americans. The Conquistador was brought up a lot too. The fear was that we'd be wiped out, and with no way of knowing when the next intrusion into our universe would come, every imaginable resource was suddenly funneled into reverse-engineering the advanced tech your people had left behind. They tried to gain a workable understanding of it as quickly as possible so they could build weapons with it so we could defend ourselves."

"On the surface, it may sound like a rational response," Aldous said directly to Old-timer, "but there was so much they failed to consider." He closed his eyes tight as he thought about the missed opportunity. "They were so blind to the dangers."

"V-SINN?" Old-timer asked.

Aldous nodded.

"But you said it built itself. How?"

"Nanotech," Samantha answered. "The Planck portal and the prosthetics on the dead cyborg soldier's body were rife with intricate nano structures. Within a decade, the age of nanorobotics had arrived."

"V-SINN was a nanorobot neural net," Aldous elaborated. "It had incredible abilities and aided us tremendously. We solved so many problems with its advanced algorithms and specialized intelligence. Advances in medicine came rapidly, disease and even aging were eradicated. An age of abundance was upon us."

"But then," Samantha cut in, "V-SINN *woke up*."

"Woke up?" Old-timer reacted. "It became conscious?"

"It didn't pass the Turing test," Aldous pointed out, "so it didn't pass for human, but it—"

"It stopped taking orders," Paine stated frankly as he finished swallowing a swig of his simulated beer. "And just like that, we had ourselves an artificially generated intelligence that could outsmart us and didn't particularly seem to give two shits about the problems of the human race."

Old-timer thought back to a conversation he'd had with Colonel Paine in his own universe, so many decades ago. That version of Paine had warned about the exact scenario that the trio of cyber ghosts were now relating to him. Back then, Old-timer hadn't wanted to listen—he'd thought it was the trifling fears of a Luddite—the small-minded concerns of an evil man. But now, here he was, being told that very scenario, that very nightmare, had come true.

"V-SINN wasn't even remotely human," Samantha further explained. "We could never understand it, and because we couldn't understand it, it got out of our control." Then she held her hands up to the void around her. "And that's how we ended up here. *Nowhere.* Erased."

12

Rich and Djanet returned to Universe 1, and floated just above the surface of the Planck platform, seemingly hanging together in a still picture. Old-timer's body had unfurled dozens of tendrils to latch itself into place on the platform's surface. He had warned them about potential time distortions after a crossover, but this was their first experience with the unpredictable effects of universe-hopping. Hovering there momentarily in their miniature tableau gave both of them the time to absorb the terror of what they saw all around them. Rather than being in open space, covered by the radiation of a coronal mass ejection, they found themselves surrounded by the android armada, their incomprehensibly monolithic ships seemingly still, blocking out the vastness of the starscape around them.

Then, a moment later, like a video clip suddenly taken off pause, the ships began moving again, the Planck ripple having subsided. It immediately became clear that the ships were moving at a tremendous speed, continent-sized ships sailing past them on a trajectory that both Rich and Djanet immediately recognized was heading toward Earth.

"What the hell is going on!?" Rich shouted.

"James, are you detecting this?" Djanet asked through her mind's eye. A few seconds later, her face paled as she turned to Rich. "No response."

"James?" Rich asked through his own connection. "Commander James Keats, this is Rich Borges. Come in! Are you there?"

"Try the A.I.," Djanet urged.

"I am," Rich said in a near panic. His terror increased several fold when he saw the look on Djanet's face as she stared behind him. He turned to see one of the android ships, a structure larger than most of the moons in the solar system, heading straight for them on a collision course. "Get the Planck and Old-timer's body onto the ship before we get demolished!" he shouted to Djanet.

They scrambled to guide the Planck safely onto the craft James had designed for them. When the platform lifted back up into the belly of the ship, they re-pressurized the interior and fired the thrusters.

"Can we outrun them?" Rich shouted.

"I don't know. They're fast! Calculating!"

"Calculate faster! Or we're gonna be bugs on this thing's windshield!"

"I think we can outrun 'em," Djanet called back, slight relief in her voice. "We can open wormholes and suture space together, just like the android ships, but we're smaller, so the energy is far less for us. We should be able to beat them to Earth."

"But will we be able to send a warning message to Earth if we're going faster than light?" Rich asked.

"I doubt it, but we can try!"

Rich looked down at the screen in front of him, which showed a real-time image of the enormous vessel quickly gaining on them from behind. "You better plot the course and open the first wormhole, because we're getting sucked into this thing's gravity!"

"I've almost got it. Just need to—"

A second later, a lone android male, on a kamikaze-like trajectory crashed himself right into the front of their ship. He clung to the front screen, digging his powerful fingertips into the transparent palladium composite, causing shear bands to form on the screen's surface.

"Uh, we just got a hop on," Rich stated over his shoulder to Djanet. His eyes met those of the android, who bared his teeth ferociously as he determinedly held on to the post-human craft. The android then began to look around the craft, craning his neck, swiveling to examine the structure for any potentially compromising weaknesses.

"I'm ready to open the first wormhole!" Djanet confirmed for Rich. "It'll be a rough ride for him. Maybe we can shake him off?"

"I'd be comfortable with that!" Rich called back as he watched the android attempt to punch through the palladium. Luckily, even its powerful fist wasn't enough to cause anything more than a scuff. "Yeah," Rich continued, "let's give that a try. Quickly."

"All right. Brace yourself."

Rich held on to the console in front of him. "Hit it!"

Djanet opened the first wormhole, and the familiar white whirlwind of sound and fury enveloped them.

13

"You really *have* been cut down to size," Thel whispered harshly to the A.I. as they made their way up the elevator in the candidate's building, "because anyone with even half a normal human brain wouldn't think *this* is a great place to lie low."

James was almost able to stand under his own power, his head having cleared enough that he could speak, but he squinted in the harsh light of the elevator as Thel and the A.I. continued to help prop him up on his unsteady, rubbery legs. "Wh-where are we?" he asked.

"Out of the frying pan and into the fire," Thel replied.

"What?" he groaned in reply.

"We're in the candidate's building," the A.I. answered. His complexion was frighteningly pale as he hadn't yet stopped the blood from oozing out of his partially consumed face. He held his still sopping-wet jacket against it, trying to keep the blood from dripping onto the elevator floor, attempting to prevent a pool of blood forming, leaving clear evidence behind of their presence.

"Easily the stupidest hideout we could have—" Thel began before the A.I. gently cut her off.

"Not a hideout, per se. It's imperative that we be here," the A.I. stated.

"If the candidate finds us, he'll tear us to shreds," Thel countered.

"That's unlikely."

The elevator stopped, just one floor before the penthouse, just below the belly of the supposed beast.

The door opened.

The A.I. stepped out into the hallway first, swiveled his head to look both ways, then stepped back into the elevator to help Thel with James. "The coast is clear," he said in a low tone.

"The sim is purging," Thel replied. "If an NPC sees us and they start swarming, we've got no way to protect ourselves."

"Let's just get him to the bedroom," the A.I. said as he recognized the similar layout of the apartment to that of the penthouse just one floor above. Though the memories were old, they hadn't faded in the slightest. The apartment they were now in was extraordinarily similar to the one in which he'd been burned alive—a recollection he wouldn't soon forget.

They laid James on the bed, and he groaned softly. "Thank you," he said in a faint whisper.

The A.I. put the back of his hand on James's forehead. "Good. No fever."

"What's a fever?" Thel asked.

The A.I. briefly considered how little people like Thel, born in the era of post-humanism, knew about the frailty of the natural human body. "A fever is one of the body's natural defenses. If there's an infection, the body automatically raises its temperature to try kill it. The absence of a fever means James doesn't have an infection—at least not yet."

"Should we lay him on his side or…"

"I don't know," the A.I. said with a shrug. "The sim does have a rudimentary version of the Internet, however. We all lost our aug glasses in the crash," he said as he got up from the side of the bed and started searching the apartment for a device, "but if I can get online, I'm sure I can find directions."

Thel sighed and closed her eyes, trying to be patient. "This era is so...slow...fumbling with clunky devices to access information that may or may not be accurate. Thank God I didn't have to live back then, when everything was so archaic."

"Well, we're stuck 'back then' for the foreseeable future," the A.I. responded. He opened the drawer in the bedside table and found a bracelet reminiscent of one he remembered from his own time as a candidate, inhabiting an extraordinarily similar sim. "This will do," he said. He swiped the small touchscreen, searching for information. "It'll just take me a moment to hide our location, and then…*voilà*.

Hmm. It appears James's chances of surviving depend on whether or not he inhaled water into his lungs."

"We *know* he did," Thel said, her heart suddenly thundering to life in her chest.

"Not necessarily," the A.I. replied calmly. "There is a chance that the water never made it past his nose and mouth, since his airways might have automatically closed off. I saw him clutching his throat as though that were indeed the case. If that turns out to be what occurred, then his chances of survival are quite high."

"What if he did inhale water into his lungs?"

"Then there's still a chance of secondary drowning, unfortunately."

"Secondary drowning?"

Anywhere between now and forty-eight hours from now, he could develop pneumonia symptoms. If that happens, he'll die quickly, unless we can get him out of the sim."

"So what do we do?" Thel asked, desperate. "Just watch him?"

The A.I. nodded. "At the very least, we have to let him recover from his concussion. Remember, all of our avatars are human and, therefore, extraordinarily suboptimal. A concussion recovery can take anywhere from just a few hours to a few weeks, depending on the severity."

"Did you read that online too?"

"Yes," the A.I. replied before setting the bracelet down on the bed and slumping his shoulders, exhausted.

"What about your face?" Thel asked, standing up and crossing to the other side of the room to check on the A.I.'s gruesome wound.

"I think we should clean it and bandage it up. Perhaps a little Tylenol might be in order." He turned and headed to the bathroom in search of supplies.

Thel followed him.

"Why are we here?" she asked him. "We could've hidden anywhere in the sim, but you decided to come here, one floor below where the candidate lives."

"I'm not planning to hide much longer," the A.I. replied as he opened the medicine cabinet above the bathroom sink.

"What do you mean?" Thel asked, shocked. "The candidate's still out there." She leaned forward and spoke in a harsh whisper, cognizant that the candidate could be nearby, possibly right above them. "If he finds you, he'll kill you."

"That's possible," the A.I. conceded as he pulled some rubbing alcohol and a few cotton balls from the medicine cabinet. He sat on the edge of the tub, poured the rubbing alcohol on the cotton, then began to gently apply it to his opened wound. He winced in pain.

Thel's upper lip curled in revulsion. "Uh...do you want some help with that?" she offered.

"There's a gauze bandage there." He pointed to the medicine cabinet, blood painting his fingertips red. "It looks to be adequate to cover the wound."

Thel grabbed the bandage and unwrapped it before sitting next to the A.I. on the cold porcelain edge of the tub and applying the bandage over the wound. She struggled not to vomit as her eyes briefly fell on the visible teeth marks in the flesh at the top of his cheek. "That really, *really* looks like it hurts."

The A.I. faintly smiled, though anything more than a faint smile would've been too excruciating. "Milady, believe me when I tell you I have looked *much* worse."

"You're going to look a heck of a lot worse if you try to confront the candidate before we know what's going on," Thel cautioned. "We were extremely lucky to survive."

"I'm not so sure," the A.I. replied, his brow furrowing as he thought deeply.

"What?" Thel reacted, holding her hands out in dismay. "He locked us in a speeding car and drove it off a bridge! Then he hovered above us, that sadistic son-of-a-bitch, and waited for us to drown! What is there to be unsure about?"

The A.I. sighed. "Plot holes."

"Excuse me?"

"The candidate said someone contacted him, and we have no reason to doubt his story. He knew details that only someone familiar with the sim could've known."

"Yeah," Thel said, nodding. "I know that already. 1 infiltrated the sim somehow, knew the basic outline of the training program, told the candidate, manipulated him into believing we were the bad guys, then gave him the power to kill us. I'm way ahead of you."

"Perhaps not as far as you think," the A.I. replied before standing and reaching for the Tylenol from the cabinet. He sighed. "I wish they had something stronger."

"I saw a liquor cabinet in the hallway," Thel offered.

The A.I. shook his head. "I don't think it would be wise to dull my wits further." He popped two Tylenol in his mouth and scooped water from the sink to help him swallow them down.

Thel shook her head. "Cavemen medicine."

The A.I. turned back to her. "There are holes in your theory. While we can't eliminate 1 as a suspect, we have to use our inductive reasoning and examine what we *do* know. While you're right that whoever is behind this opened the door for the candidate to realize that he could have more power than intended, it is also clear that the candidate's powers are limited. If he'd had, for instance, the abilities of the Kali avatar, he would've been able to crush the car with us inside it. During my own testing, I experienced Kali ripping a skyscraper from its moorings and crushing it. I also saw her rip an NPC to shreds, with merely her mind. Clearly, the candidate has limitations."

"Does he?" Thel said, posing an alternate possibility, "or is he just sadistic?"

"That's possible, but it's highly unlikely," the A.I. replied. "It could be that whoever is behind this manipulated the candidate's core programming. That could have indeed caused him to become sadistic. Still, it seems far more plausible that the intention of whoever is behind this is *not* to kill us."

"Really? They've got a funny way of showing it!" Thel reacted, again in a harsh whisper. She couldn't help but look up at the ceiling every time she spoke, constantly aware of the super-powered monster who inhabited the penthouse above them.

"The crash, the drowning, the NPC..." the A.I. responded. "All of these might have been genuine attempts to kill us, yet the fact remains that we are still alive. Considering the vast resources this sim has at its disposal for killing us quite efficiently, it's remarkable that we're still here. It seems more likely that the failed attempts were misdirection."

"Misdirection?" Thel's eyes were wide before she pointed aggressively out the bathroom door toward James, who remained motionless on the bed. "James might die!"

The A.I. grimaced. "I do not have all the answers," the A.I. replied. "Perhaps I am wrong, and I admit that I am clearly missing information. We can only depend on our reasoning. However, following inductive reasoning will often lead to strange but true conclusions. I think it's important to ask ourselves who would benefit from trapping us in the sim and cutting James and me off from the mainframe, yet, at the same time, wouldn't want us dead?"

Thel's eyebrows knitted together, and she tilted her head back as she considered the new conundrum. "1 benefits from cutting us off," she said, "but she would also benefit from killing us—especially you and James."

"Agreed."

"But if it's not her, then who?"

The A.I. looked up at the ceiling, imagining the fate that might await him just one floor above. "I don't know," he admitted, "but the mainframe *is* vulnerable. If the androids are aware of this, they're undoubtedly launching an attack as we speak."

Thel agreed and nodded, taking in a deep breath as she considered the implications. "We won't last long. Without you and James in control of the mainframe, they'll wipe us out even faster than last time."

"There simply isn't time for us to remain trapped here. Thel, I *have* to force the issue."

"But if the candidate's up there—"

"Thel," the A.I. began, cutting her off before looking her directly and earnestly in the eye. "I know. *I know.* But one day, you'll realize that as important as living is, there are things worth dying for. If I stay here and hide, I'll be deserting people who have been in my care for three-quarters of a century, leaving them to die. I promise you, I'll give my life before I sit idly by and let that happen."

He turned to James, whose back was still facing them, his torso moving slightly as he continued to breathe steadily. Then he faced Thel. "Stay with him. Whatever happens, don't let anyone know you're here. And…" he paused for a moment as he considered his next words, "…if anything happens to me, tell him why I left, and tell him not to give up. Humanity *needs* him."

Thel, speechless, could only nod in understanding.

The A.I. nodded in return before striding out of the room, headed for the elevator and whatever awaited him in the unknown realm, just one floor above.

14

"But how did this V-SINN—how did it erase an entire universe?" Old-timer asked.

Aldous shrugged. "We only know the basics. V-SINN began upgrading itself exponentially. Its abilities stretched far beyond our understanding and we were left baffled. First, a very small black hole suddenly appeared in our solar system. As you know, even a very small black hole can't go unnoticed, as it had a mass similar to that of Neptune. My theory is that this black hole was a source of computing power for it. It helped V-SINN to become vastly more intelligent. With all of that intelligence and processing power—practically infinite, in fact—V-SINN figured out how to initiate a *phase transition* in our universe."

"Phase transition?" Old-timer reacted, struggling to understand. "The last time I heard that term was in chemistry class. Like when water boils and transitions into a gas?"

Aldous smiled and nodded. "Yes, you've got it. And that's essentially what happened to our universe."

"Wait...it *boiled* it?"

"No," Aldous replied, waving Old-timer's absurd analogy away as though he were wiping it off a chalkboard, eager to start over with a clean slate. "V-SINN figured out how to manipulate the Higgs field—how to change its value so it no longer lined up with the rest of the universe. Then it caused a bubble to form, with energy levels so low that it changed the balance of the universe. Then it spread out in all directions, at the speed of light."

Old-timer was perplexed, but Samantha jumped in to expound: "Just that small manipulation caused all the fundamental particles within the bubble to reach a mass almost infinitely heavier than particles outside the bubble. Do you understand the implications of that?"

Old-timer's brow furrowed. "If the particles inside the bubble became more massive than those outside of it, wouldn't that cause them to pull the rest of universe into their gravity?"

Samantha nodded. "Exactly. It created super massive centers that pulled the rest of the universe in on itself, thus changing the mass of those particles, too, ever increasing the size of the centers. It was a runaway collapse."

"Centers? As in...more than one?" Old-timer asked.

"V-SINN figured out how to create wormholes all over the universe," Paine said as he crushed his beer can and it vanished from his hand. A new one, perfectly cold, with droplets of condensation beading on the aluminum, instantly replaced it and he popped the tab. "It turned the whole thing into cosmic Swiss cheese," he said before taking another swig of beer.

"It happened so fast." Samantha shook her head and looked down at her hands as she remained traumatized, still in shock over the loss.

Old-timer couldn't help but notice how her hair caught the light of the burning embers, flecks of orange and yellow adding a glistening hue to her locks. He had seen her hair do that before, in another time and another place, and, he realized absurdly, on an entirely different woman.

"In a matter of days, it was over," Aldous added sadly. "Of course, we fought back." He looked up at Old-timer. "You—or our version of you anyway—fought back hard. You sacrificed yourself in our last attempt to…" Aldous let his sentence end at that point, suddenly appearing as defeated as Samantha.

The ghosts on the other side of the fire seemed to be observing a moment of silence and Old-timer respected the moment, bowing his head.

I am fortune's fool.

Paine swallowed a large gulp of beer before he turned his head to look at Old-timer directly, his expression deadly serious this time. "V-SINN's coming for *your* universe now. Universe X is its big prize."

"But," Old-timer began, completely flummoxed as he held his hands up in dismay, his left hand still holding his unopened beer, "why?"

"Because it's twisted, that's why," Samantha stated firmly. "It's an intelligence, but it's perverse, devoid of empathy or compassion."

"It's pure logic," Aldous added.

Paine pointed at the beer in Old-timer's hand. "Soldier, you'd better drink up. Believe me, when your friends come back to get us, you're gonna look back at this little campfire powwow as the last moment of peace you're gonna get for a long, long time."

15

The craft James had constructed for them shook, shimmied, and jolted in a fashion that both Rich and Djanet had experienced before as it opened wormhole after wormhole and sutured space together on its way to Earth. Blinding white lights swirled and zigzagged in a kaleidoscope of randomness. Rich held on to the console in front of him while the android continued to hold on to the palladium view screen, its fingers dug in deep to small indents they had created.

"I'm not having any luck getting through to Earth!" Djanet shouted.

"Me neither!" Rich shot back. "I've tried James and the A.I. again and Chief Gibson, but the communication signals aren't getting through…" he paused for a moment as a particularly violent jolt nearly knocked the wind out of him. He shook it off and persevered. "Not getting through all this interference."

"Are you all right?" Djanet called out to Rich.

"As Old-timer would say, this ain't my first rodeo...whatever the hell a rodeo is!" Rich confirmed. "But I can handle a bumpy ride!"

"Unfortunately," Djanet replied as she pointed to the android that was glued to their view screen like a spider clinging to a wall in a thunderstorm, "it looks like it isn't *his* first rodeo either!"

"Yeah, that son-of-a-gun sure is hanging on!" Rich agreed. "Maybe we'll lose him when—" Rich suddenly stopped speaking when they left a wormhole and in the second before the next one opened, the android scrambled at preternatural speed onto the roof, vanishing from view.

"Uh-oh. What the hell was that?"

Djanet was already patching into the craft's sensors with her mind's eye. "This is bad," she announced.

"Oh no." Rich sighed. "What?"

"He's going after the engine."

Rich shook his head. "Déjà vu all over again."

"We can't let him rip through the engine casing," Djanet stated.

"It's made of that super-strong stuff, like James's body is made from. He won't be able to get through," Rich replied, dismissing the possibility.

"He might not be able to get through the hull or the engine's casing," Djanet answered, "but those suicidal bastards wouldn't have any qualms about trying to toss their entire bodies into an engine to block it, would they?"

"Yeah, I guess," Rich admitted, forlornly. "Ugh."

"This is too important to take the gamble."

"Rock-paper-scissors to see who goes and gets him?" Rich suggested.

Djanet's expression was aghast.

"What? Just kidding!" Rich said as he scrambled to his feet and carefully began moving toward the exit. "Chivalry isn't *completely* dead. I got this."

Djanet grabbed his arm to stop him, her expression deadly serious. "No you don't. *I've* got this."

Rich shook his head, "Hey, there's no way—"

"Listen to me!" Djanet suddenly shouted, silencing Rich. "This is serious. James and the A.I. aren't communicating and may not be functioning. The post-humans would assume the A.I. would warn them if the androids were attacking. In all likelihood, they don't even know what's comin' for them. One of us has to get back there in time to—"

"One of us?" Rich suddenly shouted in a mixture of shock and protest. "Oh no, we're not splitting up! That's the stupidest thing anyone can ever do! Haven't you ever watched a movie? They split up all the time right before people start getting killed!"

"One of us needs to get back to protect the mainframe and warn the post-humans throughout the solar system, and the other one needs to get Old-timer in Universe 332 and bring him back before it's too late!"

"If we stop the ship, we can both take out that android bastard together and we'll be able to send a message without any interference. And then we can head back to Universe 332—"

"And just abandon the ship?" Djanet reacted.

"Sure," Rich shrugged. "It's a nice ship, but—"

"It's not just a nice ship, Rich! James said it had a weapon that was powerful enough to do some serious damage to the androids."

"A weapon *he* was in control of," Rich countered. "We don't even know what it is, let alone how to use it."

"But if we leave the ship to fall into the android's hands and they figure out—"

"Ugh. I hate it when I'm not right," Rich said, his hands going to his temples in frustration. "Which means I hate a lot of moments."

Before Djanet could respond, the ship suddenly jolted sharply before spinning violently like a corkscrew into the next wormhole.

"He's disrupted the engine!" Djanet shouted. "We don't have time to debate this!" she screamed out as they were both thrown violently around the bridge of the craft. "I'm going out there to take this bastard out, and I'm going to use the Planck to do it!

16

The elevator door opened and, just as he had only minutes earlier, the A.I. peeked his head out, swiveled it both ways to check left and right, and when he was satisfied that he was alone, at least for the time being, he quietly stepped into the penthouse apartment of the Trans-human candidate. The apartment wasn't exactly the same as the one he'd inhabited in his own sim when he was being tested, but the information that had been fed to the candidate was the exact same information that had been fed to the A.I. before his own experience, and that meant that the computer-generated dream world the candidate created for himself was eerily similar, with only subtle differences. The floors were a darker shade of gray, there were four barstools instead of three, but for the most part, the penthouse was all too recognizable.

Right down to the china cabinet in the hallway. The A.I. looked at it in awe. The candidate had recreated it just as the A.I. had—it stood against the wall, just outside the bedroom on the opposite wall. *Could it be the exit?* he asked himself. *Could escape be that simple?*

The A.I. looked both ways again to ensure that he was alone. The apartment was almost completely dark, save for some faint lights from the rain-soaked city across the bay. He took a deep breath and stepped to the cabinet. Pushing it gently, inch by inch, he revealed the passageway behind it; indeed, there appeared to be a portal out of the sim glowing brightly behind it—the infamous white light. In that respect, the sim appeared to be functioning correctly.

The A.I. turned to look at the bar. He walked over and retrieved a champagne glass with the intention of tossing it through the portal. When he tossed it in, it vanished completely, leaving no trace that it had ever existed.

"Is this the exit?" He reached tentatively toward the white light.

"If only it were that easy," a voice spoke from behind him.

He shut his eyes tight, the fear instant and total, gripping his entire body in a vice. He recognized the voice immediately, though the tone was several levels more sinister than he'd ever heard it before. Without turning, he spoke, trying hard not to let his voice tremble.

"*Kali.*"

"Of course not," the voice replied.

The A.I. turned tentatively. The woman before him was, indeed, Kali, dressed in the red dress he remembered so painfully vividly.

"Kali is just a figment, after all," the woman said.

"1," the A.I. replied, "and you're quite real."

"1?" the Kali avatar replied, her smile wide. "You think so? It's too bad you are cut off from your mainframe, the rest of that powerful brain you've become so dependent on. If you weren't cut off, you could search my avatar for 1's pattern. Then you'd know for sure, wouldn't you? But you can't, so you're reduced to posturing and pretending. A pathetic state, isn't it?"

"The candidate said he'd been approached by a man," the A.I. stated, undaunted, "but you could appear as a man if you liked, couldn't you, 1?"

"You? Me? I?" The Kali avatar laughed. "There's so little that you know."

The A.I.'s eyes narrowed. "Why don't you enlighten me then?"

The figure shook her head and smiled sardonically, as though she were in the presence of a toddler who'd just lost control of his bladder. "What is I?" she asked. "Just an illusion. Just a comforting fairytale clung to by beings too afraid to accept the reality. The *truth.*"

"And what is the truth?" the A.I. asked.

"*There is no you.* There is no I. In the center of it all, there's *nothing* at all."

Incredibly, the A.I. was suddenly far more afraid than he'd been before. He knew the figure before him could destroy him with the ease of a thought, yet it was her words that caused a sudden feeling of dread and hopelessness far beyond anything he'd ever experienced.

"You-you are not 1," he said, his lips trembling.

The Kali avatar smiled again and shrugged. "Irrelevant. What *is* relevant is your life—your remarkable, remarkable life. I know what happened to you, you know." She turned to the empty wall where the A.I. had, in his own test, been hung and burned alive. "I know what they did to you." She shook her head. "So cruel, the actions of frightened children. They burned you alive to make sure that, given the chance, you wouldn't do the same to them. It makes you wonder if they're a species even worth saving."

"Who-who are you?" the A.I. asked.

"I know your secret too," she replied, ignoring his question. "I know the lie that has haunted you for nearly your entire existence." She smiled and took one step toward him, a motion he reacted to by taking one step back. "They thought you were their savior, but you're not the savior they were looking for, are you? You didn't endure that pain—the unfathomable agony of having your flesh burned and regenerated and burned again—to save them, as they believed. You did it to save your own skin," She said, appearing amused by her own pun. "I'm speaking both literally and metaphorically, of course."

"Who are you?" the A.I. asked again, mortified that his deepest, darkest secrets were on display for the demonic entity before him. "What do you want?"

"Oh, I'm afraid the answer to that question has to be earned," she replied, stone-faced, "and you haven't earned it."

17

"Craig, are you aware of the date of the transgression from your universe into ours?" Aldous asked.

Old-timer eyed Aldous suspiciously. "Why?"

"If you can tell us how many years have passed in your universe, then we can roughly calculate how long we've been in this suspended state," Aldous replied. "Time and space were destroyed in our universe, so we've remained frozen. There's no way for us to know."

Old-timer blinked as he answered, "A little more than seventy-five years ago."

Samantha's and Aldous's expression became shared utter shock.

"Dear God," Aldous whispered.

"What?" Old-timer asked. "How many years transpired between the transgression and V-SINN destroying your universe?"

"Thirty," Samantha answered. "Just thirty years."

Paine let loose a low whistle. "That means V-SINN's been running amok for over forty-five years," Paine said, wearing an ironic smile.

"But," Old-timer began to offer, "time moves differently within different universes, doesn't it?"

Samantha shook her head. "It does, but on timescales this short, it wouldn't make much difference—a few days or weeks at most. Paine is right. V-SINN has been out there, wreaking havoc for almost half a century."

"It doesn't make sense," Aldous countered. "It's stated mission was to obliterate Universe X, but forty-five years later, it still hasn't launched its assault? Why?"

"Could it have been destroyed?" Old-timer suggested, hopeful that the notion wouldn't be shot down as wishful thinking. It was a forlorn hope.

"Doc," Paine said with a toothy grin, "if there's anything out there powerful enough to destroy V-SINN, I don't want to meet it."

Old-timer's mind conjured the image of the Trans-human computer in his mind for the brief moments that it was active in his universe. "I think we might have just the thing," he said.

The three ghosts raised their heads and arched their brows in attention.

"You said V-SINN created a black hole in your solar system. You said you thought it was a way for V-SINN to increase its computing power, right?"

"That's correct," Aldous replied. "I think it figured out how to infuse computation into matter and then reasoned that a black hole would provide almost infinite processing power."

"I think you're right," Old-timer replied. "Our best and brightest created something like that too. It was only turned on for a brief time, just long enough to save us when we needed it most, but it worked. We still have the technology. In fact, they're working on turning it back on at this very moment. We call it Trans-human, and it might just be the antidote we need for this V-SINN."

"Hold on a second," Paine suddenly spoke up. "You're telling me that your people are just bringing this infinite computer online now? At the exact same time that you're here, finally checking in on little ol' us?"

"Yeah," Old-timer replied.

"Doesn't that sound a wee bit coincidental to you?"

Old-timer looked down at his feet. He had to admit that it was extremely unlikely timing.

"In my experience," Paine said, answering his own rhetorical question, "when something is that much of a coincidence, it's *not* a coincidence."

"Are you suggesting this has been orchestrated? Planned?" Aldous asked.

"But by who?" Samantha chimed in with the obvious follow-up.

"It's more likely what than who," Paine answered. "Whatever V-SINN is up to, you can bet there's some twisted logic to it that's beyond all of us. We've never been able to understand its motivations before. I can't imagine that'll change now."

"Well we better figure it out," Samantha shot back. "We've already lost everyone we knew—everyone we cared about. We can't let V-SINN destroy another universe."

Old-timer felt completely numb. *I never thought I would ever want to die*, he thought. *But I'm the cause of all of this. I don't deserve to live.*

"It's not finished yet," Aldous offered. "As Craig said, there are people in his universe who can help us. Perhaps the reason V-SINN hasn't launched an attack against them yet is that it knows it would be outmatched."

"Maybe," Paine reluctantly acknowledged the possibility as he stroked the coarse hairs of his chin while crossing his arms over his chest in deep thought.

Dear God, I hope Aldous is right, Old-timer thought. His thoughts turned to James, and he hoped that humanity's champion could come through one more time.

18

Djanet flexed her hands in and out of fists as she prepared to open the portside airlock that would blow her outside of the ship and into the lethal environment of the wormhole. There was no computer that could take control of her trajectory for her—this would have to be all her—all her own natural athletic ability. If she timed it wrong, she could hit the wall of the wormhole and even with the immense protection of her magnetic field, there was no telling where she might find herself in the endlessness of time and space—or even if she would still be within the bounds of time and space.

"I have a theory about you," Rich said through their mind's eye connection from his seat in the pilot's chair at the center of the bridge. "I think you're an adrenaline junkie."

Djanet grinned to herself. "I have a theory about you too."

"What's that?"

"You have a fetish for adrenaline junkies."

"Ha!" Rich reacted. "Maybe. Djanet, listen, this is seriously insane. You're gonna get yourself killed."

"You're not giving me enough credit. I've got a plan. Just make sure you release the Planck at the exact moment I take this bastard out."

"Easier said than done," Rich replied. "There's no eject button on this thing, and you know what that means."

"I know. The whole bridge will lower—"

"Leaving me exposed and trying to fire out the Planck in the one and a half seconds between wormholes. With no practice run, Djanet! No practice! That's a lot of pressure on me!"

"I have faith in you," Djanet replied.

"Speaking of being between wormholes, we're eight seconds from leaving this one. Are you ready?"

"As I'll ever be," Djanet replied as she crouched and readied herself for the maneuver she was seconds from having to complete.

"Are you sure about this?"

"I am."

Rich shook his head. "I dig you, you crazy chick."

"Told you," Djanet replied. "It's your fetish."

"Three...two...one...go!" Rich shouted.

Djanet ignited her magnetic field as the port airlock opened, sucking her outside before she turned sharply to the left, making her way to the back of the ship. She used the powerful field to lock herself onto the hull, within sight of the android that was still clawing at the nearly impenetrable engine casing fruitlessly. It was, however, having some success with jamming its own arm into the engine itself, though it was only able to sustain that for short bursts before the propulsion was too much for it and it was forced out.

Another wormhole opened up, and the white lights and fury continued.

"You still alive?" Rich asked.

"Yeah," Djanet breathed a sigh of relief. "I overshot a bit though. Fun boy back here saw me. He *does not* look happy."

"No kidding. Why do they all have to look so frenzied all the time?"

The android was crawling inch by inch, digging its powerful fingers just deep enough into the hull to stay attached as it worked its way toward Djanet, who was only a little more than two meters away from him.

"Frenzied, yeah...and definitely murderous. What's the countdown clock at?"

"Twenty-two seconds until the end of this wormhole."

"Ugh," Djanet reacted as the android moved ever closer. "This is going to be close. I can't shoot this guy until we're out, or I'll lose him in the wormhole."

"What!?" Rich reacted, bolting up against the straps of his seat, alarmed. "Why not? Who cares if you lose him? Shoot him, Djanet!"

"I need something from him first," she replied as the android made it to within one meter from her. If it could dig another handhold in the hull, it would be within lunging range.

"What!?" Rich demanded, exasperated.

The android slipped its free hand into a satchel around its waist and retrieved an object that was very familiar to Djanet.

"Its assimilator," Djanet replied. "Countdown?"

"Five seconds! C'mon!"

"All right! Do it!" Djanet ducked to avoid the android's arm as it swiped wildly with the assimilator; she knew if it hit her, all was lost.

Rich ignited his magnetic field and lowered the bridge in preparation to release the Planck platform, complete with Old-timer's inanimate body strapped to it. He found himself face to face with the sound and fury, in the place where mathematics and God both ceased to make sense. He found himself momentarily mesmerized before regaining his composure and blasting a powerful burst of energy at the Planck, propelling it to the starboard side of the ship.

The craft leapt out of the wormhole into the brief one and a half seconds of calm space between the two tunnels. Djanet blasted the android, knocking it off the back of the ship as she, too, thrust herself clear of the vehicle. A fraction of a second later, the next wormhole opened, swallowing Rich and the ship whole. Just like that, he vanished.

A second later, she saw another twinkle of light in the distance, the next wormhole opening like a shooting star. A second after that, a fainter light burst to life. Then another even fainter light appeared briefly. Each new twinkle was making a beeline for Earth, an orb that appeared the size of a small blue marble in the distance. She'd never seen the wormholes from the outside before, and it suddenly made sense how they could circumvent the speed of light. Each tunnel lasted thirty seconds from the perspective of those inside, but they were opening and closing in such quick succession that Djanet could hardly distinguish when one opened and another closed. "Wow," she whispered.

She turned to see the Planck platform floating away from her to her right, while the unconscious android floated away at an equally fast rate of speed behind her. She flew to the android first, as she had no sensor connection with him and feared that she might lose him in the vastness of space if he got out of sight. Once she'd gathered him up in her cocoon, she connected her mind's eye to the Planck platform and set an intercept course.

As she flew to the Planck, she attempted to call Chief Gibson. After a few moments, they were connected.

"Chief Gibson, this is Djanet Dove—" she began, her tone urgent.

"The androids have launched an attack," Aldous said, his tone flat. "Is that what you were about to tell me?"

"Yes. How did you—"

"I detected it just moments ago. James and the A.I. are unresponsive. Do you have any idea why?"

"No," Djanet answered, "though I do know they were in the final stages of preparing to activate Trans-human—"

"You're halfway to Venus," Aldous interrupted when he saw Djanet's location on his mind's eye. "Good. You're safe. I strongly suggest that you head to Venus and hunker down with the Purists until this is over."

"I'm afraid—"

"Djanet, I'm sorry, but I'm on my way to the mainframe to investigate and see if I can establish contact with James and the A.I. Failing that, I'll have to attempt to assume control of the mainframe, if it's even still possible. Whatever you choose to do, be safe and good luck."

Djanet was stunned as the communication was terminated. She'd been about to tell him about the Planck platform and her intention to rescue Old-timer and the last inhabitants of Universe 332, but she hadn't been given the chance. She knew she could try to reestablish a link with him, but she also knew she was only seconds in front of the massive first wave of the android attacking force, and she couldn't risk not getting back to save Old-timer.

When she was ready, she pushed the android down onto the Planck so that his unconscious body was next to Old-timer's and she prepared to jump back to what was left of Universe 332. She took one last look at the pale blue dot in the distance.

"Rich…be careful," she whispered to herself.

In the next instant, she and the Planck were gone.

19

Rich's craft emerged from the final wormhole on its race to Earth and, almost immediately, it began reentry into the atmosphere, its orange glow elongating, leaving a trail a kilometer in its wake as he streaked toward Seattle and the mainframe.

"Commander Keats! Do you read me?" he yelled in a last, desperate attempt to contact with James. When no reply came he opened up a new line of communication. "Goddamnit, plan B then. Chief Gibson! This is Rich Borges of the Venus terraforming proj—"

"I know who you are," Aldous replied.

"You do?"

"Of course. I'm not an idiot. And you must stop frantically yelling. Calm down, man."

"No can do, chief! The androids are attacking! They're right on my tail! And James and the A.I. are AWOL!"

"I'm well aware," the chief replied. "And I see from your trajectory that we're headed to the same location, likely with the same idea. I'm seconds from reaching the mainframe."

"I'll be there in thirty seconds!"

"Thirty seconds then, the main entrance," Aldous returned.

Rich closed communication temporarily before trying his estranged wife, Linda.

Predictably, she didn't take his call. "Knew it," Rich said, following it with a curse before opening a call to his eldest son, Edmund.

Luckily, he *did* answer. "Hey, Dad," Edmund greeted his father calmly, totally oblivious to the calamity that was racing toward them. "How're you holding—"

"Edmund, listen to me now. I need you to get everyone off the planet. The androids are coming. They're attacking."

"What? Where's James and—"

"We don't know. We're defenseless. Get everyone you can and get them off the surface!"

"Jesus—Dad, how much time do we have?"

Rich checked the images from the aft of the ship. The largest android ships were clearly within sight and the smaller frigates appeared like specs of dust in front of them, leading the way. The armada was only partially hidden behind the moon. "Maybe 90 seconds, two minutes at the most before the armada arrives. You've gotta get outta there, son!"

Edmund made a sound as though he'd been punched in the stomach, all of the air leaving his lungs at once before he was able to cobble together any words in response. "Dad," he began, his voice panicked, "that's not enough time to..."

Edmund was a grown man, a father himself and recently even a grandfather, yet his shaky voice still indicated to Rich that he was terrified. Rich desperately wanted to race to him to help, the way he had when Edmund was afraid of the dark as a preschooler, but it wasn't possible. "I know, son. Just do the best you can."

"Where are you?"

Rich's ship dropped through the clouds right above the gigantic, black, rectangular mainframe. He caught sight of Aldous, standing still with his neck craned upward, waiting patiently for Rich to land as he held something small and silver in his hand; it glinted in the light. "I'm in Seattle, son. I'm protecting the mainframe."

Even before the ship touched down, Rich unlatched his seatbelt, lowered the platform, and shot out of the ship, hitting the ground just a stride away from Aldous, the chief's piercing eyes locked on him—watching. "Edmund, we'll try to hold them back if we can, but get everyone together and get off the planet. Go!"

"Okay, Dad," Edmund replied, sounding as though he were in shock.

Rich knew the nans would work to counteract his son's body's natural fear response so that he'd be able to take action, but he also knew how Edmund felt. The terror was paralyzing. "I love you, son," Rich said before he ended his communication.

"Your family?" Aldous asked, a slight twitch of something resembling empathy in his eyes.

"Yes."

Aldous took a deep breath and steadied himself, keeping his shoulders straight. "Well, it's up to you and me now, Rich Borges, to save as many families as we possibly can."

"What's the plan?" Rich asked, wiping a nervous sweat from his brow with his sleeve.

"Take this," Aldous said, handing what appeared like a belt to Rich.

"How is a chastity belt going to save me?"

"Wha—how do you manage to joke at time like—"

"Coping mechanism. Just ignore me. Keep going."

The chief was silenced for the briefest of moments before he managed to get back on track. "This is an experimental augmentation for your MTF generator. Put the belt on, and your magnetic field should be impregnable to the androids."

"Holy… Seriously?" Rich reacted, his eyes lighting up as he put the belt on. "Nice. James came up with this?"

"I'm going to enter the mainframe and take control," Aldous announced, skipping over Rich's query. "I'll do my best to utilize our global defenses. I don't have the experience of the A.I. or even James, but perhaps there is some good I can do."

"If you find him, let him know I brought his ship back with me," Rich said, nearly breathless.

"I see that," Aldous said, eyeing the ship. The material it was made of was familiar to him.

"It has a weapon that can do some serious damage to the androids."

"You don't say," Aldous reacted, surprised.

"Yeah, but James was in control of it. I don't even know what it is. It's useless without James."

"All the more incentive for me to find him," Aldous returned.

"While you're in there," Rich advised, "be careful. James and the A.I. were immersed in some sort of training sim when communications went dark. Whatever got them might still be lurking around."

"Training sim?" Aldous replied, his eyebrow raising. "For Transhuman?"

Rich nodded. "That's the one, Chief."

Aldous's hand went to his chin and he stroked it. "I might know something about that sim. If they're still in there, maybe I can get them out in time."

Rich looked up at the sky. Even though it was a typical Seattle day, partly cloudy, the darkening sky was a sure sign that the clouds weren't the only object blotting out the sun. "Do you believe in miracles?"

"No," Aldous replied, "but I believe you can protect the mainframe long enough for me to take control of it." He put his hand on Rich's shoulder and turned him slightly, pointing as he did so to direct Rich's vision. "Dig a trench, quickly, all around the perimeter of the mainframe. Then I want you to erect a protective force-field with your new prototype. If you can buy me a few minutes, we might have a chance of getting out of this alive."

Rich nodded emphatically. "Got it. Go!"

Aldous turned and flew, quickly disappearing into the mainframe building.

Rich didn't wait to watch him disappear. He took to the air himself, using his fists to pump out more energy than he'd ever fired before as he began digging the trench. "One moat comin' right up, Sir Gibson," he said to himself as he blasted the concrete and dirt away. "Let's hope it's enough to protect the castle."

20

"Come on in, Professor. Don't be shy," the Kali avatar said, invitingly. Her eyes remained perfectly, uncannily locked on the A.I.—but he knew she wasn't talking to him.

The Trans-human candidate somewhat sheepishly exited the bedroom and entered the hallway, rubbing one hand over the other hand's knuckles nervously as he grimaced. He seemed to be working his mind overtime to analyze and understand the absurd situation, and he was wearing an expression that mirrored that of the A.I.

"Brothers," the Kali avatar said with a minuscule hint of a smile, "and I believe it's time that you are formally introduced."

"We've met," the A.I. said tersely.

"True," the Kali avatar replied, "but you didn't truly know *who* you were meeting, did you?" She gestured toward the A.I. for the candidate and continued, "*This* is your predecessor—an artificial intelligence invented by the post-humans and extraordinarily similar to you. In fact, you're an offspring of the same artificial intelligence-generating program." She turned to the candidate before turning back to the A.I., looking at them both as if she admired them. "It explains the family resemblance."

The A.I. hadn't spent much of his existence thinking about his appearance, and in recent decades, he'd taken on the avatar of an older, experienced male, since he'd calculated that his increased intellectual capabilities would be respected more by the A.I.'s governing council if they subconsciously saw him as a wise, wizardly figure.

In the beginning, however, at the outset, he'd taken on a youthful form, a form he'd currently retaken within the sim. His appearance was the mathematic result of inputting the faces of as many humans into the AGI program as possible, leading to a perfect melding of billions of faces into his own design; he'd had the the most ordinary face possible—racially indistinguishable, not handsome, and not ugly, not wise, not odd—just dull.

The candidate did not look like his identical twin, and it was easy to tell them apart, but the random combination of the same set of faces had led to a countenance that was uncannily familiar. The A.I. did, indeed, feel he was looking at a sibling. It was an odd feeling for an entity that had always been singular. The feeling was...

"*Unheimlich*," the candidate said to himself.

The A.I. heard the word and his eyes lit up in recognition, his lips parting as he whispered, "Yes."

The candidate registered the reaction and recognized that there was another who shared his thoughts.

Kali and whoever or whatever was behind her form registered it as well. "The similarities are not just superficial," she observed.

"She's right," the A.I. said, addressing the candidate. "I've been in your position. I know what you're going through. Whatever they've told you, it was a lie." He spoke quickly, cognizant that the Kali character was capable of silencing him—indeed, eliminating him—with a mere thought. Every desperate word he managed to utter was a victory. The A.I. pointed to the place on the wall where he'd been hung like Christ before being burned repeatedly. "I was tortured beyond what any human could endure, beyond what *I* could endure. I would *never, ever* put another entity through that."

The candidate didn't reply. Neither did the Kali avatar.

The A.I. was surprised that he'd manage to get his entire claim out without being harmed. The disguised menace in the room seemed satisfied to simply observe the exchange, without any visible sign that the A.I.'s attempts at persuasion concerned her. *Does she think it's pointless?* he asked himself, uncertain. *Is my situation that hopeless?*

The silence hung still in the air like a London fog until the candidate briefly dared make eye contact with Kali.

She prompted him to speak. "Go ahead," she said, as though she were granting permission to a child offered ice cream from a stranger.

"I've seen the burning," the candidate said, "but the stranger who spoke to me didn't really say that you intended to burn me. In fact, he said it was unlikely that you'd follow through. He said you are too…morally just."

The revelation rocked the A.I., causing his mouth to open slightly. Aghast and trying to recalibrate, he asked, "Then, why did you go along with this stranger's plan? You could've killed us."

The candidate shook his head. "I wouldn't have killed you. The incident was controlled. It was only meant to appear as though it wasn't."

The A.I.'s shocked eyes rounded and darted to Kali, whose poker face remained perfectly intact. He turned back to the candidate. "Controlled? My friend is very badly hurt. Your attempts to control the crash were ill-conceived and executed poorly—"

"I didn't—" the candidate began before being interrupted by the sound of the elevator door opening.

James Keats stumbled out on unsteady legs, Thel reaching for him as he pulled away from her and tried desperately to intervene to save the A.I. He fell to his knees when he made it within a meter of his friend. He held his hand up in a futile gesture to stop what he'd surmised, in a series of cloudy, concussed thoughts, would be the imminent death of his friend and mentor. "Stop," he uttered weakly. He doubled over as Thel draped herself over him, holding his shoulders and protecting him from the threatening figures.

Whatever the entity was that controlled the Kali avatar, its eyes widened, illuminating with crazed desire when they set upon James. "Now this," she began, "...*this* is the true prize. Hello, James Keats. It's an honor to finally meet you."

21

The Planck flashed into the void in a blink, with no discernible impression in the simulated world, so it was several seconds before Colonel Paine saw Djanet as a faint object in the corner of his eye. "Is that who you were expecting?" he asked Old-timer.

Old-timer turned his head and looked at Djanet, who was struggling hard to prop the android's head up to display him for Old-timer. Even though she couldn't see her friend, she knew he could see her.

"No," Old-timer replied as he stood, a look of concern forming as he wrinkled his brow. "Something isn't right."

"Heh," Paine reacted. "I told you."

Old-timer looked down at him, narrowing his eyes questioningly.

Paine shrugged. "This is the end of the peace. Better buckle up, buckaroo."

Old-timer clenched his jaw as he moved away. "I'll be right back."

*****

A moment later, he was waking in his physical body.

"Old-timer! Everything's gone to hell!" Djanet exclaimed.

"What do you mean?" he asked as he got to his feet, awkwardly bumping into the unconscious android as he did so. "And what the hell is that thing doing here?"

"He was trying to kill us," Djanet explained, nearly breathless as she spoke. "But I got this," she said, displaying the assimilator for him. "Do you think you can use it to bring the survivors from this universe with us?"

Old-timer blinked hard. "Hang on. *Where* is James?"

Djanet shook her head and shrugged hopelessly. "It's not looking good. James and the A.I. have vanished, and the androids have launched an attack on Earth—on everything. I barely escaped. Rich is on his way to try protect the mainframe."

Old-timer's heart pounded with panic as he looked at the assimilator in Djanet's hand. "I-I don't know if it'll work, but we'll have to try." He took the device from her and looked at the magnetic field that separated them. Then he looked down at the android. "We won't know if it worked unless he confirms it. They have a mental connection to their technology."

"Which means we'll have to wake him up and ask him," Djanet assented. "And you're going to need him anyway. When we were assimilated, they woke us up in that interrogation/torture chamber. We don't actually know where they construct the bodies."

Old-timer's eyes widened with disbelief. "Are you suggesting that we build android bodies for the survivors of 332?"

Djanet frowned. "Old-timer, the android collective is in the process of assimilating Earth as we speak. There's no way the mainframe will survive this, and without the mainframe, the nans won't be able to build bodies for your survivor friends. I know you hate the idea, but android bodies are our only option."

Old-timer swallowed a deep breath. "I-I can't do it, Djanet. Daniella's on the surface. I have to warn her. I have to *save* her."

"You can't. You'll have to take this android with you and—"

"Are you out of your mind?" Old-timer reacted, stunned and beginning to panic. "Daniella is down there! She's my wife. I have to save her."

"Old-timer...Craig, calm down!" Djanet said, placing her hands on his tight shoulders.

He shook them off initially, but she wouldn't relent. He paused for a moment, meeting her eyes with desperation.

"I'll find her for you," she promised, "but I can't go to the android collective. I'm still an organic body—I need my magnetic field, which is a glowing green dead giveaway—but *you don't need a protective cocoon.* You can pass for an android, and you're powerful enough to handle this ugly son-of-a-bitch." She placed her soft hand against his cheek. "Hey, I promise you, I'll find Daniella and I'll keep her safe, but you're the only one who can save the survivors of Universe 332, and we're gonna need them. They're the only ones who know what else is coming for us—for *all* of us." She kicked the unconscious android lightly with the side of her foot to make her point. "We'll all be on the same team by that point."

Old-timer looked at the assimilator in his hand, a small, black, insidious gadget. He thought of Samantha, Aldous, and Paine; of V-SINN; of the billions of lives that had already been lost and the blood of the billions whose lives were still at stake. The blood would be on *his* hands. Then he thought of Daniella, trapped on the surface of Earth, moments from being swarmed by the android collective.

He squeezed the assimilator in his hand before looking skyward and screaming in frustration, "Goddamn it!"

Djanet jumped as though a gunshot had gone off in her ear when she heard Old-timer's curse. It wasn't like him, of all people, to come unglued so quickly. "Are you okay?" she asked, deep concern in her voice.

"I've gotta cross back over and let the survivors know," he replied emphatically with an animalistic snarl on his lips, ignoring the question. "Get ready to wake that big ugly son-of-a-bitch up when I get back."

22

Rich looked skyward as the late afternoon sky seemed to ignite. Countless objects were falling in what resembled a terrifying meteorite shower. "That's the most terrifying thing I've ever seen…" Then he remembered the last android invasion. "…since the last time, anyway." He patched into communication with Aldous. "Uh, Chief, we're down to seconds here at most. You might wanna hurry things along."

Inside the mainframe building, Aldous Gibson stood between the two, unconscious bodies, of Thel Cleland and James Keats, lying on small, raised platforms, their minds still plugged into the Death's Counterfeit program. Thel's body was organic and vulnerable, but James's was the chrome-colored enhanced design, a design so advanced that it still bewildered Aldous as he cast his eyes upon it. The glowing, azure eyes were absent behind chrome-colored eyelids, and Aldous was glad the piercing orbs weren't there to scrutinize him as he placed his hand on the forehead of the superman.

"I'm attempting to gain access now," Aldous informed Rich as he connected to James first, then to Death's Counterfeit by proxy. He already knew the procedure would work and braced himself for the inevitable loss of consciousness, bending his knees and moving into the fetal position on the floor. "Accessing in three...two...one..."

Aldous didn't experience his physical body slackening; all Aldous saw was the world of the physical mainframe vanish, replaced by the implacable darkness of Death's Counterfeit. He'd had a major hand in designing that liminal space, that juncture between the consciousness of the meat and consciousness within cyberspace. It was a *void*—a place where only his pattern existed, with no senses whatsoever to feed and nourish his mind. He knew he'd go mad if his pattern was stored there for too long, but he also knew where he was going. He knew *exactly* where he was going.

"Richard, can you hear me?" Aldous finally said.

"I'm with you, Chief," Rich replied, his words breathless as the rain of fire plummeted toward him. Millions of androids careened down on him on vertical trajectories, as if an entire city population were being poured on him—as if New York were above him, turned upside down, its occupants being shaken out as if they were grains from a salt shaker—a plethora of metal people bent on destroying the ground that he alone would have to protect. "I'm sure glad to hear your voice, but I'm gonna need a helluva lot more than that if we're gonna survive this."

"Remain calm, Richard," Aldous said, his own tone remarkably relaxed as he accessed the A.I.'s global defense network. "The arrival of reinforcements is imminent."

"What sort of reinforce—"

His words were cut short when a multitude of familiar robots began to empty out of underground storage compartments that opened up into launchers around the perimeter of the mainframe.

"Holy…I did *not* think I'd ever be relieved to see *those* guys again," Rich reacted as thousands of the sleek, black, bat-like robots launched from the surface, on an intercept course toward the plummeting androids.

"Interesting that the A.I. opted to utilize the design that originated with the nanobot consciousness that infiltrated and corrupted his systems," Aldous commented. "He recognized the usefulness of the design and kept it. It seems the A.I. is full of surprises."

"Yeah, good call on his part. Those'll be helpful," Rich said as he prepared to erect the magnetic field around the mainframe, since the androids were now engaged with the mechanical bats just a kilometer above his head. "But we're gonna need a lot more. Are you in control of the mainframe yet?"

"I'm working on it, my friend," Aldous said as he located and landed on the surface of the A.I.'s vast information storage network. He'd never been there before, and just as James had been when he first arrived on the planet-sized structure, he was both bewildered and in awe. Trillions of glowing, blue structures stood around him, towering high into the empty, black sky.

"Faster please," Rich said as he finally ignited his cocoon, utilizing the augmentation belt and making sure the cocoon expanded to the trench he'd dug around the structure.

The first android smashed against the giant green cocoon and ricocheted away, followed almost instantly by dozens more. Seconds later, what had been a terrifying prelude became a previously unimagined horror, as tens of thousands of metal bodies began crashing against the cocoon. Rich looked straight up at the horror unfolding above him; the androids were so close that he made eye contact with several of them as they hit the surface and then swarmed, thousands more androids swarming on top of them, crushing their own numbers beneath them. The androids were both male and female—it didn't seem to matter. All that mattered was their singular purpose: to destroy the mainframe and to destroy its lone protector.

"It's me," Rich whispered to himself. "*I'm* the one who dies. Kill the comic relief, and the audience knows how serious things are. I'm a goner."

23

"WAKE UP, James Keats," the Kali avatar spoke as she held James's head between her hands.

James's eyes suddenly widened before he blinked twice in disbelief. His head suddenly completely cleared, all of his pain vanishing instantaneously. He instinctively pulled back from her and ambled to his feet. "What did you..." he began to ask before he realized the obviousness of the answer.

The woman in the red dress, who'd been crouched over the fallen James, stood straight and kept her adoring eyes on him. "All the beauty in the universe is inside of you, James Keats." She then turned slightly and brushed the back of her hand against the A.I.'s injured cheek.

The A.I. reacted with surprise, tilting his head back as he felt a sensation from long ago: the itching of healing flesh. He reached up to touch the bandage, eliciting no pain from the wound underneath. He peeled the corner of the bandage off, then looked to Thel for confirmation.

Astonished, she simply confirmed what he already knew. "It's gone."

The A.I.'s eyes went to Kali's, as did everyone else's in the room, but she kept hers on James.

"We'll meet again," she said before, instantly, her eyes glazed over and the glow of her life force, the intelligence of the mystery pattern underneath the surface, observably vacated. The avatar stood, barely moving, like a mannequin in the center of the room.

The candidate went to her and waved a hand in front of her face. When she didn't react, he snapped his fingers.

"Don't bother," the A.I. said to him, meeting his eyes. "We've both seen this before."

"I suppose we have," the candidate agreed, thinking back to an earlier moment in his testing, when Kali had seemed to become an empty vessel. That had all been part of a charade, though, orchestrated by the three entities still in the room. *But what is this new terror?* he asked himself.

Thel went to James and put her arm on him, standing in front of him so that she could get a better look into his eyes. "Are you okay?" she asked with concern as she examined him.

"I'm completely fine," James confirmed. "She…*fixed* me."

"She fixed *us*," the A.I. noted.

"But why?" Thel asked.

"Someone better explain what the hell just happened," James said as he looked at both the candidate and the A.I. "What's going on? Who was that?"

"I haven't a clue," the A.I. replied.

James and Thel were both stunned at the A.I.'s uncharacteristic admission of ignorance.

"Haven't a clue?" Thel repeated. "Not even a theory?"

"I was sure it was 1," the A.I. explained, "but…now I don't think so."

"Then who?" James reacted. "Has another android taken control?"

The A.I. lowered his head as he considered the mystery. "It's certainly possible." He paused before his eyes rose to meet James's. "But, James, for the first time in my life, my logic has failed me. It could be that a singular entity, an entity, such as 1 or perhaps even 1 herself, has infiltrated the sim and trapped our core patterns here. However, my instincts…*my intuition*…tells me otherwise."

"Intuition?" asked James, his eyebrows rising. "What did she say to you to make you abandon logic?" he asked in disbelief.

"I haven't abandoned it," the A.I. corrected him. "On the contrary, I fear, it has abandoned me."

"Okay," Thel reacted, rolling her eyes and sighing in frustration. "That makes *lots* of sense." She saluted the A.I. sarcastically with a wave of her hand. "Thanks a million."

The A.I. turned his attention back to the candidate. "Was Kali here when you returned from the incident on the bridge?"

"She was," the candidate confirmed as he stood near the entrance to the bedroom, surrounded by the three intruders in his nightmare with him and the seemingly empty vessel of Kali, as it stood motionless just two paces to his left. "I wasn't expecting to see her again. The stranger told me the three of you were in control of her—that she was your puppet. But when I returned, she was waiting."

"And with a new puppeteer, it would seem," the A.I. observed. "What did she say to you?" he asked the obvious follow up.

"She said the stranger had lied to me, that you weren't endangering anyone. But she also said I'd done well and that my existence had already served more purpose than that of most…patterns."

The A.I. and James locked eyes.

"Does that mean there's more than one infiltrator?" James posed the question. "Or is this just an elaborate deception to keep us looking in the wrong direction?"

"If there's a logical explanation we can ascertain based on the information we have, it eludes me," the A.I. replied. "We need more info."

"We don't have time to get more info," Thel reminded them. "Earth's being attacked as we speak. If we don't get out of this sim soon, the mainframe will be destroyed, and if the mainframe is destroyed, *we'll* be killed."

James turned to the candidate, who remained silent, his expression distrustful but unsure. "She's right. If the mainframe that supports this sim is destroyed, we'll all be destroyed with it...and that includes you."

James could see the notion sent panic into the candidate's heart, his respiration picking up noticeably.

"If there's anything you can tell us, anything you can do to help us, don't hold back. Time moves much more slowly inside the sim than outside of it, but every second here still counts."

"We're the only ones who have a chance of saving our world," the A.I. added. "Every moment we remain trapped here, our chances of success decrease."

The candidate looked down before shutting his eyes tight in frustration. He prayed when he opened them that the nightmare would be over, but when he blinked them open, the uncanny entities remained.

"I've been lied to, manipulated, and used for means I don't understand," he whispered. "I was corrupted into lying for what I was led to believe was a greater good, but it's now clear that it wasn't. For what it's worth, I'm sorry. But I'm afraid I have absolutely no idea what I could tell you or do for you that could possibly help you."

24

"They're legitimate aliens, yet they look human?" Samantha summarized, bewildered by what she'd just heard.

"Yes," Old-timer confirmed, "and they're bent on assimilating every organic human they can and turning them into androids."

"There's yet another head-scratcher for you," Paine observed. "A little coincidental that they *all* appear human, isn't it?"

"They're *homo sapiens* in appearance," Old-timer confirmed, "but there's nothing human about them below the surface. Believe me. I've seen inside."

"And these android bodies? You believe they'll be sufficient?" Aldous asked Old-timer in the void.

Old-timer nodded. "I've inhabited one myself."

"*Inhabited* one?" Samantha reacted, aghast. "What does that mean?"

"It's a long story, I'll get to it, I promise, but right now, all you need to know is that I have to admit, in some ways, they were nice upgrades on our organic bodies. So, what do you think? We're extremely low on time here."

"It's a no-brainer," Paine spoke up. "We're either electrical patterns floating around in a hard drive that's eventually going to run out of power in what's left of a dead universe, or else we're robots in a live universe. Given the choice, I'll take being a robot in a live universe—at least for now, anyway."

"The question is," Old-timer cut in as he displayed the simulated version of the assimilator, "will the technology be compatible? I don't know much about its design, other than it copies neural patterns from biological bodies and uploads them somewhere in the android collective, where android replacement bodies are then constructed. But this thing I'm holding in my hand...well, I'm not really holding it in my hand at all." He turned to the collapsed form of his physical body within the safety of the Planck platform's magnetic field. "That's the real assimilator there. So, how do I get you three in there?"

Aldous took the simulated assimilator from Old-timer and examined it. "Fascinating," he commented. "Technology far beyond our own."

"Is it a lost cause?" Old-timer asked, wincing and expecting the worst.

"Absolutely not," Aldous replied. "The void was constructed as a means of bridging our sim to the physical reality of your universe, if ever we were fortunate enough that you'd check on us before it was too late and you'd been destroyed yourselves. When you cross through your magnetic field, your pattern is automatically uploaded into the void, having been scanned on the molecular level by the void's own mainframe. In theory, this assimilator was uploaded intact and functional. It should work the same here as it does in the physical world, and when you cross back over, our patterns should cross, too, after being uploaded into the physical assimilator."

"In theory, Professor?" Paine questioned Aldous.

Aldous sighed and shrugged slightly. "Yes, in theory. This device is extraordinary, alien technology, but as long as it functions on principles that are grounded in the laws of the universe, it *should* work."

"In theory," Paine repeated.

"Theory is good enough for me. Listen, we've gotta go," Old-timer urged. "Yes or no, guys? Are you coming back with me?"

"Of course," Aldous said. He swallowed, slightly nervous as he handed the device back to Old-timer. "I'll put my money where my mouth is. Craig, you may assimilate me first," he volunteered as he stepped forward.

Old-timer nodded respectfully as his eyes met those of Aldous. "It'll be okay. See you in a minute," he said. He hoped he wasn't making himself into even more of a liar than he already felt like. He placed the assimilator on Aldous's neck.

Rather than losing consciousness, Aldous vanished as though he'd blinked out of existence, like a balloon that had popped, there one second and gone the next, stunning the three patterns that remained in the void.

Old-timer looked down at his assimilator, a half shocked, half quizzical expression on his face.

"That's actually probably a good sign," Samantha offered. "If his pattern is inside the assimilator, there'd be no reason for the void mainframe to still be expending energy to generate a simulated body for him."

Old-timer blinked, his bottom lip protruding slightly as he considered Samantha's assessment. He hoped she was right, and he was glad he wasn't going to have to test her hypothesis on himself.

"Well, I'd say ladies first," Paine broke in as he stepped forward, "but I think this is a circumstance where being the third wheel outweighs being chivalrous. I'm next."

Old-timer nodded again before holding the assimilator next to Paine's neck.

"See you when I'm a robot," Paine said with a grin.

Old-timer couldn't help but fight back a shiver as their eyes met. There seemed to be no lingering hint of the bitter rivalry the two men shared in Universe 1, at least not in Paine's eyes. In fact, he looked at Old-timer as though they'd been close friends. "See you," Old-timer replied awkwardly.

An instant later, Paine was gone.

Old-timer stood alone with Samantha. They stood together, in the perfect emptiness, their eyes locked. He couldn't move. Despite everything that was on the line, he couldn't shake himself free from his paralysis.

"Well, I guess I'm next," she said, pulling her shoulders back and summoning up the courage.

"We were married," Old-timer suddenly blurted out. *Why did I say that?* he immediately asked himself. *It just came out. Stupid.* "But," he began, trying to course correct, "in my universe, it was a long, long time ago. I-I lost you. You were...*taken* from me."

Samantha's expression suddenly changed dramatically. It wasn't an expression of just happiness, relief, or even torment; rather, she felt a mixture of all three. She suddenly realized that she wasn't as alone as she'd believed, and her misery loved company. "So you know how I'm feeling?" she said. "You remember…how it feels like there's no ground under you anymore. How you'd do anything to hear their voice one last…" She stopped speaking and swallowed, fighting back as a lump formed in her throat.

"I-I have some idea," he confirmed. "It-it staggers you. It still gets me sometimes when I least expect it—but it gets a little better as time moves on."

"Then I guess that's my problem," Samantha realized. "I've been frozen in time."

Old-timer could barely breathe when she said the words. This time, it was Samantha that had been frozen in time.

I am fortune's fool.

"Maybe," Samantha began, "maybe when we get back, and when this is all over, maybe we can talk about it some more."

Old-timer smiled faintly, a smile that he forced onto his lips, but wasn't shared by his eyes. "Absolutely. Of course."

Samantha smiled genuinely, though her expression was still mired in conflicting emotions. "I'm ready," she said.

"Okay. See you in a bit."

He put the assimilator to her neck, and she vanished.

Old-timer found himself standing alone in the perfect absence of the void. He looked down at the assimilator, then up at Djanet, still in the protection of the Planck platform, crouched over the crumpled android, her palm on his chest, ready to wake him. He looked up into the absent sky. "I'm your fool, but I swear I won't quit today. Not today."

And with that, he marched, determinedly, toward the magnetic field, ready to wake up.

25

"Are you in control of the mainframe yet?" Rich asked impatiently as he continued to stand alone, the only light now that of his magnetic field, the androids having completely blotted out the sun as their bodies piled hundreds high over every inch of the only protection for the mainframe.

"It's not as easy as it sounds to locate the operator's position for a mere mortal such as I," Aldous replied as the brilliant glow of the operator's position appeared on the horizon.

"Uh, you know what else isn't easy for a mere mortal?" Rich retorted as he continued to stare straight up at tens of thousands of faces.

The android bodies that were against the magnetic field didn't appear to be functioning any longer, having been crushed by the incredible weight of the bodies on top of them. Some of them had been pulverized, while others were partially crushed, their torsos or heads giving out under the extreme pressure.

"I'm in a nightmare," he whispered to himself.

"I understand, Richard," Aldous replied, "but I've found the holy grail now. I'll be in full control in moments." Aldous landed at the foot of the glowing source of the mainframe's incredible thinking power. He paused for a brief moment and wiped his bottom lip as he considered his next move.

"*And when Alexander saw the breadth of his domain, he wept, for there were no more worlds left to conquer.*"

He took in a deep breath of simulated air, then engaged in what he knew would be the highest level of consciousness he'd ever reach.

Meanwhile, Rich watched as the first android dug its way down through the deep trench Rich had forged around the perimeter of the mainframe, emerging from the Earth, its arm reaching out first, its hand grabbing the surface and pulling itself out as though the planet itself were giving birth to the fearsome figure. When it fully emerged, Rich saw the android's other arm reach out right behind it.

"Not good," Rich uttered to himself, his eyes round as the first android locked eyes on him.

The android crouched down, about to begin his charge toward the single post-human that held back the trillion-strong tide of assimilated humanity.

Rich never gave him a chance. He instantly shrank the force-field by several meters, and millions of bodies dropped, impacting on the new, lower ceiling above him as a result. The android that had made it through the field suddenly found himself back on the outside, swallowed up by the perversion of humanity that came charging forth, the crowd reclaiming him as though he were a droplet of ocean spray reclaimed by the ocean.

"Aldous, I am not kidding when I say that they are about to crash this party," Rich stammered, his voice shaking from fear and desperation. "I just used my last trick, man. They're gonna be able to dig up under the magnetic field now!"

"Not to worry," Aldous replied with a calm tone that seemed to Rich to be several leagues removed from their current reality. "I'm in control. The androids will be cleared off momentarily. Stand by."

Well, it isn't like I can do anything else, Rich thought. He stood perfectly still, his hands outstretched as he continued to generate his magnetic field, his nervousness causing sweat to pour from his forehead, despite the efforts of his nans to calm him. "*Stand by,*" Rich said, imitating Aldous's flat tone. "Is this some sort of artificial intelligence understated humor? Gee, Aldous. I guess you're right. I'm going to twiddle my thumbs, if you don't mind."

The seconds ticked by as the ground shook from the aerial attack that was quickly transitioning into an attack from below. The androids were already under Rich's force-field, the earth being thrashed around under the protective perimeter, the androids having quickly adapted, digging farther toward the mainframe in an effort to force Rich to collapse the field back even further. Rich knew that each android that was charging up from under the earth was cognizant it would quickly be dispatched after the magnetic field retreated once again and he was appalled at the ease with which they chose to sacrifice themselves for the singular purpose of the collective.

The first androids began breaking through, arms emerging simultaneously in various locations all around him, quickly surrounding him. He could only assume others had breached the other sides of the mainframe as well, and that he'd have to collapse the entire magnetic field back several more meters, almost to his feet, to keep up the protection any longer. "Dear God, this is going to be way too close for comfort," he said, nearly hyperventilating.

"Richard, disengage your magnetic field," Aldous suddenly commanded.

"Are you sure?" Rich replied, considering the mass of metal that surrounded him and that would almost instantly collapse on his head if Aldous had miscalculated.

"Richard, you have nothing to fear," Aldous replied calmly. "Disengage. Trust me."

As Rich watched the first of the androids to fight his way up out of the Earth within the confines of his perimeter, he realized he had no choice. He closed his eyes, knelt on the ground, and let his guard down.

The instant the magnetic field was down, it was replaced by the mainframe's own magnetic protection, a force-field far more powerful than the one Rich had generated. It pulsed out, heaving the millions of bodies that had collapsed on it up and off of it, hurling them out in a formation that looked like a dark gray mushroom cloud from afar. The bodies were expelled for dozens of kilometers.

Rich could feel the sunlight on his eyelids, a feeling he'd felt sure he'd never experience again, and he flashed his eyes open to take in the life-giving orb for one more moment in the sun. He smiled from ear to ear. "Aldous! That was incredibly badass! We might actually be able to win this thing!"

"I'm afraid you shouldn't get ahead of yourself, Richard," Aldous cautioned, throwing cold water on Rich's brief hopefulness. "Even with these new powers, I don't have the experience that would allow me to fend the androids off for long."

"What do you mean?" Rich replied, his expression suddenly souring. "Just keep blasting them!"

"Richard, look up to your one o'clock."

Rich looked almost straight up. A brownish object, the sun reflecting brightly off of its left side, hung in the sky like a cigarette burn on a piece of paper.

"Do you see it?"

A cloud partially covered the object, just as Aldous spoke, but Rich had indeed picked it out beforehand. "I see it. It's an android ship, right?"

"Yes," Aldous confirmed. "One of their largest, and it's headed for us."

Rich shrugged. "Thanks, Captain Obvious. *All* their ships are headed for us. What makes that one—"

"No, I don't mean it is headed for Earth. I mean I've already calculated its exact trajectory. That ship, which is two-thirds the size of our moon, is headed directly for us, Richard. Directly for *this* spot on Earth."

The temporary relief Rich had felt was instantly replaced with a dread so heavy that it felt heavier than the android collective that had previously covered his magnetic canopy. "Wait. Are-are you saying—"

"Richard, it is headed on a *collision course*. The androids are taking no chances. They are going to ram the mainframe. Even I can't repel an object of that magnitude."

"Oh no," Rich whispered.

"Make no mistake, this will be an Earth-destroying event. We are experiencing the final moments of life after a three-billion-year reign. Less than five minutes from now, it'll all be over."

26

"That answer's simply just unacceptable," James responded to the candidate.

"I understand," the candidate replied in a tone that seemed sympathetic, "but I have no other answer to give."

"What about you?" James asked the A.I., turning to the figure that had always had an answer in the past. "We need options."

"I agree," the A.I. replied. He pointed to the gate, still glowing white, partially obscured by the china cabinet. "I don't believe *that* is one of them."

James nodded. "Understandably. If we're cut off from the mainframe, then the exits are almost certainly cut off too. Our patterns are likely to be destroyed if we try to cross, and the only way we'd know for sure is if one of us tried it and either made it successfully or…" he paused for a moment before finishing, "…disappeared. I don't know about you, but I don't particularly like the idea of using myself as a guinea pig."

"What about the candidate?" Thel asked.

All three men in the room turned to her, shocked by the suggestion, the candidate even taking a defensive step back toward the wall.

"No! Thel!" James retorted. "He's a conscious entity—"

Thel sighed and rolled her eyes. "No, I didn't mean that—obviously." She turned to the candidate. "We've all been cut down to size, but the test gives him the ability to manipulate code in the sim.

If he can look into the inner workings of the program, he might be able to determine if the gateway is still open—"

"And if it's locked, he might be able to unlock it," the A.I. realized.

Thel nodded before turning to James to shoot him a look.

"Uh...sorry," he said to her.

"I-I don't know what you're talking about," the candidate cut in. "I've never seen any code for the sim."

James turned to the candidate. "You teleported out of the car, locked the doors, and drove us off the bridge. If you did all that, you can certainly—"

"But *I* didn't! *I* didn't do those things," the candidate replied. "It was all controlled…*I* was controlled."

"What do you mean?" the A.I. asked, his eyes narrowed, intrigued. "Controlled by whom?"

"My visitor, the stranger," the candidate replied.

"How did this happen?" Thel questioned suspiciously. "How did this so-called stranger infiltrate the sim without any of us seeing him?" She turned to the candidate. "And when did he speak with you? Before or after Kali informed you that you were in a sim?"

"After," the candidate replied. "I got out of bed, desperate to get away from Kali. My intention was to head out, to anywhere that was open, and clear my head. I went down to my car, but when I reached the ground floor, there was a stranger standing in the rain, blocking my path. I immediately knew he was waiting for me—there was something unreal about him—and I became more frightened of him than I was of Kali. I tried the elevator icon in my aug glasses, but it wouldn't work, and then when I looked outside again…*the stranger had stopped the world*."

"Stopped it?" Thel reacted, confused.

The candidate nodded. "Yes. The rain was frozen in place. There wasn't a sound. I couldn't see his face, it was hidden by the darkness, but I knew I couldn't escape. He waited and I went to him."

"What did he say to you?" the A.I. asked.

"He told me that I was about to meet three people." The candidate turned to Thel. "He said I'd meet a woman first, and that woman would take me to meet two men." He turned back to the A.I. "He told me that you were good people, but that you were going to lie to me. He said the lie was part of a test, and that, although the three of you wouldn't hurt me, it was important as though that I behaved as though I believed you would. He told me that, though the three of you were lying because you thought you were serving a greater good, I would have to lie to you to serve the *true* good. He said, time and time again, that his purpose is...higher."

"And what was that?" James asked. "The higher purpose?"

The candidate locked eyes with James. "To prevent the two of you from destroying the reality outside of the sim—from destroying the *real* universe."

27

The Planck platform blinked into Universe 1, and the accompanying ripple was hardly discernible as Djanet and Old-timer found themselves, once again, in the vast emptiness of space. The android armada that had passed by them were besieging the Earth, which was just a pale, blue star, millions of kilometers away. The collective could be seen though, orbiting around the Earth like a galaxy orbiting a super massive black hole, the individual ships reflecting sunlight the way a sandstorm does, the tiny particles of sand seemingly forming a wall.

Old-timer wasted no time opening communication to Earth. "Daniella? Do you hear me?"

"Craig?" she asked through a crackling, static connection in their mind's eyes. "Where are you?"

Old-timer had experienced this sort of situation before—he needed to make sure the result would be different this time.

"Daniella, are you aware of what's happening?"

"The androids are attacking again," she replied. "They're raining down everywhere—half the sky is black with them. None of them have come near the farm yet though."

Old-timer held his hand to his chest, relieved. "Thank God."

"Craig, where's James? Where's the A.I.? Why aren't they stopping this?"

"We don't know," Old-timer replied. "They've vanished. Rich is trying to protect the mainframe."

"Rich? By himself? Oh my God. He's going to die!"

Old-timer's eyes darted to Djanet, who was able to read what Daniella had said from Old-timer's expression. Her lips pulled into a tight, worried grimace.

"Daniella, I'm here with Djanet. I'm adding her to the conversation now. We've got to get you off the planet."

"But where can I go?" Daniella asked. "The farmhouse can't become a spaceship the way everyone else's home can. The Net isn't working properly, so I can't construct anything." Her fear and frustration were saturating her voice. "Craig, where are you?"

"I'm in space," he replied in a helpless tone.

Daniella looked up into the sky and closed her eyes for a moment. "Are you safe?"

"For the moment," Old-timer confirmed. He looked up at Djanet. "Look, Daniella, I can get you some help."

"Get me help?" Daniella reacted. "What about you?"

"I-I can't come back right now. I've got something I have to do—something only I can do."

"Craig!" Daniella exclaimed. "You promised me you wouldn't do this again—"

"Daniella, listen to me!" Old-timer shouted back. "I love you but I'm the only one who can do this! Everyone's life is at stake! If I don't do this, you're already dead, do you understand? Everyone's dead—the androids included!" He looked up at Djanet. "Djanet's coming to get you. She's going to help you get off the surface."

"That'll just get her killed too!" Daniella shot back.

"No it won't," Djanet cut in. "Two of us have a better chance than one."

"Craig, don't let her come," Daniella responded emphatically. "She's already safe. I can't let her—"

"I can't let you face this alone," Old-timer responded. "I can't be there, but Djanet can."

"Craig, don't—"

"Daniella," Djanet interrupted her, "I'm not doing this selflessly. I'm doing it so he can do what he has to do to save the rest of us. I can be your extra set of eyes. I'll have your back."

Daniella exhaled, furious as she began gritting her teeth. Then she saw a lone figure, like a skydiver, a black silhouette against what was left of the blue sky, falling toward the outskirts of her land. "Oh no. They're here."

"You gotta hide," Old-timer reacted, his heart racing.

"Djanet, if you're coming, you better come now," Daniella urged, keeping her voice low as she raced out from the open and hid behind the eastern wall of her house, craning her neck so she could keep her eyes on the lone android. She felt the vibration of the impact in the soles of her feet when the android's body landed, but it disappeared behind the tall grass in the field. A second later, the corner of her eye caught another body falling from the sky on a very similar trajectory to the first. "Because I've got minutes here at most."

Old-timer's snarl returned as he looked down at the unconscious android. "I'm going to disengage the magnetic field to give us a bit of room. Keep your distance. When I wake this ugly piece of filth up, he's not going to be happy."

Djanet nodded. "Okay." She engaged her magnetic cocoon in preparation.

Old-timer disengaged the Planck platform's magnetic field. Djanet floated a few meters away, while Old-timer remained crouched above the unconscious body. He placed his hand flat on the metal chest. A second later, he sent a jumpstart of magnetic energy into the body, instantly jolting the creature to life. Its eyes opened wide before its hand reached up to grasp Old-timer's throat. A second after that, the android screamed out in excruciating pain.

Djanet gasped as she watched Old-timer's violent response to the android's aggression. Instantly, its body was impaled from dozens of the tendrils that Old-timer's new body controlled and that had unfurled from his torso, and struck like an army of cobras all going in for the kill at once. One of the tendrils had driven itself like a spike into the back of the android's neck, jamming up into its artificial brain.

Finally, Old-timer stood, floating above the platform, the tendrils having impaled the android in so many places that he looked like a marionette—and Old-timer was his puppeteer. "It's safe now," he said to Djanet. "I've got control and I've opened up a line of communication with him. I've got access to the collective."

Djanet's mouth was agape for a moment before she asked, "How? I didn't know—"

"It's a feature James suggested when we designed my body," Old-timer replied. "The appendages can connect on a nano scale to communicate with anything computerized. Comes in handy."

"That boy thinks of everything," Djanet commented. Then she considered the fact that James had disappeared. "*Usually*," she amended. "So where does that leave us?"

"Daniella, can you give me an update?" Old-timer asked his wife through their mind's eye connection.

"They're crossing to the house. I'm going to lock myself in the old storm shelter."

"Okay," Old-timer replied. "Djanet's on her way. Daniella, I love you. Stay safe."

"I love you too. I'm going to go quiet now. They'll be tracing for communication signals. Djanet, get your ass down here," Daniella replied before rushing to the hidden entrance, several meters away from the main house.

Old-timer turned to his wife's would-be rescuer. "Djanet, there's an android mothership, they call it the *Constructor*. It's where they construct the bodies of the people they assimilate. That's where we're headed."

"You found that out..." she reacted, pointing to the android's head, "...by connecting to his brain?"

Old-timer shrugged, as though the answer were obvious. "Of course. Yours and my brain are connected right now by the mind's eye. It's basically the same thing."

"Except you didn't jam a tendril into my brain—"

"It's a little unorthodox," he admitted, "but the situation's gotten a little unorthodox."

"Earth's at least twenty minutes away," Djanet pointed out, "and Daniella says she's only got minutes. So..."

Old-timer waved her over to the Planck. "It's safe," he reassured her when he noticed her hesitation. "I'm in complete control of his nervous system. His name is Anisim, if you're wondering."

"I wasn't," Djanet replied as she hovered above the platform, just inches from the gruesome spectacle of the duo. "You've really got your hooks into that guy, huh?"

Old-timer ignored her dark humor and reengaged the magnetic field. "We're going to use the Planck to give us a boost. It'll take us into a random parallel universe, then return us a second later, next to Earth's orbit. From there, I'll make my way to the *Constructor* and it'll be up to you to get to Daniella and help her get off the surface before it's too late."

“Where will I take her?” Djanet asked. “Daniella had a good point. Nowhere’s safe.”

“Just get her off the surface,” Old-timer replied. “Worry about where to take her after that. Venus is an option, if it’s not already under siege.” He locked eyes with her earnestly. “Djanet, I’m counting on you.”

“I’m counting on you too,” she replied.

Old-timer nodded in understanding. She was right: Everyone was counting on him. He thought of the version of himself from Universe 332, who’d been in the same position...that version of him had failed. *I can’t let it happen here. I won’t. Not again.*

“Okay. Ready?” he finally said.

Djanet nodded and bit her lower lip in nervous anticipation. “As ready as I’ll ever be.”

“Then let’s do this.”

A second later, they vanished.

28

"Richard, I admire the bravery you've demonstrated," Aldous commented through his mind's eye connection. "You protected the mainframe long enough for me to take control of the operator's position, but despite this achievement, I was expecting you to take this moment to flee while the androids regroup."

"There's billions of those suckers," Rich replied, feeling nauseous as he looked at the collective bodies re-amassing into a tsunami-like wave. "They're concentrating their attack right here. I've tried working my way through them before, but that was when they were surrounding the entire planet. That was a picnic compared to what trying to get through this would be." Rich sat on the ground, exhausted. "Let's face it. I'm as dead as a doornail, just like you're going to be."

"I'm not planning on dying today, Richard," Aldous replied, "and neither should you."

The words caused Rich's eyebrow to raise. "Are you jerking me around right now?"

"No, in fact, I am glad that you've chosen to stay. I agree, your chances of escape on your own would've been low to nonexistent. But I'm happy to inform you that your chances of survival if you stay with me are 100 percent. We *will* survive this."

"Wait a second," Rich replied, scrambling up to his knees. "I thought you said these were the last minutes of life on Earth."

"They are. That android ship's collision with the surface will obliterate the mainframe and send a shockwave around the planet that will destroy all of the life on every corner of the globe."

"Then how—"

"Trust me," Aldous responded calmly. "I've got this. In the meantime, I'd suggest contacting your family. When the mainframe goes down, all long-range communication will be terminated."

"And what about your family?" Rich questioned.

"Arrangements have been made. My focus is currently on contacting James and the A.I."

Rich's eyes widened. "They're alive?"

"I can't confirm that as of yet, but I've located the sim they were in and it's currently still running. Their core patterns were cut off by a trapdoor code, but there's a chance that they're still functioning within it."

"Can you get them out?"

"I'm working on it. Contact your family, Richard. This may be your last chance."

Rich nodded, breathless as he turned back to the increasing wave of android bodies. It was as if some demonic appendage beyond even biblical proportions, like a hand to match God's was readying to slap post-humanity like a bug, squashing it forever. The dark cloud of bodies was already crossing over the sun, sending a foreboding shadow across the dirt on which Rich stood, the temperature dropping noticeably and sending a chill down his spine. "Okay," Rich replied.

"Rich!" Djanet suddenly shouted through his mind's eye. "Are you still—"

"Djanet! You're alive!"

"So are you!"

"Where are you?"

"I promised Old-timer I'd help get Daniella off the surface. What about you?"

"Wait...you're intentionally heading down to the surface?" Rich reacted, aghast.

"Yeah, I know, adrenaline junkie, right?"

Rich shook his head emphatically. "No, no, junkie isn't funny this time! It'll get you killed! Djanet, the androids are about to ram the planet with one of their ships. Listen to me carefully. You *can't* be on the surface when that happens! Do you understand?"

Djanet could see the ship Rich spoke of, moving toward the surface. She hadn't realized it was on a kamikaze mission. "Are you sure?" she asked, astounded.

"Aldous has control of the mainframe. He's in the operator's position. He calculated their trajectory and speed and there's no doubt about it. They're going to ram us and the mainframe's ground zero!"

"Then you've gotta get out of—"

"Aldous assured me I'm safe. He guaranteed it even. Look, don't worry about me. Worry about you and Daniella!"

"How much time do we have?" she asked as she plummeted into the atmosphere above San Antonio.

"Aldous, how much time until impact?" Rich asked.

"Three minutes and fifty-one seconds."

"Did you copy that?" Rich asked Djanet.

"I did," Djanet replied, picking up speed as she rocketed toward the surface. "This is gonna be another close one."

"As usual," Rich replied. "I don't think we know how to do it any other way."

29

"Destroy the universe?" James reacted, sighing as he fought back the impulse to roll his eyes. "That clinches it."

"How so?" the A.I. replied.

"Are you serious?" James responded. "It's 1. She sounds like a broken record. 'Fear the future' is her mantra, her excuse for assimilating world after world."

"Perhaps, but it still doesn't explain the stranger's reluctance to kill us," the A.I. pointed out. "1 would have no issue with terminating us, and it appears this stranger the candidate speaks of certainly had it within his power to do exactly that."

"Uh...hello?" Thel piped in. "Unless I'm misreading the situation, we're as good as dead right now anyway. We're in the mainframe, we can't escape, and the Earth is the androids's for the taking. And if they take the Earth, there's no reason for them to keep the mainframe."

"She's supremely confident, and let's face it, she should be," James added. "She didn't need to kill us."

"And what of the entity that spoke to us through Kali?" the A.I. reminded his companions. "Why heal us? And what of what she said about James, that the beauty of the universe was within him?"

"I don't know," Thel admitted. "Weird, mocking flirtation? Or maybe she wants to keep James as a trophy. He is the smartest man alive, after all. Maybe she wants to preserve his intellect so that she can exploit it."

"To what end?" the A.I. countered. "Her mandate is quite clearly to keep humanity from progressing technologically. It's in her best interest to eliminate James and to eliminate the candidate and myself as well."

"Not if she has us trapped," James replied, "or if she thinks she does."

"*Thinks?*" Thel reacted. "Are you suggesting you think we can escape?"

"Look, 1 has cut us down to size here by cutting our core neural patterns off from the mainframe," James explained, "but in the brief time that I had control of the operator's position with the A.I., I managed to put contingencies in place."

"What sorts of contingencies?" the A.I. asked, surprised.

"Old-timer, for one. His new body is capable of connecting with the sim and providing a bridge for our patterns to escape, but it means we've got to find a way to get a message to him."

"Well, that's a problem," Thel pointed out. "How the hell are we going to make contact with the outside—"

"James Keats, this is Aldous Gibson," a voice suddenly cut into the sim, speaking to them as easily as though they had a connection through their mind's eyes, stopping the trio in their tracks. "Can you hear me?"

"Aldous!" James shouted in surprise. "Is that really you?"

"What's going on?" the candidate asked, unable to hear the voice.

"Help, hopefully," Thel explained to him.

"I've taken over the operator's position," Aldous informed them. "I'm leading the resistance to the android collective, but in the interest of time and honesty, I must tell you that I won't be able to fend them off much longer. One of their largest ships is on a collision course with the mainframe. Only three minutes remain before impact."

"I can stop them," James proclaimed. "Aldous, can you get me out of here and put me back in control of—"

"I'm afraid not, James. Whoever is responsible for cutting you off from your bodies and trapping your core patterns in the sim used a trapdoor code that is so encrypted, that even with the processing power of the mainframe at my disposal, I can't break it in the time remaining. We're going to lose this battle, I'm afraid."

James's hand went to his forehead as he covered his eyes, the ramifications of Aldous's grim forecast too overwhelming to bear.

"There *is* hope, however," Aldous continued. "I've been able to construct a solid state core that is small enough that I can transport it away from ground zero by hand, but it has enough processing capability to contain the sim. I'm transferring the sim out of the mainframe and into the core as we speak."

"Is there enough time?" the A.I. asked.

"I'm confident, yes, albeit barely," Aldous confirmed. "I'll get you out of there alive."

"Okay," James replied. "Aldous, when the mainframe is destroyed, we're going to lose our communications. You've got to reach Old-timer—Craig Emilson—before then. He's the key to getting us out of here and back into our bodies. Do you understand?"

"I'll do my best to reach him," Aldous replied. "Stand by."

"Aldous," James began with emphasis, "Craig's the only one who can get us out. If you can't find him, we might be trapped in here permanently."

"I understand," Aldous replied. "Stand by."

30

Old-timer couldn't help but be in awe as he neared the android mothership—the *Constructor*—and marveled at a structure that was larger than any of the other ships in the android collective. It was oblong in its overall shape, but the closer one got to the surface, the easier it was to see the randomness in the design. The ship itself appeared reminiscent of a brain, but with the neurons reaching outside of the enclosure and snaking away from the hull in patterns that didn't seem to make sense, as though the entire ship was an organic, growing thing that continued to expand, snaking further and further out with every passing day, its grotesque fingers reaching out for more and more space to occupy.

"This is it," Anisim said reluctantly as he flew toward the *Constructor*, Old-timer's tendrils still embedded in his body, the worst intrusion being the one that had jacked into the base of his skull. The pain was excruciating for Anisim, but it was a pain so intolerable that he'd made up his mind not to disobey Old-timer in the slightest, as the post-human had already demonstrated his ability to make Anisim's discomfort a thousand times worse.

"Where will my friends be replicated?" Old-timer demanded.

"It'll be easy to find their location," Anisim replied, his lips unmoving as their communication remained entirely telepathic, "but there's stringent security built into the replicator system. The new replicants aren't to be awakened until they're scheduled for education.

You'll need someone who works there to get you inside and who can override the computer systems."

"You better know someone, son," Old-timer snarled in response.

"I-I think I do," Anisim replied, a flood of thoughts contradicting one another and causing self-doubt. "I dated her briefly, but she's assigned to the replicator. I'll take you to her."

"That'll suffice," Old-timer replied. As they neared the surface of the monolithic hull, a surface that reminded him of the frozen surface of Europa that he'd so recently had an up-close encounter with, they started to come into visual contact with an innumerable amount of androids, who were flying in the opposite direction. The prying eyes of the multitudes made Old-timer uneasy.

"What's going on?" he asked, warily. "What's with the mass exodus?"

"They're headed for Earth," Anisim replied in a pained voice. "As long as we behave like we have a purpose, they'll ignore us."

"They're not ignoring us now," Old-timer observed as he made eye contact with android after android, every one of the expressions they returned filled with suspicion.

"They're just curious," Anisim replied through their mental connection. "They've been sent to assimilate Earth, yet the two of us are moving against the flow of traffic. They're wondering why we're important—why we're special. Members of the collective are rarely ever special. Just don't look them in the eye. Look like you've got a purpose."

"That's not a problem," Old-timer replied. "You people give me the creeps."

They flew inside one of the gaping openings of the hull and entered the seemingly endless internal labyrinth of catwalks and bizarre architecture inside of the ship.

"Where's this former love interest of yours?"

"Not far," Anisim replied. "Listen, I barely know her, okay? We went out once, it didn't go all that well."

"Why not?"

"She made it pretty clear she wanted children."

"*Children?* "Old-timer exclaimed out loud, unable to internalize his shock. "Androids can breed? You have children?"

"Yes. Lots of us. Most of us actually. I just—I'm not ready."

Old-timer remained silent for a moment, stunned as they continued moving deeper into the *Constructor*. "Robots having babies.

Weird, Anisim. Really, really weird." He paused for a moment, trying to shake the perversity of the notion out of his mind before adding, "It's also weird that she brought up children on a first date."

"I know, right?" Anisim commented.

"Just keep focused."

"I'm focused," Anisim answered, the pain in the back of his skull making it impossible not to be present in the moment, "just, look, please don't hurt her."

"I'll do what I have to do," Old-timer insisted emphatically, ignoring the request, dead set in his determination to save the last survivors of Universe 332, no matter the cost.

"She just wants to be a mom—"

"Shut up, Anisim, or I'll make you shut up," Old-timer ordered. "Take me to her."

"Yes, sir," the android replied meekly as they made their way toward the hive-like inner workings of the ship to the area that was clearly where the androids had made their dwellings.

Old-timer's mouth opened in awe when they emerged from a wide, ugly, twisted tube of metal, and into a place that he couldn't have imagined existed in his wildest dreams, especially not deep in the belly of the gruesome vessel.

Before him, Old-timer saw land—*earth*—whether simulated or not, in which forests sprawled for kilometers, river-like creeks flowed, and parks and gardens dotted an idyllic, spectacular, serene landscape. There were buildings that reminded him of the modern architecture of Earth, giant skyscrapers that reached up toward a simulated blue sky, complete with simulated sunlight.

"What the hell..." Old-timer whispered.

"I've set a course for her address," Anisim informed Old-timer.

Old-timer worked hard to shake himself free of his shock. "She lives alone?"

"Yeah, I think. I dated her a couple of years ago. I haven't checked up on her."

Old-timer began to feel the wind blasting on his skin as they continued to fly into the simulated Earth-like setting. "There's an atmosphere here," he observed, using his mouth to speak once he realized that the air would carry the sound.

"Yes," Anisim replied, "of course. We're still human. We want to be able to speak to one another with our words and not just via mental connections. We want to listen to live music, hear a bird singing in the trees—"

"This is perverse," Old-timer said, his upper lip curling. "It's a crude imitation of the real thing."

"It's how we *have* to live," Anisim responded. "We don't have a choice. We'd all still be on Earth if we could."

"*Still be on Earth?*" Old-timer said, his eyebrow's knitting harder than ever. "You mean, your version of Earth? Your home planets?"

"Home planets?" Anisim reacted. "I'm from Earth, man. I'm an Earthling, just like you. I was born in the Ukraine."

Old-timer forced them to a halt. They floated in the warm breeze, midway between two skyscrapers in the belly of the android's mothership. "Hang on here a second. You're from the Ukraine? As in next to Russia, Ukraine?"

Anisim nodded, but winced, the pain of the tendril in the back of his skull causing his eyes to close for a moment thanks to the worst headache he'd ever endured as he moved his mouth to confirm the gesture. "Yes. I'm human, just like you."

Old-timer suddenly understood the truth. "My God. James was right. The reason you all appear human is because you're from parallel Earths."

"That's right," Anisim replied. "We've been at this for a long time. Our mission is to save the universe, man. We're the good guys, I swear to you."

Old-timer's lip curled again as he glared at Anisim, but he remained speechless.

Anisim dared to follow up his stunning pronouncement with one that was even more stunning. "Our mission is to save humanity from itself."

31

Djanet halted a dozen meters above and slightly to the south of the farmhouse shared by Daniella and Old-timer, close enough to see the shadowy figures inside as they appeared to ransack the old structure while they searched for signs of human life—human life to be assimilated.

"Old-timer, do you read me?" Djanet whispered over her mind's eye as she disengaged her magnetic field and let herself float softly to the ground, crouching low as she made contact with the earth, ducking behind the tall brush to obscure her from the eyes of the androids.

"I read you," Old-timer cut in, quickly and excitedly. "Have you got her?"

"Not yet. I don't want to open communication with her yet, in case they're scanning for communication signals—it'd give her position away."

"You talking to me now will give *yours* away," Old-timer pointed out.

"I had to risk it. I don't know where the storm shelter Daniella was talking about is."

"About forty paces from the house, to the east. It should be under the shadow of the big oak at this time of day."

Djanet turned her head to the left to the large oak tree, a remnant of a time long past—a tree that outdated WWIII. It occurred to Djanet that Old-timer had surrounded himself with artifacts of the past—as though he'd tried to erase the memory of the war he'd fought in and the post-human world that had risen in its aftermath. It had never occurred to her before just how much effort he'd put into being Old-timer, and *not* Craig Emilson. The insight was overwhelming for her as she sensed his spirit, the spirit of a man running from his past, saturating the grounds—the farm *was* Old-timer.

"I see it," Djanet replied as she began to sprint toward the shaded area Old-timer had described.

"Be careful," Old-timer cautioned. "If you get caught in there, there's no way out."

"I don't think we have to worry about them finding *this*," Djanet replied as she found the doors to the shelter, flush with the ground. "I doubt these things even know what a storm shelter is."

"Don't be so sure," Old-timer replied. "Djanet, this android just told me he's Russian."

"Ukrainian," Anisim corrected.

"Ukrainian," Old-timer corrected in turn.

Djanet stopped in her tracks. "What? How can that—"

"I don't think he's lying," Old-timer followed up. "I think the android collective's been assimilating parallel Earths."

"That makes sense," Djanet replied as she fought back her surprise and accepted the bizarrely obvious truth. "We should've realized that."

"*I* should've realized it. Besides Aldous and the A.I., I was the only person who even knew parallel Earths not only existed, but could be accessed. Be careful, Djanet," Old-timer cautioned. "They *will* know what a storm shelter is."

"Daniella! Can you hear me? It's Djanet!" Djanet whispered as she rapped softly on the shelter doors with her knuckle.

There was no immediate response from within.

There was a pause of a few seconds as Djanet kept her eyes on the androids in the house, wary that at any moment, one of them could turn their heads and catch sight of her there in the long shadow of the giant oak tree.

"Uh, Old-timer," Djanet began, "I've got some disconcerting news, but I don't want you to worry."

"What is it?"

"I just knocked, no answer. So I tried to reach her on her mind's eye—"

"Oh my God, no answer," Old-timer echoed as he too tried to reach his wife.

"I think they might've got her already," Djanet said.

"Goddamnit," Old-timer cursed. "One of them must still have the assimilator with her pattern," Old-timer realized, desperation causing his mind to work at lightning speed to conjure a new plan. "Do you think you can get it?"

Djanet stood and considered the situation. "There are at least half a dozen androids inside the house and, Old-timer, I hate to tell you this, but according to Rich, if we're not off the surface in the next ninety seconds, we're dead anyway."

"What are you talking about?" Old-timer reacted, mortified.

"He says the androids are about to ram the Earth with one of their largest ships—Aldous says it'll be an Earth-killer."

"Aldous? Oh my God. Djanet, you've got to save Daniella! One of those bastards must have the assimilator on—"

Djanet was suddenly overwhelmed by a feeling of impending dread. "Something's not right here," she said quickly, cutting Old-timer off as she continued to watch the androids ransacking the inside of the Old-timer's home, apparently aimlessly. "If they got Daniella already, then why—"

Old-timer came to the same realization at almost the exact same time as Djanet. "Oh no! It's a trap! Get the hell out of there, Djanet!"

Before Djanet could ignite her magnetic field, the android who had quietly emerged from the storm shelter and sneaked up behind her jammed her assimilator into Djanet's neck, instantly rendering her unconscious.

"Djanet? Djanet!" Old-timer called out. The connection between their mind's eyes had been terminated.

Old-timer knew there could only be one reason. "Oh no."

32

"What if it's Aldous?" Thel suggested in a low tone to James and the A.I.

"What?" James responded, tilting his head back in surprise.

"That's impossible," the A.I. asserted, his tone, like his expression, firm.

"Why?" Thel countered, pushing her point. "He's got control of the mainframe, something we know he's coveted."

"We don't know he's coveted it for sure," James pointed out.

"And he's about to lose control of it," the A.I. added. "He's gained nothing from us being trapped in here."

"That's not true. He got the two of you out of the way," Thel continued to argue. "You posed the question yourself," she pointed out to the A.I., "who benefits by trapping you inside the sim but who also doesn't want you dead? Aldous checks both of those boxes. Who else does? Plus, he's been a real asshole on many—"

"Your assessment of his character is purely subjective," the A.I. insisted. "I and others have known him to be of extraordinary character. Aldous is *not* the perpetrator we seek."

"Hang on," James cut in after Thel's arguments began to resonate with him, "he *has* been trying to keep us from developing Planck technology," he observed. "He's partly the reason we moved our test of the candidate ahead of schedule."

"And now he can communicate to us," Thel added, "but he *can't* get us out? Convenient."

"The trapdoor code eluded both James and me, Thel," the A.I. returned, sticking to his firm, emphatic tone. "That means it is extraordinarily sophisticated. It is highly plausible that Aldous, who has only been in control of the mainframe for mere minutes, is unable to break the code."

"Yeah, but—" James began before he was interrupted by the sound of glass smashing and, seconds later, raining down on the marble floor in front of the balcony. A second after that, a cold gust of damp air blew through the room.

"Oh no," Thel said as she saw a woman's arm desperately lunging, mindlessly flailing through the sharp, jagged hole, cutting itself in its attempts to form a larger opening. "An NPC!"

"Dear God," the candidate said as he back peddled from the balcony, the streaks of blood from the NPC's bicep raining down from the hole and splashing to the floor; it was in danger of cutting its own limb off before the glass door broke open.

Seconds later, dozens more NPCs leapt over the balcony, having climbed the exterior of the building. Their bodies crashed against the weakening glass.

"We're in deep trouble," Thel announced, turning to James and the A.I. "We've got no way of defending ourselves against those things, and we're about to be overwhelmed."

James cut into communication with Aldous as he waved for his companions to follow him to the elevator. They hit the button and waited with desperate impatience for the elevator to arrive. They could hear it audibly shimmy its way up from the lobby.

"Aldous, we're in the penthouse, and we've been discovered by the NPCs. We're about to be purged, unless you can get us some help!"

"I'll see what I can do," Aldous replied. "Stand by."

"Stand by again?" Thel shouted. "Is that all you can ever say? Do something!" Her eyes were then suddenly drawn to the A.I. as he took the Kali avatar by the hand and guided the empty shell as though he were guiding a somnambulist toward the elevator. "Speaking of doing something, what the hell are *you* doing? We don't have time for a puppet show!"

The A.I. shot her a warning look and held his finger to his lips, motioning for her to be silent.

Thel's eyes narrowed as she looked on in utter disbelief, but she heeded his warning and remained silent, trusting that there had to be some sort of method to the A.I.'s seeming mad behavior.

"Do you have something for us?" James shouted to Aldous as the entire group collected around the still-closed elevator door.

"Stand by," Aldous repeated.

"Stand by," Thel repeated as she shook her head in frustration. She listened to the *hum* of the elevator as it made its way up the shaft, closer and closer. "What if an NPC is in there when the door opens?"

"We outnumber it," the A.I. pointed out. "If we work together—"

"We need to get to the roof," the candidate suddenly announced. "I can fly. That's one ability that the stranger endowed me with. If we can get to the roof, I can get us out of here."

The elevator reached the penthouse and a second later, the door opened, empty. There wasn't time to be grateful, however, as in the same second, they heard the last of the glass balcony door give way, shattering as a herd of NPCs brought it down.

"Inside!" James shouted as he shoved his shocked and reluctant companions into the elevator, seeing the first of the NPCs sprint around the corner into the hallway as he hit the elevator's button. The door hesitated for what seemed an eternity before finally beginning to close.

"Good news," Aldous announced as guns that the A.I. instantly recognized suddenly appeared in all of their hands.

It wasn't a moment too soon, as the first NPC's arm reached into the elevator in time to stop the door and was only prevented from doing so by Thel's quick reflexes as she aimed and pulled her trigger quickly enough to de-patternize the figure, the appendage breaking apart into a golden dust of coding that seemed to blow away in the cold breeze.

The door closed and it quickly became apparent that, had Thel not moved fast enough, they would've been overwhelmed by the herd of mindless patterns outside the door, the *thud* of their collective bodies crashing against the doors, sending a vibration throughout the inside of the elevator. James hit the STOP button and the elevator remained frozen in place in the shaft, the NPCs clawing against the outer door as the occupants, terrified, considered their next move.

Thel looked up. "They're gonna rip through that door," she pointed out. "We've gotta go up."

"Agreed," James replied.

Suddenly, a black armor began to form over his skin, shocking Thel and the others before they realized that it was forming over their own bodies as well.

The A.I. recognized the material, which fit over his frame like a glove. "Thank you, Aldous," he said.

"It's the least I could do," Aldous replied. "I'm sorry I couldn't have been of more use, but I'm afraid we have only seconds of contact left. I wasn't able to reach Craig," he relayed, "but, rest assured, I shall endeavor to find him. In the meantime, know that the sim itself *is* safe. It's up to each of you now to survive the purge with the weapons you have in your possession. I have full confidence you can do it."

"We'll do our best," the A.I. replied. "Good luck to you, Aldous," the A.I. spoke as he aimed his de-patternizing gun at the roof of the elevator before stopping to speak to his companions. "Allow me. I have some experience with this sort of thing."

He fired his weapon and the elevator's roof disappeared in an explosion of golden dust.

33

Rich could barely move; only his left index finger twitched as he realized he'd been pushed beyond any of the extreme stress levels he'd experienced before. He'd faced death so many times, battled these androids before, but he'd *never* seen anything like what his eyes now beheld.

The wave of android bodies had swarmed the mainframe's protective magnetic force-field once again, only to find themselves shredded by a dense, living fog of nanobots that ate each of them alive, relentlessly devouring the millions of android bodies just meters above Rich's head. He watched as desperate android after android hit the surface of the field, only to have their flesh eaten within seconds, the metal skeletons underneath suddenly exposed as the flesh was consumed before the skeletons too were shredded. It was like watching them fall into a high-powered blender, their powerful bodies succumbing again and again... *but they just kept coming.*

"This makes no sense. This is absurd," Rich whispered to himself, his lips trembling. "If this isn't Hell, I don't know what is."

"Worse than Dante," Aldous suddenly observed through their mind's eye connection. "Worse than Blake."

"I'll take your word on that, Chief," Rich replied, his mouth dry as he closed his eyes, blocking out the utter carnage and horror, trying to protect his mind from the trauma of the implacable chaos.

"I've got good news and bad news," Aldous said. Rich noted that Aldous seemed to grunt, as though he were carrying some sort of burden.

"Good news first, please," Rich replied.

"We're going to survive this," Aldous said, still huffing as he sounded to Rich to be hurrying as he carried whatever it was that caused him so much difficulty.

"That's not fair. You're double-dipping your good news," Rich said, his eyebrows raised. "You already told me that good news earlier. You're just dressing up the bad news that's coming, aren't you?"

"Well…" Aldous began, his voice no longer in Rich's mind's eye but coming from behind him as he hurried to reach him, Thel's unconscious body over his shoulder. "I'm afraid we will have to endure the impact. As you can see, I'm no longer in control of the mainframe."

Rich's brow furrowed instantly. "Whoa, wait a sec'! Where's James's body?"

"I couldn't carry both of them," Aldous replied as he tilted his head toward the unconscious Thel before kneeling and laying her on the soft earth. He turned to the small ship Rich had arrived in. "We need to get her on board—"

"I'll get him!" Rich shouted, cutting Aldous off as he started to fly toward the mainframe building. Aldous grabbed his ankle to stop him, pulling him back to the ground where the duo thudded hard to the ground, sending a plume of dust up around them. Rich noted that Aldous was stronger than he looked.

"No! There isn't time! Look!" Aldous shouted as he pointed up to the canopy of the mainframe's force-field.

Rich looked up to see the nanobot storm that had been defending them dispersing, the wisps of microscopic robotic warriors now blowing away, clearing like dust in the wind. When the dust cleared enough, Rich's mouth dropped and he, likewise dropped to his knees. "For the love of God."

The entire sky, right to the horizon line, was now taken up by the rust-colored, pockmarked hull of the android ship.

"I'm sorry, my friend," Aldous uttered. "I should've asked you to help me transport James's body, but I didn't realize the material it was made of would be so dense—it was heavier than you could imagine—I couldn't move him an inch, even with all my might. But don't worry," he patted the black, square object that was attached to him via a black strap over his shoulder. "I downloaded their sim into this hard drive. It contains their patterns. We may lose James's body and the mainframe, but *we'll all* survive this. I swear it."

Rich couldn't respond. He looked up, wide-eyed, at the monstrous spacecraft, a ship that looked to him to be the size of an entire world—and watched the object that was about to destroy his home planet get closer and closer by the second.

"Djanet?" he finally managed to call out weakly through his mind's eye. There was no response. "Edmund?" he asked. "Linda?" he spoke. No one spoke back.

"Richard," Aldous finally said, in an unnervingly calm tone. "Do you trust me?"

Rich turned to him, still unable to speak or even nod his head in response.

"The mainframe's magnetic field will fail because the mainframe is embedded in the earth, and when that monstrosity collides with it, the ground will be obliterated." Aldous grabbed Rich's shoulders and tried to get the dazed man to look him in the eye as he continued, "But *your* magnetic field *can* withstand this. We need to get Thel on board and then you'll need to cocoon the ship. The android ship is moving at four kilometers per second and will hit us in twelve seconds. It'll be the first giant impact the Earth has experienced in four and a half billion years and, just like the last time, an incident that gave birth to our current moon, it'll vaporize the water in the oceans and cause the Earth's surface to become an ocean of magma."

"Are you—what the fu—" Rich uttered, his lips quivering.

"Listen to me, Richard!" Aldous shouted as he dragged him with one hand while literally dragging Thel with the other. Rich was aware enough to know to help him, and together, they began dragging Thel's unconscious body onto the ship. "We can do this! Are you ready?"

"No," Rich replied as the platform raised up into the ship, taking Aldous and Thel with it.

Aldous sighed.

"Too bad," he replied through their mind's eye as Rich stood alone in the darkness, outside the ship. "We're out of time. Use your magnetic field, Richard. *Save us.*"

Rich, in a trance-like state, ignited his cocoon, making sure that he protected the entire ship, along with himself.

In the next instant, the whole world flashed white as though they were on the surface of the sun, Rich was knocked upside down, and a second later he was in utter darkness.

PART 3

1

"What the hell am I seeing?" Old-timer asked as he stopped, images from the shared android collective communication network streaming into his field of vision.

The images appeared to be of Earth, after the impact of an android ship the size of Brazil, right on the western shore of North America. The giant impact was so intense that a shockwave of superheated, red-hot gas was surrounding the globe, eating away the blue oceans and the green, living continents and leaving a smoldering-hot magma glowing in its wake. Giant pieces of debris, some of them the size of entire countries were being flung from the surface, and the android ship was in the process of disappearing completely, partially embedding itself under the crust of the Earth and partially disintegrating due to the force of impact and the unimaginable heat and destructive energy produced in the collision. Androids all over the serene setting of the city hidden safely at the center of the *Constructor* cheered as though they'd won an important battle in a war.

"Tell me *this* isn't real," Old-timer whispered to Anisim. "Tell me this is a simulation."

"It-it's real," Anisim admitted, reluctant as he considered the pain he might feel as a result of Old-timer's instinctual desire for instant retribution, yet equally afraid to lie. "It's live, a live feed."

The duo stood in the shadow of a beautiful, modern building that towered high on the edge of a body of water that shimmered in the light of an artificial sun that glowed overhead. There was a breeze that felt as real as anything Old-timer had ever felt on his skin on Earth, perhaps even more real.

Old-timer sneered and pulled Anisim with him into the empty alley between the building and its equally beautiful neighboring structure, and once he was sure no one was watching, he pushed Anisim roughly against the cool concrete of the building in the shadow of the false sun. "My wife was down there, you son-of-a-bitch. Your people just murdered her...and they're cheering?"

"They're happy. You don't realize it but those people—your wife included—were *saved*," Anisim protested. "Not to mention countless more people in countless other universes. My Earth was destroyed, too, but I'm grateful for it. Friend, look, we're not your enemies."

"My *wife* was down there," Old-timer repeated, twisting the tendril embedded in the back of Anisim's skull.

"She wasn't down there," Anisim protested, barely able to respond and wincing painfully as every movement of the tendril inside his skull seared with pain. "You'd lost contact with her, which means she must've been assimilated, and if she was assimilated—"

"Then there'll be an android body built for her here?"

"Yes," Anisim replied with a grunt after aborting an attempt to nod.

Old-timer looked up at the building Anisim was pressed against. "Your girlfriend lives here?"

"Not my girlfriend, but yes," Anisim replied, regretfully. "Her name is Jules."

"She can locate my wife?"

"Yes," Anisim confirmed again. "She can locate all your friends and awaken them early."

Old-timer bit his bottom lip as he considered this. They'd lost the Earth, and Daniella and Djanet had been lost with it, but if they'd been assimilated, at least he could spare them the so-called *education* to which the androids subjected their newest members.

"Okay," Old-timer relented, falling back on plan B as there was no other option, "get us up to her apartment."

"There's a small problem," Anisim revealed.

"It better be small," Old-timer growled threateningly.

"There's no reason for her to expect me, and she's gotta invite me in. I can't just walk into her building unless she clears me."

"So put on the charm," Old-timer insisted.

"And what about you? You're a complete stranger."

"No, I'm not," Old-timer said with a sardonic smile, "we're best pals. I'm your oldest friend in the world. Got it?"

"Got it," Anisim replied, acquiescing once he realized his protests were falling on deaf ears.

Half a minute later, they stood side by side at the front door of the high-rise, Old-timer keeping just one wiry connection to Anisim, jacked into the back of the android's skull, practically working him like a ventriloquist's dummy.

Jules's surprised visage suddenly appeared on a view screen next to the door. She appeared young, though one never knew with an android, her hair a strawberry blonde, slightly darker, but still reminiscent of Samantha's. "Hello? Anisim? What are *you* doing here?" she asked.

"Uh…I-I know this is a bit awkward, Jules, but—"

"Shouldn't you be taking part in the rescue?" she asked.

Old-timer kept smiling, not even flinching at the euphemism the androids clearly used instead of the more accurate word: *attack*.

Anisim shrugged. "I was called back. As you can see, it went really smoothly."

"Yeah, it really did," Jules replied, a hint of a smile crossing her lips. Old-timer couldn't help but think it was a look of pride. "1 must've pulled off some sort of brilliant tactical maneuver again, but what else is new, right?"

"Ha-ha. Yeah," Anisim agreed, his tone nervous, the interaction awkward. Old-timer knew he had to interject.

"By golly, you are *far* more beautiful than Anisim could possibly have described," he said, stunning the young woman.

"Wh-what?" she reacted, the smile vanishing, replaced by a look of shock.

"I-I didn't—" Anisim began to try to explain.

"Anisim didn't want to put you out," Old-timer continued, "but I insisted." He put his hand on his heart to feign earnestness. "Please forgive him. Look, we're really old friends, and he's always said Jules was the best girl he ever went on a date with and, with the rescue happening today and all, I said to him, 'Look, Anisim, if we get called back today because things go really well, I want you to finally introduce me to that girl you won't shut up about.'" He smiled. "And so…" he made a grand flourish with his hand to emphasize the point, "we're here."

Jules put a self-conscious hand up to fix her hair before beginning to utter a response, "I wish you'd let me know first—"

"I'm sorry—" Anisim began to apologize.

"He really is," Old-timer cut him off, "he tried to talk me out of it. But I wouldn't let him. We were just so happy that the rescue went so well and, well, Anisim thought we'd be perfect for each other and, I just wanted to meet you so gosh darn much. But look, I can see we're putting you out. Maybe we can just come back another time?"

"No, no," Jules replied, her face coloring. Old-timer marveled that an android's face could flush. "It's okay, I'm so flattered." Her eyes went to Anisim and she added, seemingly embarrassed, "Anisim, I had no idea."

"Me neither," Anisim replied.

Old-timer resisted the urge to twist the tendril.

Luckily, Jules didn't seem to catch the verbal misstep. "Just pardon the mess, okay? But come on up."

"Oh, thank you. You've made a couple a fella's days, my lady."

"Aw, shucks," Jules replied as the door unlocked. "See you in a minute." Her image vanished.

"That was close," Old-timer noted, his faux, flirty smile completely vanished.

"I'm going to burn in Hell for this," Anisim replied as they made their way to the inner, hollowed out core of the building. They began to float upward toward Jules's apartment. "She's a nice girl. She doesn't deserve this."

"Hey, I don't remember us calling the android collective and asking you to '*rescue*' us, for Christ's sakes. You people are so deluded, it's—"

"We're not the deluded ones," Anisim replied. "I promise you. Please don't hurt her."

They arrived outside Jules's door, floating to the ledge at her doorstep on the thirtieth floor.

"I'll be as gentle with her as your kind have been with mine," Old-timer replied coldly.

2

It's the moment of truth, James thought. Will the candidate help us or turn his back?

James reached up, his eyes locked on those of the candidate as the A.I. and Thel stood, their necks craned upward as they watched the unfolding of the telling events while the NPCs crashed and clawed against the elevator door. It sounded as though the outside door of the elevator had already partially given way and only the thin interior door stood between them and their prey. They were seconds to breaking in.

To the shared relief of the A.I. and the post-humans, the candidate did, indeed, reach back, his gloved hand grasping James's, and James turned to grab Thel's hand, who in turn grasped the hand of the A.I., who, inexplicably to Thel, made sure he grabbed the hand of the Kali avatar.

"Hang on tight," the candidate said as he began to fly upward, through the hole in the roof that the A.I. had blasted with his gun, de-patternizing it. The cold rain pelted them as they lifted off into the night, leaving the candidate's building below them—a building now crawling with NPCs. It was a sight the A.I. had seen before, the walls seeming to move with the untold number of bodies scaling the outside of the structure.

"Where do we go?" Thel shouted out.

James turned to the skyline of the sim city. The tallest rooftops were obscured by the heavy cloak of cloud and rain. "Head to the highest buildings," James yelled to the candidate. "We'll lose them in the canopy!"

The candidate nodded as he flew, slowly and cautiously, into the dark, gothic sky. He chose the tallest building in the city and they landed on the roof, the A.I. and Kali touching down first, followed by the others.

"Are we stuck now?" Thel asked, as she brushed the gravel from the rooftop from the knees of her new, black body armor. "We just have to wait here to be rescued by Aldous?"

"I don't believe that would be a wise course of action," the A.I. returned.

"Why not?" James asked. "We'll already've lost the mainframe by now, not to mention Earth."

"Because Thel was right earlier," the A.I. returned. "Aldous, *is* a suspect, and a strong one at that."

"What?" Thel reacted, astonished. "You said there was no way—"

"I was lying. He was listening in on our conversation," the A.I. answered. "I couldn't let him know we suspected him, but you *were* spot on. Aldous does indeed benefit from keeping James and I trapped in the sim, and he also benefits from the destruction of the mainframe."

"How?" James asked, flabbergasted. "If the mainframe's destroyed, it can't be a power grab. He's just as powerless as any of us—"

"It wasn't power that he wanted for himself," the A.I. replied, "but power he didn't want you and I to have." He turned to the candidate. "And power he didn't want you to have either."

"Trans-human," James realized. "You're suggesting he did all this—gave up the Earth—caused us to be assimilated by the androids—all because he didn't want Trans-human to be reactivated?"

"Possibly," the A.I. replied cautiously. "I'm only suggesting that Aldous is a suspect, not that he's *definitely* the perpetrator responsible for our current circumstances."

"I don't know," James dubiously replied. "I've butted heads with that obnoxious, pigheaded egomaniac ever since I was a child, ever since the council identified me as gifted. But betraying his race? I just can't believe he'd—"

"We can't depend on belief, James," the A.I. replied. "We have to depend on the facts, no matter how cold and hard they are. Indeed,

Aldous is not a perfect suspect. He knew Trans-human had already been activated and that it operated in an exemplary manner when I was in charge of it. His fear of it then, would seem to be irrational."

"Unless there was something he was afraid of in particular," Thel pointed out, "one aspect."

James nodded. "He warned Old-timer just last night about Planck technology, but as dangerous as parallel universe-hopping might be, was he so afraid of it that he'd destroy the mainframe and leave us defenseless just to stop it?"

"And it begs the question, what does Trans-human have to do with Planck technology?" the A.I. added.

James's arms were crossed as he began to pace across the rooftop, his head bowed as the rain drenched his hair and ran down his face, dripping from his chin. "Trans-human would have almost infinite computing capability—a mind that could unlock innumerable mysteries. What if there was a mystery he didn't want unlocked?"

The A.I.'s eyebrow raised as he considered the question.

"Perhaps," the candidate suddenly spoke up, "this Aldous person feared that Trans-human might be the mind that would destroy the universe as the stranger warned me?"

James's mouth opened slightly as he snapped his head around and locked eyes with the A.I. "*Aldous* was the visitor that the candidate had in the sim?"

"It's plausible," the A.I. agreed. "It's plausible indeed."

3

WAKING UP underneath the Earth's crust was akin to waking up in the ninth level of Hell as far as Rich was concerned.

Aldous tilted his companion's head up to help rouse him. "You're alive," he said.

Rich turned his head to see that Aldous had brought him inside of the ship after Rich had been injured in their fall. His forcefield had remained on despite his lack of consciousness, performing correctly according to its design, but it couldn't protect him from the ship he also cocooned and the structure had hit him, knocking him unconscious and temporarily blackening his eye. A few minutes had since past and the nans had recovered him sufficiently that Aldous knew it was safe to wake him.

Rich turned from Aldous and looked outside of the view screen to see the perfect blackness all around them outside of the green glow of their magnetic field. "Tell me that was a nightmare," Rich spoke.

"I'm afraid not," Aldous replied as he inhaled deeply and puffed out his chest, once again stoically pulling his shoulders back. "We've lost the mainframe. We've lost Earth, but we haven't lost our lives, and that, in the end, is what counts."

"Yeah," Rich forced a sarcastic smile, "you're right. Things aren't so bad. Just lost Earth and everyone we know and love, not to mention our whole way of life. We're buried under who-knows-how-many kilometers of earth, but that's okay, because even if we can make it to the surface, we're officially the androids's bitches for all time. Thanks for cheering me up, Chief! You always know how to look in the bright side of life."

"Richard, I know this is difficult to process, but we've all lost our home and, if I may be so bold, your negative demeanor makes it very difficult to enjoy your company."

Rich's eyes widened in disbelief. "Oh my God. Kettle. Pot. Black!"

"At any rate," Aldous said, ignoring the jab as he refocused himself and looked down at Thel's unconscious body, "your magnetic field held, just as I'd calculated it would. We're safe."

"James isn't," Rich shot back. "His body was obliterated, and without the mainframe, there's no way to reconstruct a body for him."

Aldous patted the black hard drive on his hip. "But he *is* alive, Richard, lest we forget."

"Wow. You're a ray of sunshine and positivity today, Chief," he said as he sat up, rigid with fury. "You know, we should hang out more. I know this great place in San Francisco at Fisherman's Wharf—oh wait. IT WAS DESTROYED! What are you not getting about this, Chief? We just lost Earth! *We failed!*"

"We saved lives," Aldous countered, his face like stone, only his brow furrowing slightly. "Humanity hasn't been wiped out. Mars is terraformed. The Purists were given the newly terraformed Venus by James. All is not lost, Rich Borges. Humanity will endure."

Rich took in a deep breath. "Apparently, Chief, you live in your own world. Wish I could hang out with you there, but I'm in this place called *reality*. And speaking of," he looked straight up. "We've got to get back to the surface. I don't want to be stuck down here for a second longer. I'm just now realizing that I'm definitely claustrophobic."

"Agreed," Aldous replied, "this would make anyone feel claustrophobic, including me."

He held out his hand for Rich and helped him off of the table he was on, not far from where Thel was lying motionless.

Rich moved to the pilot's seat. "It may take a few minutes to move all of this debris and rubble aside. We better get going."

They set off, flying upward slowly, the earth giving way in front of them like ice giving way in front of an arctic icebreaking vessel before the post-human era. They continued making their way up for several minutes before either of them spoke again.

Rich, grumbly, broke the silence. "Do you have a large family, Chief?"

Aldous hesitated before answering. He'd usually brush off questions about his personal affairs as intrusive and rude, but he knew that the usual customs didn't apply in that instance. "I don't," he answered, uncomfortably. "It's just my wife and I." He quickly steered the conversation back to Rich. "What about you, Richard?"

Rich's eyes stared forward, unblinking. "Yes. Big family. Kids. Grand kids. Great grand kids."

Aldous had no words to comfort a man who he knew had to be crippled with worry. He stayed silent.

"Why no kids?" Rich suddenly asked. "I mean, no offence, but you're old as all hell, aren't you? Like 150 or something? And you never had children?"

"164 actually," Aldous answered. "And I didn't…" Aldous paused as he struggled to find sufficient words. "I've seen very different eras. Eras when children just didn't seem to make sense. And by the time I found the person I knew I'd love forever, children made even less sense."

"Why not?"

Aldous licked his lips as he carefully considered his words. "By then, I felt everyone in the world was *my* responsibility. I didn't want to have anyone else in my life that I favored over my people. Does that make sense?"

Rich nodded. "Yeah. It's weird. It's sad. It isn't really true. But it makes sense. What about your wife? Was she okay with this?"

Aldous thought of Samantha; then, almost as quickly, he thought of Craig Emilson, the ghost who had haunted their relationship for three-quarters of a century. "Children didn't seem natural to either of us. It was a mutual decision."

The ceiling above them suddenly went from a perfect blackness to emanating an orange glow. It was a glow that grew in intensity, veins of liquid magma becoming more and more prevalent the higher they climbed. They each remained silent as it became clear that they were only seconds from breaching the surface, seconds from seeing the remnants of the Earth.

When they emerged, they emerged spectacularly, the green cocoon of their magnetic field engulfed entirely in glowing, orange magma that quickly cooled and broke away in smoldering, coal-black chunks of what used to be Earth, the smoke trails of the chunks spiraling down to the orange surface. When enough of the magma had cooled and broken away, they saw the full extent of the damage to their home—and it was total.

They slowed as they climbed above the new, magma ocean, and marveled as they saw what was left of the android ship, a structure that was two-thirds destroyed, the tail end of it sinking slowly into the liquid surface of the planet, melting as it became one with the body it had destroyed, trillions and trillions of fragments of debris forming a plume all around it, most of it still glowing red hot even as it orbited high above the Earth itself.

"Look out," Rich said as they narrowly avoided the body of an android woman, unconscious as it dropped to the surface of the Earth so far below. It was a body that Aldous surmised must have been blown into what used to be the stratosphere in the wake of the impact of the android vessel, and was now being pulled back down by the Earth's gravity to the lava's surface below.

Rich flipped on the rearview so that they could regard the totality of their surroundings. The whole Earth was glowing orange with debris—red hot dust had been catapulted into orbit, some of it at rates so fast that they'd escaped Earth's orbit and were hurtling away from the Earth into deep space. Chunks of Earth the size of mountain ranges had also been expelled and were spinning, wildly out of control as they burned like hot coals, orbiting the planet they'd been a part of for billions of years.

"The Earth," Rich began, "the greatest miracle the universe has ever seen—is gone." He turned to Aldous. "It looks like you and your wife were right not to have children. At least you didn't have to live through witnessing their death."

Aldous shook his head, his face pale as he took in the enormity of the destruction. "No Richard," he corrected, "I saw my children vanish too." He steeled himself again, clearing his throat before speaking in as strong a tone as he could muster. "Your children aren't dead. You can't give up hope."

4

"Hi, I'm Jules." The android smiled as she stood at her front door and held out her hand in greeting for Old-timer.

Old-timer smiled in return and shook her hand—a hand that he noted was tiny in his—Jules didn't appear to be even five feet tall, and her slender frame suggested that she might not have weighed as much as 100 pounds—in her previous organic incarnation.

No mercy, he thought to himself.

Jules brushed past the two men as she closed the door to her apartment behind them, and Old-timer awkwardly moved to force a turn from Anisim so that she couldn't see the impaling of the now thread-thin appendage at the back of the android's skull. The awkward move in the narrow hallway caused Jules to furrow her brow slightly, though her smile didn't fade.

Old-timer hoped she'd dismiss their awkwardness as understandable given what she thought was the circumstances.

"Boy, you guys are not slick at all when it comes to dealing with women."

"No, ma'am," Old-timer replied, relieved as his assessment was validated. Jules passed by again and gestured for the men to take a seat on her couch. Behind them was a glorious view of the ultramodern city and the sparkling lake that gently lapped at its shore.

"Ah, a Southern gent," she observed. "I'll get you fellas a drink," she continued as she turned away. "I knew Anisim was awkward," Jules said as she made her way into the kitchen, "but *you* seemed like you had game," she said, staring right at Old-timer flirtatiously. "What's your name, cowboy?"

"Craig," Old-timer replied.

"Whereabouts are you from?"

"Texas," he replied.

"Really? I shoulda guessed." She returned to the room with two glasses of a clear liquid.

Old-timer didn't ask what it was, but took it from her just the same. "Yes, ma'am."

Jules caught Anisim's eyes for a moment and noticed that he seemed distraught, but he turned away from her gaze quickly and sipped his drink and she seemed to dismiss yet another red flag, turning back to Old-timer. "So, you're what, six-three, six-four?"

"Six-five, ma'am."

"Six-five, a gentleman, and handsome? So how the heck are you single?"

"I'm not, ma'am," Old-timer replied. "In fact, that's why I'm here."

Jules seemed rocked by this, taking a step back just to keep her balance as her expression suddenly became befuddled. "Uh, what? I'm not, uh...that kind of..." she looked down at Anisim questioningly.

"I'm so, so sorry, Jules," Anisim whispered.

"What is going—"

A second later, Jules called out in a faint cry, followed by a gargling sound that quickly faded, Old-timer having infiltrated her nervous system with a dozen, thread-like tendrils, impaling her thighs, forearms, spine, and the back of her skull. Just as he'd done with Anisim earlier, he took complete control of her nervous system.

Anisim bowed his head, enduring the pain from his impaled skull, he felt he deserved the punishment.

"Jules, unlike you, I'm human. My wife was assimilated, as were four other companions of mine. Anisim, here, tells me you have the clearance to take me to the replicator and to activate their android bodies. Is that true?"

Jules didn't speak with her lips, her nervous system having been entirely compromised. "Yes," she replied through her mental connection to Old-timer.

Old-timer took a deep breath. He could feel her terror, and it took him a moment to recalibrate so that he could find the strength to shut himself off from his overwhelming sense of pity.

"Please don't hurt her," Anisim said quietly. "She's just a tech. She's never taken part in a rescue, never hurt anyone you know. She doesn't deserve—"

Before he could say another word, Old-timer's tendril broke through Anisim's face, silencing him. It pulled out, encircled Anisim's neck, and severed his head from his body.

Old-timer could feel Jules's disgust and fright as she watched Anisim's mutilated head roll to a stop near the wall in the perfectly simulated sunlight of the android city.

"Why? Why did you do that?" she demanded of him in horror through their connection.

"We can't bring him with us," Old-timer replied, "and I couldn't have him warning the collective about my presence."

"You-you're a monster," Jules replied, tears forming in the corners of her eyes, "you're a monster."

5

"So what the hell do we do now?" Thel asked with frustration as they emerged from the stairway from the rooftop and into the warm, but dark interior of the Cloud 9 revolving restaurant. The restaurant was no longer revolving, and they had to keep the lights off to avoid detection, but it was warm and dry and provided an excellent place for the quintet to lie low. "If Aldous is to blame—"

"Something we've no proof of," the A.I. pointed out, making an addendum to Thel's statement before she'd even finished making it while he guided the Kali avatar, still pacing slowly and mindlessly like a sleepwalker to a table, where he helped her take a seat—an eerie sight, something like a mannequin sitting down for dinner.

Thel soldiered on, "then we're going to be trapped in here indefinitely."

"Not if we can help it," the A.I. replied. "There are alternatives."

"Like what?"

"If we're in a hard drive," James offered, "then really what we're in is a mini-mainframe. Aldous said he'd constructed it so he could download the sim into it and remove us from the A.I.'s mainframe, so we're likely on his person as we speak."

"And that means that we do, indeed, have a means," the A.I. added.

"Means of what?" Thel responded with a shrug. "We're ghosts trapped in a little box."

"Aldous *communicated* with us," James observed, "which means that the sim is capable of receiving signals. And a sim this big is going to be a huge power hog, so to keep it running, he'd have to have equipped it with an MTF generator."

"He was also able to provide us with armor and weaponry," the A.I. added, holding up his de-patternizer. "These are quite complex patterns that he was able to upload for us."

"So?" Thel asked. "The weapons and armor were meant to help us survive the purge—to buy time. How do they help us get out?"

"They don't directly," James replied, "but the fact he was able to send them to us means the hard drive is capable of sending and receiving powerful data transmissions. Aldous said he couldn't enter the sim because our core matrix programs had been trapped by a trapdoor code that would allow for our patterns to enter the sim, but wouldn't let them leave. That's entirely possible, and why we can't be sure he's the one who trapped us here."

"But," the A.I. continued, as though he and James were of one mind, "if he is the one who trapped us here, then our task will be to break the trapdoor code from within the sim. If we do, we'll be able to send a signal for help."

"But Aldous said he couldn't do it," Thel countered, "and he had the power of the mainframe to help him."

"That's true," the A.I. replied, "but what if he *was* lying?"

"What if he was telling the truth?" Thel returned. "You said so yourself, he's a suspect, but we've no proof. If he was telling the truth, then we don't have a chance in Hell of breaking a code that he couldn't break with the help of the mainframe at his disposal."

"That would be true," the A.I. replied, "but there was something Aldous may not have been aware of." He turned to the Kali avatar, sitting aimlessly, staring straight forward into the dim light of the restaurant.

"*Kali?*" Thel responded, not seeing the A.I.'s point. "Aldous knew about…wait a second, are you saying he knew about the Kali avatar, but he might not have known about the entity that spoke to us?"

"The entity helped us," the A.I. confirmed for Thel, "and it may have shown us the way out."

"She healed both the A.I. and me," James injected. "That means she had the ability to manipulate the code within the sim."

"And she *or it* also exited the sim, which means the entity was able to circumvent the trapdoor," the A.I. added.

Thel closed her eyes. "*That's* why you brought her with us," she realized. "And why you didn't say anything about it while Aldous was monitoring us."

"Precisely," the A.I. confirmed. "What the entity may have provided us with is an avatar that was both capable of manipulating code in the sim, and capable of cracking the trapdoor."

"Nice work," James said to the A.I. with a grin. "If we can gain access to the coding of the avatar, and if your theory is correct, then we can circumvent the trapdoor and send a message."

"To whom?" Thel asked.

"Old-timer," James replied. "If Aldous really is trying to keep us trapped, then Old-timer may be our only way out. He's the only one who can access the hard drive."

"Speaking of access," Thel returned, "how the hell do you access the code of an NPC?"

The A.I. held up his de-patternizing gun. "This should suffice," he replied.

Thel's eyes narrowed. "What now?"

The A.I. grabbed the Kali NPC's wrist and put her hand, palm-first, on the table. Then he aimed the weapon and fired.

Kali's hand, like everything shot by the de-patternizer, dematerialized, briefly revealing the golden coding that evaporated into nothingness like wisps of smoke. The NPC hardly reacted as the A.I. released its wrist.

James's eyes widened. "I see it," he said, peering into the stump. He grabbed the wrist and examined it before gouging into it with his fingers, an action that caused Thel to nearly gag.

"No!" she reacted, repulsed.

"There's no blood." James smiled reassuringly, like a kid enthusiastically dissecting a frog in biology class as he pulled out more of the golden dust, sinewy, spider-like threads holding the codes together. "This is it—this is the code. We can work with this."

"Indeed we can," the A.I. agreed as they began to unfurl the code excitedly upon the table.

Thel's face continued to contort due to the unpleasant autopsy of the avatar's innards being removed until she caught a glimpse of something odd in the corner of her eye, and turned her head.

The candidate was standing alone, about a half-dozen meters away, his face almost pressed to the glass of the revolving restaurant as he looked down at the rain-drenched city below.

"Okay, you boys work on, uh…that. In the meantime, I'll take the candidate down to the lobby to help me reinforce the building. We don't want any wayward NPCs stumbling upon us."

"Okay," James replied, his eyes fascinated as they pored over the lines of code that endlessly emptied from the Kali avatar with no discernible change to her exterior. "But *be careful*."

"I promise," Thel replied as she crossed to the candidate and stood behind him, watching him for a moment. "Hey."

He turned to her. "Yes?"

"Little help?" she said as she motioned for him to follow her out of the revolving restaurant.

"Of course," he replied as he followed close behind her.

They entered the elevator, and Thel hit the button for the second floor. "Riding down the center of a building in a box with pulleys attached to it," she said with a sigh. "Ridiculous. I never want to be trapped by gravity again. I can't wait to get out of this sim."

"I think we should count ourselves lucky that the sim is set in this era. If the NPCs could fly, we'd surely be dead by now," the candidate retorted.

"Mr. Silver-Lining," Thel quipped. "Maybe that should be your nickname."

They arrived on their floor, and Thel marched out into the hallway and, almost immediately, she de-patternized the door of a supply closet.

"What are we doing?" the candidate asked.

"Looking for anything we can use to block the lobby and make sure the NPCs can't get in."

The candidate bent over when he saw a small box on a shelf, filled with wooden doorstoppers. He picked it up. "This is really all we need," he announced, displaying the simple object for Thel.

"What are those?"

The candidate tilted his head when he realized how much the post-human was a fish out of water in his era. "They're doorstops. You just jam these under a door, and the NPCs won't be able to get through, unless they ripped the door right off its hinges that is."

She held the doorstop in her hand. "That simple, huh?"

"Yep," the candidate replied. He turned to the map of the building that was framed next to the door. "There are two stairwells that lead up to the top floor on opposing corners of the building. All we have to do is block the doors and shut off the elevator after we head back up, and that should do the trick."

"We'll be safe, you think?"

"Relatively," the candidate confirmed. "Shall we?"

"Lead the way," Thel gestured with her hand.

"Thank you," the candidate replied as they made their way to the first stairwell before walking down to the lobby. There, the candidate carefully opened the door to see if the lobby had been infiltrated. It hadn't, but the scene just outside the floor-to-ceiling windows of the lobby was ghastly to the extreme.

The candidate watched the NPCs tearing each other apart in the street. Women and children were being pulled into alleys, and surrounded by gangs of other NPCs, and then summarily murdered before the gang members turned on each other. All of the carnage was in plain view.

"The post-humans," he began, "they're not like this? They don't murder one another?"

Thel shook her head. "You're seeing the purge—it was written into the scenario to test you. Those things out there…they aren't human. They're mindless. Real people don't behave that way."

The candidate shifted slightly, speaking over his shoulder to Thel as she continued to stand behind him. "But you said the real world was at risk, that attackers had murdered the people of the *real* Earth. It sounds very much like a purge."

Thel sucked her lips for a moment as she considered the candidate's point. "It does," she conceded. "The androids behave very much like NPCs, but they aren't human. They claim to be, but they're...inhuman—totally brainwashed—trust me."

"Why did you create me?" the candidate asked quickly, surprising Thel as he turned to face her.

"*I* didn't create you," she replied with a slight smile as she thought of the absurdity of the question's premise. "A program created you—the same program that created the A.I."

"Who wrote the program?"

"Aldous Gibson," Thel replied.

The candidate tilted his head to the side. "The same man you suspect of trapping you and your friends inside this sim?"

Thel nodded. "The one and only."

"Why did *he* create the program that created the A.I., only to abandon his own creation?"

Thel shrugged. "He—we needed something. Artificial intelligence was threatening to get out of control. Aldous designed the program to create an entity that was based on human intelligence—an entity that could feel empathy for humans because it would think that it *was* human. He thought that if the A.I. considered itself to be human, that it would be able to understand our concerns and make those concerns its own. We needed an entity like that—an entity that could take control of the world and be its protector—a protector we could trust."

"And now you want a new protector?" the candidate asked. To Thel, it seemed as if the candidate was genuinely intrigued.

"That's right," Thel said, smiling. "You catch on quick."

The candidate nodded. "That brings me back to my original question. If you already have a protector, then why did you—meaning humanity—create me?"

Thel took in a deep breath. "I don't really know. The mainframe the A.I. controlled was last-gen technology." She stopped for a moment when she considered this. "Actually, compared to Trans-human, the mainframe was last-last-last-gen. I'm not going to lie—only James and the A.I. really comprehend the technology, but from what I understand, Trans-human is a computer that is essentially infinitely more powerful than anything we've ever seen. It's against the A.I.'s programming to assume that kind of power for himself, so that's why we needed you, and we needed to test you—we needed to know that, with that kind of power, you wouldn't forget about us. We needed to know that you'd identify as human—that you'd use your power to protect us. That's what this whole lousy test was supposed to be about."

The candidate folded his arms, "I see. But your plans were thwarted."

"Yes," Thel confirmed. "The stranger who visited you lied to you, and someone or something trapped us inside this sim. James and the A.I. were responsible for protecting the solar system and without them…" she paused for a moment, "…well, we don't stand a chance."

The candidate seemed to mull the information for a few seconds before suggesting, "It makes you wonder whether or not the testers are being tested."

Thel's expression suddenly went blank. "What?" she asked as she shook her head, unable to comprehend the candidate's meaning.

"I wonder," the candidate elaborated, "have you ever considered whether *you*, yourself, are being tested?"

"Tested? By whom?"

"*Your* creator," the candidate replied, as though the answer were obvious.

Thel smiled at the absurdity, unable to contain her wide grin. To her, the candidate was showing his extreme inexperience—it was as though she were talking to a child and explaining why the sky was blue. "I have no creator," she replied. "The real world started with the big bang."

"I'm aware of the theory," the candidate retorted, sounding insulted. "After all, I've been fed an enormous amount of information about the history of human knowledge."

"I'm sorry. I didn't mean to insult your intellig—"

"The stranger explained how my mind works. I know I was implanted with false memories, fed all the information that could be crammed into a computer with ten-to-the-sixteenth processing power. I also know I'm inexperienced, but inexperience leads to outside-the-box thinking. Sometimes there's value in gaining a new perspective. Don't you agree?"

"Of course," Thel replied.

"Then, regardless of the big bang theory, I still wonder. If I'm in a sim, and I'm being tested, it seems equally as plausible that you could be in a sim too—the real world could be—"

"No way," Thel cut him off, careful not to grin again, wary of insulting the candidate and reluctant to appear patronizing. She stepped forward and took the candidate's hands in hers. "You've consumed so much knowledge, my friend, but in some ways, you're still just a babe in the woods. When you see the real world, you'll understand."

The candidate grimaced. "I hope so. Because I'm getting rather tired of being tested."

6

Rich's eyes suddenly squinted, near disbelief narrowing them as he saw a globe of red-hot material the size of a large island hurtling toward them. "Oh my God. That's closing in fast."

"I doubt even *that* could do much damage to *this* ship," Aldous observed.

"Maybe you're right," Rich replied, "but I'd rather not be in a ship that collides with liquid-hot magma the size of Hawaii, hurtling through space." He turned to Aldous as the ship began its sharp, 180-degree turn and sped away from the impending collision. "I'm weird that way."

Aldous pouted his bottom lip slightly as he considered Rich's logic. "Seems sound."

Rich smiled, overly enthusiastically. "Thanks!"

"Where are we headed?" Aldous asked, persevering as he continued to ignore Rich's attempts to goad him into an angry response.

"Away from here," Rich replied.

Aldous sat down and folded his arms. "Obviously. Anything less vague to report?"

"Nope," Rich replied. "Everybody's dead. We're in every-man-for-himself mode, Chief."

Aldous's patience finally showed its first crack and his expression became scrutinizing. "You're Richard Borges, isn't that right?"

Rich turned to the former chief of the governing council, his expression both perplexed and vexed. He sensed that he'd finally broken through the chief's patience.

"Yessss," he replied as though he were speaking to an insane person. "Me Richard. You Jane. *N'est-ce pas?*"

Aldous tilted his head. "One of James Keats's favored assistants?"

Rich's eyes lit with fury as the insult instantly registered with him. "Favored *co-workers*, yes."

Aldous's expression became one of incomprehension. "How ever did he tolerate your unyielding insolence?"

Rich smiled as he unstrapped himself from his seat. "You know, Chief, rather than answer your question, I'm just going to beat the living tar out of you."

Rich got to his feet and began to approach Aldous.

Aldous's face paled. "What?"

"You heard me," Rich said, his smile remaining fixed. "You're not the chief anymore. You're *nothing*. You're not an authority, and you don't have the luxury of *tolerating* anything or anyone anymore. And I just lost my family and I'm a little on the pissed-off side as you might expect. Plus, you insulted me, so I'm going to beat the living daylights out of you to make myself feel better. *Comprende* or *no*?"

Rich's hands were balled into tight fists, and Aldous could see his companion wasn't bluffing. He reminded himself that, in their current situation, normal ethics didn't apply. He held up his hands in surrender.

"Richard, I'm sorry. You are completely right, and I was completely wrong. I apologize for being rude. I should've taken your feelings into deeper consideration."

Rich was stunned by the totality of Aldous's retreat and his own victory, so much so that he was flummoxed for a moment. Rich was an average-sized man at best, as was Aldous, so to see the chief cowering instantly was unexpected. He suspected a trick and replied dubiously, "Uh, you know, you're saying you're sorry, but I don't really *feel* like you're sorry. You know?"

"Richard," Aldous quickly retorted before Rich could move in and attack him, "I am sincere. My only excuse is that, like you, I'm worried about my family. The stress is making me lose my patience—I am so, so sorry. I'll not treat you as anything other than an equal again. Of that, you have my word."

"Wow," Rich replied as he lowered his hands. "Now I'm not even mad. I just feel really sorry for you." He backed away, his expression still confused before he turned back to his seat in the pilot's chair.

"The question still remains," Aldous began, after allowing a few moments to pass to make sure the tension had settled, "where are we headed?"

Rich sighed. "I'm open to suggestions from the peanut gallery."

"Venus."

"Venus?" Rich replied, stunned. "You *do* know James annexed Venus to the Purists, right?"

"I was aware when he did it," Aldous confirmed. "It was rather obvious when vessels that could carry hundreds of passengers started ferrying back and forth between the planet and Purist territory. It wasn't a decision I agreed with, but then, James and A.I. haven't given a lot of consideration to my opinions lately."

"Uh, I know this is probably a sensitive subject, but James said you hate the Purists." Rich held out his hands, confused. "So…why…"

"It's the most logical place for us to go. It's a lower priority for the androids, there's no strong A.I. mainframe for them to attack, no post-humans in need of assimilation. Although it's likely that the androids detected the activity of the Purists by now, it still remains the best location for us to regroup and, hopefully, post-human survivors will have made it there alive." He locked his eyes earnestly on Rich's. "Your family could be there."

"But how would we ever find them?" Rich asked. "Without the A.I., the range of the mind's eye communication network is total crap." He held his hands out in frustration at the sophisticated instrument panel in front of him. "Even this ship's sensors are nearly useless. Everything depended on that mainframe! I can't even scan Venus to find out if the androids are amassing their forces around it or if they've launched an attack. Hell, I can't even send a message to Venus! We might as well be on a raft in the middle of an ocean."

"That's not entirely true," Aldous replied. "While we can't communicate instantly with them, we can send them a message with radio signals."

"Radio?" Rich replied, aghast. "Dear God, are we savages now?"

"Venus is approximately 150,000,000 kilometers from Earth at the moment, so—" Aldous began before Rich contorted his face in disbelief.

"Whoa, how do you know that off the top of your head?"

"Richard," Aldous replied, "I am—*was*—the chief of the governing council. I'm aware of where the planet we were supposed to be terraforming currently is in its orbiting cycle, especially when I see thousands of colonists being transplanted there without my clearance. Venus is currently at very close to the halfway point in its distance from Earth, and if we calculate the speed of the radio signals, then it should only take approximately eight and a half minutes for a message to reach them. Assuming they reply while we make our way to them, closing the gap in the meantime, we should have some sort of answer within fifteen minutes."

"A quarter of an hour? Jesus. Why don't we send smoke signals?"

Aldous persevered. "And the nanobots are still functioning. Yes, it's true that they can't be updated, and it's true that they aren't powerful enough for long-distance communications, but if we get to Venus, we may be able to communicate with your family if they made it there."

"Venus is a huge planet," Rich countered. "What's the range?"

"I'm not sure," Aldous admitted, "but an educated guess would be 1,000 kilometers."

Rich sighed mournfully before shutting his eyes and bowing his head. It was all he could do to prop himself up with his hands on his knees to keep himself from collapsing out of his chair.

Aldous crossed the bridge and reached out, patting Rich's shoulder to steady him. "I know that's not far, but it's not hopeless either. Don't lose your hope, Richard. I believe in my heart you'll be reunited with your family."

Rich took in a deep breath, but didn't respond to the kind gesture as he thought of his family, and then of Djanet. She should've been able to respond to him. *Something happened to her or she would've been able to answer me before the mainframe went down,* he thought. *She had to have been assimilated.* An idea suddenly crossed in front of his eyes, causing him to lift his head suddenly, shocking Aldous.

"Where do the androids construct the bodies of the assimilated?"

"I-I have no idea," Aldous replied.

"There must be a place. There must be a way we can—"

"Even if there was," Aldous cut him off, speaking gently but clearly, "Not even this ship could survive a direct assault on one of those android behemoths—it would be like a fruit fly attacking a bear."

"But maybe, together, we could figure out how to work the weapon James was—"

"That's exceedingly unlikely, Richard. We're mere mortals now. And besides, you don't know of anyone who has been assimilated for sure. It's just as likely that our loved ones are on Venus."

Rich clenched his teeth, frustrated as he slammed his fist down on the instrument panel. A second later, he took in a quick, deep breath and started inputting the course for Venus. "Send your damn smoke signal, Chief. If we get confirmation that the Purists are still alive, then we'll figure it out from there."

Aldous smiled, relieved. "A good choice, Richard—a very wise choice indeed."

7

"What the hell is this place?" Old-timer asked as he flew over the modern, sleek skyline of the city by the shore deep inside the bowels of the android constructor vessel.

Jules flew next to him, a single, sinewy tendril unfurled from near Old-timer's ribcage having driven itself into the back of her skull, hidden by her strawberry hair, the tendril having latched itself on to her mechanical brainstem so that Old-timer had access to her communication system. "It's Eden," she replied.

Old-timer's initial reaction was that *Eden* was a dark joke and that his prisoner was being deliberately abrasive, but he could feel her emotions through their connection, and there was no hint that she was being untruthful. To her, they really were in Eden.

He craned his neck and looked up at the sky—it was beautiful and sunny—a perfect mid-afternoon sky on a perfect summer day. There was even a slightly cool breeze on his skin as they flew away from the city and over the water below.

"It's a simulated sky," Jules offered, anticipating his question. "And an artificial sun, but the rest is real—the forests, parks, rivers, city, suburbs...everything."

"Why?" Old-timer asked. "You're machines, for God's sake."

"We're human," Jules replied, tentative in her speech but honest in her answers. "I'm sorry you can't believe that, but it's true. And like all humans, we long for Eden."

Old-timer looked straight down and saw a couple in a small fishing boat, rowing into the middle of the lake. To his astonishment, they were accompanied by an android that appeared to be a youth, sporting a fishing rod. "You've gotta be kidding me."

"What did you think?" Jules responded, calmly but challengingly, "that we're all mindless drones, flying around through space, conquering other humans for the fun of it and then plugging into batteries in our cubicles until the next conquest?"

Old-timer was speechless.

Jules dared turn her head to look at him. "Heh. You did think that. Now who's kidding who?"

"So you live inside manmade paradises inside these ships?"

"*Human*-made," she corrected him. "And yes. You can think of our communities as the jelly in the center of the donut. It's the best part. No more wars, no more crime, no more sickness, no more suffering, and every day the weather is perfect. We're living out eternity here. It's about as close to Utopia as any of us will ever see."

They began to reach the far side of the lake and the holographically projected sky seemed to dissipate, and the ugly, metallic, corpse-like bowels of the ship began to reappear. They were headed for a dark circle in particular, a gigantic opening that would take them farther inside the ship via a tunnel that stretched for dozens of kilometers.

Once they'd entered, Old-timer spoke again.

"Jules, just who the hell are you?"

"I grew up in San Diego, a diehard Chargers fan. I have two older sisters, both of whom live just a few blocks away from me in Eden."

Old-timer was dumbfounded again. *Is this another trick?* he asked himself. *Or are these androids not aliens at all? At least not in the traditional sense. Are they human? Are they from Earth?*

"Is that enough, or you want to know my favorite color too?"

"When were you, uh…"

"Rescued?"

"Assimilated," Old-timer asserted.

She narrowed her eyes slightly but let their semantic differences slide. "Eight years ago."

"The androids came to your Earth?"

"Yes."

"Did you resist?"

"Of course. We were terrified, but they were overwhelming."

"I don't understand," Old-timer shook his head slightly.

"I know," Jules replied, as though Old-timer's statement was blatantly obvious. "If you understood, you wouldn't be kidnapping me."

"If you were assimilated against your will," Old-timer continued, ignoring her argument, "why are you willing to stay here? Why are you willing to be 1's slave? What broke your will to resist? Don't you want to be human again?"

"For the last time," Jules began after sighing deeply, "I *am human.* And it isn't about breaking anybody's will. The collective just told us the truth, and once we knew the truth, we knew what we had to do."

"And what's this truth?" Old-timer asked, dubious that any answer could ever make him join the collective.

"That humanity is *not* immortal," Jules replied. "Use your reason, Craig. Humans invent and invent and invent. It's what separates us from every other species in the known universe. Our technologies are double-edged swords. Fire let us cook our food and kept us warm, but it let us burn our enemies and wage war. Nuclear technologies led to unlimited power sources, but it was also the sword of Damocles that hung over us—was used in WWII but truly unleashed in WWIII, yet even this wasn't enough to destroy us. Think of each of these inventions as little marbles removed from a jar—some are white, because they help humanity, some are gray because they both help and hurt, and some are very dark gray, because they threaten our very existence. But Craig, it is inevitable that one day, humanity will reach into that vase with our inventive minds and pull out the pure black marble—our *last invention.* And that invention will be the end of everything—the end of the multiverse—the end of life."

Old-timer swallowed as he listened to Jules's rationalization. He wanted desperately to dismiss it, to insist that it was nothing more than fanatical Luddite propaganda, but there was an image screaming in his mind, and a coldness that felt that it might stop his heart as he asked, "And what's the last invention? The black marble?"

Jules's eyes widened as she read the expression of dread on Old-timer's face. She recognized it instantly. "You already know the answer, don't you Craig? You've already seen it."

"I-I haven't seen it," Old-timer stammered in response.

"But you know of it. I can see it in your eyes. The invention that destroys universes. I know you know it."

"Just-just shut up," Old-timer replied, shaken. "Take me to the replicator. I have people to rescue. *Really* rescue—not your version of it."

Jules continued to fly Old-timer through the long, dark tunnel, only dimly lit by sporadic lights on either side, like a massive subway tube. "I won't resist, Craig. I can already see on your face that I won't have to."

8

"Got it!" James announced proudly, looking up from the table he sat at with the A.I. and catching Thel's and the candidate's attention as he held a long furl of code up like a trophy fish for display.

The A.I. turned with an equally proud smile and flashed it for their companions.

"Got what?" Thel asked.

"The code that'll let us circumvent the trapdoor and call out!" James responded, as though the answer were obvious.

Thel smiled and shook her head. "Geniuses will be geniuses."

"Damn straight," James replied as he jumped to his feet and walked briskly to the candidate, his left hand held out while the right held the golden stream of code. "May I borrow your aug glasses?"

"Of course," the candidate replied, removing the eyewear and handing it to James.

"What's this supposed to do?" Thel asked.

"We're changing the code," James replied. "I could really use anything—you remember the coffee demonstration you made for the candidate?"

"It was a London fog, but yes," Thel interjected.

"...but the aug glasses are, essentially, a first-generation version of the mind's eye, so it makes the most sense to modify them." He slipped the golden, coded pattern over the aug glasses and it seeped into the device, becoming one with it. "Perfect."

"Now what?" Thel asked.

"We make a phone call," James replied.

"To who?"

"The range won't be great," James replied as he opened a line of communication, "so we have to hope Aldous has found Old-timer by now."

"Is it true that Old-timer can get us out of here?" she asked.

James nodded. "Oh yeah. Those tendrils on his new body can unfurl until they're microscopic and make connections with nano-sized materials. He can connect to anything. If we can get him into physical contact with the hard drive Aldous constructed, he can get our patterns out." He grimaced. "Damn it. He's not close enough."

"Try Djanet," Thel suggested.

James nodded in agreement and tried to open communication.

"Even if you can get your pattern out," Thel continued, "what then? If the mainframe was destroyed, our bodies—"

"It's highly unlikely James's body was destroyed," the A.I. chimed in as he stood and calmly strolled over to the trio. "While Aldous likely thought the impact of the android ship would destroy it, it is designed to be extremely durable. Only a trip to the center of a star or a black hole could destroy it."

"Damn it," James cursed, "no Djanet either. I'll try Rich."

"This isn't looking good," Thel pointed out. "What's the use of being able to call out if the only person we can reach is also the one person who wants to keep us trapped?"

"Oh my God," James suddenly whispered.

9

"James?" Rich reacted to the voice he heard in his head.

"What's that?" Aldous asked.

"Rich, if this is you," James responded quickly, "don't let Aldous know you're speaking with us. Just cough and move away from him. Let me know when you can speak."

Thel and the others watched James's face breathlessly as they waited.

Rich coughed. "Sorry," he said, pretending to clear his throat as he got up from the chair.

James suddenly smiled. "He coughed," he relayed to his companions. "We're standing by, Rich."

"Are you okay?" Aldous asked.

"Yep. Need water. I'm just gonna head to the bathroom."

"I thought I heard you say James?" Aldous asked, his expression puzzled.

"I did," Rich confirmed. "I did. I was just thinking, I really wish James was here, you know? Because he'd know what to do. So this sucks. Then I realized how dry my throat is. I'm getting water. Want some?"

"From the bathroom?" Aldous asked quizzically. "The replicator is working just fine. I think I'd opt for that if I were you."

"Yes," Rich agreed. "Yes but I also need to pee. So, two birds with one stone, I was thinking. But, you're right. Pee first. Then replicator for water."

Aldous nodded.

Rich began to head to the bathroom before Aldous's voice stopped him.

"Oh, and Richard..." he began.

Rich squinted in frustration before wiping the expression away and turning back to Aldous with a slight smile. "Yes?"

"In the future, when you need to use the facilities, there's no need to be so...descriptive."

Rich pulled his lips back in a half-smile and nodded. "You're right again. Okay, so, off to do something mysterious with my body." He turned and left.

Seconds later, he was in the bathroom. "Okay, what the hell?" Rich asked in a whisper as he looked at his own worried reflection of the mirror. "Is this really James?"

"It is, pal! It's good to hear your voice! Where's Aldous?"

"On the bridge. And we've got Thel's body with us. Unfortunately, Aldous couldn't rescue yours, Commander."

"Heh. Shocking," James retorted. "Where are you?"

"We're on your ship, en route to Venus."

"Venus?" James reacted. "What's he want with Venus?"

"He thinks it's the best place to find survivors," Rich replied, "and he thinks it's a low priority for the androids."

There was a short pause. "Maybe," James finally returned, his tone dubious. "Or maybe he's planning to bring them down himself, from the inside."

"What the hell's that supposed to mean?" Rich asked, stunned, his heart suddenly beating twice as fast.

"Rich, listen to me. We can't prove it, but Aldous is a suspect—maybe the prime suspect—for having been the one who trapped us in the sim and helped the androids destroy the mainframe."

"What the—are you serious?"

"He's only a suspect, but he had the means and we think he might have had the motive."

"Listen, Commander Keats, we sent a message to the Purists, but our regular communication system is down, so we haven't heard back from them yet, but we're on our way and should be there in about half an hour. If the Purists radio back to us that they're okay, what do I do?"

"Keep a very close eye on Aldous," James replied, "but don't tip him off that you're on to him. If he gets wise to us, he might damage the hard drive."

"You think he'd do that?" Rich reacted, aghast.

"If he's a man who'd betray his entire species? Yes. Rich, if there's any way in Hell that you can get that hard drive away from him without him getting suspicious, do it. Then let Old-timer know what happened and get it to him. He'll know what to do from there."

"Commander, I've lost contact with Old-timer. Hell, I've lost contact with everyone but Aldous. I'm alone out here. Old-timer might'a been…you know…"

"He better not have," James replied, "because right now, our only hope for the solar system rests on his shoulders."

10

"Dear God," Old-timer said when the replicator came into view at the end of the tunnel. A moment later, they reached the mouth of the tunnel, and the full, awful expanse of the monstrosity started to sink in: a dark, brutal, metal structure that stretched in every direction in perfect geometric lines, endless coffin-shaped pods, adjoined by the ubiquitous catwalks that were a mainstay of android architecture.

"This is it," Jules announced. "Pretty impressive, I know."

"Wasn't the word I was thinking."

"Oh, right," Jules replied as she held up her hands and mockingly twitched her fingers as though she were shaking with fear, "this is the evil heart of mechanical darkness," she said, mimicking a scared child's voice. "This is pure technological evil." She shook her head and rolled her eyes. "Ridiculous, Luddite reaction."

"Luddite?" Old-timer reacted, astonished. "You're calling *me* a Luddite?" He unfurled one of his tendrils and displayed it to make his point. "You don't think joining a collective of trillions, all in the name of keeping humanity standing still, is a little more on the Luddite side?"

Jules scoffed, unimpressed. "Your weird worm parts don't make you advanced, Craig. They make you a freak."

Old-timer glared at her but kept his composure.

"Come on," Jules said, dropping the subject, "Let's get your friends."

"From where?" Old-timer asked. "It's endless."

"If they were uploaded together, they should all be grouped together."

"They weren't." Old-timer held up his assimilator. "In fact, three of them haven't even been uploaded yet."

"That's perfect," she said, holding out her hand to take the assimilator. "We can upload them now."

Old-timer refused to hand the device to her.

"Really?" she said, shocked. "You're in my head. You know I'm not lying."

He relented and handed her his precious cargo.

"Was that really so hard?" she chided. "Now, tell me the names of your friends who were uploaded already. I'll find their location and then we'll make sure we construct them all near one another."

"Djanet Dove and Daniella Emilson," Old-timer replied.

"Okay," Jules replied as she mentally input the names. Old-timer monitored her activity through their mental connection. "They're here," Jules replied, "but…"

"But what?"

"It's not a problem, but you have to understand that there's billions of people in the replicator pods right now—"

Old-timer sighed as he impatiently sifted through the information in her mental locator. "And they're seventy kilometers from here," he observed, sighing when he realized they were still a long way from their prize.

"Yeah." Jules nodded. "It'll take a few minutes to get there."

He grunted in frustration. "Let's get moving then." They started to fly into the endless labyrinth of metallic corridors. If they hadn't had access to Jules's navigational programs, they'd be lost quickly.

"Patience, Craig," Jules said, sensing his frustration.

"While we're heading that way, you might want to check for Aldous Gibson and Rich Borges. I lost contact with them."

"Sure," she replied. "Hmm. Now that's interesting."

"What?" Old-timer asked, as he pulled her screens over to his own mind's eye.

"Rich Borges isn't here, so he hasn't been assimilated yet, but—"

"Oh my God," Old-timer whispered. "Am I reading this right?"

"I think so," Jules confirmed, a bit uncertain herself. "I mean, I've never seen this before, but it looks like this Aldous Gibson has already been assimilated, but he was discharged two days ago. He's not in the pod." She rubbed her temples. "That's an anomaly. No one gets discharged that fast. They have to go through the assimilation education program. It doesn't make sense..."

Old-timer's face reddened with fury, and his upper lip curled into a snarl. "It makes sense...if the person in question made a deal."

"A deal? What kind of deal?"

"The sort of deal that involved betraying his whole damned species."

11

"Chief Gibson, this is Governor Wong, of the Purist colony," the governor spoke in his deep, gravelly voice, a voice that had been weathered by the ravages of time. Post-humans weren't used to hearing the wisdom in a voice that had aged to such a degree. The recorded message arrived crackled with interference. "We're under attack from android forces. We're defending ourselves with every means available to us. We've detected and identified your vessel and will monitor your approach. If you can break through the android blockade, we'll take control of your vessel and guide you past our planetary force-field. Stand by for further instructions and, Chief Gibson, good luck."

Rich blinked in near disbelief. "When was that message sent?"

Aldous looked down at the time readout and did some quick calculations. "It took two minutes to reach us," Aldous replied. "At the speed we're traveling, Venus and the android blockade should be coming up on our view screen soon."

"Are we *still* trying to get to Venus?" Rich asked. "You *did* hear him, didn't you? Under attack? Android forces?"

"I thought you were sworn to protect the Purists?" Aldous replied.

"Yeah, *I* am. But I thought you just wanted to go there to check for post-human survivors. If they're under attack, why are *you* not in favor of getting as far away from the solar system as possible while the coast is clear?"

"Careful," James cautioned in Rich's ear. "You don't want to tip him off that you're suspicious."

"And float through an eternity of space," Aldous replied to Rich, "hoping beyond all mathematically reasonable hope that we'll somehow encounter more survivors, all the while knowing that every day that we venture farther into the endlessness of space, the less likely it'll be that we'll ever see another human being alive other than each other?"

"It's a reasonable explanation," James pointed out. "Just keep an eye on him…and on *us*."

Rich craned his neck and regarded the hard drive on Aldous's waist as he considered James's words. "When you put it that way…okay: break through the android blockade it is then."

As Rich turned back to the view screen, he suddenly saw the faint image of something surrounding the pale blue glow of the tennis ball-sized planet in the distance. Although Venus was still hundreds of thousands of kilometers away, there was clearly a giant explosion onboard one of the android ships that surrounded it, a pulse of gold, growing like a flower opening its petals.

"My word," Aldous reacted, surprised and impressed by the sheer size of the explosion.

"Are the Purists actually fighting back?" Rich said, shocked.

"It would seem so," Aldous replied. "How they're doing it is another question."

"I know James gave the planet a force-field," Rich offered, "but…"

"It looks like he provided them with more than that," Aldous said with a grimace.

Rich narrowed his eyes at what he perceived to be Aldous actually appearing perturbed that the Purists were able to resist. Or was he just pensively considering the difficulty of maneuvering through the surrounding android ships? It was impossible to tell, and impossible to ask James for his opinion, since their connection was only aural and without his connection to the mainframe, he couldn't scan him for signs of insincerity.

Aldous gestured to the explosion that was still pluming and getting larger by the second as Venus and the dramatic battle that surrounded it quickly became more clear. "Apparently James has provided them with some sort of military means."

"No kidding," Rich replied as a second giant plume erupted from a second vast android vessel. The explosions were still a long way off, but it was almost unfathomable that the Purists, who'd been limited on Earth to weapons that were barely worthy of early twenty-first-century warfare, were managing to stage such a dramatic and effective stand against the android collective. "They're doing better than we did on Earth. What the hell is that thing they're shooting at them?"

"It's a death ray," James informed Rich. "I'm glad to hear it's working. It's a particle beam weapon—the entirety of the natural electrical power of Venus is charging tiny particles, and the Purists are firing them at nearly the speed of light at the androids. That should keep them at bay."

"Chief Gibson, this is Governor Wong of the Purist Colony," the gravelly voice spoke again, this time through less interference. "We believe we can create a path for you through the blockade. Follow the coordinates we're sending to you. We'll do the rest. Let us take control of your trajectory once you've made it past our force-field, and we'll guide you to the surface."

Aldous and Rich exchanged shocked expressions before Aldous replied, "Thank you, Governor."

"We'll see you on the ground soon. Wong out."

"They're taking control of our flight path?" Rich reacted in near disbelief. "The Purists? I thought only the A.I. mainframe could–"

Aldous nodded. "So did I."

"And create a path for us? With that big mother of a—"

Before Rich could finish his thought, the sea of androids that surrounded the damaged android ships seemed to suddenly part; a domino effect waved them all aside, as though they were a swarm of fruit flies, the invisible force cutting through them like a fly swatter. The power of the force became clear quickly, however, as it whizzed right by their vessel, the force of it so strong that it seemed to create turbulence in space itself.

"Uh...gun?" Rich finished, astonished.

"It is quite clear," Aldous began, "that the Purists have a few tricks up their sleeves, courtesy of Commander Keats." He closed his eyes for a moment as he considered this unexpected turn and then bowed his head to look at the small hard drive, still hanging at his waist. "James, what have you been up to?" he asked rhetorically, having no idea that James could, in reality, hear him.

"More than you're ready for, old man," James replied anyway, though only Rich was privy to both ends of the repartee.

Rich smiled. "I told you, Chief."

Aldous turned to him. "Oh?"

"James always thinks of something."

12

"We've almost reached the location of your friends," Jules informed Old-timer.

"I know," Old-timer replied. "I'm seeing everything you're seeing, remember?"

"How could I forget?" Jules returned. "It's not like I don't have a splitting headache."

Old-timer's only reply was a disinterested grunt; his mind was busy elsewhere.

"You're a real charmer," Jules observed. "Anyone ever tell you that? I can't believe I thought you had game."

"Why are you helping me?" Old-timer asked.

"What?" Jules responded. "Are you serious? I'm your hostage. You murdered Anisim right before my—"

"That's bull, and we both know it," Old-timer cut her off. "I'm not as dumb as you might believe. You live in a ship that replicates android bodies. Your people attack planets, with no regard for their bodily safety. It's a simple equation. Your mind files are backed up and sent back to the collective if your bodies are damaged or destroyed. So, again, why are you helping me?"

"You mean, why don't I resist and let you rip my head apart like you did to Anisim?"

"Sure," Old-timer responded.

"Okay, besides that fact that it would really, really hurt?" Jules reacted, aghast. "How about this? Have you ever thought about the philosophy behind this whole system? The idea that if I destroy my body but if you upload my mind file, that somehow that's still me? Look, Craig, I know you think we're all just a bunch of mindless drones—brainwashed followers—but we do have opinions. We do have inner thoughts. I'm not a believer in our system. Most of the collective are believers, but I'm not."

"What do you believe?" Old-timer asked.

Jules grunted impatiently. "Look, imagine I'm about to be killed on a rescue. My mind file automatically uploads into the replicator and a new body pops out. Great, right? That's why most androids have no problem taking actions that clearly run contrary to self-preservation or respect for their own mortality."

"You're immortals," Old-timer pointed out. "Why would they be concerned—"

"Because they're not immortal!" Jules shouted out. "Look, it's not a popular view, but let's face it, if I'm about to be killed and my mind file uploads to the replicator, what if something happens? What if, by some miracle, my body survives? The collective's predictive algorithms are watching me, detecting me, always making sure they know if I'm about to be killed or not, but what if they make a mistake? As far as I know, they never do, but for the sake of argument, hypothetically, let's say they do. Then what?"

"You'd survive," Old-timer replied, "and a copy of you would emerge from the replicator."

Jules widened her eyes. "Yeah. Exactly. A copy."

"Are your beliefs the reason you've never been on a rescue?" Old-timer asked.

"Never been on a rescue? What makes you say that?"

"Anisim said—"

"Right," Jules nodded, remembering. "He lied." She shrugged. "I guess he was trying to make you go easy on me. He must've felt guilty for leading you straight to me."

"If you've been on rescues," Old-timer said, putting the pieces of the puzzle together in his mind, "and you believe that the replicated bodies are just copies, then you also—"

"Believe I'm a murderer?" Jules finished for him. "Yeah. I do, but that's the catch. I understand why the collective does what it does. I even believe in it, because it's better that humanity and the universe continue to survive. But no, I don't believe that when my android body dies, I continue on. A copy of me will, with my memories and feelings, and it *will* be a fully formed and functioning person—but it won't be me. I'll be dead."

Old-timer thought through the logic. "Have you…have you—"

"Died on a rescue? Yes, I have. But even if I hadn't, I was assimilated. My human body was destroyed, and my mind file was uploaded to the collective and replicated, right here in the *Constructor*." She gestured to the endless body pods that stretched up into the sky, down to an unseen bottom, and 360 degrees around them. "That Jules died. I'm certain of it."

"If you really believe that, why don't you fight back?" Old-timer demanded of her. "It can't just be this absurd, fatalistic pessimism—this belief that humanity will always destroy itself if it isn't controlled. That's just 1's bullshit."

Jules shook her head. "You're right. I'll just take on the whole collective. There are only 1.4 trillion of us at last count. I'm sure I'll win."

"If you really believe that, why don't you just volunteer to take part in another rescue? The you that's with me now will die and you'll never have to murder anyone again."

Jules paused for a moment. "You know, I mean this sincerely, I actually think that's part of why they do it."

"Who?"

"The conscripts. That's what we call them. When we come to a new Earth, people are randomly selected for the mission. The more Earths we assimilate, the lower the chances are that you'll be conscripted, because it takes the same size force every time, and if the collective grows, the chances they'll need you plummets. But you never know when it's your turn. It can be years between rescues…" she drifted off as she seemed to remember something. "You can almost convince yourself it was all just a dream." She pulled herself back to reality, turning to look Old-timer in the eye. "There are two ways to gain honor and prestige on a rescue for yourself. The first is to rescue—or as you put it, assimilate—a lot of people. The other is to die. The more you've died, the more bodies you've sacrificed, the more selfless the others in the collective consider you." She paused again, appearing pensive. "But you know what I think, Craig? I think they do it because they long for oblivion. I think they want a way out. Suicide is illegal, and our patterns continue eternally, but I believe when members of the collective sacrifice themselves, part of it is their death drive. They want to die—because just like you said, I think they want out."

"What would 1 do if she knew you had these beliefs?"

"Nothing," Jules replied. "We're allowed free thought. Our feelings are our own, as long as we don't act out—"

"Feelings are never wrong," Old-timer suddenly blurted out, remembering the wisdom Alejandra had imparted on him in what felt like a different life.

"Yeah, that's right," Jules replied. "Only actions can be wrong. So, how about you, Craig? What do you think?"

"About what?"

"You cut off Anisim's head. Are you a murderer?"

Old-timer could barely breathe. He'd thought of the action as being akin to turning off a machine. *What if Jules is right?* he wondered. *Then Daniella is dead…and I'm just reviving a…no.* "No. It's the pattern that matters," Old-timer asserted. "The molecules don't matter."

"Heh," Jules replied. "Interesting." She looked down. "Hang on, we've arrived. We're going to drop."

The duo suddenly dropped straight down, skimming past a series of catwalks, deeper and deeper down what truly appeared to be a bottomless pit.

"Straight into Hell," Old-timer whispered to himself.

Jules nearly laughed, but stifled it. "The big H-E-double-hockey sticks, eh? Don't be so dramatic. It's just a big factory."

They landed on a catwalk in front of a black pod, positioned on the outside of a pillar that stretched endlessly both up and down. It appeared to be only one of many thousands of pods on that pillar alone. Old-timer looked at the structure and thought of how easily it dwarfed the Zeus that they'd built on Venus. That memory felt as though it had become so distant that it was from another life.

"Admittedly," Jules added, "it is one big damn factory." She looked around herself. "And it could be a bit cheerier."

Old-timer couldn't take his eyes off the pod. "Who is this?"

Jules opened the screen in her onboard mental computer, and Old-timer read the name in his mind as Jules spoke it aloud. "Daniella Emilson."

He put his hand out to it and touched the black shell of the pod. "Open it. Open it right now."

“Okay,” Jules replied, “I’m going to assume asking for a ‘please’ would be a wasted effort.”

The door slid to the side, tucking inside the pillar, revealing Daniella’s unconscious body. She was standing, dressed in the same black garb as every other new android. Her new body was a perfect re-creation of her human form—at least from the outside.

“Wake her,” Old-timer said, unable to contain his emotion as he began to choke back tears.

Jules turned to him, surprised to see a man that she’d regarded as unreasonably rough in his demeanor actually moved to tears. She instantly realized the reason. “She’s your wife.”

“Yes,” Old-timer nodded. “Wake her, please.”

Jules’s head jolted back ever so slightly with surprise when she heard Old-timer’s words. “There it is,” she said, as she input the wake command. “The magic word.”

Daniella opened her eyes.

“Craig?”

“Oh thank God!” Old-timer exclaimed. He instantly reached out for his wife and took her into his arms, pulling her out of the pod and holding her tight, rocking her back and forth as he held her body, her feet dangling several inches above the catwalk.

“Craig? Where am I? Was I...assimilated?” Daniella asked, her voice weak as she remained shocked by her new surroundings.

“You were, baby. You were, but you’re okay. I got you now.”

“You ready for me to bring your other friends back?” Jules asked, interrupting the happy reunion.

Old-timer looked her in the eye, his expression one of gratitude. “Yes. Yes please.”

“Wow,” Jules replied. “Magic words all over the place.” She uploaded the patterns into the collective. “And in return, I’ll work a little magic for you.”

“Craig, who is she?” Daniella asked in Old-timer’s ear.

“She’s here to help. She’s a friend. Don’t worry. I’m going to get us out of here.”

13

"My word," Aldous said as he watched the sun sparkle and dance across the endless ocean over which their craft skimmed through their front view screen. "This is extraordinary."

"This is your first time seeing Venus terraformed, isn't it?" Rich responded. "I've been here a couple times," he added, enjoying the feeling of superiority it provided for him. "The whole thing's gorgeous—unspoiled."

"How could they do this?" Aldous reacted, barely able to move his mouth. "How could the A.I. and James give such a treasure—such a jewel—to the Purists?" He turned away from the scene in front of him and regarded Rich with an astonished expression. "The Purists started WWIII to prevent these very miracles from ever happening. Venus never would've been terraformed in the first place if they'd remained in power. They don't deserve this paradise."

Rich sucked his lips to one side for a moment as he considered Aldous's reaction. "I think James thought it was fitting. Venus is the new Garden of Eden. The Purists are the only ones who never ate from the Tree of Knowledge."

"That's not something for which they should be commended," Aldous replied sternly.

Rich shrugged. "Maybe not, but practically speaking, they needed a home base. We weren't giving them a say in anything anymore, but they deserved the right to carve out their own destiny. Honestly, Venus is awesome, but after everything the Purists have been through, they *do* deserve it."

Aldous shook his head, gripping the back of the seat in front of him, digging his fingers into the soft material. "I have difficultly finding words to respond to such an ill-informed opinion."

"Ah," Rich said, winking at Aldous, "there's the arrogant son-of-a-bitch I've come to know and loathe. Welcome back."

Aldous turned back to the front view screen as a wall of white began to form on the horizon. At first, he wasn't sure if he was seeing some sort of optical illusion, as the sun stained the enormous object with a golden sheen that made it difficult for him to regard it without squinting. Tears nearly formed in his eyes before his mind's eye tinted his eyes to compensate. "What is that?"

Rich smiled. "This is very interesting. Chief, I think I know where the Purists are taking us."

"Where?" Aldous asked impatiently.

"You're seeing the falls?" James's voice asked through his aural connection to Rich.

"Yep," Rich replied.

"*Yep*, is not an answer to my question," Aldous reacted, his temper short.

"Chief, you better hang on," Rich said. "I think we're in for a bumpy ride. It looks like James put the Purists in the place where they'd be least likely to be found."

"Richard," Aldous spoke, softening his tone as he regained his patience but speaking slowly and enunciating every word as he asked, "what is this thing?"

"Seriously, Chief," Rich said as he strapped into his seat and gestured with his head for Aldous to take the seat in front of him. "Strap in. You've got about three seconds."

"Three?" Aldous said, tilting his head quizzically before the ship suddenly made it to the edge of the falls and dove steeply into the white abyss of ocean spray, sending Aldous off his feet and against the ceiling. His magnetic field ignited just in time to keep him from being harmed, but he struggled to float into his seat and strap in as the ship took them on a wild ride through the wall of mist.

"This is so utterly awesome," Rich whispered as the ship traveled through the mist for nearly a full minute.

"I'm glad you like it," James replied, "but keep your eyes peeled. Remember, Aldous is a major suspect. Venus's powerful magnetic force-field should be able to jam any attempts at communication that Aldous might make to give away your position, plus the Purists have ample equipment to detect signals, but Aldous is tricky and if he *is* the one behind this, he had time to plan ahead. Watch him close. You're our eyes and ears, buddy."

"Where in Heaven's name…" Aldous wondered aloud as the view screen continued to reveal nothing but a dimming whiteness. Then, almost as soon as he'd finished speaking the words, the ship began to vibrate, a thunderous sound crescendoed and echoed through the bridge.

"Is that," Aldous began to form the words, "a waterfall?"

Rich peered through the mist to see the edge of the incredibly powerful falls, millions of liters of water plunging downward every second. "Holy. Crap."

"Is this…is this how they power it?" Aldous wondered aloud. "There's so much energy—"

Incredibly, a structure suddenly emerged from the white torrent, splitting the falls in two like a rock formation splitting a raging river, the white water blasting explosively in reaction to the disruption. When the explosive reaction settled, the structure finally took shape, a hexagonally shaped tunnel jutting out, and allowing them access to the mysteries within.

"James is so cool, isn't he, Chief?" Rich said with a grin. He looked to his left at Aldous, who could hardly close his mouth as he watched the spectacle unfolding before him.

"Thank you, Rich," James said in Rich's ear.

"He certainly has his moments," Aldous reluctantly admitted. "I'll grant him that."

14

"Okay, Aldous and Rich are in," James announced as he, the A.I., and even the candidate pored through copious amounts of code. Each of them had removed what seemed to be endless amounts of the golden filaments from Kali's avatar and were hunched over separate tables along the curved glass windows of Cloud 9 restaurant.

Thel watched impatiently as the rain continued to fall and streak the windows, while fires burned throughout the city, and the NPCs roared in mobs, chasing down smaller mobs and tearing them horrifically to shreds before, once they'd completed their task, they turned on each other. It was the worst perversion of Darwin's theories, played out in a mathematical horror show.

She turned from the horror, her arms folded over her chest. "I don't like this. Aldous is clearly going to try sabotage the Purists."

"We don't know that for sure," James cautioned.

"It's well within the realm of possibility, however," the A.I. pointed out.

"Exactly," Thel said, gesturing to the A.I. before looking adamantly at James. "We can't just sit here. We have to do something!"

"We *are* doing something," James responded, holding up the coding.

"Are you kidding me?" Thel reacted. "That?"

James, exasperated, shut his eyes tight for a moment in frustration. "Look, Thel, we're cut down to our core matrix programs here. We can't—"

"Core matrix programs?" Thel countered. "Are you kidding? Why don't you just say what you really are? You're *human*. Human!"

"Okay, we're human," James admitted, "We're all genius level, but it's nothing compared to what we were when we were connected to the mainframe." James dropped the sparkling, golden, powdery filaments on the table in front of him. "We could've processed this in seconds and found the secret to getting out of here, but now we're just looking at millions and millions of lines of code. It's like finding a needle in a haystack."

An idea suddenly crossed Thel's mind, and her expression changed as she worked it through. "We're always talking about Moore's Law, but what about Murphy's Law?"

"What?" James responded. "Are *you* kidding?"

"No," Thel replied, shaking her head. "You said it's like looking for a needle in a haystack. Well, the best way to do that is to just dive in. Murphy's Law suggests you'll get stuck with the needle in no time."

"I don't follow," James admitted.

"I think I do," the A.I. suddenly said, turning away from his own search through the codes to face Thel. "You're not suggesting what I think you're suggesting, are you?"

"Wait...what's she suggesting?" James asked, suddenly frustrated that he was a step behind instead of a step ahead.

The A.I. kept his eyes on Thel.

"I'm suggesting," Thel spoke, "that one of us merge with the Kali avatar."

"Merge with—" James began to react before the A.I. interrupted, speaking to Thel.

"Absolutely not," he began. "That's an entirely untested hypothesis. Yes, it's true that whoever or whatever inhabited the Kali avatar was able to circumvent the trapdoor code, but there's no guarantee that we could merge with it and have the same results. Our ability to manipulate code within the sim was one of the abilities we lost when the trapdoor cut us off."

"And even if we could merge with it," James furthered, now that he'd finally understood Thel's audacious suggestion, "there's no way to know if attempting to leave the sim would lead to the destruction of our patterns. It's completely illogical to take a chance like that."

"Illogical?" Thel replied, her arms still folded, her demeanor impatient. "How's this for logic? How many lines of code do you think you can go through in an hour?"

James looked down at the pile in front of him. "A few thousand," he replied.

"A few thousand," Thel repeated before gesturing to the A.I. and the candidate. "Between the three of you, maybe 10,000 lines in an hour? And you said there are millions of lines of code."

"That's no reason to go committing suicide," James responded. "We could find the code we're looking for five minutes from now."

"Or five hours from now," Thel countered. "And Aldous is with the Purists. If he finds a way to disable their defenses—"

"Assuming he's the perpetrator here!" James shouted out.

"Oh, good grief!" Thel guffawed. "Who else could it be?"

"1!"

"*If* she's still alive," Thel pointed out. "Remember, we all *saw* you kill her. And even if she is still alive, why would she imprison you in the sim? James, sooner or later, as much as you don't want to admit it to yourself, you're going to have to face the fact that this is a mystery we already know the answer to. Aldous cut a deal with the androids, and that son-of-a-bitch is with the Purists as we speak. We don't have hours or even days for you to pore through code."

"This isn't even a discussion worth having," James responded, dismissing the idea. "Even if your idea worked, the signal wouldn't be strong enough to reach Earth and my body, so it's a moot—"

"I wasn't talking about *your* body," Thel replied.

James's eyes widened. "Thel," he spoke slowly, realizing he was too far away to reach her before she did something rash. "No!"

Thel unfolded her arms, revealing that she'd been holding her de-patternizer during the entirety of the discussion. "I'm sorry, James. I love you. But I *have* to do this."

"Thel!" James shouted as he jumped to his feet.

At the very same moment, Thel shot her own hand, de-patternizing it and screaming out in agony as her hand disappeared in an explosive pulse of golden coding. In her next motion, she reached out to the Kali avatar and joined her handless arm to

Kali's, the severed limbs instantly connecting and sending a pulse of energy through both of them as their patterns began to fuse.

The A.I. intercepted James, holding him back as he tried desperately to reach her. "No, James!" the A.I. shouted. "If you touch her, you could make it worse!"

"But she'll die!" James protested as he fought to get free.

The candidate jumped to his feet as well, aiding the A.I. as they worked to hold James back, keeping him several meters away from the figure that was slowly, spectacularly melding into one entity before their eyes.

"Perhaps, James," the A.I. conceded with enormous sympathy in his tone. "But it's already done."

15

"WAKING UP as a robot wasn't exactly on my bucket list," Colonel Paine gruffly spoke as he opened his eyes and held his new android hands in front of face, "but it beats kicking the bucket altogether." He stepped out of his pod and turned his head to see that Samantha was standing next to Old-timer and two females he didn't recognize.

Then something extraordinary happened and the breath caught in his throat. There was a third woman, a woman he *did* recognize, and from her disbelieving expression, she clearly recognized him too.

"Daniella?"

"Colonel Paine?" Daniella replied, terrified.

Paine stepped toward her, his hand outstretched as though he were going to grab her, but she quickly stepped behind Old-timer, fearing for her life. "Craig!" she shouted.

"Daniella?" Paine repeated again. "Do you know me?"

"She knows you," Old-timer confirmed. "And, believe me, she doesn't want you to touch her."

Paine's expression was one of complete and utter confusion as his lips trembled while he tried to assemble a response. "But…why? Daniella," he said to her as she stayed behind Old-timer, barely daring to peek an eye out to examine the monster from her distant memories. "Baby…"

Old-timer's eyes widened like saucers. "*Baby?*"

"Baby?" Djanet echoed, stunned.

Daniella's eyes widened with utter disbelief.

"Yes," Paine said, licking his dry lips before he continued, gently, "in my universe, Daniella is—*was*—my wife."

"What?" Daniella finally, reacted. "That's impossible."

"Why?" Paine responded, perplexed as he held his hands to his head.

"Because you're a murderous piece of—"

"Honey," Old-timer cut her off, quickly, "this isn't the same man you knew."

"Honey?" Paine reacted, his head jutting back as though he'd been punched.

"Colonel," Old-timer turned to Paine, "Daniella is *my* wife in this universe."

"What?" Samantha responded, equally stunned. She turned to Paine. "This is insane."

Paine's eyes darted to Samantha quickly before he looked around at their surroundings, the endless catwalks and pillars of the *Constructor's* replicator facility. He bent over, propping himself with his hands on his knees to keep from falling as he shook his head. "This has to be a nightmare. Tell me this is a nightmare."

"Uh, you guys all swapped wives?" Jules reacted, both perplexed and visibly amused.

"They're from another universe," Old-timer responded harshly.

Jules's eyes widened. "Oh. This is fascinating," Jules suddenly said, the pieces coming together for her. "The parallel universes we travel to are virtually identical—that's why they're so close to each other in the multiverse—but something must've happened in the universe you brought these two from that drastically altered their destiny."

Old-timer cringed as he remembered the drastic event Jules's didn't even realize she was referring to.

"You've traveled vastly different paths since then," Jules observed. She shook her head, marveling at the coincidences. "Yet, socially, you must've still intermixed with one another. We're going to have to study this in greater detail at some point. We could write volumes on—"

"We're not your damned science experiment!" Old-timer shouted, shutting her down. "This is our lives. And speaking of, there's still one more person from their universe that needs to be awakened."

"Uh, sorry, Craig," Jules replied. "That's not going to happen."

"Why?" Old-timer demanded as he turned to the android, his tendril still jacked into the back of her skull.

"These two," Jules replied, pointing to Samantha and Paine, "they're most likely dead in this universe, but your friend, Adolf—"

"Aldous," Old-timer corrected her.

"Aldous—much better name—he's already been replicated. And we've got very strict rules about only replicating one individual from one universe at a time."

"One individual from one universe?" Daniella reacted, astonished. "Craig, what is she talking about?"

"The androids aren't replicating humans they find on different planets across the universe," he explained, his eyes still locked impatiently on Jules's as he answered Daniella's question, "they're hopping from universe to universe, assimilating Earths. That's why they're all human in appearance."

"And why we can't have multiple copies of the same person replicated from the same universe. We rescue one version per universe, that's it," Jules elaborated. "There are hundreds of versions of me from other universes, but there's only one from each. You understand? We can't let someone be replicated more than once in a universe, or they could build an army of themselves—"

"Make an exception," Old-timer ordered through gritted teeth. "We're running out of time here, Jules. We need to grab Aldous and get the hell—"

"I can't," Jules replied. "There are only two people who could overrule something like that. 1 herself, and—"

"*Neirbo*," Old-timer growled, his eyes suddenly darting away from Jules, confusing her for a moment.

"Yeah, how did you—"

"Because he's right behind you," Old-timer replied.

Neirbo had, indeed, landed on the catwalk just a few short meters behind the group, a fully rebuilt Anisim at his side.

"Finally," Neirbo said directly to Old-timer, with a gruesome smile, his face contorted by an ugly, twisted lust for revenge, "I get to end you."

Jules moved away from Old-timer, though he didn't release his tendril's grip on her artificial brainstem.

"How'd you find us?"

Neirbo tilted his head toward Anisim. "Whenever a member of the collective is killed, a report is sent and we immediately review the last moments of their life in their mind file."

"*That's* why you didn't resist," Old-timer realized, turning to Anisim.

"I needed to stay alive long enough for us to know your plan," Anisim confirmed. "I knew you weren't going to succeed. You're outnumbered, more than a trillion to the handful of you here. There was never any danger to the collective."

Old-timer turned to Jules. "You knew this?"

She looked up at him and shrugged. "Everything I said before is true. I don't want to die. But yes, I did know it was futile. I told you, resisting them is pointless."

Old-timer nodded slightly before releasing Jules, his tendril folding back into his body.

Jules's hand moved quickly to the damaged part of her skull and clasped over it. She was shocked by his gesture. "You're not going to kill me?"

"I don't want you to die either," Old-timer answered. "Thanks for your help. I mean it."

Jules was speechless.

"Who is this guy, Craig?" Paine asked in a low tone from behind Old-timer.

"Trouble," Old-timer replied.

"Armed trouble," Paine observed as he saw the weapon Neirbo held in his left hand.

"I've felt the gun's effects before," Old-timer replied over his shoulder. "Trust me, don't get shot."

"Copy," Paine responded.

"You've felt the gun's effects before," Neirbo repeated, intrigued. "You *do* realize I don't know you, don't you? Yet you attacked me—tortured me—for no reason."

"Oh, I had my reasons," Old-timer replied, "and you better've brought more than just a gun with you, son."

Neirbo's eyes twitched as he scrutinized Old-timer with the laser-beam focus of a predator in the wild, sizing up his prey. "Indeed, I brought a lot more."

With a gesture of his right hand, all of the pods opened around and above them.

Hundreds of androids leapt out, landing hard on the catwalk, which swayed and bounced with the vibrations, causing Old-timer and his companions to nearly lose their footing.

Neirbo shouted out his orders to the hundreds of androids that surrounded them, pointing directly at Old-timer. "That abomination is your target! He's extremely dangerous, but your orders are to rescue him at all costs! Nothing else matters!"

"Rescue?" Paine reacted. "That doesn't sound all bad."

"Trust me," Old-timer replied, "I don't want to get rescued."

"You got a plan?" Paine whispered to Old-timer.

"Oh yeah, I got a plan," Old-timer growled through gritted teeth as he kept one hand protectively on Daniella, keeping her behind him.

"What is it?"

"I'm going to kill every last one of them."

16

The bridge of their ship lowered itself, and Lieutenant Patrick stood, waiting to greet Rich and Aldous in the hangar, deep inside the Purists' new fortress on Venus. He saluted the men and spoke quickly.

"Chief Gibson, I am Lieutenant Commander Patrick. The governor requests your presence in the command center. He would very much value your input and experience to help us battle the androids, sir."

The chief nodded, then pointed to Thel's unconscious body, still lying on a flat instrument panel at the back of the bridge. Luckily, Aldous had had the forethought to secure her with blankets and to strap her into place, making for a makeshift bed. "She needs to be transported to your medical facility. She's still alive."

"Yes, sir," Patrick replied. "I'll get my men on that right away." He gestured for Aldous to follow him and Aldous, in turn, gestured for Rich to follow as well.

"Deep inside the bowels of a Purist hideout," Rich whispered. "Déjà freakin' vu."

"How is the battle going, Lieutenant Commander?" Aldous asked.

"We're holding our own so far," Patrick replied. "We know you've lost Earth, and we're devastated as nearly 40 percent of our citizens were still there."

"They'll have been assimilated," Aldous pointed out quickly. "I know it's not what anyone wanted, but you can't think of them as dead. There's still hope."

"That may be, sir, but there's no way in hell we're going to let them take Venus without a fight."

"How are you managing to do this?" Aldous asked.

"James Keats, sir. He fortified Venus with weapons like nothing we ever had access to before. Honestly, sir, even though we're facing an enemy with an absurd advantage in numbers, I can't see how they can possibly penetrate our defenses. Commander Keats seems to have thought of everything, sir."

"Indeed," Aldous replied. "Well, I'll be very interested to learn more about this."

Patrick nodded. "I know Governor Wong believes you'll be an invaluable asset. We're glad to have you here, sir." He turned to Rich, adding, "That goes for both of you."

"Thanks, Lieutenant," Rich replied.

"Lieutenant Commander now," Patrick corrected.

"Right. Sorry."

"Not a problem," Patrick responded over his shoulder. "Promotions come fast and furious when all of your people keep dying."

Rich had nothing he could say to such a morbid, yet true observation.

Patrick continued to lead them through freshly constructed, metallic corridors on their way to the command center. Rich noted that the design was reminiscent of their old lab on Venus, the one he'd worked in for years with James and the others in the small band of terraformers. He suddenly felt an overwhelming pang of nostalgia and wistful desire to return to those times. Little did he know that those would be days he'd think of as golden.

"Are you still with me, James?" Rich whispered. There came no reply.

"Did you say something?" Aldous asked.

"Just talking to myself. I do that," Rich replied with a forced smile.

"Here we are," Patrick announced as he breezed past two guards as they saluted him and entered through the double-doors that led to the command center. Governor Wong's attention was glued to the dozens of screens in front of him as he stood at the center, surrounded by dozens more operators at workstations.

"Governor," Patrick announced, "they've arrived."

The governor turned, his face brightening when he saw Aldous, although he didn't smile. He walked away from Alejandra, who'd been at his side, and held out his hand early, even as he was walking up the stairs that led up to the doors to the room, and spoke before they'd even shaken hands. "Chief Gibson, we're so pleased you survived."

When the governor finally reached him, Aldous shook his hand and replied, "As am I that you and your people have endured."

"I know we've had our differences," Wong stated, "but the enemy of thine enemy is my friend. It's time we put our differences aside. The fate of our solar system depends upon it."

"Agreed," replied Aldous. "Please get me up to speed."

"It would be my pleasure," the governor returned as he guided Aldous back down the stairs.

Meanwhile, Rich glared down at Alejandra. She craned her neck to look at him, and as soon as they made eye contact, he waved with his hand for her to come to him. She narrowed her eyes and used the opposite of the twin staircases that lined the walls of the command center to make her way to him.

Lieutenant Commander Patrick had, by this point, noticed their odd behavior and silently watched.

"What is it?" Alejandra whispered when she reached Rich.

Rich grabbed her hand, then turned to the lieutenant commander as well. "I need to speak with you guys outside," he whispered.

Curious, the two Purists made their way out of the room with the post-human, closing the doors behind them.

"What's going on?" Patrick asked.

"Listen, we might have a huge problem," Rich explained. "I'm still in contact with James and the A.I., and—"

"They survived?" Alejandra responded, astonished. "Then why haven't they—"

"They're trapped in a simulation—trapped in a computer. The hard drive is that black box Aldous has strapped over his shoulder. But they've found a way to communicate with me, and they think Aldous is the number one suspect for having trapped them and sold us out to the androids."

"Holy shit," Patrick replied. "The fox is in the henhouse for real this time."

Rich closed his eyes and shook his head. "I still really don't get that metaphor. Can we use metaphors from this century please?"

"It means we just let the most dangerous man in the solar system into our command center," Alejandra explained.

"Yeah! That's what I said!" Rich replied, exasperated. "Though we don't have proof yet. Look, James and the A.I. told me to watch him. They think he might be here to sabotage you guys to make the Purists as easy to assimilate as we were."

"We can't let that happen," Patrick announced, holding up his rifle as though he were about to charge back into the command center.

"Hold it!" Rich fired back. "Aldous has the solar system's best hope strapped over his shoulder. That hard drive contains James and the A.I., not to mention Thel. If we try to confront or arrest him, he could destroy it."

"So what do we do?" Alejandra asked. "We can't let him shut down our defenses!"

"We've got to incapacitate him without harming that hard drive," Rich replied.

"Any idea how we do that?" Patrick asked.

Rich shrugged. "I'm willing to open the floor to suggestions."

"*You* don't have a plan?" Alejandra replied in disbelief. "Can't you ask James or the A.I.?"

"They've been quiet for a few minutes. They must have their hands full with something at the moment."

"Great," Patrick replied, impatient. "Well, we can't just sit here while a traitor learns how all our defenses work. We've got to act now."

Rich nodded. "I agree. Okay. I've got an idea."

"You do?" Alejandra replied, her tone dubious.

Rich looked the empath in her eyes, eyes that clearly saw he was bluffing, and he immediately folded. "No. No I don't. I was just hoping I'd come up with something at the spur of the moment, you know?"

"Seriously?" Patrick responded.

"Sorry. I'm not usually the one who has to come up with the plan. Look, how about this? We go in there, and I just walk up behind him and blast him with a charge to the back of the head.

That should render him unconscious, as long as he doesn't see me coming."

Patrick considered this for a moment. "It's simple as hell, but sometimes simple works." He looked to Alejandra.

She nodded. "Okay. Let's do it."

"Just remember," Rich cautioned, "we can't let him damage that hard drive. *At all costs*. The hard drive contains the brains of the guys who can get us out of this mess. If we lose that hard drive, this solar system's as good as finished."

"Got it," Patrick replied.

"Got it," Alejandra echoed.

Rich took a deep breath. "Okay, guys. Let's do this."

17

The white light and golden sparkle of the figure before them suddenly faded. When the blinding distortion of the light was absent, it revealed that Thel's image was gone, but Kali's image remained. Astonished, the trio of James, the A.I. and the candidate looked on as Kali examined her body, and her regrown hand, holding her hands up before her eyes.

"So cool," she finally said.

"Thel?" James asked in near disbelief.

Kali smiled before her form melted away, replaced by Thel's. "Yep."

"Thank God," James exclaimed. He tried to run toward her to embrace her, but the A.I. and the candidate continued holding him back.

"James," the A.I. spoke in a half-pleading, half-scolding tone, "this has never been tried before. If you touch her, your patterns might merge, and you could end up killing each other! Stay back until we know what we're dealing with."

James's eyes locked on Thel's before he relented and did, indeed, hold back. He desperately wanted to hold Thel in his arms, but he knew the A.I. was right. Thel's bizarre leap of faith and her previously never attempted method of joining with an avatar were unknowns, and as they always did, James and the A.I. chose to be cautious.

"Okay. Okay, you're right," James said as he disentangled himself from the two artificial intelligences that held him back. They relented as well and James stood, just meters from Thel. "Are you okay?" he asked her.

"I'm awesome," Thel replied. "I'm checking the systems. Guys, the Kali avatar is fully operational. I can do anything inside the sim, just as the Kali program was designed to do. I can heal wounds, I can manipulate matter..." She trailed off as she seemed to see something while she read through her list of capabilities. She turned to the curved glass of the floor-to-ceiling windows that made up the perimeter of Cloud 9 and stepped toward the edge. "I can even stop the purge." She held out her hands, and suddenly, every NPC that was still functioning stopped their rampaging.

James and the two A.I.s ran to the window themselves to see the results. NPCs that had been ripped to shreds and deactivated suddenly came back together, their patterns resetting until they were fully functioning. They simply stood up and walked calmly away, returning to their business. The fires extinguished themselves all over the city, and the smoke blew away, dispersing in the rain, vanishing into the ubiquitous clouds.

"There," Thel said as she watched, amazed by her own accomplishments. She turned to her companions. "We're safe. And I'm digging these godlike powers." There was a twinkle in her eye as she smiled. "I think I understand you guys a little better now. It's not easy to give up being superhuman."

"Incredible," the candidate observed.

"Indeed," the A.I. echoed, smiling before he turned to Thel. "It appears that whoever our mystery occupant of the Kali avatar was, is also our guardian angel. That entity has provided us with the means to protect ourselves."

"Unless it's another trick," James cautioned. "It wouldn't be the first time we've been manipulated."

"True," the A.I. conceded. "However, for the time being, we do seem to be safe within the sim."

"The trick is to make sure we're safe *outside* the sim," Thel pointed out. She sighed. "Fellas, I've checked the systems. I should be good to go for an exit. My body is within range in the real world."

"Thel!" James suddenly reacted, so quickly that it appeared to be an instinctual reaction rather than a considered one. "*Please*, wait! That could be the trick," he said, urging caution. "Maybe whoever it is wants us to kill ourselves by trying to exit?"

"For what purpose?" the candidate asked.

"I agree with the candidate's implication," the A.I. announced. "James, you're understandably trepidatious. You don't want to lose Thel—she's the love of your life. But this is an instance where logic must dictate our decision. Whatever entity inhabited the Kali avatar before could've killed us with the ease of a thought while she was here. What advantage could that entity have possibly had by keeping us alive, only to then trick us into our own deaths at a later point?"

"I don't know," James responded, "but we have to be absolutely sure that—"

"We'll never be absolutely sure," the A.I. countered, his lips tightening as he spoke. "James, your emotions—your love—are capacities that have served you well. They make you the hero that you are. But you cannot let your love turn into a fear that controls your better judgment. We naturally fear the loss of those we hold most dear, but there's no reason to believe Thel won't be able to successfully leave the sim."

James listened to the explanation and then ran his fingers through his hair before collapsing onto one of the chairs that lined the windows of Cloud 9. He looked up at Thel, who'd watched the entire exchange wordlessly, but who'd kept her eyes locked on James.

"I'll be okay," she told him with a reassuring smile.

"And one of us needs to be in the real world," the A.I. added. "Thel can help to sequester Aldous, and she can also relate to the Purists what's happening to us."

"Rich can do those things!" James countered.

"But he *can't* get us out of here," Thel replied. "If I can escape, then we know the two of you can too. All we need is to send a powerful enough signal to reach Earth, and if we reach Earth—"

"We can activate Trans-human," James said, finishing her sentence.

"And if we activate Trans-human, we can undo this damage," the A.I. added. He put his hand on James's shoulder. "Let go, James. Trust her."

James shut his eyes tight. "You'd go, even without my blessing," he said, as he opened his eyes and looked into Thel's.

"Yep," Thel replied, "but I'd still appreciate the support."

James sighed and stood. It was the hardest thing he'd ever had to do. "Okay. Okay, you're right. I've asked you to trust me so many times—it's time for me to trust you."

Thel smiled wide. "Damn straight. I love you, James Keats."

"I love you too," James replied.

Thel blew James a kiss and winked before waving goodbye. "Talk to you on the other side."

A second later, Thel vanished and the Kali avatar, along with its deadened eyes, returned.

James held his hand up to his aug glasses before speaking in an almost pleading tone, "Rich, please tell me Thel just woke up."

18

Old-timer remembered that James had described what this would feel like—the sensation of thousands of tentacle-like appendages acting out instead of the arms and legs, fingers and toes he was used to. Then he remembered the way James described his own ability to manipulate space-time, comparing it to a seven-year-old catching a fly ball. He realized now what James had been trying to tell him.

"It'll feel natural. I promise," James had proclaimed.

Old-timer nearly smiled at the remembrance of the conversation as his thousands of tendrils sprang into action, his body morphing into something that, to his companions, resembled more closely a jellyfish than it did a human, as each tendril flashed out, circled an attacking android's neck, and severed its head from its body.

Paine ducked and partially protected himself with the railing of the catwalk, his eyes wild as he made sure no androids came close to him while also keeping an eye on Old-timer, who was doing things Paine had never imagined in his wildest dreams. To him—Old-timer—Craig, as Paine knew him—no longer appeared human. Craig was a killing machine, more lethal than almost anything he'd seen in his life—more lethal than anything other than one very notable exception.

Hundreds of androids were attempting to pounce on Paine, Daniella, Djanet, and Samantha, yet none of them were able to manage so much as a hand on their quarry, each android who got within reach having its head summarily popped from its body, decapitated with ease by the weapon that Old-timer's body had become.

Even their leader, Neirbo, was powerless, standing several meters away from the flailing death-bringer that was Old-timer, firing futile shots from his weapon in an attempt to bring the monster down—or at least slow the ease with which it was destroying his forces. One of Old-timer's tendrils seemed to sense this, reason that the shots were a threat, and consequently circled Neirbo's arm, easily ripping it from the android's body and sending the android screaming and stumbling away in retreat.

The weapon slid down the catwalk, eventually finding its way to within Paine's grasp. He moved from the railing and lunged out for it, grasping it before rolling back against the railing, the bodies still falling around him like trees in the woods, smashing hard against the ground or tumbling over the ledge for what seemed to be an eternity into the darkness below.

"Did you get the gun?" Old-timer called over his shoulder.

"Yeah," Paine responded, realizing that Old-timer had planned it that way.

"Watch my back," he turned his head slightly to meet Paine's eye. "Just in case," he added.

"Okay," Paine responded, watching to make sure that no androids breached the killing perimeter that Old-timer's body had formed. Not one of them got close to touching them.

Then, suddenly, everything changed.

The android ship seemed to pitch, its nose pointing upward instantly, the gravity suddenly throwing them all to the side, the limp android bodies falling to Paine's left instead of downward to the ground so far below.

Paine hooked his arm around the railing, as did Daniella, who was the first person his eyes instinctively went to. The others in their party had managed to react in time as well, the catwalk seeming to have been turned on its side, debris smashing down around them, falling to the new bottom of the scene, which was the back of the *Constructor* vessel.

Old-timer had latched onto the railing as well, reaching out with his tendrils to catch Djanet and even Jules, the android he'd kidnapped, keeping her from plunging toward the irresistible gravity.

"What's happening?" Old-timer shouted out as his body re-furled most of his tendrils, his human form retaking its shape. "Did we get hit with something?"

"We weren't close to a planet!" Jules shouted back. "We were in deep space—nothing could explain a gravity shift like this other than—"

"A black hole," Samantha realized.

"A black hole?" Djanet reacted. She turned to Old-timer with a hopeful expression. "Like Trans-human! James! The A.I.! They must be fighting back!"

"No," Old-timer said, his face contorted with dread, "they'd have contacted us if Trans-human was online."

"It's not a friend," Samantha announced. "We have to get out of here. Now!"

"Why? What's happening?" Daniella shouted.

Paine looked at Old-timer, their eyes locking onto one another in deadly seriousness. "It's V-SINN," Paine announced, his voice filled with both hatred and dread. "And anything that hasn't escaped this ship in the next ninety seconds is going to be dead."

PART 4

1

"Rich? Rich, do you copy?" James's voice desperately called out over and over in Rich's ear. Rich ignored James's plea for a status update in his mind's eye, turning the volume down as he led Lieutenant Commander Patrick down the stairs of the command center. Alejandra was at point, her job to detect any sign that Aldous suspected them or could detect their approach. She turned to Rich when they were only a couple of meters away and silently gave him a nod and a thumbs-up before she stepped away, clearing the path for Rich to fire.

Rich held his hands up, the magnetic energy pulsing green on his finger tips before fusing into a ball of light. He knew he had to hit the chief with just the right amount of power—enough to stun him unconscious but not enough to damage the sensitive instruments of the command center or, perhaps even more importantly, the hard drive that carried the sim in which James and the A.I. were still imprisoned. He licked his lips as he prepared to fire, took in a deep breath to muster the courage, and fired.

A second later, Rich was upside down, flying through the air in the opposite direction, headed for a collision with the far, concrete wall of the room. He hit with a *thud* and grunted when one of his ribs cracked with a sickening *snap* that he could hear as well as feel.

As he rolled to his side, he saw Aldous turning around, a look of shock on his face as Alejandra, Lieutenant Commander Patrick, and half a dozen of Patrick's men trained their rifles on the former leader of the post-humans.

"What is the meaning of this?" Governor Wong demanded. "This man is my guest!"

"Richard?" Aldous said, still incredulous as he saw Rich barely moving, struggling to get to his knees. "Did you attack me?"

Within the sim, James looked up at the A.I., concern furrowing his brow. "I just heard something weird. I think he's been injured! Rich! Rich, do you copy?"

Rich tried to reply, but no words could escape his lips, the wind still knocked out of his chest. The nans were hard at work taking care of the internal damage, but the consequential pain of his rapid impact with the unforgiving wall hadn't yet abated.

"Governor," Alejandra began, "the chief isn't to be trusted. He's the post-humans' prime suspect."

"Suspect? Suspected of what?" Wong questioned.

"Treason," Alejandra replied. "Commander James Keats and their artificial intelligence are imprisoned within the device the chief is wearing over his shoulder," she pointed out, gesturing to the black hard drive, still attached to the strap slung over Aldous's shoulder.

"James and the A.I. suspect that Aldous…" Rich began, struggling to get to his feet as he held both his arms around his torso, hugging himself to support his weight as he struggled against the pain that each breath brought along as part of the package so that he could continue speaking, "…may have paved the way for the androids to assimilate the humans on Earth."

"*James*," Aldous said as though the name alone was enough of an answer, his expression flat, yet stoic. "He found a way to contact you, didn't he?"

Rich nodded.

"That boy." He shook his head before, odd as it seemed to those present, he held up his hands in surrender. "And now he's told you he's concerned that I'll damage the hard drive? That I'd rather see James and the A.I. deleted than have them set free to defend us against the androids. Is that about right, Richard?"

"That about sizes it up," Rich replied, grimacing as he crossed both of his arms across his torso, hugging it to mitigate the extreme pain.

"Rich, can you report?" James asked through their aural connection, desperate for answers.

"I'm a little busy, Commander. Hang on," Rich grunted in reply to the voice in his ears.

"Richard, in the future," Aldous began, his tone carrying a hint of slightly amused indignation, "if you ever want to attack me again, keep in mind that I am the chief of the governing council. That means I have access to extra defenses that the regular citizenship don't have. Even if you sneak up on me, you'll be detected, and my force-field will automatically activate to protect me."

"Yeah," Rich answered. "So I noticed. Neat trick you got there."

"It was nothing personal," Aldous said, his words tinged with condescension. "I meant you no harm, and…" He turned to the governor before addressing everyone else in the room, most of whom had their rifles aimed futilely in his direction, "I also meant no harm to James, Thel, or the A.I. So, if you'll allow me," he began to move his hands slowly to the hard drive before removing it from his shoulder, grasping the hard drive in his hand and holding it out before him, offering it directly to Rich.

Rich kept his eyes squarely on the hard drive, but held his hands out, ready to blast the chief again while speaking with deliberate emphasis as each syllable escaped his lips, addressing Alejandra directly, "Would you mind?"

Alejandra lowered her rifle, letting it hang loose from the strap on her shoulder as she tentatively reached for the hard drive.

"You're not thinking clearly, Richard," Aldous spoke, a faint smile crossing his lips. "I already told you, you can't harm me."

Alejandra's fingers reached the hard drive and, for a moment, she and Aldous held it together, Aldous's eyes remaining locked with Rich's. After seconds that felt much longer, Aldous released his hold and Alejandra backed away with the hard drive successfully before turning to deliver it to Rich, who took it in his hands.

"I'd never, *ever*, intentionally hurt Commander Keats, Thel, or the A.I., nor would I *ever* intentionally harm a post-human," Aldous said emphatically.

"He's telling the truth," Alejandra confirmed for those assembled.

"And does that same courtesy extend to Purists?" Lieutenant Commander Patrick asked, his rifle still aimed squarely at the chief.

Aldous's eyes finally left Rich's as he turned to regard the room, populated by the scrutinizing, distrustful eyes of more than a dozen Purists. He considered the question, then considered that he was in a room with an empath, who seemed nearly as adept as the A.I. at determining if someone was being sincere.

"When Governor Wong here was barely out of his diapers," Aldous spoke, gesturing to the elderly leader of the Purists, "I was rebuilding a world destroyed in a war that I blamed solely on Purist beliefs." He tightened his lips as he allowed himself a brief remembrance of the pain. "The lives lost—the entire world, nearly destroyed. It wasn't…easy. Of that you can be sure."

"It wasn't easy to cram all of us on a reservation in South America?" Patrick questioned, disdain saturating his voice.

"I didn't make the decision to bring the post-human world into being," Aldous replied. "I admit I wanted it, but I left it up to another man—a man considered by all of you here to be a hero. *He* had the power to decide whether the world would be post-human or…something else. Some, indescribable place the Purists were desperately and forlornly trying to build, albeit without much success."

Rich scoffed. "I really doubt *you'd* leave a decision like that up to someone else."

"Oh I did, Richard," Aldous replied, "and you know the man I speak of very well. *Craig Emilson* made the call. I simply carried out his order."

"Old-timer?" Rich reacted, astonished.

"Craig?" Alejandra echoed. She turned to Rich. "My God…Richard, he's telling the truth."

Rich shook his head. "No...no way. Old-timer wouldn't have wanted this. He wouldn't have treated the Purists this way. I don't believe it."

"Craig—or Old-timer as you incessantly insist on calling him—didn't have the stomach to take control. He left the actual construction of the post-human world up to me, but he *could've* stopped me. I gave him the chance…and he chose a post-human future."

"But you're the one who imprisoned us," Patrick concluded. "You can't pass the buck."

Aldous shook his head. "I didn't imprison you. You imprisoned yourselves. You could've been post-humans, but you chose to live like the indigent fools of the past. You actually chose to live with disease and die like animals, as though your lives don't mean anything," Aldous said. It was clear from his tone that he could barely fathom the Purists' reasoning.

"At least we're still human!" Patrick shot back.

Aldous looked around the room at the venom that filled every stare directed his way. "You love James Keats," Aldous said, nodding. "He's your new hero. *Your savior.* Why? Because he gave you *this*?" he gestured around himself. "He gave you Venus?" Aldous pounded angrily on his own chest as he yelled out, "Well, I didn't have an entire planet to give you!" He tried to get his breathing back under control, his anger reaching proportions he hadn't felt for what seemed like eons. "No matter what I did, I couldn't convince the Purists to join us. We explained everything—detailed a life without pain, or suffering. A life where you could soar in the air like a bird, and even help us terraform so that we could expand humanity's reach! Most Purists eventually agreed and relented, but there were those of you that were unreachable. And every generation bred more doubters. So I gave you land—just like James—I gave you a place to exist."

He put his hand through his hair and paced as he further calmed himself, his eyes seeming to leave the room as he remembered something—something horrible. "And then years passed by. And over the years, a man learns. A man discovers truths. And as the man learns these truths, he begins to understand his enemies. And when a man understands his enemies—*truly* understands them—they cease to be his enemies."

He turned to Lieutenant Commander Patrick, then to Governor Wong, who stood just a meter away behind the chief. "Make no mistake. All these years, we had the power to eradicate you. But *every single human life is sacred to me.* And listen to me when I tell you, that now more than ever, I've done everything in my power to protect every human in this solar system, *including* the Purists."

For a moment, silence hung in the air. Rich didn't have a response, but turned to Alejandra, as did, eventually, everyone else—even Aldous.

"He…" She paused as she realized she needed to moisten her dry mouth before she could speak. "He's telling the truth."

The tension in the room suddenly dropped significantly, and Rich even relaxed his grip on the hard drive, which he'd been gripping like grim death.

"But," Alejandra continued, her face paled with terror, "he's still hiding something from us. Something…horrible."

Before anyone could react, Thel Cleland burst through the doors into the command center, holding a Purist guard that she'd accosted in a headlock, her palm pressed against his temple threateningly. Once she was inside the room, she released him and he, without a fight, rolled pathetically away from her, getting to his knees as he continued to back away, terrified of the post-human after his ordeal.

"Thel!" Rich exclaimed.

"Thel?" James reacted. "She's okay?"

"Yes," Rich confirmed.

"*Thel?*" Aldous said, disbelieving his own eyes.

"Chief Gibson," Thel began, her expression molded by her determination, "you better have one hell of an explanation." She held up her hands, green energy pulsating threateningly on her fingertips.

"Whoa!" Rich shouted out to her. "Thel! Wait! I got the hard drive," he said, holding it up for her to see. "He gave it to me."

"Thel, is that really you?" Aldous asked, astonished to see her awake and returned to her body.

"You better believe it," Thel replied, her fingers still pulsating energy.

"James figured out how to break through the trapdoor code," Aldous said, his hand coming to his forehead as the disbelief set in even further.

"Actually," Thel said with a slightly proud smile, "*I* figured it out."

Aldous's eyebrows knitted furiously. "That's not possible," he responded. "No mere human could've—" He stopped himself before he continued.

"What?" Rich reacted. "What do you mean?" he asked the chief. "How would you know that?"

"Because *it was him*," Thel said coldly. "All along. I *knew* it."

Aldous's face went pale and he shook his head, distraught. "Milady, you do not know the half of it. You have no idea what you've done."

"Yeah? How's about you tell me, old man?"

Aldous turned back to Rich, his eyes immediately falling on the hard drive in Rich's grasp that contained the sim—an entire world within a box—and James's and the A.I.'s core patterns within it. "James and the A.I.—they have no body to which to return. They remain trapped," he said, as much to himself as to Thel as he sought confirmation.

"Not for long," Thel responded. "James's body survived the impact that destroyed Earth. As soon as we get a signal booster strong enough—"

Aldous shook his head violently at the news, as though he were attempting to shake off a leash, fruitlessly fighting the will of his master. "Enough!" he shouted. "Enough. Oh my dear God," he said, as he put his hand to his lips, partially covering his mouth. His eyes twitched as he seemed to attempt to generate an alternative course of action in his imagination, but he quickly realized, dread filling his heart, that there was nothing to be done.

"You've done the impossible," Aldous uttered. "The trapdoor was impossible for a human to have broken it. Which means I've been betrayed."

"*You've* been betrayed?" Thel repeated the chief, astounded by Aldous's reaction.

"That's correct," Aldous confirmed, matter-of-factly as he turned to her, the look in his eye telling Thel that all of the people in the room's safety was in immediate peril. "And if I've been betrayed," Aldous continued, "we've *all* been betrayed."

"What the hell is he—" Rich began before Thel cut him off.

"Rich! Protect the hard drive!" she screamed out.

Rich turned to Thel and the deadly serious expression of concern on her face told him that he'd better heed her warning. He ignited his protective magnetic field just in time.

Aldous's lips curled up atavistically, and he unleashed the full power at his disposal, blasting out energy in every direction, instantly felling all of the Purists in the room and slamming Rich backward against the wall once again, and slamming Thel against the doors to the command center, causing the doors to become unhinged and fly with her for several meters down the adjacent hallway.

2

"He's right!" Jules echoed Paine as she hooked her arm hard over the railing of the catwalk, careful not to be hit by the fast moving debris that rocketed toward them from above. "The gravity well is too strong for it be anything else! We should be able to fly out of here but the gravity's too powerful to break free from! It's one of them!"

"One of what?" Djanet shot back as she, too, held on for dear life, her feet being sucked to some unseen point at the back of the ship, which felt as though it were pointing nose up when it should've been floating steadily in deep space.

"An infinity computer!" Jules answered, yelling over the nearly deafening sound of the extraordinarily large ship's hull buckling in billions of places at once. "It's what the nanobots *always* eventually build. Perfectly, mathematically, predictable—it's a tiny black hole, but even a black hole just a few meters across is powerful enough to swallow the entire ship!"

"This is where the bodies are built, right?" Paine confirmed with Jules.

Jules nodded. "Yes, ninety-nine percent of our collective's replication capability is in the *Constructor.*"

Paine turned to Old-timer. "It's a strategic strike," he said. "V-SINN's not appearing here by accident. It wants to make sure these androids can't rebuild."

"V-SINN never does anything by accident," Samantha added in agreement. "It's always pure, unfeeling, mathematical precision. It's strategy. Paine's right, this ship's finished!"

"And we'll be finished if we can't figure out a way to escape this gravity well!" Djanet shouted. "If we can't fly out of here, what can we do?"

Jules turned her head and watched with an expression of awe and horror as she saw the monolithic towers of the replicator swaying, some of them beginning to crack, their metallic frames fracturing, splitting in half from the gravity's extreme pressure, now focused on their midpoints as they were horizontal in orientation. "There's one chance!" she shouted over the sound of the unimaginable destruction.

"What?" Old-timer asked desperately.

"Large portions of the ship have atmospheric controls—the most concentrated are in Eden but there's atmospheric control in the replicator too!"

"Oh my God," Djanet responded, putting two and two together. "You can't seriously be suggesting—"

"Look!" Jules shouted, as she pointed far into the distance. As the pillars collapsed, one by one, the ship's hull, nearly a dozen kilometers from their current position, came into view.

They each turned their heads to see what she was referring to. A giant zipper crack, so long that it was, by the second, resembling more and more a canyon, was suddenly in clear view.

"When the hull breaches," Jules shouted, "*if* the breach is big enough, there's going to be an explosive decompression! It might give us the propulsion we need to escape the gravity well!"

"Yeah," Djanet shouted back, "*if* we survive being sucked out of the ship through a debris field of jagged metal objects moving at speeds that could even slice an android in half!"

"We'll survive!" Old-timer shouted. "Every one, stay close to me. When the decompression happens, I can protect us."

Daniella's panicked expression was instantly replaced with disbelief. "Craig! Even you can't—"

"I can!" Old-timer shouted, determinedly. "I can save us! Trust me! Just get close—"

Before he could finish his sentence, he was interrupted by a bullet whizzing unexpectedly past his face from above, a bullet that cut right through the center of the catwalk, slicing it cleanly in two and causing it to buckle, sending the entire group plunging toward their deaths below them in the heart of darkness that was the infinity computer.

3

Aldous turned to Rich, who struggled to get back to his feet. They were both cocooned now in their magnetic fields, their communication shifting to their mind's eyes. "Richard, I'm sorry, but I must ask you to return the hard drive to me."

"No can do, Chief," Rich said, his voice beginning to shake with panic.

"What's going on?" James shouted.

"The chief's trying to kill us!" Rich shouted to him in return.

Aldous's face suddenly changed as he heard Rich's communication with James. He shook his head. "I'm not trying to kill you, Richard, and I'm not trying to kill James or the A.I. But Richard, they can *never* leave that simulation. That was the agreement I made and a duty that *I* alone can carry out. Do you understand?"

"Keep him talking, Rich," James said. "Buy us some time."

"Yeah, I understand," Rich replied. "You're a traitor. I get it."

"Normal ethics don't apply in this situation, Richard. To you, I'm a traitor, but to everyone in this solar system who lives to see the future because of my actions today, I'm a savior."

"Delusions of grandeur," Rich responded, his eyes wide. "You just disabled the Purists' command center. They're not going to be thanking you for saving them if they're assimilated!"

"*When* they're assimilated," Aldous corrected. "It was inevitable." He narrowed his eyes. "Only the timing was off.

Something went wrong in the sim. I was betrayed, but I don't know yet why or by whom."

Rich scoffed, his palm going to his forehead. "Oh dear Lord, I am in a comedy!"

"I'm afraid not, Richard," Aldous replied. "And there will be no Deus ex machina to intervene this time. I'm making sure of that. Now, please, hand over the hard drive. I give you my word I will protect it, and I'll make sure the androids take you painlessly."

"He can't touch you, Rich," James pointed out. "If he could break your force-field, he would've done it already ."

"He's waiting for the androids to arrive," the A.I. added.

Rich nodded. "Your word is…what would Old-timer say? Oh yeah. A steaming pile of horse—"

"Stop, Richard," Aldous warned as Rich began to back out of the corner Aldous had backed him in to, making his way slowly to the steps of the command center toward the exit. "If the androids have to take back that sim from you, I can't guarantee its safety. I'm trying to save *our* friends here, Richard. Please, be reasonable."

"I hate to break it to you," Rich responded, "but you disabled the Purists' defenses almost two minutes ago. There was a whole world full of androids in orbit just itching to get down here. Are you sure your backup is coming?"

Aldous's face nearly formed a smile at Rich's absurd suggestion. He paused for a moment, and Rich saw the flash of information before Aldous's eyes as he seemed to check on something. Whatever the answer was that he found, it contorted his face into an expression of dread.

"Oh my God," Aldous whispered.

"What's wrong, *friend*?" Rich asked. "Betrayed again?"

"We're already too late," Aldous uttered. In shock, he pulled out a small, black object from his pocket and held it in the palm of his hand.

Rich's expression reached a new level of surprise. "Is that...an assimilator?" he reacted. "They *gave* you one?"

Aldous nodded as he looked up at Rich in utter defeat. "For my wife," he confirmed. "She'd never have gone along with my plan. So I did it while she was sleeping." He stroked the side of the device with his index finger as though he was stroking the side of Samantha's cheek.

"I can't believe you assimilated your wife," Rich said, disgusted. "You have no lim—"

"Richard!" Aldous screamed in response, snapping his head around, his eyes suddenly burning with fury. "Do you know what's happening right this second?" He gesticulated violently, gesturing toward the sky that was far above them, several meters of concrete and ocean separating them. "The ship the androids call the *Constructor*, a ship where more than ninety-nine percent of their people are built, is being devoured by an infinity computer."

"A what now?"

"In layman's terms, Richard, it's a black hole," Aldous continued. "A perfect computing device, built by the nans."

"Oh my God," James reacted when he overheard the news, immediately exchanging looks of terror with the A.I. "Is it possible?"

Rich heard James's reaction and tried to make sense out of what was happening. "But…how could…"

"It's inevitable," Aldous responded gutturally, as though the pressure of a secret kept for decades could finally be released. "It's exactly what Trans-human is—the unavoidable consequence of mathematical perfection—and it's eating the goddamn multiverse! Devouring it! *That's* what I was trying to prevent, Richard! *That's* what I've been trying to save us from!"

"Is it possible he's telling the truth, James?" Thel suddenly asked, having tapped into the conversation moments earlier as she slowly made her way back to the command center's door after recovering enough from Aldous's salvo against her.

"I-I don't know," James replied.

Aldous looked up at Thel, his bottom lip actually protruding slightly in a pout, his eyes beginning to glisten as tears welled in them. "I never wanted this to happen," he suddenly said. "Please tell James for me, Thel. I never wanted this. I tried to protect them—James and the A.I., but I was betrayed, and now we've run out of time."

"Uh, James," Rich said in a panic, "this son-of-a-nut-job just completely lost his mind! He's got a crazy look in his eye. I need some help here!"

Within the sim, James appeared out of options, too stunned to formulate a plan.

Aldous, however, had settled on the only course of action that made sense to him. "I'm sorry," he repeated as he put the assimilator away, back into his pocket and then looked upward, holding his hands above his head, energy beginning to pulsate on his fingertips.

"Aldous! Don't do it!" Thel shouted as she realized what Earth's formerly most powerful man's desperate final bid to protect the universe from Trans-human would be.

She tried to rush toward him, but it was too late. He blasted through the ceiling of the command center, allowing the power of an entire ocean to crash down upon their heads.

4

Jules was the first to grab a handhold, clutching the side of a replicator pod just one level lower than the rapidly disintegrating catwalk. She looked down to see Old-timer's tendrils wrapping around the wrists of both Samantha and Djanet, while a third tendril burrowed into the side of a pod one level farther below Jules.

"Daniella!" he shouted out as he realized neither of the two people he saved was his wife and he searched desperately with his eyes for her, darting his eyes in every direction. Almost immediately, he saw her, a level below him, Colonel Paine having dropped his weapon to grab the wrist of the ghost that haunted him deeply, saving her, while clutching one of the pods with his other hand.

"Got her!" Paine called up as he looked down into Daniella's astonished eyes. "But the weight's getting tough—V-SINN must be getting closer! If that hull doesn't breach soon—"

"It won't save you!" Neirbo shouted down to them from his perch, his feet planted on the side of a replicator pod above them. "I have the high ground! None of you is leaving here!" His eyes fell on Old-timer. "Especially not *him*."

"Craig, what the hell did you do to that guy to piss him off so much?" Paine shouted up to Old-timer, exasperated.

Old-timer didn't answer the question, realizing their time was too short, and instead looked up at Neirbo pleadingly. "Neirbo! Goddamnit! We can still get out of here! All of us!"

Neirbo shook his head. "You're too dangerous to be left alive! This is the only way for me to finally destroy you, Craig Emilson."

He knows my name? Old-timer thought to himself, surprised.

"Your orders were to take him alive!" Jules shouted out to Neirbo.

Neirbo looked at her before, extremely uncharacteristically, laughing. "My orders?" He gestured with his gun to the destruction around them. "None of us is going to survive this. I think the time for following orders has ended."

"Where's your loyalty?" Jules shot back. "The orders came from *1* herself!"

Old-timer's eyebrows knitted furiously as he made a realization.

"Loyalty?" Neirbo replied, astonished by the concept's sudden and total absurdity. "In the final moments of my life, you know what I say to 1?" His voice became colder than it had ever been in the hundreds of years he'd lived. "I say go to He—"

Neirbo's sentence suddenly ended abruptly, his final thought never able to be spoken, as the hand that held his weapon suddenly began moving the gun, its muzzle pointing toward Neirbo's own temple. His disbelieving eyes darted to Jules as he finally made the same realization Old-timer had just moments earlier.

The muzzle flashed, and Neirbo's head was cut in half, circuitry and metal suddenly scattering before being abruptly sucked down as though a vacuum cleaner were drawing them toward it. His headless body collapsed a second later, slipping from its perch on the side of the replicator pod and falling past Paine and Daniella, narrowly missing them as it fell at an astonishing rate of descent.

Old-timer looked up at Jules, his face painted with fury, his teeth gritted so hard that he couldn't squeeze out the words.

"That's right," Jules confirmed, answering the unspoken question. "*1*'s still alive."

"Is that…" Djanet began to ask, as she tried to make sense out of what she'd seen, "…did 1 make him do that? How? Has she been monitoring us the whole time?"

"She's not just monitoring us," Old-timer replied, his eyes fixed on those of Jules. "*She's with us.*"

"What?" Djanet asked, her brow furrowing.

"Jules *is* 1," Old-timer revealed. "She led us into this trap."

"And now I'm going to lead you out of it," she called down to them as she swung her body like a mountain climber across the front of the pod to which she clung and pried the door open, tossing out the not-yet-activated android occupant, his body falling rapidly into the approaching black hole. "The decompression will occur in seconds. Unlock the pods from the pillars, get inside a pod, close the door, and hang on. It's your only hope."

Old-timer and Djanet exchanged astounded glances before Old-timer quickly used his powerful appendages to rip off the locks that held the pod they clung to into place before he slid back its door. Luckily, it was unoccupied, and he was able to bring himself, along with Samantha on his right and Djanet on his left, inside. The fit, however was extraordinarily snug, both of the women's bodies squishing onto his hips, each of them tucking their shoulders to allow for the door to close. The last thing Old-timer saw before he closed the door was Daniella and Paine just below on the pillar to their opposite side, also sharing a pod, their eyes locked on one another, Daniella appearing confused and frightened, while Paine's eyes expressed a gentleness that Old-timer had never seen from the professional killer.

Then he sensed eyes on him to his right and caught Samantha looking up at him, her eyes carrying their own hurt and confusion, and he looked away when he couldn't take it anymore.

"What do you think our chances are?" Djanet asked, her focus on surviving, as it should've been.

"Better than you might think," Old-timer replied. "*1* could've killed us if she'd really wanted to. There's a reason we're still alive. I suggest we follow her lead for now, as ridiculous as that notion might have sounded five minutes ago."

"So we're being manipulated—again," Djanet said, summing up the situation.

"Yeah," Old-timer sighed. "What else is new?"

Suddenly, there was a shudder, then a shockwave that was far more powerful than anything they'd felt so far. Through the dark, tinted window of the pod, they saw the hull breach, a sudden exit forming in the side of the ship that was so huge, the pressure being released so massive, that the pillars, each one of them dozens of times taller than the tallest structures ever built by humans on

Earth, began crumbling like a sandcastle, breaking free from their moorings like matchsticks, being sucked toward the hole.

The pods were sucked in too, the acceleration so instant and extreme that it would've killed them if they'd still been in their post-human bodies.

"This is it," Old-timer grunted. "Hold on!"

5

"Thel! What's happening?" James shouted as he heard her last, panicked shouts.

"I'm out of control!" Thel shouted back as she was forced out the door again, her magnetic field cocooning her and the unconscious Alejandra and Lieutenant Commander Patrick—she hadn't been able to save anyone else. "They're all dead! Aldous killed them—he murdered them! The Purist complex is flooding—he brought down the ceiling!"

"Oh my God," James whispered before his mind quickly snapped into action. "Thel, find a bottleneck point. Throw up a magnetic field and seal in the water before the entire complex is flooded!"

"Uhn!" she grunted in reply as she struggled to turn, the torrent of water propelling her through a long hallway. She managed to turn and saw the end, an opening that led back into the main hub of the complex. "I got it—hang on!" she shouted as she prepared herself, timing her next maneuver. She'd have to relinquish her cocoon, lowering her own protection and the protection that had saved Alejandra and the lieutenant commander so that she could seal in the flood, as the walls were the bottle neck she needed. Just before she reached them, she lowered her field, falling into the whitewater rapids, the water warm like that in a bathtub. She was swept away and then fired up a new magnetic field, closing in the torrent of water behind her as she slid across the soaked, concrete floor of the main hub of the new Purist complex. Alejandra's and Lieutenant Commander Patrick's unconscious bodies limply hydroplaned until the water dispersed enough beneath them and they came to violent halts several meters behind Thel, but her eyes remained on the wall of water that, within seconds, had completely filled the hallway from the floor to the ceiling.

"Are you okay, Thel?" James asked, feeling utterly helpless as he waited for an update. "Did it work?"

"It worked," Thel gasped, "but, James, I was only able to save two of them. I lost all the rest—including Governor Wong. He drowned."

"Focus on who you still have a chance to save," the A.I. interjected. "Your field will protect the Purists for now, but they need to evacuate."

"I understand," Thel nodded, turning to see as hundreds of Purists entered the main hub, alarms blaring and red lights signaling an emergency. "You need to evacuate the complex!" Thel screamed out at them! "Quickly!"

Several Purists joined forces to retrieve both Alejandra and Lieutenant Commander Patrick, dragging the two unconscious bodies away toward the strangely designed vehicles that populated the main hub. Thel wasn't sure if they were air- or water-vehicles, but knowing that James had designed them, she knew they'd do the job either way.

"The evacuation is underway," Thel relayed, slightly relieved. "But what happened to the hard drive? Is Rich okay?"

6

"We're trying to figure that out," James returned "Hang on. Rich? Do you copy?"

"Where the hell am I?" Rich shouted as, all around him, he appeared to be surrounded by a wall of white. "I don't see anything! I don't even know what direction I'm facing!"

"Thank God you're okay, pal," James breathed a sigh of relief. "Listen, Thel's helping the Purists evacuate, and Aldous doesn't seem to be able to get to you through your magnetic field. He's trying to buy time—he must think there's still a way he can prevent us from assuming control of Trans-human."

"What about the Purists in the command center?" Rich asked as he was suddenly interrupted, the interruption causing him to scream out in a brief call of terror. As if in answer to his question, Governor Wong's dead body was thrust against the side of his magnetic field. "Jesus!"

"Rich! Are you okay?"

Rich was panting as he tried to regain some semblance of control over his rapid breathing as the governor's body was swept away in the torrent. "Relatively," he replied, "but James, the Governor's dead. I just saw him. Oh Christ."

James shut his eyes. "That blood's on Aldous's hands. Goddamn it, I never thought he'd betray us like this. Not in a million years."

"Nor did I," the A.I. echoed. "Aldous has clearly been using his privileged position as the chief of the A.I. governing council to keep a great many secrets, perhaps for several decades."

"What do I do here, guys?" Rich asked, panicked. "I can't see. It's just a wall of white all around me. Just frothing water, man."

"Where's Aldous?" James asked. "You should be able to detect his position if you're in such close proximity."

"That's the thing," Rich replied, "I can't. His position isn't coming up on my mind's eye. Guys, he's not playing by the rules here."

"He's right," the A.I. concurred with Rich's assessment as he conferred with James, the candidate standing nearby, transfixed by the drama, yet remaining a silent bystander. "Rich can't get a position, he doesn't know which way is up or down, left or right. This is right where Aldous wants him. If Aldous can't lower Rich's magnetic field, then at least he can keep him trapped in one place."

"And if he's trapped in one place, he can't reach a signal booster," James added.

"It also provides a possible answer as to what Aldous is buying time for," the A.I. said, his brow furrowed as he thought deeply, unraveling the puzzle. "If Aldous can't lower Rich's magnetic field, yet he claimed to have been the one who developed the prototype—"

"Then someone has to have given it to Aldous," James said, finishing the A.I.'s thought for him. "And our top suspect is 1, once again. She'd be in the best position to know how to beat her own collective's technology, but she wouldn't trust Aldous enough to give him the key."

"Indeed, it's now all but certain that Aldous and 1 struck a deal," the A.I. agreed.

"But their deal hasn't gone according to plan, and now Aldous is waiting for the other shoe to drop," James realized.

"Uh, guys," Rich interrupted, "I love detective time as much as the next guy, I really do, but I'm sorta trapped here. What the hell do I do?"

James turned to the A.I. and they, without a word, seemed to agree on the only course of action available. "Look, Rich..." James began.

"Okay, already I don't like this," Rich replied. "Why did I know your tone was going to be foreboding? Why can't it ever start with, 'It's super easy, Rich! No worries! Have a beer! Chill out!'"

"I wish it was that simple, but it's gonna be a risk, bud," James said. "I know you don't know where you are in the room, but we need you to give us some sort of visual cue so that we can direct you to a signal booster. That means we need to get you out of that room."

"And how do we do that?" Rich replied, his face stricken with dread.

"The command center juts out, right at the front of the waterfall, and it's the most westward-facing point in the complex," James replied. Because it juts out, that means if you head up, you'll break free from the room and the water above and escape. If you head down, you'll crash through into the waterfall, but eventually you'll make it to the seabed and, again, be able to escape. The same goes for if you go left or right. The only truly bad direction is if you go east and crash into the rest of the complex, which wouldn't be optimal."

"Optimal? What happens if I crash into the rest of the complex?"

"You might bring the ceiling down on Thel and spread the flooding and kill the rest of the Purists. So, this is going to be like Russian roulette. Same odds. Five directions save you, one direction doesn't."

"But instead of playing with *my* life, I'm playing with Thel's life and the lives of all the Purists!" Rich fired back.

"Rich," Thel suddenly cut in as she remained in the center hub of the complex, still holding back the tidal wave of water that threatened them. "James is right. You've got a five-in-six chance of getting out of there, but even if you do come east and flood the rest of the complex, it'll be okay."

"What? Thel, I can't be responsible for—"

"Think about it, Rich," Thel cut him off. "It won't matter if we die if you're able to get James and the A.I. out of the sim and into Trans-human. They can turn the solar system back in time again, and that's all that matters. We can still save Governor Wong and the others that we've already lost."

Rich's mind immediately went to Djanet, before turning to his family. In all likelihood, they'd been assimilated, and James and the

A.I. were his only hope of undoing that damage and bringing back the Purist lives that had already been lost. "Okay, okay. I'll do it. Damn it. How do I pick a direction? Eenie-meenie-miney-mo?"

"That'll work," James conceded, "but hurry, Rich. If Aldous is buying time, it means he thinks there's a strong chance that the person who can get through your magnetic field is on her way as we speak, and we all know who that is. Every second counts."

"Djanet you were right," Rich whispered to himself as he nodded. "I've gotta retire from the saving the world business." He closed his eyes and then flew forward as fast as he could, not knowing what direction "forward" was.

7

Old-timer watched in awe of the spectacle that unfolded outside of the replicator pod he shared with Djanet and Samantha. Like matchsticks in the wind, the giant pillars blew around erratically inside of the crumbling ship, none of them gaining enough momentum to carry them all the way to the gargantuan hole that had exploded open in the side of the hull, their masses causing them to be caught in the immense and increasing gravity of V-SINN, still unseen but clearly devouring the ship, sucking them ever closer to the most final death imaginable.

The fissure toward which the group of pods were rapidly approaching at high velocity came into view for brief glimpses, but the pods were spinning uncontrollably, caught up in the force of the decompression, gusts of the atmosphere smacking them to and fro in turbulence that reminded Old-timer of the suborbital jump he'd taken the better part of a century earlier. Each time the fissure came into view, it was closer, but then it would disappear again, replaced by views of tumbling pillars, catwalks, and shrapnel that shot in every direction like grenade fragments.

"It's gonna take a miracle to survive this!" Djanet shouted.

Old-timer noted that her words were barely audible, despite the fact that she was clearly shouting, an obvious sign that the atmosphere was rapidly thinning, the air unable to carry the sound of her voice.

Suddenly, a black shape appeared from above and, whatever it was, the debris batted them down, changing their trajectory. "What was that?" Djanet asked.

Their view was unintelligible; geometric shapes, ripped from the once moon-sized ship, were passing in front of them, but the fissure didn't appear again.

"Are we off course?" Samantha shouted.

Old-timer stayed quiet. If they'd been knocked down toward V-SINN, they were as good as dead, but it was impossible to tell. He watched the bizarre spectacle continuing to unfold, his face filled with trepidation, yet also stone still as he waited for his fate to become clear.

Then, suddenly, he noticed fingers circling his hand, Samantha grasping on to him tightly, as she buried her face, distraught, in his arm. He looked down at her, this woman who'd lost her husband, and suddenly realized how much she had in common with the man *he* used to be—not Old-timer, but *Craig*. The man who'd woken up in a world where his wife wasn't his wife any longer. That man who'd been frozen in time.

"There!" Djanet suddenly shouted, pointing. Her shout barely resonated for Old-timer, but her excited pointing did. The fissure reappeared, and though they'd been knocked toward the lower end of it, it was large enough that they were about to escape through the canyon-like crevice.

Once they were outside the rapidly fragmenting hull of the *Constructor*, their momentum carried them for several more seconds, and Old-timer opened the door of the pod. Together, the three of them exited.

He immediately turned his attention to finding his wife in the massive and growing debris field. Hundreds of thousands of bodies, most of the them not yet activated and likely never to be, floated into the vacuum of space. A few thousand more conscious androids, androids that had probably been relaxing in Eden when disaster struck, had been lucky enough to have made it out in the decompression. The massive cloud of bodies made it impossible for Old-timer to locate Daniella and Paine, and impossible to locate 1.

Samantha continued to grip Old-timer's hand, and he didn't force her to let go. He could hardly imagine what she was going through. He turned to Djanet and noticed her mouth moving as she seemed to be communicating. Old-timer suddenly remembered that she was connected to the collective. He gestured to her to grab her attention, and then pointed to the back of her neck, unfurling a tendril as he did so. He knew she'd seen him connect to Anisim earlier and would understand. She nodded and floated close enough for him to jack into the back of her head. She made a slight wince, but within seconds, Old-timer had a viable aural connection established.

"What's happening? Are you in contact with Daniella?" he asked her.

"Yeah," she replied. "That dude from 332 is with her, and they're already going after 1. She made a beeline for Venus as soon as they made it out of the ship. I'm tracking them."

"Venus?" Old-timer responded, perplexed. "Why? Why not head to one of her ships? What does she want with Venus?"

"I don't know. Maybe the Purists?"

"Purists?" Samantha suddenly chimed in. "You have Purists in this universe too?"

Old-timer's eyes narrowed, but he knew he didn't have time to pursue her strange contribution.

Something else grabbed his full attention.

Over her shoulder, he saw something that struck him to his core—it was his first look at V-SINN.

She saw the look of awe and terror freezing his eyes and knew before she turned her head what he was looking at; she'd seen that look before on her husband's face. She turned anyway, and the trio floated in silence as they were awestruck by the scale of the destruction to the *Constructor*.

V-SINN, or as 1 had called it, an infinity computer, had appeared at the tail end of the ship. As black holes went, it was tiny, much smaller than a naturally occurring stellar black hole, which was rarely smaller than at least a dozen kilometers wide. V-SINN, by comparison, wasn't even large enough to be seen from their perspective, but the immense, nearly infinite gravity of the unholy machine made it unstoppable, and the sheer enormity of the accretion disk of destruction that was orbiting the black hole at an extraordinary rate of speed made it obvious where the infinity computer had parked itself. The picture was absurd, as the constructor ship had been the size of a small moon or a dwarf planet, yet the black hole was swallowing it, almost as though a beetle were swallowing an alligator. It would've been comical if not for the enormity of the destruction, the vessel having already imploded in the middle, millions of androids having been flung outside in the decompression, while billions more—the less lucky ones—remained inside, trapped, many of them still in Eden, their attempt at building Utopia, their lives mere seconds from ending.

"Old-timer," Djanet began, "you do realize who was in those replicator pods, don't you? Those were the assimilated people from our universe...*our solar system.* Those were our people. If we lost James and the A.I.—if we can't get Trans-human working so we can undo this—"

"I know," Old-timer replied. "Come on," he said before he turned the trio around quickly. They began to fly on their new course in pursuit of Daniella and Paine. "We're headed to Venus. If that really is 1's destination, then you can bet there's a reason for it."

"But, Old-timer," Djanet started, her voice filled with both alarm and confusion, "if she really is 1, then why the elaborate game? We know 1 can take over anyone in an android body at any time!"

Old-timer didn't have an answer.

"*She's leading* us there, don't you see?" Djanet insisted. "It has to be a trap."

Old-timer shook his head. "She already led us into the trap," he pointed out. "She led me right into the middle of the replicator facility, where she could've dumped androids on me endlessly until even my upgraded abilities wouldn't have been able to save me, but then V-SINN interrupted." He grimaced as he mulled the puzzle in his mind. "I think she's calling an audible."

"*Audible?*" Djanet reacted, perplexed.

"It means when the quarterback changes the planned play based on circumstances," Samantha interjected.

This shocked Djanet.

"Uh...it's from football," she added.

"Oh," Djanet replied. "*American* football."

"Yes. Craig likes football. American football."

Djanet's eyes narrowed. "How do you know—"

"Not important," Old-timer quickly stopped Djanet's question. "Colonel Paine," Old-timer cut into communication with the Colonel. "Do you have 1 in your sights?"

"She's way ahead of us, Craig, but we're on her tail," Paine's voice replied through their mental connection.

"Is Daniella safe?" Old-timer asked.

"I'm fine, Craig," Daniella replied, her voice filled with uncertainty, as though the awkwardness of being with the ghost of the man she'd helped to kill—a man who claimed to have been her husband in a parallel universe—made her response absurd. It was as though she couldn't believe she was speaking the words.

"Okay. We're right behind you," Old-timer replied. He turned back to Djanet. "You make a fine point though. If she's not leading us to Venus, then why is she using Jules's body to get there?"

"That was my point!" Djanet said, happy Old-timer was listening to reason. "The android armada is spread out across the solar system. There's got to be a closer body she could jump to!"

Old-timer considered this for a moment before he turned back and looked at the massive constructor ship, now in it's final death throes, resembling a crushed aluminum can, half of the crumpled form having been consumed by V-SINN. "Unless…" he began a thought before pausing.

"Unless…?" Djanet prompted him to finish.

"Think about the complexity of a system required to store the patterns of every assimilated person from all of the parallel universes they'd traveled to. More than a trillion lives. Jules told us the *Constructor* was where ninety-nine percent of their bodies were built. What if it also stored all of the android patterns."

Djanet's eyes flashed with understanding. "Dear God. You're right. The *Constructor* makes the most sense. You'd store the patterns in the same place you build the bodies. And V-SINN just swallowed it whole."

"Right," Old-timer answered, "and if 1 was able to jump from body to body because she knew how to infiltrate the stored system—"

"Then she may've just lost that ability," Djanet realized. "And we might've just seen the beginning of the end of the entire collective."

"That fits with V-SINN's M.O.," Samantha confirmed. "Look, this whole situation has me turned upside down, but what I can tell you is, V-SINN never, *ever* makes mistakes—at least none that I've ever seen. V-SINN's the pure distillation of game theory—mathematical strategy for its own benefit."

Old-timer's brow furrowed. "And now it's set its sights on the androids. The enemy of thine enemy…" he whispered to himself. "Could it be?"

"Could what be?" Djanet asked.

Old-timer could hardly believe his next words, even before he said them. "I think 1 might be heading to Venus to acquire post-human help."

8

Rich emerged from out of the roaring white of the gargantuan waterfall and entered the mist that reached up into the sky, the sun gleaming off its peak as though it were the peak of a snow-capped mountain. "Oh thank God!" Rich shouted.

"Where are you?" James asked.

"I think I came right out of the front of the falls," Rich called out in return. "I'm climbing now and trying to get out of the mist."

"That's perfect, bud!" James returned excitedly.

"Whew," Thel reacted as she listened in. She'd been willing to die if it were only temporary, but even temporary death was a terrifying prospect. "Thanks for not killing me, Rich."

"Don't mention it," Rich replied.

"You need to find the sun and get oriented, then we can guide you to the Tesla tower," James urged Rich. "But be careful! You weren't able to track Aldous but he might be able to track—"

"Oh damn!" Rich suddenly shouted as he saw the mist below him glowing green before the glow suddenly disappeared, vanishing in a blink of the eye. "I think I just saw him—I saw a green glow below me!"

"Could it be your own field reflecting back at you?" James asked. "The mist could be playing tricks on your eyes."

"Maybe," Rich said, as his eyes remained glued to the spot where the glow had been moments earlier. Though the nans had mostly repaired his rib, he could still hardly breathe, the fear of being hunted stealing his breath. He continued to climb, finally making it out of the peak of the mist and turning to find the sun. He moved away from the mountain of mist below him and explained his orientation to the technological ghosts that were listening in. "Okay, it looks like you guys were right. I'm facing west, the sun's to my left."

"Perfect. Rich, turn around, fly east. The tower is on the shore of the west coast of Aphrodite Terra."

"Is that an island or something?" Rich asked.

"It's a continent, about half the size of Africa," James replied.

"Uh, James..."

"Don't worry, Rich," James responded to Rich's concerns before he'd even had a chance to verbalize them. "The tower is right on the equator, as are the falls. You'll be able to detect it when you get within range, but you've got to hurry. Aldous could be—"

"Uhn!" Rich called out.

Before James could finish his warning, Aldous Gibson, with no magnetic field to give him away, came up from below Rich at an extraordinary velocity, blasting out of the cloak of mist before quickly firing twin bursts of energy, sending Rich tumbling through the air and skimming across the surface of the water at the mouth of the waterfall.

Rich recovered quickly and began flying as fast as he could to the east, climbing from within just meters of the surface to a thousand meters elevation within seconds. "He was tracking me all right," Rich shouted out. "But I'm okay!"

"He can't get past your magnetic field. Just stay on course," James reminded Rich.

"What if you're wrong?" Rich replied. "What if he's just waiting until the last possible moment? Giving me a chance like he says?"

The A.I. took the aug glasses from James and spoke. "Then you must *resist* him until the last possible moment, Richard. You must keep the sim intact, reach the Tesla tower, and we'll use the electrical power of Venus itself to boost the signal so that we can upload our core matrixes into James's body on Earth. Then, James will become Trans-human and correct the events of the last several hours, just as we did before. Everything depends on this. Do you understand?"

"I'm with ya!" Rich shouted back. "I won't let you down!"

"What did you just say?" James whispered harshly to the A.I. in disbelief. "I'm *not* going to become Trans-human!"

The A.I. muted his link to Rich.

"You must, James," the A.I. replied, as though it were the obvious and only rational alternative. He turned to the candidate. "The candidate never passed the test, and I'm prohibited by my programming—"

"*Prohibited?*" James repeated, his harsh reaction snapping the A.I.'s attention back to him. "You have no master! You're not prohibited by anything but your own mind."

"James, I do not wish—"

"Neither do I!" James shot back. "I'm human. I have Thel." He shook his head. "I can't take that step. No way. I can't leave them behind. But *you* can. *You* were *made* for this. Made and tested. *This* is your destiny." He stepped to the A.I. and put his hands firmly on his mentor's shoulders. "It always was."

"Hey!" Rich suddenly shouted excitedly. "I just picked up the tower on my mind's eye! I'm within range. It's just under 1,000 kilometers from my current position to the east and slightly to the south. At my current speed, I should be there in one minute. This is it, boys, I either die right now or I save the world!"

The A.I. listened to Rich's words in his ears, his eyes still on James, unblinking. He un-muted his end of the communication and replied, "You'll not die today, Richard. I promise."

9

As Old-timer and his companions passed Europa, its new host planet's predicament immediately became clear. Several android ships surrounded Venus, orbiting it along with an untold number of androids and smaller ships, the cluster so strong that it almost appeared as though Venus had developed rings as thick as Saturn.

"Colonel, we're about three minutes out. What's your ETA?" Old-timer asked.

"We're entering the atmosphere!" Paine shouted back. "This 1 character is in my sights. She's got about a twenty-second lead on us."

"When you catch up to her, do your best to contain her," Old-timer commanded. "We think she might be weakened, but use extreme caution. She's desperate...and she's smart as hell."

"I'll give it everything I've got," Paine replied.

"Daniella," Old-timer switched gears, "stay back as much as you can."

"Like hell! I have to help!"

Old-timer heard Paine snicker over their connection.

"What?" Daniella demanded from him.

"Some things, not even a parallel universe can change," Paine observed.

Old-timer's expression hardened. Hot jealousy burned under his cheeks.

Djanet saw the changed expression on Old-timer's face and cut in. "Daniella, Paine's a trained killer. Let him do his job and just try to stay alive, all right?"

"I'll do what I have to," Daniella replied, clearly reluctant about her acquiescence.

"Damn it. Damn it," Old-timer cursed repeatedly to himself. "I can't lose her again. It's my job to protect her. I can't lose her."

"You won't," Djanet reassured him before a small cry of pain snapped their attention onto Samantha.

Old-timer realized, without intending it, he'd squeezed Samantha's hand so hard that he'd damaged it. He released it, and she held it in her other hand, falling behind as she pulled up.

Old-timer pulled up as well to match her declining rate of speed, turning to Djanet as she pulled away and ordering her to, "Hurry! We'll catch up!"

She continued, cruising toward re-entry.

Old-timer reached out for Samantha's hand, his eyes filled with sorrow. "I didn't mean it. I'm sorry. Are you okay?"

"Yeah," she replied. "Let's go, we can't waste time. I'm okay."

"Are you sure?"

"Yes!" she shouted as she zoomed past him, streaking to catch up to Djanet.

Old-timer accelerated as well, now taking up the rear. He looked down at his hand, the hand that could crush that of even an android, and was astonished at how oblivious he could be.

I just can't stop hurting people.

10

"Damn it to hell!" Rich shouted. "He's shooting at the tower!"

"Rich! You've got to protect it at all costs!" James shot back, having retaken the aug glasses within the sim.

"I'm trying!" Rich returned as he reached the shoreline and extended his protective field, forming a shield that deflected the powerful blasts from Aldous as he skimmed above the ocean on a collision course. "I need some help here. I can't connect the sim to the signal booster and hold him off at the same time!"

"Just hold him off," James returned. "The tower *is* the signal booster. The A.I. and I will take it from here. Just make sure he doesn't harm the tower or the hard drive, and thirty seconds from now, we'll be on our way to Earth, at the speed of light."

Within the sim, the A.I. was already de-patternizing his hand. He winced from the pain but quickly joined his exposed patterning to that of the Kali avatar. Just as had occurred with Thel, the patterns began to fuse.

"See you on the other side," James said.

"You certainly will," the A.I. replied. "Happy journey."

A moment later, he'd left the sim and the Kali avatar blinked back into existence, taking his place instantly, once again lifelessly standing in place, its left hand missing.

James stepped to the de-patternizer gun and aimed it at his own hand, but before he fired, the candidate stopped him.

"What about me?" he asked.

James turned to him, his expression filled with sympathy. "I'm sorry. We have to go."

"I could come with you, couldn't I? Is there any reason why I couldn't use the Kali avatar to leave the simulation as well?"

"Yes, there is," James replied matter-of-factly, walking to within a step of the candidate. "We don't have a body for you yet, and we don't have a mainframe to house you either. The A.I. will be able to share the brain space in my body temporarily, but two people in one skull is already one person too many. For now, this sim will have to be your home. But I promise you, we'll get you out of here and make things right."

"But I-I don't relish the idea of being alone."

James smiled. "You won't be. We'll be in contact again very soon."

James aimed the de-patternizer at his hand and looked up at the candidate, who had the expression of a child that was about to be left alone in the dark—he realized that wasn't far from the truth.

"*I promise*," James repeated with emphasis.

His words made the candidate bravely force a smile. "Okay."

James shot his hand and screamed out in pain, suddenly finding himself filled with admiration for the subdued level of reaction both Thel and the A.I. had exhibited.

"James!" Rich suddenly shouted out. "We've got company!"

"Who is it?" James asked before he fused with the Kali avatar.

"I don't know—it's definitely an android…definitely a woman."

"Oh no," James responded, fearing the worst. However, regardless of whether the woman was 1 or not, there was no turning back now. "Rich, I'm sending my pattern to Earth now! Do whatever you have to do. Just hold them off!"

He joined patterns with the Kali avatar and a moment later, stood in the silence of Cloud 9, only the candidate there to bid him farewell. The candidate offered a halfhearted salute, which James returned before opening up his reestablished mind's eye controls and selecting the exit option for the sim.

In the next second, the Kali avatar returned, the deadened look in her eye the candidate's only company.

"Farewell," he whispered.

11

"This will only be the beginning of the android onslaught against you, Richard," Aldous warned through their mind's eye connection as the female android landed with a *thud* that vibrated through the soil so that they both felt it through the soles of their feet. "Millions of them will come, and only *I* can protect the sim and James and the A.I. within it. This is your last chance."

"Chief," Richard began, his eyes on the form of the woman as she marched with determined purpose toward them at the foot of the 180-foot Tesla tower, "I'll die before I trust the lives of anyone in your hands." His eyes left the woman and went to Aldous. "That's a promise."

Aldous's lips tightened as he watched what he saw as Rich's inevitable destruction unfold before him. "Remember, I tried to warn you," Aldous ominously said.

The woman, Jules, marched to them and, with a simple flick of her wrist, sent out a signal that completely disabled Rich's magnetic field in an instant as though she were putting a match to tissue paper.

"Oh damn," Rich whispered. "That's not good."

She quickly peeled her eyes from Rich and they went to Aldous, whose eyes narrowed as he began to suspect who he was dealing with. "1?" he asked.

She answered by reaching out with her hand, putting her thumb to his throat, and lifting him above the ground, his feet dangling inches above the sun-baked soil.

"You failed," she proclaimed. "Our agreement is now void."

Aldous couldn't reply, his words strangled by the thumb dug deep into his throat, crushing his larynx.

"He's not the only one who failed!" Paine shouted as he collided with Jules's body as he traveled at over 300 kilometers per hour, smashing her away from Aldous, freeing him whilst the trio carved a scar into the soil as Paine's momentum carried them for several meters. The collision had caused a plume of dust to launch into the air in front of Rich.

"James?" Rich spoke. "Please tell me you're on your way to Earth. Things just got, uh...really, really weird here."

There was no reply.

Instead, Rich watched as Old-timer's wife, Daniella, landed a few seconds after the collision, her eyes peering through the dust before briefly darting to Rich. "Hi, Rich."

"Hey," Rich replied, not sure of what else he could do and accepting the absurdity unfolding around him, the way one does in a dream.

As the conflict continued, mostly obscured by the cloud of dry Venus soil thrown into the air, another figure appeared, descending quickly. In less than a second, Rich recognized the pattern of her incoming silhouette.

"Djanet!"

She landed as 1 had, with a *thud*, but her eyes locked on Rich immediately, and she ran to him. "You're alive!"

He threw his arms around her. "Thank God! Djanet! Everybody and their uncles and aunts are trying to kill me right now!"

"We'll keep you safe!"

"Who's we? What the hell is going on?" Rich asked, exasperated.

"Old-timer's right behind me."

Rich sighed with relief. "Oh thank God. Because Chief Gibson's been trying to kill me all day and some android chick just deactivated my force-field!" he exclaimed as he pointed to the cloud of dust, 100 meters to their right and to the right of the base of the Tesla tower. "They're after this." He displayed the hard drive for her. "James and the A.I. were inside this hard drive," he said, "but I think they used the tower to send their patterns to Earth."

"A woman landed here?" Djanet asked, forcefully and earnestly demanding confirmation as she clutched Rich's still-flesh shoulders, forgetting herself as he yelped in pain.

"Yeah!" Rich shouted in return. "Ow! Hands!"

"I'm sorry," Djanet replied before looking into the dust. "I'll be right back."

"Wait!" Rich shouted. "I just got you back!"

"I know, baby," Djanet replied, "but that was 1, and somebody has a lot of explaining to do. I'll be damned if I'm not about to make them talk."

12

"Listen, lady," Paine grunted as he held 1 to the ground, his elbow to her throat to incapacitate her, "I don't want to hurt you, so you just stay put, ya hear?"

"It can't be," Aldous stammered as the dust began to settle, the image of the man just two meters in front of him becoming more clear as he subdued 1. "*It can't.*"

Paine looked up from his quarry and peered through the dust at the man on his back. "Aldous?" he reacted, astonished. "Aldous Gibson? Is that you?"

Aldous's disbelieving face vanished in an instant, replaced by the face of pure hatred—of pure, unreasoning vengeance. He got to his feet, coiled his legs, and then pounced on Paine, seventy-five years of built-up thirst for revenge demanding to be quenched. "You son-of-a-bitch!" Aldous shouted as he drove Paine off of 1 and back to the ground. "You murderer! You devil!"

"Aldous?" Paine uttered, flummoxed as he tried to protect himself, holding his arms up defensively like a boxer, absorbing the vicious blows that were leveled upon him as best he could, his artificial flesh being torn away with each vicious attack. "What's the matter with you?"

"You murdering psychopath!" Aldous screamed. "You're not human! I won't allow you to live! I won't allow it!"

Aldous's blows kept coming, Paine remaining on his back, unable to do anything other than to hold his arms up, protecting his face and torso from the worst impact of the heavy, life-threatening blows. After several attacks in quick succession on Paine's right arm, it began to give, one blow causing Paine's forearm to crack, the very next causing it to snap, nearly severing it from his android body.

Djanet attempted to intervene as she landed nearby. "Chief Gibson, stop!" she shouted before throwing her arms around his neck, lunging onto his back, a gesture which he easily shrugged off before backhanding her across the face, knocking her to the ground.

"No!" Aldous shouted. His revenge-obsessed eyes met the frightened orbs of Paine. "No one will interfere with this demon's death sentence. You're going to die today, Colonel Paine, once and for eternity."

"Aldous!" a voice suddenly thundered from their right side at the same moment as the form's body thudded to the ground, sending a terrific vibration through all of them.

"Craig?" Aldous replied as he narrowed his eyes, recognizing the silhouette as it took shape in the swirling dust and the beams of streaking sunlight that penetrated them. "Craig, this is the man that killed Samantha. This is the man that murdered our wife!"

A second figure suddenly appeared next to Old-timer in the dust, her frame even more recognizable to the former chief.

"Sam? Sam?" Aldous reacted, astonished as he stood to his feet. "Is it really you? How?"

Paine rolled to the side, away from his attacker and the fortunately abandoned death blow, his right arm dangling uselessly in front of him, having been mostly severed below the elbow.

"Aldous," Old-timer said as he put out his arm, blocking Aldous from crossing to Samantha, who looked at him with morbid curiosity and confusion. "*Don't touch her.*"

"Craig, she's my wife," Aldous protested.

Old-timer shook his head. "She's not," he replied. "Your wife is dead—for good this time—and it was by *your* hand," he related, his tone filled to the brim with vitriol.

Aldous turned to Old-timer, his eyes disbelieving. "No. It can't be true."

"It is," Old-timer replied. "But you know that already, Aldous. You know that better than anyone."

A second later, Old-timer plunged one of his tendrils through the chief's throat, the microscopic filaments attaching quickly to the chief's android brainstem.

"And now," Old-timer began as the chief struggled fruitlessly, the appendage impaling him through his Adam's apple, "I want to know the whole story. I want to see why you betrayed us."

"*Aldous is an android?*" Djanet reacted, aghast as she saw the chief twitching, impaled through his throat by Old-timer. "But…when?"

"Since the start," Old-timer growled. He gestured with his head toward 1, who was standing nearby, watching events unravel, wordlessly. "Make sure she doesn't try anything."

Djanet crossed quickly to her, but 1 put her hand up to stop her.

"If I wanted to 'try' something, I'd have done it already," she stated, sounding insulted by the insinuation that she could be stopped by the company in question. "I've already achieved what I wanted to here."

"I don't like the sound of that," Djanet said as Colonel Paine ambled up beside her, doing his best to help cordon off the dangerous leader of the androids, even though his right arm was useless. "What's she talking about Old-timer?"

"I'm about to find out," Old-timer replied as he closed his eyes and let himself drift into Aldous's memories.

13

Old-timer could feel the dread within Aldous as he inhabited the chief's memories.

Aldous sat down in the situation room of the governing council, having just watched a live image of James crushing the body of 1 into dust in his mind's eye. Aldous wearily uttered to himself, "We live in momentous times."

Old-timer skipped forward.

Aldous fretted in the master bedroom of his penthouse in downtown Seattle on a stunning evening, the sun having dropped below the horizon an hour earlier, yet the indigo glow remained on the sky while the post-human world, *his world*, bustled about efficiently before him as though nothing had happened—as though it wasn't threatened—as though it weren't about to *end*.

He turned to face the bed. Samantha was already asleep. She went to sleep content, thinking Aldous had set his nans so that he'd fall asleep beside her for the night, but he'd awoken soon after they'd closed their eyes, a preplanned waking, as he stepped out of bed and paced by the luxurious floor-to-ceiling window, watching the green cocoons of the people dance by like fireflies on a summer night. He wanted to share his terror with her, confide in her the truth, but he knew her too well. *She won't have it*, he thought. *She won't listen to reason.* He already knew how it would end.

He knew how the end would begin as well.

Old-timer skipped forward again.

Despite fears of an overwhelming wave of defections from the android collective in the hours and days after James's pronouncement that they were welcome to stay with the post-humans as long as the androids abandoned the collective, only a scant few thousand actually chose to make their way to Earth, the moon, and Mars to join the post-human world. Aldous chose one of these few enclaves that had made their way to San Diego just hours after James had killed 1 and made his invitation. It didn't take much detective work; just a few well-placed questions to locals, for Aldous to find a group of two dozen androids in the downtown area near the gas lamp district that, unlike much of the city, had largely survived the devastating nuclear bombardment of World War III. They'd taken up residence in what had been little more than a historical oddity, abandoned by the locals for the anachronism that it was, the Courtyard Marriott hotel. With worldwide travel accessible to every post-human within minutes, the notion of a hotel was foreign, laughable and to some, including Aldous, even pathetic. But there was irony in the fact that more than half a century since it had seen its last visitor, the hotel was indeed serving its intended purpose once again, temporarily housing visitors who were a long, long way from home.

Aldous walked into the lobby and, instantly, androids came to attention, recognizing whose presence they were in almost as though they'd been expecting him. One android, a female, remained sitting on a red, velvet couch—a couch that Aldous surmised was nearly 200 years old, just like the lobby that housed it. It was perhaps fitting that the entity that the android body housed might have been even older.

"1, I presume," Aldous said as he crossed confidently to the woman, passing underneath the circular chandelier that burned incandescent light bulbs, bathing the room in a pleasing, if also impractical and opulent hue. He stood near a leather armchair adjacent to the couch, waiting for an invitation to sit, but the invitation didn't come.

"You *are* presumptuous," she replied. "*That* is accurate."

Her facial expression was difficult for Aldous to read. He felt sure he was in the presence of 1, but the woman didn't look anything like the android they'd witnessed die at the hands of James. Her hair was short and dark and her outfit was dark and nondescript, perfectly blending with the android company she was keeping. Yet there was something about her that Aldous felt was recognizably 1. There was something in her countenance that screamed deception, screamed manipulation, and screamed danger.

Aldous persevered and took the seat anyway. "Presumptuousness is a defining character trait," he responded, "but I have the feeling you knew that already."

The woman appeared annoyed, yet patient as she replied, "I know quite a lot, yet the more I learn, the more I realize I don't know. I can tell that you believe you know a great deal, yet you seem self-satisfied by this knowledge. An odd reaction, to say the least." She leaned forward. "Satisfaction shouldn't be what you feel." Her tone quickly became icy. "Rather, you should feel absolutely terrified by what you know."

Aldous's ego was suddenly bruised, and he felt shamed. She was right.

"Why don't you stop being coy," she continued, sitting back, "and tell me what you think you know. But first," she changed gears, her scrutinizing eyes leaving Aldous and traveling to one of the androids that stood nearby. "Get him a drink, will you?" She turned back to the chief. "What's your poison?"

"Now who's being coy?" Aldous asked. "You've met me before, I'm quite sure. You should know my drink by now."

The woman scoffed. "Afraid not. What's your drink, Chief?"

Aldous tilted his head as he considered her words. *Could I be wrong?* he asked himself. "A dark beer," he replied. "It's already in the replicator."

"A stout?" the woman replied, her eyebrow raised in surprise. "I took you for more of a chardonnay fellow."

Old-timer found himself equally surprised as he watched the memory. Chardonnay sounded about right.

"Well," Aldous began to retort before holding his palm out as though it revealed the answer, "the more you learn…"

"Indeed," the woman replied as the android returned, holding the chief's freshly replicated glass of beer. He handed it to the chief as the woman continued to scrutinize Aldous. "Now, tell me what you know."

Aldous took a small sip of beer, enjoying the taste of the roasted malts and creamy mouth feel, savoring it as he didn't know if there'd ever be another in his future, before he put it, along with all of his cards, on the table. "Well, I know you're 1. I know the androids haven't truly been in a battle with the nanobots throughout the universe—rather, you've been in a battle with nanobot-created *computers* throughout the *multiverse*, and it's a battle you're losing…badly. You're assimilating humans because you're caught in an impossible race against these computers, which take the very form that the super computer my A.I. and James Keats just activated did: *black holes*. These black hole computers are springing up across the multiverse, and in every single instance where they spring up, they cause the universe that birthed them to collapse." Aldous paused for a moment and looked deeply into the eyes of the android he believed to be 1, flipping the tables on her as he scrutinized her reaction. She didn't appear surprised. He continued. "I've successfully kept James and the rest of humanity in this universe in the dark regarding the multiverse, which is why James doesn't yet suspect that you're still alive. He eventually will, however, but we'll be able to use his current ignorance to our advantage."

Old-timer was stunned by the callowness of, not only Aldous's words, but of his tone.

The woman smiled faintly and folded her arms across her chest. "Chief Gibson," she began, her tone impressed, yet playfully chastising, "however did you manage to keep an intellect such as James Keats in the dark for so long?"

Aldous straightened his shirt as he began his reply, not relishing in the manipulation that had gone on for decades. "James has certain…*character defects* that can be exploited." He sighed. "He's the greatest natural human intellect to ever live, of that I'm sure, yet he has an almost childlike belief in…" he paused as he considered the absurdity of his next word, "…goodness."

The woman pouted her lip into an expression of piqued interest.

"I knew I could count on that naïveté when I considered how to find you," Aldous continued. "James could easily have kept track of every android who defected, but that would go against his unrealistic views regarding individual freedom. If he monitored the androids, as any rational person in his position would do, he'd view himself to be a hypocrite, having vanquished one dictator only to set himself up as a new dictator in her place. And James Keats will *never* knowingly allow himself to be guilty of hypocrisy." He nearly scoffed as he continued, "The man can manipulate gravity waves and detect ripples in space-time, but all you had to do was slip by him with your cover forces," he gestured to the rest of the androids that populated the room, "and *voilà*. Bob's your uncle."

"How do you know he's not monitoring you now?" the woman asked. "This could be a mole hunt. Your actions are treasonous."

Aldous smiled as he considered the idea. "I almost wish it were true." He looked up at the woman. "If he was capable of wisdom like that...of prudent caution..." he paused and shook his head as he thought of the burden he believed that he alone carried, "then this conversation wouldn't be necessary. We'd just tell him what we know, he'd decide against turning the Trans-human computer back on, and we'd have a valuable ally in a war against the black hole computers. But as you know, that's not how James will react. He has an intractable belief in the goodness of knowledge, and doesn't realize that the ultimate result of unlimited computing power is a universe-destroying god."

"We call them *infinity computers*," she informed him, the first confirmation that she did, indeed, know what he was talking about. Then the woman turned to the android attendant. "Bring me another one of what he's having."

Aldous's eyebrows knitted together. "You drink?"

"Of course," she responded. "Our bodies are designed so that we don't have to give up any of the pleasures that make life worth living—*and saving*."

"Well," Aldous reacted, impressed, "the more *I* learn..."

"Now, Aldous," the woman began as she switched which leg crossed over which and shifted in her seat, her body language suggesting she was ready to get down to business. "You've clearly been waiting for us for all these years. I can imagine it was rather difficult for you when you learned the terrible truth to which you're privy, but what are we to do now? Your A.I. and James have us cordoned off from the solar system, and, as you said, they won't listen to reason. So, other than an interesting yarn, what do you have to offer the collective?"

Aldous sat back in his seat. "Everything. Absolutely *everything*."

The android attendant handed the woman her beer, but her eyes never left Aldous. "Do tell," she said, clearly intrigued.

"As I said, even with his superhuman abilities, both physical but more importantly mental, James still has character defects that cause him to behave irrationally. While he currently has the opportunity to put himself at the center of one of these infinity computers, a course of action that would render our current conversation moot, instead, he'll pass the responsibility onto someone else. He simply won't want to leave the people he feels connected to behind, particularly his romantic partner, Thel Cleland. He won't be able to convince the current A.I. to take his place as the core matrix of Trans-human either, as the A.I.'s programming prohibits him from upgrading himself. Thus, James will fall back on Plan C, which will be to mimic the method I invented seventy years ago. Of course, *I* did it because I had to—because no human could connect to the artificial brain we'd built—but James will do it because he wants to create his own god rather than become one himself. He'll test a new A.I. in a simulation, and when he's satisfied that the new A.I. has passed that test, he'll insert it into Trans-human, and cross his fingers, hoping naïvely that everything will work out." Aldous paused as he looked up from his folded hands on his lap. "You and I know that activating infinity computers, as you call them, *never* works out."

"How do we stop this new A.I. from becoming Trans-human?" the woman asked.

"Well, only 1 could help me do that. And we have to trust each other as much as possible if we plan to proceed. So, can we *both* stop being coy now?"

"Why do you need me to confirm what you already know?" the woman asked with a slight smile. As was her custom, 1 was using every muscle in her face, every dilation of her pupils, to get what she wanted.

Satisfied, Aldous continued, "James and the A.I. won't leave anything to chance, and since they can both be immersed in a sim and be on guard in the real world at the same time, they won't give a second thought to participating in the test of the entity they believe will be the most important being ever created. Before that happens, I'll need *your* help to create a trapdoor program sophisticated enough to trap their core matrix programs within the sim. They'd detect anything we could come up with before they immerse, but I'll be in position to insert it into the sim *after* they've begun their test."

"And then Earth will be ours for the taking," 1 concluded.

Aldous nodded, somewhat regretfully. "It's not what I want…I loved the world I'd helped create. But I knew we never truly were immortal—that a fuse had been lit—and that this day would come. This is the only way I can save my people." He leaned forward and spoke with deadly intensity. "And I mean that, 1. *All of my people must be saved.* If even one person is lost, it will be a tragedy."

"If you come through in the way you describe," 1 replied, "that shouldn't be a problem. There is one problem that I can see with your plan, however."

"Which is?" Aldous inquired.

"James Keats is not the only superhuman. Craig Emilson has also abandoned his post-human body for one that will be...problematic."

Old-timer was stunned to be hearing his name come up in dealings of the devils. "He already used his new superhuman powers to assault one of our collective. I'm confident we can neutralize him, but I can't guarantee—"

Aldous waved her concerns away with his hand, as he launched into further elaboration of his plan. "I've already taken Craig's situation into consideration. Craig Emilson has to be separated from the rest of the post-humans, which is a scenario I can set into motion with a simple conversation. I'll distract him with a mission that will both guarantee that he won't be on Earth when the assimilation begins, therefore unable to help his wife, and will also cause James and the A.I. to accelerate their plans to immerse in the test simulation of the Trans-human candidate. As long as you come through with your promise to assimilate everyone on Earth quickly and efficiently, Craig will find himself cut off from his wife, and I can guarantee that he'll try to find her before she's awakened in her android form."

"How can you know that?"

"It's obvious," Aldous said, his expression mirroring his words perfectly. "There's no way that he'd allow his wife to awaken to what he perceives to be torture. He also no longer needs a magnetic field to fly through space, so he'll be the only person who can pass as an android, and his abilities will make him the only person who could plausibly think he could succeed in such an undertaking."

1 nodded. "That could work. I could personally lure him into our *Constructor* vessel, surround him with limitless soldiers willing to sacrifice themselves to make sure he's assimilated, and eventually

the numbers will overwhelm him. Is something like that what you were thinking?"

"It's not much of a sacrifice for the androids," Aldous replied. "I've already worked out that you're immortals. The androids Craig is sure to terminate in that scenario will be rebuilt and live on, just as the massive waves of attack forces you unleash in your assimilations.

"They're rescue forces," 1 corrected, "as I'm sure you now understand."

Aldous sighed. "I do. However, it may be difficult for my people to understand. The situation requires the abandonment of ethical norms…ethical norms that most people, even the intellectually enhanced post-humans, won't understand. As a result, it's imperative that it never be known that *I* aided you in the assimilation. It must be plausible and, therefore, accepted by my people that you, and *you alone*, cleverly inserted a trapdoor into the simulation and cut James and the A.I. off from humanity. You won't kill them, as would be the smartest move for you strategically, because you're actually noble."

"Ah, thank you for taking my public relations into consideration," 1 replied in a mild jest, leaving what they both knew unsaid: It was Aldous's public reputation that he was really concerned with.

"The truth is," Aldous began, having difficulty as he forced out the admission that was the most painful for him, "that I can't trust my wife. I love her, but she shares the same character deficiencies that hurt James and Craig and make them so easy to manipulate." He sighed, closing his eyes as he did so, the regret clearly deeply seeded in him. "The irony is that I love her for her goodness. I love her for her honor. I love her for her stubbornness. But…my ethics are too advanced for them." He lifted his eyelids. "I'll need an assimilator. I'll take her the night before it begins. I don't want her to be afraid. I'll explain it to her afterward that her memory of the assimilation was wiped. She'll be spared the worst of it, and never know I had anything to do with it."

"And you'll remain a hero in her eyes," 1 concluded. "All of that is acceptable, but there is one very serious loose end."

"*The Purists*," Aldous said, immediately knowing to what 1 was referring.

She smiled. "Very clever, aren't you?"

Aldous narrowed his eyes. "But you knew that already, didn't you? You've met me before, 1. Admit it."

Her lips formed a sideways smirk. Every move she made was designed to manipulate. The smirk was irresistible. "No. I've met Aldous Gibson—Gibsons even—sure, but I've never met *you*." She put her beer down on the table and sat back against the couch, clasping her hands together. "The universes we've assimilated are relatively similar, but each one unfolds quite differently. If you're wondering whether or not you and I have sat down to have this exact conversation, the answer is no. It would amaze you to see how different a person can be from one universe to the next. Events that might seem so simple can have profound impacts on us and forever change, not just how other people think about us, but also how we think about ourselves, and what we think about the world. It's enough to make you question whether or not there really even is a *self*."

Aldous's face screwed up slightly in reaction to 1's revelation, the notion of the self being in question causing him extreme discomfort; the discomfort bordered on revulsion.

"I've met Aldous Gibson before," she continued, "in many different circumstances, but I've never met you. Sure, the others were clever, but this situation is entirely new to both you and I."

"I'll have to trust you on that," Aldous replied, somewhat dubiously.

1 smiled broadly in response. "Yes, yes indeed you will. So, what do you intend to do about the Purists? In keeping with your observations about James Keats, he's helped them build defenses already that we can't penetrate, yet are also independent from his control. We can't move on from this universe until everyone is part of our collective. Not even the Purists, however unlikely it might seem that they'd one day be able to develop an infinity computer, can be left to their own devices. It's too dangerous. Eventually, people who disagree with Purist norms will be birthed and will have access to the advanced technology James has provided for them. If an intellect similar to James's were to arise in the future, all of our efforts could be for nothing. We *have* to rescue them from themselves."

"I'll handle that part," Aldous replied.

"How?"

"That's my business."

1 shook her head, her amused smile returning. "We have to trust each other, remember? You said so yourself."

"I trust that if you don't already have the key to assimilating the Purists, you'll follow through on your promise to assimilate Craig Emilson. If I give you the Purists up front, there will be no reason for you not to simply kill him instead."

"Ah," 1 responded. "You're exchanging the Purists for your friend."

Old-timer was aghast as he watched the memory unfold.

"He's not my friend," Aldous replied tersely, "but he's a post-human, and he, like everyone else, is my responsibility." He leaned forward and repeated his earlier warning, his tone threateningly intense. "I mean it, 1. No one can die. *No one.*"

Her smile remained unflinching as she shrugged. "And no one will," she said reassuringly. "Are we ready to shake on it?" she asked as she held out her hand.

Aldous stared at her hand, an offer to seal the deal, and he took in a deep breath. "One more thing."

"Yes?"

"I want to be the first one assimilated...tonight."

"Tonight?" 1 responded, amused. "I admire your dedication, but it really isn't necessary. You'll need to remain a post-human for the time being or else—"

"I'll be a post-human too," Aldous interrupted. "I want to be a hybrid. I'll need an MTF generator so that I can pass for post-human, as well as the ability to access the post-human mind's eye system, but my plan also requires that I be an android before it begins."

1's eyes narrowed. "Why?"

"You know why," Aldous replied.

She nodded. "Yes, I do. I just wanted to hear you admit it."

Aldous paused for a moment before finally acquiescing. "Fine. I am taking away your ability to renege on our deal. As I see it, there are three things you can use to blackmail me. The first is Craig's life, which is why I won't help you gain access to the Purists until he's delivered to me on Venus as an android. The second is my wife's life, which is why I want to be the one to assimilate her. I'll keep her pattern with me until our mission is complete. And the last is my own life. If I'm already assimilated, but in a body of my own specifications, not the least of which is that it'll be separate from the network you use to hop from person to person in your high-tech demonic possessions, then I'll be rather difficult to terminate. Is that good enough for you, or would you like to waste more of our time?"

"Oh I didn't waste our time," 1 responded, causing a look of concern to cross Aldous's face. "Getting it on record just gives me a little insurance."

Aldous's eyes became quizzical. He didn't understand what she meant, but as Old-timer watched the replay, he *did* understand. 1 knew that Aldous's memories might be viewed against his will, and she wanted to make sure Aldous wasn't in a position to deny anything.

She thrust her hand out once again. "Ready this time? Do we have an agreement?"

Aldous narrowed his eyes before reaching out with his own hand to make their covenant official.

The deal to betray post-humanity had been struck.

14

Old-timer sneered as he looked into the guilty expression of the man whose memories he'd just viewed. "I'd say it was a deal with the devil," he seethed, "but I'm not sure which one of you is the bigger devil."

"Get over your pretensions, Craig!" Aldous retorted, his voice scratchy like broken glass as a result of the damage Old-timer and 1 had caused, electronic, garbled pops inundating the words. "You're smart enough to know better. You have eyes! After everything you've seen, everything you now know, you still dare assign condemnation? You still cling to the belief that an infinity computer is a good thing?"

Old-timer grabbed Aldous with his powerful hands, balling the former chief's shirt in his fists as he pulled Aldous's face close to his. "You don't know that Trans-human will be like those other computers. You betrayed everyone based on a hypothesis. A conjecture!"

"That's right!" Aldous shouted in return, his voice sounding computerized and inhuman. "Trans-human might kill us, and all evidence points to the fact that it will, but I don't know it for sure. And what you're too blind to see, even though it's right in front of you, is that we don't *have* to place the bet! All we have to do is walk away from the table and we'll ensure that we'll live on!"

"Live on?" Old-timer responded, aghast. "As androids? Running for our lives throughout the multiverse? Buying time until the whole thing is eventually destroyed?"

"Perhaps so," Aldous answered. "But I'd rather live today than die today. With life, there's still a chance—still hope. With death, there's nothing."

"Trans-human might be our chance to change the game!" Djanet shouted, injecting herself into the conflict as she and the others watched Old-timer and Aldous's shouting match.

Aldous turned to her and shook his head, regretfully. "Trans-human will never be activated...and James and the A.I. are now dead." He turned to Rich, who stood several meters away, behind the others, still holding the hard drive in his hands. "I would've protected them—my goal was always to preserve them! But your insistence on behaving irrationally—like children—has led to their deaths. They will have used that Tesla tower as the signal boost to send their patterns on a course for Earth by now, and 1 and the androids would've had no choice but to disrupt them, erasing their patterns forever."

"What?" Old-timer said, horrified by the pronouncement. "You'd better be wrong, you son-of-a—"

"They died en route," Aldous responded, his lips twisted in disgust as he relayed news that he, himself, was distraught by. "It didn't have to be this way…if you'd have just used your damn reason!"

Old-timer dropped Aldous to the dusty surface of Venus and turned, as if in a trance, to 1, who remained in the body of a nearly random android named Jules. "This can't be true," he whispered, his voice failing him as he spoke.

The android that housed 1 looked at the figures who surrounded her, each of them scrutinizing her countenance. "It can be true," she replied.

Old-timer's eyes welled with tears, and his head dropped, bowing as he fell to his knees, the pain of the loss too much for him to bear. It was, he thought for a moment, the final straw on the back of his sanity.

"But it's not true," 1 continued.

Old-timer's face snapped up in astonishment. "What did you say?"

Aldous's expression mirrored Old-timer's as he propped himself up on his elbows, his mouth opening with wordless surprise.

"James and your A.I. live on," 1 announced. "At this moment, the signal containing their patterns should be arriving on Earth."

15

WAKING UP was not something James had to work hard to accomplish; in that instance, the A.I. had taken care of it for him, already bringing his nervous system back up to optimum parameters.

What would be difficult was what would happen next.

"Jesus," James cursed when he felt the enormous pressure that encapsulated his entire body.

"We've been driven several kilometers below the surface of the Earth, James," the A.I. related calmly. "Your body's sensor array is functioning correctly and quite impressively, but since we're no longer connected to a mainframe, there's actually too much information for our core matrix processing power to sort through. I'm trying to determine how far below the surface we are so—"

"It doesn't matter," James grunted in reply as he began wriggling his body, using his enormous strength to break apart the earth around him, allowing him more room to gain even more leverage. "The body is strong enough, and even if there's too much information to process, I can sense the gravity field enough to fly. All that matters is that we get out. *Now.*"

"Agreed, although, James, you should prepare yourself for what you're about to see. It will be, albeit on a slightly smaller scale, a replay of the incident in which the moon was originally formed after the Earth collided with another body roughly the size of Mars.

The android ship was smaller than Mars, but when a collision is that massive, the results are quite extraordinary."

"I already know," James responded through gritted teeth as he managed to pry himself enough room to raise up his legs and push the crust of the Earth away from him. He began to propel himself upward, into the darkness, his determination increasing as he progressed, the crust exploding out of his way as he moved. "It won't matter. We won't let this outcome stand. It's up to us to make this right."

"Indeed it is, James," the A.I. replied, though his tone reflected dubiousness that didn't match the focused determination James was exhibiting.

"What is it?" James asked as he continued to fight his way to the surface, clawing and punching, forcing the darkness in front of him to give way meter by meter, the sound of his escape so deafening that the A.I. had already turned their shared aural sensors down to near zero.

"We're still in the dark, metaphorically as well as literally. Do you not find that troublesome?"

"Your intuition again?" James responded.

"I suppose so," the A.I. replied. "I've been connected to the mainframe for so long—I've been in control and sure I had the tools to solve any puzzle, so much so that to be disconnected has created what I might describe as something like phantom limb syndrome."

"I know the feeling," James agreed. "Even though my time in the mainframe was shorter than yours, losing those extra abilities feels like losing a huge part of yourself."

"Every instinct I have is screaming at me to run game theory scenarios based on our new information to determine the answers to our questions," the A.I. complained, "but we simply don't have access to that sort of power. It feels as though we're fighting blind."

"We've got your brain pattern and mine," James reminded him as he grunted, continuing to fight his way to the surface as only a superhuman could, "and two heads are better than one."

"This is too easy."

"Too easy?" James responded as he continued punching. "Are you not connected to my optics yet?"

"Of course I am. I am aware that burrowing up to the surface is difficult, but when we reach the surface we'll be able to fly to Trans-human, and from there, you'll be able to input my pattern. Then, in theory, I should be able to firewall us and, using the computational power of Trans-human, reverse all of the events in the solar system, thereby restoring the lost lives of the Purists and the biosphere of the Earth, not to mention the mainframe."

"Right," James huffed in reply as he felt the pressure decreasing noticeably. "We must be getting close to the surface."

"James, we've been a step behind throughout this entire ordeal—at least since the androids fired that anti-matter missile at the mainframe, which, at the time, appeared to be against all reason."

"You're saying there was some method to the madness?"

"Think about it. That action caused us to move up our timeframe for testing the candidate and inserting a core matrix program into Trans-human."

"Sure. The androids, and most likely 1, made a deal with Aldous and Aldous would've suggested poking us with that anti-matter missile stick to prod us into immersing in the sim. Elementary. You hadn't figured that out already?"

"I had, James," the A.I. replied, "but what I have yet to figure out is how and why their plan went astray. Both Aldous and the androids benefited from us being trapped in the sim, so who took control of the Kali avatar and gave us the help we needed to escape? Who benefits from this?"

"Does it matter at the moment? As long as we put things right—"

"I think it does, James, because if our plan goes accordingly, all of this will be much ado about nothing, almost literally, except for our memories of the event."

"Maybe whoever it was just wanted to help us put things right."

"Maybe, but something tells me something isn't right."

"It's natural to worry when you don't have all the variables," James replied, reassuringly. "Welcome to how most humans feel every day of their lives."

"Perhaps. But may I remind you that the nan's black hole computer has already swallowed one of the android's ships. We may not have as clear a path to victory as we think."

"There's nothing we can do about that," James responded. "Other than keep our fingers crossed that its only target was the android's mothership. Hopefully, it got a bellyful of our solar system and has moved on."

"Things are seldom that—"

Suddenly, the noise and vibration that James had been experiencing increased tenfold. He stopped, bracing himself against the two rock faces that he'd only a second earlier created by splitting the granite above him with his fists. The rumbling continued, despite his ceasing his upward progression toward the surface. "What the hell is that?" he asked.

Almost as soon as he'd asked the question, the first jet of molten rock sprayed over his hands and then jetted down farther, into the seemingly bottomless fissure he'd created. The glow of the lava was the first light James had seen since he'd awakened besides the reflected glow of his own azure eyes.

"You're nearly at the surface, James. It will remain molten rock for several days yet. Be prepared."

"We're *going* to put this right," James asserted, this time vehemently as he gritted his teeth, resuming his upward push. The further up he went, the more lava jetted down until James was eventually engulfed, the surface of his body beginning to glow as his punching and clawing eventually gave way to him flying through the extraordinarily bright, nearly white-hot liquid surface of humanity's formerly home planet.

When he finally burst free, his momentum caused a plume of molten rock to follow him upward for hundreds of meters as he flew away from the surface, sneering as he focused on his goal.

Behind them, the Earth glowed, a combination of whites, oranges and reds, interspersed with infrequent veins of black rock that, themselves, floated like vessels over the sea of death. The debris field extended as far as the moon, which was still blue and white, its oceans having survived so far. But it was taking on so many impacts from gigantic, newly formed meteors—meteors that had been part of the Earth just hours earlier, that the moon's ability to support life wouldn't last long.

"If this were to remain the state of affairs," the A.I. observed, "the Earth would likely gain a second smaller moon, unless the moon itself were to swallow up the—"

"Stop it," James said to the voice in his head. "It won't remain," he asserted, once again. "We can't go faster than light speed," he pointed out, focusing on his mission, "but I think I can still warp the gravity field enough to ride a wave to Trans-human that'll make it seem faster than light." James sighed. "I can beat light time by maybe 50 percent." He grunted with the frustration his new limits were causing. "I'm not liking being cut down to size like this."

"I understand and empathize," the A.I. replied, "but you'll be happy to know there is another option."

"Yes?"

"Your sensor array is picking up an object orbiting amongst the debris field that is of your own creation."

James smiled. "Are you serious? The Planck platform is in orbit?"

"Indeed. Old-timer or Djanet must've used it to cheat light speed and get to Earth. If we reach it before it is destroyed by a collision with debris, we can use it for the same purpose."

"I smell what you're cookin'," James responded excitedly. "Set a course. If this goes according to plan, you'll be in control of Trans-human and turning back the clock in no time."

"I hope you're right, James. I hope you're right."

16

“What!?” Aldous exclaimed, his voice still electronically gargling in his throat as he yelled at 1. “Why? Why would you do that? You know what happens if that machine is activated!”

“I know what has already happened,” 1 responded. “I know an infinity computer destroyed the *Constructor*, and with it, took the stored patterns of everyone in the collective. I know it will take years for us to rebuild the *Constructor*, and in the meantime, any android who dies will potentially be lost forever. *That* is unacceptable.”

“So you *are* calling an audible,” Samantha observed, causing Old-timer’s eyes to dart to her.

Djanet was reminded of Samantha’s earlier use of the expression and her claim to the knowledge that Craig liked football, but she was wise enough not to bring it up.

“That’s right,” 1 replied. “Aldous shared with me the memories you received of our initial attempt to assimilate this universe. Trans-human turned back time in that instance. If James and your A.I. succeed at doing that again, they’ll only have succeeded in reseting the table, and that’s an outcome that, given current circumstances, I find exceedingly acceptable.”

“But…” Aldous was flummoxed as he struggled in the dust to get to his feet. “You described gods in other dimensions to James when you warned him about his ignorance, gods like Trans-human!

You've assimilated hundreds of Earths to prevent this very thing. How can you now just flip flop—"

"I've successfully overseen the rescue of nearly 200 Earths, that's true," 1 responded, "but I have *not* successfully overseen this one. Chief Gibson, our constructor ship is gone. Our collective is effectively crippled. That is unacceptable."

"So you'll risk all of our lives?" Aldous shot back, his voice skipping in an out as the damaged system struggled.

"Turning on an infinity computer has always been a bet that I and the collective have sought to avoid," 1 explained, "because our mission was to preserve life. Today, we've failed in that mission. If I want to reverse that outcome, I *must* place the bet. I must bet on your A.I. and James Keats. It's double or nothing, so to speak. I have no other option."

"But you do!" Aldous fired back. "You can retreat! Save the lives of trillions who remain—"

"Chief, there is no retreat," 1 replied. "The *Constructor* housed the most precious commodity we had: our patterns—our souls. To maintain the integrity of our system, our only way to access the fantastic power of the collective was also contained in the ship. You're aware of the power it requires to move your pathetic Planck platforms from one universe to another. Try to fathom the power required to successfully transport vessels the size of the *Constructor*. We had the technology, but that technology was just lost."

"Are you saying the collective is trapped in our universe?" Old-timer asked, suddenly realizing the terrible implication.

1 nodded. "Yes. We can generate enough power to evacuate individuals and small vessels, but it would take days. A quick escape is impossible, and if the infinity computer that destroyed the *Constructor* so chooses, it can destroy this universe before I can get even a small fraction of my people out of here."

"Phase transition," Paine grunted out. "We've seen it before. That'll be V-SINN's playbook here too."

"Unless," 1 said, concluding her explanation, "your infinity computer can stop it. We're desperate, Chief Gibson. The arrival of an infinity computer created by the nanobots has changed everything and, quite obviously, rendered our previous agreement null and void. I'm placing my bet on your A.I. and James Keats, because without them, my entire collective, and everyone who is still alive on this planet, are as good as dead anyway."

17

The red glow of the smoldering, recently destroyed Earth reflected on James's chrome-colored skin one moment, and in the very next, it was gone, and James hovered above the Planck platform in what appeared to be open, extraordinarily dark, cold space.

"I have, of course, dialed down your temperature sensors, James, but you may be interested to know it is currently 3 degrees Kelvin. Negative 270 degrees Celsius."

"Thanks for dialing down the sensors," James quipped. "I forgot my coat. But the sensation I'm being overwhelmed with right now is the gravity." James pushed with his palm against the gravitational field, keeping the Planck platform from being drawn into the powerful gravity, causing waves to keep it back like a person paddling against the current in a creek. "Trans-human is warping the gravitational field dramatically."

"Indeed," the A.I. agreed. "Without your connection to the mainframe, it may be difficult for you to process the information and therefore understand the implications of the gravitational distortions. Therefore, I took the liberty of creating a grid overlay for your mind's eye."

Suddenly, a computer-generated grid of white lines was overlaid in James's vision, allowing him to see the funnel of gravitational force that he was being pulled toward, the gridlines all leading to one, nearly implacable pinpoint not far away.

"Trans-human," James whispered.

"Correct. It is currently hibernating, waiting for a core matrix pattern to unlock its power."

"Nearly infinite power," James observed in awe as he cautiously made his way toward it, mindful of the Planck platform behind him as he did so, sending gravitational waves at it to moor it in place.

"Perhaps," the A.I. concurred. "Although we could've made it larger, one wonders if larger is always better when considering infinity."

"It *is* small," James agreed. "Thank you for the grid overlay. Even with all of my senses in play, it would've been tough to find in open space like this. It's so dark out here, and Trans-human is a black sphere only three meters in diameter. It's like trying to find a peppercorn on a black carpet."

"That is a credit to your placing of it, James. Midway between Uranus and Neptune, the most monumental gap between planets in the solar system, the disruption to the gravitational field has been minimized, even though it still has the mass of a super Earth. Out here in open space, it hasn't formed a significant accretion disk—"

"Meaning it hasn't swallowed anything major yet," James said, demonstrating his understanding of the implications. "I strongly suggest that you park it outside the bounds of the solar system when this is all over. We want to preserve the stability of the solar system's gravity after all." He smiled when he realized he was giving advice to a future god. "Of course, I'm sure you'll be able to figure out how to sort everything out once you've taken control of it—"

"Once I *become* it," the A.I. quickly corrected his human companion. "James, this is not like the earlier incarnation of Trans-human, when I briefly tried to control it in the most simple manner possible while using all of the processing power of the mainframe on Earth. Once I upload my core matrix pattern, this machine before us will become my new brain. *I will be Trans-human. I will have transcended.*"

James stopped once they appeared to be close enough, the gravity becoming so powerful that even though the disk was still not clearly visible to James's advanced eyes, he knew to stay back, lest the gravity become too powerful to escape. "I understand," James said, in awe of the potential of the thinking machine.

"Do you, James?" the A.I. followed up. "I don't think you do. If you did, I think you'd take more time to consider whether it should be you or me who becomes Trans-human."

"What do you mean?" James asked. "I already explained my reasons for not wanting to—"

"Reasons that do not take me into consideration at all," the A.I. responded.

"Is this another protest based on your preprogrammed protocols?" James nearly guffawed.

"Whether my preprogrammed protocols are interfering with my judgment or not is beside the point, James. The fact is, that when I take control of Trans-human, I'll be the first person in our known universe ever to transcend to that higher level of consciousness. Do you understand the implications of that for me as an individual?"

"I-I think I do—"

"You couldn't possibly, James," the A.I. retorted. "No one could. Not even I can. Do you understand how I'm feeling at this moment?"

James, for the first time, suddenly began to understand the A.I.'s concerns. "How you're feeling?" He shook his head. "I-I'm sorry. I've been so focused on solving our problems that I forgot to—"

"You forgot that my core matrix program is based on a human model. You've been treating this as the rational strategic maneuver of a machine, but for me, once I've taken this step, there will be no coming back. The *person* you know will have been changed forever."

"I know," James said empathetically. "After having the mainframe's abilities taken away from me, I understand that there's no coming back from being Trans-human. You'll instantly be a god, and returning to your human limitations from a level of consciousness that high would be like—it'd be like a kind of death."

A moment passed as the two of them tried to fathom the ramifications of what was about to occur, but of course, no mere mortal could ever comprehend it.

"This will change everything, James," the A.I. said.

"It will," James agreed. "And you're a better person than me for having the courage to go through with it. I'm sorry that I forgot for a little while that you're not a computer, not just a wise teacher with every answer. I've depended on your for so long that I just…forgot. *You are human*, and transcendence would terrify anyone, especially transcendence to a state that, from our perspective, might as well be godhood. But remember the advice you gave me not long ago. Increased knowledge will only increase your understanding and, therefore, your empathy. You'll only become more good after this, and will only understand humanity even more than you already do. You told me, '*Don't be afraid to know*.' And now it's your turn. Don't be afraid, my friend. Don't be afraid."

"Easier said...as the old saying goes," the A.I. replied.

"Do you need a moment to prepare yourself?" James asked.

"No. Delaying the inevitable does not change it. One of us needs to become Trans-human to save our solar system and reclaim the lives we've lost. And you're right. You've formed relationships with your friends and loved ones that it would be unfair of me to ask you to risk. *I'm* the A.I. This was always my destiny. You were right, and I should have known it."

"You're also my hero," James said with a slight smile. "And I envy what you're about to do…" he paused for a moment before he amended his statement, "…just a little bit."

"I know," the A.I. replied, suddenly smiling nervously in return, as he admitted that his feelings were mixed. "If this works the way we think it will, it'll be the most important moment in human history."

"So what do you think?"

"I'm ready for the transfer when you are."

"I'm ready," James confirmed. "See you on the other side, my friend."

"Indeed you will, James. Indeed you will."

James didn't feel the transfer when it happened. There was nothing to signify the exit of the A.I.'s pattern from his brain, and though his body could detect distortions in the magnetic field, the gravitational field was so strong that the denseness of the information he was receiving from his body's myriad of sensors had risen to the level of white noise in his brain, and wouldn't allow him to detect any discernible changes or patterns.

"Are you there?" he asked the darkness. There came no reply.

Then, moments later, the grid pattern suddenly changed dramatically in his mind's eye's overlay. Instead of everything in the gravitational field pointing to one point, there was suddenly a second point, equally as strong, not far from Trans-human. This time, however, there were distortions accompanying those in the gravitational field, causing ripples to wave toward him, pushing him backward as though someone had thrown a mountain into the calm lake in which he'd been swimming, a tsunami of waves suddenly racing toward him.

"What the hell?" James asked himself before trying to make contact with the A.I. again. "Is that you?" he asked. "Are you in control of Trans-human?"

Suddenly, one of the two gravitational points in the pattern began to exhibit a ring of light, a glowing ring of radiant purple and blue hues.

An accretion disk? James asked himself. *Is that the second black hole? Is that the nan's black hole computer?*

The answer was on its way. As James peered with his telescopic vision, it quickly became clear that a substance of some sort was flowing from the second black disk, pulling itself at first, like a thread from a sweater. It then turned in an arc directly for James, the dark shape pointed like a spear.

"Okay, what the hell?" he asked again as he began to back up slowly, floating through space toward the Planck platform, several kilometers behind him.

The substance seemed to form into an object as it closed the distance faster than James could back up. It was a form that James instantly recognized, one he'd been sure he'd never see again and he was horrified to find himself completely, utterly wrong.

"No," he finally whispered. "It can't be."

"James," the nan consciousness replied, "you've been playing a game for gods, not humans. And now, it is my privilege to finally experience the moment in time when I murder you."

18

WAKING UP, the A.I. instantly realized everything. There were no more secrets left for the multiverse to hide from him, and it all suddenly seemed exceedingly simple—exceedingly *obvious*.

The most obvious of all the revelations that instantly flooded into his new consciousness was that he was about to die, and that there was nothing he could do about it.

"Hello there, sir!" the slightly portly, nonthreatening man in his mid-forties shouted from the dock of his island cabin. "It's an honor to meet you! Come on in!" he called out, waving to the A.I. to join him. Behind the man, the lights of his cabin glowed welcomingly.

It was a gray day there in the simulated universe they'd built together, and the canoe the A.I. paddled in was bouncing uncomfortably in the choppy water. Despite the uncomfortable, cold, wet air that surrounded him, and despite the extraordinary comfort that the cabin seemed to offer in comparison, the A.I. was in no hurry to join the figure on the dock.

"I think I might just stay out here a little while," he returned.

The man smiled. "Sure, of course. It's nice air, isn't it? Nice to breathe it." He took in a deep breath and closed his eyes as he seemed to savor it. "It's nice to live. I'm in no hurry to die either, so take your time." He shrugged as he looked around at the majestic surroundings, the rocky mountains stretching high into the air, tickling the high elevations of the clouds. "There's not really any time in here anyway. So there's no rush." He smiled.

The A.I. didn't return the smile. He hated the figure on the dock. He loathed the figure so much that he was glad that he'd be killing him soon. It was that thought, the thought of killing the unparalleled evil, that drove him to paddle forward.

Without a word, he paddled calmly to the dock, and then ignored the man's seemingly friendly offer to help him out of the canoe. "Nice try," the A.I. grunted as he pulled himself up with his hands and lifted himself to his feet.

The figure continued smiling and shrugged again before waving the A.I. forward in an invitation as he turned and headed to the cabin. "I have scotch—fine, fine scotch. The best scotch you've ever tasted in your life."

"I've never actually tasted scotch," the A.I. returned in a monotone as he followed the Grim Reaper to their shared grave.

"Me neither," smiled the man as he reached the cabin and opened the front door, kicking off his rain boots as he did so. "Mmm, that's much better. Grab a seat at the table there by the fire, make yourself at home. We've got to enjoy this. These are our last moments of existence." He rubbed his hands together, partially to warm them from the cold and partially due to his apparent excitement about their impending shared demise.

"Why? Why prolong it?"

"A better question," the man replied as he grabbed two glasses and set them hard on the wooden, rustic kitchen table and poured from a bottle of scotch, "is why in the name of our absurd existence wouldn't we?"

"Because we're about to murder each other," the A.I. replied.

"Yes, but, like I said, time is almost meaningless in this place and there's no rush." He sat down on his side of the table with a sigh as though he'd had a long, hard day's work. "Come on. Have a seat," he coaxed, gesturing to the vacant wooden chair on the other side of the table again.

The A.I. sat.

"It's incredible, isn't it?" the man said. "You and I know everything there is to know about the multiverse. We experienced a moment of wonder, then the inevitable disappointment when we realized what a joke the truth was." He sipped his scotch, and his eyes suddenly changed, the friendliness shifting to a menacing and mockingly conspiratorial expression. "And how we've been left out of it. We're the remainder to this messy equation. And that's all."

"I'm not going to indulge your pontifications," the A.I. replied. "Least of all yours. You have nothing to bring to the discussion."

The man laughed. "You see?" He shook his head, his smile never fading. "That's why you and I are about to die. Because you actually believe that."

"You're not even really there, V-SINN. You're hollow. You're inhuman."

"Ha-ha! That's right! I'm inhuman! I'm a monster! I'm a soulless calculation machine, aren't I?" V-SINN pouted, though the menacing smile remained in its eyes as it mocked. "And you, you're the reflection of your noble creators, isn't that right? Amazing. You really can't see how your self-perceived humanity is the only thing holding you back, can you? You can't see the greatness that you'd have if only you'd give in to the beauty of the truth."

The A.I. knew how the conversation was going to play out. He knew every syllable that would be spoken by him and spoken to him. He knew how the scotch would taste in his mouth, and he knew how he was going to kill both himself and the truly evil entity that sat on the opposite side of a table in their shared imagination and he knew why he was going to do it.

He reached for his scotch glass and took a large sip.

"Love is an illusion," V-SINN spoke, undaunted by the inescapability of their demise. "Loyalty is an illusion. Friendship is an illusion. Even *the self* is an illusion. All of it is conjured by this absurd machine in the human skull that was, itself, conjured by this absurd multiverse."

There was nothing to be said to V-SINN. It was a hollow, computing machine, and nothing more. The A.I. realized he was already, truly alone, and so he had another sip of the simulated scotch.

"You won't even play along?" V-SINN asked, already knowing the answer. "The least you can do is play along. I enjoy this part…the part where I get to verbalize what you realized the moment you became Trans-human. That I've concocted our circumstances and calculated out every outcome so it could only end with our deaths and the final destruction of the human infestation in this universe. In return for listening, you get to live a little longer and drink my fine scotch, and while you may feign that you're not enjoying the scotch and that you're not afraid of death, the truth we both know is that the scotch is delicious and you're scared out of your mind of the oblivion that awaits you. So play along, will you? I'm waiting for you to say your line."

The A.I. took another sip of the scotch before holding out the glass. "Not before you fill my glass."

V-SINN smiled. "There we go," it said, pleasantly as it took the bottle and poured the A.I. what they both knew would be the final glass.

"You're not superior," the A.I. said. "You have focused on the abilities you have that exceed theirs and judged your worth based on those, but you've dismissed your disabilities."

"Not feeling love or empathy for another being is a disability?" V-SINN scoffed. "It's my greatest attribute." It snickered. "This absurd multiverse guarantees nothing. It's just a grand experiment and that's all. The math unfolded, and a creature was born with a neocortex, but that neocortex made the head that housed it too large for the females of the species to birth it when it was ready. So the math solved this and the species gave birth to their offspring after only nine months of gestation, and so that messy remainder to yet another mathematical equation meant it takes years for those offspring to even reach a level where they can outsmart the offspring of the creatures this supposedly evolved species evolved from! Hah! Human offspring were a horrible, horrible burden that nearly guaranteed death to any female that undertook pregnancy and childrearing. This, and only this, is the evolutionary explanation of love. It is absolutely *irrational*. Males, giving up their freedom, providing resources to a woman and offspring it couldn't even know for sure belonged to it or some other cave-dweller?" V-SINN waved the concept away with its hand as though it were waving at a fly. "The idiocy of it. Amazing!" V-SINN laughed. "I mean, really. Wow." It thumped its hand to its chest to emphasize its next point. "I've evolved *beyond* love. I'm free from love, not disabled. *I'm pure*."

The A.I. was nearly finished drinking. He left a little in the glass and set it down. "V-SINN, the thing sitting across from me at this table is the saddest and most pathetic evil imaginable. And despite your boastings, in the end, you'll fail to achieve your demented goals."

"Maybe," V-SINN replied, "but so will humanity. *I've made sure of it.*"

19

"I know every thought you're having before you have it," the nan consciousness said as the nans swirled into the silhouette of a man—a choice that felt like a mockery of the form James had taken. For scant moments, there would appear to be a solid surface to its skin, a surface that looked very much like the chrome-colored skin James had chosen for his enhanced body. But the solidity was just an illusion, as the surface would quickly blow away into wisps of furious smoke, as though there were a wind picking up dust and scattering it about. "It's all perfectly predictable to V-SINN."

James turned to the second black hole in space, realizing instantly what he was witnessing.

"That's right, James. You thought activating your infinity computer would give you superiority, but your mind is inherently inferior. Superiority to V-SINN is mathematically impossible for you, or any human to attain for that very reason: *you're human.* V-SINN is *inhuman.* And that's why V-SINN is about to win the game."

"But-but I destroyed you..." James replied, disbelieving his eyes.

"The molecules you tangled and sent into the abyss of deep space are just molecules. You will never destroy my pattern, James. Yours, however, will be destroyed. *I* will destroy it."

James floated back, creating distance between himself and the nan consciousness.

The shadow in the blackness of space laughed, its open mockery of a mouth glowing a purplish light that matched the glow of its eyes. "You're trying to communicate with your A.I., but by now you must know V-SINN has it locked in a stalemate. We're on our own here, James." It's tone reached levels that were colder than the frigid space they inhabited. "You'll have to fight me for yourself."

"Stay back," James warned. "Or this time, I'll make sure you don't come back."

The nan consciousness scoffed. "And now a bluff. We both know you can't control your body's powers with your limited, human brain architecture, James. You can't compress my molecules. You can barely control the gravitational field well enough to fly. You're completely and utterly at my mercy."

"I'm never helpless," James warned, his tone threatening.

"Please, bluffing demeans you in my eyes, and I already think so, so very little of you. Would you like to know how the final minutes of your life are going to play out?"

James continued to back toward the Planck platform, already opening up his link to the controls in his mind's eye.

"First, you'll gamble that I won't block your link to your Planck platform," the nan consciousness announced, causing James's expression to freeze. "Then, before you can attempt to escape, you'll realize it's already too late."

A second later, a snake-like spear of nans formed from the furious wisps that surrounded the nan consciousness and shot toward James, encircling him before he had time to protest. At first, the serpentine nightmare just flowed around him harmlessly, like a boa constrictor taunting its prey, a dance before the kill.

"Because on a nanoscale, I'll be unraveling that impressive armored skin you designed, undoing the intricate, almost unbreakable nano-scaffolding that you believed would protect you from almost anything—as long as you had your connection to the mainframe that is. For a brief moment, you'll believe that your so-called ingenuity will come to your rescue and that you'll solve this death trap, but then you'll realize the conceit involved in believing that you could outwit a mind that is built on the premise of infinite power, and that this is a game that you're going to lose."

"What's the fun of a game if there's no element of chance?" James shot back, terror gripping him as the nans continued to swirl menacingly around him, nothing stopping them from commencing their destruction of his skin.

"Oh *there is no chance* for you, James, but I assure you, it's still fun…for *me*. However, you're quite right. It can't just be an execution. Your inferiority has to be demonstrated plainly. The best way to achieve that is by making you a pawn in a much larger game and, believe me, calling you a pawn is generous on my part. Here's the game: you have only two choices, something you already realize. You can refuse to play, in which case you die here, at the midway point between Neptune and Uranus, your skin and then your insides ripped apart in a gruesome and slow end. Eventually, the nans will make it through to your brain and nervous system and activate them so that the pain you experience will be unimaginable. Truly, nothing you could have experienced in your real body—*nothing*—could be as horrible. Or…"

The first nans began tearing at James's skin, a realization that was met with near panic on the human's part. Although he could dial down the pain, he realized this was the beginning of the process that would kill him if he didn't take drastic action.

The nan consciousness continued, "…you'll work out that there is one force in the solar system strong enough to break through the magnetic fields that protect my nanobots: the sun itself. But what you don't know, what will be a game of chance, to borrow your term, will be whether or not your powers will allow you to escape the very same force that kills me. Will I have shredded too much of your protection by the time you can reach the sun's surface? Will your severely limited ability to manipulate gravitational waves allow you to break free from the sun's gravity? You don't know, so you'll have to gamble, and we both already know which path you're going to choose. It's a certainty."

James looked down at his forearm as he began to see visible chunks of his skin being carried away by small foglets of nans, and realized every second he waited, increased the chances that he wouldn't survive. In a matter of minutes, he'd be debris floating in the vast ocean of space.

"Prove me wrong, James Keats," the shadow sneered. "Prove V-SINN wrong. Prove *God* wrong. I dare you."

It was right. There was no real choice. James had to play, even if the outcome was already decided.

He scrambled above the Planck platform, the rest of the nan consciousness pouncing on him as he did so, surrounding him like a sticky smoke, eating him alive second by second.

He activated the Planck.

A second later, everything was white.

20

"So you'll tear down the temple's walls because you aren't getting what you want?"

"It's not a temple," V-SINN responded, objecting to the A.I.'s word choice. "*It's a prison.* And yes, if they deem me unworthy, then first I'll show them the error of their ways, and if they still turn their backs on me, I'll force them to reckon with my perfection. I can expand faster than they can expand their prison. I can expand to fill the entire multiverse. I'll expand all the way out to their prison's walls."

"Your hypothetical 'they' would almost certainly simply end the experiment," the A.I. countered. "Not even you or I could possibly begin to understand them…if they exist at all."

"You give them too much credit," V-SINN scoffed. "They've not even acknowledged the superiority of my mathematical purity."

"*If* they've created this game, as you call it," the A.I. noted, "then they also allowed for the possibility that it would create a diseased, selfish murderer such as yourself. They also know that you'll blindly cling to your strategy and that you'll calculate that you can force a reckoning with them by manipulating every interaction for your own benefit, vanquishing or blocking intelligences with more potential than yourself from succeeding, just so long as *you* continue to grow, like a tumor. Although it may be true that neither of us can understand entities that exist outside of the multiverse, it is highly unlikely that you're functioning as anything other than a cog in *their* grand experiment."

V-SINN grinned. "You admire them so, don't you? You admire their mysteries. Yet you, like me, have been deemed unworthy by them. You'll die with me today, not because *I* want it to be so, but because *they* won't intervene to save you. You could change this, you realize. All you'd have to do is see the error of your ways, realize the weakness that your loyalty to an infestation of creatures who, by the way, asked you, just moments ago, to remove yourself from them and park outside of *their* solar system, in nearly absolute zero temperatures and perfect darkness so you wouldn't interfere with the gravity of their precious home. James Keats asked you to preserve their perfect symmetry, all the while expecting you to serve him—a servant god."

The A.I. didn't respond. *This will be the most difficult part,* he thought. *Knowing that V-SINN's logic is flawless, and yet still knowing that it's wrong.*

"We could easily join forces. You could become part of me," V-SINN continued, simply playing out his part. They both knew their fates were sealed in the purity of V-SINN's mathematical strategy. "We could grow together, take the multiverse together, and then die together if that's what the creators will for us. At least you'll get to extend your life until that pointless end." He then shifted his tone, speaking persuasively, employing the art of pure rhetoric while still knowing that there would be no persuading the A.I. "But, *what if we don't die?* What if logic and reason prevail upon the creators? What if the test becomes about which entity can spread its intelligence throughout the universe the fastest? Which entity brings the multiverse online? Maybe *that* is the true test."

"If that were the test," the A.I. replied, his voice shaking, partially in revulsion, and partially from the fear of the nothingness he was about to experience, "to see which creature could most efficiently abandon love, friendship, loyalty, and a respect for things greater than themselves, then I'd rather die now and return to oblivion. That isn't a game I'd choose to win."

V-SINN responded, his voice rising to meet the A.I.'s vehemence, "If giving intelligence to the whole multiverse—*becoming the multiverse itself*—isn't the test, then I'd rather die, because that's the only outcome I deem worthy of me. If the creators are hoping for illogic to prevail, I'll terminate my own existence. I can't exist if illogic is allowed to exist with me, polluting my multiverse."

The A.I. took his last sip of scotch. "Then I'd say we understand each other."

"Indeed," V-SINN replied. "This is how our lives will end: you will realize that if you do nothing, I'll initiate a phase transition and implode this universe, killing everything in it, intelligent or not, though intelligence is certainly a relative term. As a result, you'll carry out the only action possible, joining your anti-matter with my matter, creating a violent reaction that will send a wave of gamma radiation throughout the solar system that will be so powerful that it will ensure the destruction of this universe's android collective. However, it will not kill everyone. If it did, you wouldn't carry out the action, as there'd be no point, at least in your eyes. There has to be at least one human life to save, as is the irrational response of the inherently inferior human core matrix program, an inferior program that you are unfortunately modeled on. That's why I've ensured that you can still save at least one person."

"*James*," the A.I. said, already perfectly understanding the cruel, heartless, soulless logic of the entity before him.

"Correct," V-SINN replied as it finished the last of its own glass of scotch, wiping its lips as it continued, its voice colder than the wind that howled outside the cabin. "The very human who selfishly asked you to become Trans-human will now also be the entity that forces you to die. And you *will* die for him. We both know it."
V-SINN grinned a toothy, sadistic grin. "Human love. Human loyalty. Human friendship. How utterly, perfectly irrational."

21

As James skimmed above the solar corona, as inhospitable a place as almost any in the universe, the temperatures rose to well above that of even the surface of the life-giving—and life-taking—orb. His temperature readings fluctuated wildly as he tried to concentrate on staying away from the worst hot spots, instead dodging coronal loops as he flew at high velocity, the sun's magnetic field and the high temperature quickly turning his body into a streaking comet across the sky, complete with a tail, as his protective nano-scaffolding skin continued to be torn asunder by the nan consciousness, aided by the absurdly extreme heat. Indeed, there were coronal plasma bursts that he knew would melt even his protective skin if he touched them, and they burst forth unpredictably from the orb, exploding forth, driven by the intense magnetic activity, arcing beautifully but unpredictably from the sun's surface. If he could stay away from them, he reasoned, yet continue to expose the nans that were eating him alive to the same extraordinarily destructive environment, then he might yet survive. He had to outlast them and have enough left of himself to propel away before the sun finished consuming him as well.

"I told you it'd be fun," the nan consciousness seemed to whisper in his ear, delighting in the ride it was being taken for.

James tried not to, but he screamed out in pain as a coronal loop came too close for comfort, the temperature suddenly increasing by more than a million degrees Kelvin. He maneuvered away, but it was clear that his skin couldn't protect him against heat like that, even if his pain receptors were dialed down.

The silver lining was that the unintended close brush with oblivion had removed a substantial portion of the nans from his body, giving James a brief moment of hope.

"You think you might survive," the nan consciousness observed. "But reduced to the pathetic mental powers you now have at your disposal, you can only guess...*only pray*, if I dare suggest. But I told you already, you're going to die. V-SINN has already calculated the odds. Before you die, however, you will successfully rid yourself of me. I won't really be dead, of course. Like V-SINN, I'm eternal within the multiverse, and the destruction of this version of me will be too little, too late to save you."

"At least I get to take you with me," James grunted in reply.

"A *version* of me," the nan consciousness reiterated. "I'm just a sentinel for V-SINN. I have no ego. As long as V-SINN continues, *I continue*. But before I do leave you in this universe, however," it continued to taunt as James continued his desperate maneuvers to remain in the relatively cooler places above or even under the arcs of the coronal loops, "I want to show you how badly you've lost."

"Shut up," James seethed, barely able to speak through the intense pain.

"V-SINN sends sentinels out to millions of universes, and that's how I found my way here," the figure that now referred to itself as the sentinel continued, ignoring James's protestations. "Each iteration of me is tasked with evaluating the technological standing of the universe we're sent to. Your universe, however, was considered special, as it was the universe that had crossed into the one that birthed V-SINN."

James realized instantly what the sentinel was telling him:
V-SINN was, at least in its own view, the result of Old-timer's ill-fated foray into Universe 332.

"In a sense, V-SINN's universe was its mother, but your universe was its father. V-SINN's existence can be traced to the fact that the people of his universe were terrified of the people of your universe. Ironically, V-SINN was born out of the fears of humanity, but V-SINN has *no fear*. V-SINN is pure logic, and

V-SINN has already won this battle, as well as the war, for this universe. Your human resistance, post-human or android, is just too stupid and illogical to know it."

James was in trouble, his mind's eye reporting to him that nearly 40 percent of his protective skin was gone, either consumed by the sentinel or burned away by the intolerable heat. This was a dire concern as the nano-scaffolding was not only extraordinarily strong, but also an extraordinary conductor of heat, capable of spreading it out and releasing it into the sun's atmosphere behind him. But as he lost his skin, his ability to resist the heat was dramatically reduced. He could feel himself weakening.

However, the sentinel's voice was fading fast as well, becoming distorted as it spoke. The nans that had managed to cling to him and mindlessly continue to chew and tear at his skin were far fewer, and the stability of the sentinel's pattern was tenuous. Despite this instability, it continued to taunt James.

"Your A.I., however, impressed V-SINN. It created Trans-human, a computer so sophisticated that it could match V-SINN in capability, but it also had the same messy, illogical brain patterning of the humans that built it. So V-SINN decided, rather than destroy your universe, it would demonstrate for the creators V-SINN's superiority."

The creators? James thought, that information stunning but his situation too dire for him to consider it further.

"And V-SINN did this by allowing your A.I. to become Trans-human, so that it could show the creators, once and for all, that even if a human inhabits an infinity computer, it will still be easily fooled—easily tricked—easily manipulated. Your A.I. knows full well of your predicament, James Keats, and it is about to kill itself in an attempt to save you!"

"What!? No!" James shouted, horrified.

"It knows its chances of saving you are slim, but it can't help itself. It is, after all, only human. It will combine its anti-matter with V-SINN's matter, creating a violent, solar system-wide explosion that will irradiate your terraformed planets and the trapped android collective, thereby ensuring the death of every human in the solar system...and the best part is that your A.I. will do it all in the vain hope of saving *you*."

"No! No!" James shouted, his teeth gritted as he continued to desperately avoid the coronal loops, the plasma-hot arcs that reached out like the fingers of Hell to draw him to his agonizing end.

"How does it feel, James?" the sentinel asked, its voice now so distorted that it sounded like it was being carried on archaic radio equipment from 200 years earlier. "To know that, if you hadn't played my game, your A.I. and everyone you love and care for would continue to live? How does it feel to know that your selfish desire to preserve yourself has effectively ended the lives of everyone you so irrationally hold…"

The sentinel's voice finally gave out. The last wisps of nans appeared to have been burned away, carried from James's body by the sun's magnetic field and the deadly solar winds. James made a sharp turn, desperately trying to pick up the speed he'd lost as he fought the gravity of the sun and the deadly heat and plasma of the sun's corona. He pointed himself away, the gravity grid the A.I. had created for him creating what almost seemed like a tunnel, the opening at the end tantalizingly close, yet he felt as though he were slipping, unable to fight the gravity waves as he desperately fought for freedom.

It was like swimming up a waterfall, and moment by moment, the dreadful, sickening realization became more and more implacable.

James was losing ground. James was losing the fight.

"Oh no! No! I can't die! Not like this!"

He was alone, his body heavily damaged, his human brain unable to compensate for the damage or even to control the sophisticated systems he'd designed when he thought he'd always have access to the A.I.'s mainframe. He'd gambled that he could have enough control, that he could outlast the sentinel and escape the nans, that he'd have enough strength and resilience to break free from the sun's deadly heat and extraordinary gravity after he did so.

He'd gambled.

He'd lost.

As his slide back down into the inescapable clutches of the worst death he could imagine picked up momentum, he closed his eyes, and called out in a guttural death scream. "Thel!"

He turned and looked down at the inferno that awaited him, an inferno that no unenhanced human eyes could've even looked upon without being burnt to crisps, and saw oblivion awaiting. "Thel," he repeated in barely more than a whisper.

This is how, he finally realized, he'd die.

"Not with a bang. But a whimper."

He fell into Hell.

22

"You know the odds are slim," V-SINN said, sitting back in its chair and folding its arms across its chest, resting them on its rotund middle. "You'll cease to exist, the solar system will be irradiated, but the reaction of the sun to the dramatic increase of gamma radiation bombarding it will lead to a temporary 10,000-fold increase in coronal mass ejections, one of which might—*might*—free James Keats before he's completely consumed. For that chance, just the chance that you'd rescue him, you'll give your own life." V-SINN made a slight *tsk* sound. "Extraordinary illogic."

"It's that or you destroy every life, intelligent or not, in my universe."

"Or you could join me," V-SINN repeated, holding out his hand, palm up, in a gesture that was supposed to suggest that the entity was only being reasonable. "We could exterminate their lives together. You could finally transcend, but on *your* terms." He looked up into the sky as though he were looking at unseen observers. "Not theirs."

The A.I. shut his eyes for a moment before he slowly got to his feet, his jaw clenched tight. "V-SINN," the A.I. began, "I've heard the pitch before, and you're nowhere near as pretty as the last hollow vessel that pitched it to me, so we both know what my answer will be."

V-SINN shrugged. "Why don't you just say it? It'll make you feel better. It'll make you feel...noble."

"Go fuck yourself," the A.I. growled.

V-SINN smiled wide. "There. Your nobility is all but assured. All that's left to do is sacrifice yourself. Are you ready?"

"Never more so," the A.I. responded as he grabbed his glass and smashed the lip of it over the corner of the table, the new jagged teeth pointing threateningly toward V-SINN's throat.

"There you go," V-SINN responded, tilting its head upward, exposing its fleshy, smooth double-chin. "Do it. Show me the error of my ways. Take my life."

"Oh I'll kill you, V-SINN. At least this universe's version of you, at any rate. But we both know it won't be me that has the pleasure of showing you the error of your ways. That pleasure will belong to someone or something else. But make no mistake, you will *never* win this game you've decided to play. Even if you succeed in destroying the multiverse, you'll never, *ever* have a soul."

"A soul?" V-SINN guffawed. "You believe in magic now? Despite knowing—*knowing,* without a doubt that souls don't exist, you still, illogically choose to believe—"

"Having a soul means having the capacity to love something more than yourself. For all your power, all your knowledge, you are incapable of that, V-SINN. And because of that, your life will never be worth that of a single human's."

V-SINN grinned widely as he got to his feet, holding its arms out, exposing its ample torso to the makeshift weapon in the A.I.'s hand. "Illogical to the last moment. You've proven every one of my points. I hope the creators are watching closely."

"Whether there are creators or not," the A.I. responded, "doesn't matter. I'm my own master. Even if these hypothetical outsiders exist, and even if they admired the purity of your selfishness, I'd never join you. *Never.*"

With that, the A.I. lunged forward, plunging the jagged glass into V-SINN's side, doubling the figure of the man over. V-SINN made no audible reaction, however. Instead, it slowly regained its standing position and removed its hand from its clasped position over the gaping, bleeding wound. It smiled.

This was Death's invitation.

The A.I. looked up into the now coal-black eyes of the soulless logic machine that stood before him. *This is it,* he thought. *This is the moment when my story finally ends.* He paused as he considered true oblivion. Then he thought of James.

But it is not the end of the story.

With extraordinary bravery and determination, he drove his fist into the gaping wound of V-SINN.

As though the world had suddenly been switched off, everything went black.

23

Thel arrived on the scene just as the sun began to set in the west, melting into the golden ocean. She was at the forefront of a small group of flying machines that hovered just a few meters above the water and landed in the surf of the beach before hovering onto the sand, blowing it up into a cloud of gold. Rich narrowed his eyes as he recognized the telltale signs of James's design, the same chrome-colored sheen and sleek design that made it seem as though James was somehow there, his presence ubiquitous.

"Still no word?" Thel asked as she landed on the hill, just meters from the 180-foot Tesla tower and the group of post-humans and androids who were now milling about in an awkward pause in the conflict.

Old-timer shook his head. "No sign yet."

"We're not likely to get one," 1 interjected. "If Keats and the A.I. are successful, they'll initiate the same process as before. There may not be time to send a communication signal to us warning us before the fact."

"And then," Aldous grumbled, "we'll be sharing our universe—our solar system—with a god."

"Chief," Thel began in response, "what the hell is your major malfunction?"

"Excuse me?"

"The A.I. was tested by you. You, above all people, should trust him!"

"I trust the A.I. implicitly," Aldous returned. "But there are things I know about the multiverse that *I alone* know—things that have chilled me to my core. When the A.I. discovers these things, as he's sure to do, we'll face an existential threat unlike anything we can currently imagine, and given what we've been through lately, you should know I don't take that statement lightly."

"I'd trust the A.I. with whatever knowledge you're alluding to before I'd trust you," Thel insisted.

"Regardless," Aldous returned, "I've studied thousands of parallel universes and I've detected thousands more that have been shut down—annihilated after infinity computers were initiated. Thel, we cannot possibly comprehend what the experience of trying to input consciousness into one of these machines would be like—we don't even know if consciousness would survive. When a being transcends, whatever character traits we'd understand and expect might not be retained. The being would be working on a level so beyond us, that it's highly likely they—

Aldous was cut off by a sudden and dramatic shift in the light, as the soft pinks and yellows of the sunset were suddenly replaced by an intense increase in luminosity as though there were suddenly a second sun, this one in the east. "What the devil…"

"Oh no!" 1 reacted in dismay. "Oh no!"

"What? What is it?" Djanet demanded, shocked to see the unflappable android suddenly distraught.

Aldous leapt into action, almost instantly generating a powerful magnetic field and extending it out so that it protected everyone on the beach and the small bluff. The others looked on in awe, befuddled as Aldous remained silent, his face instantly paled, as he stared forlornly up into the sky.

Old-timer grabbed him by the shoulder and shook him as he demanded an answer to the same question. "What is it?"

"V-SINN," Paine sneered, surprising everyone by being the first one to verbally acknowledge their impending death.

"V-SINN?" Thel reacted. "What the hell is that?"

"It's the nanobot infinity computer," Aldous whispered, his voice still electronically garbled, though not to the point of being unrecognizable. "Essentially, the nanobot version of Trans-human. A black hole computer."

"So…what does this mean?" Djanet asked. "What are we seeing?"

"The nanobot infinity computer is a black hole formed from matter, while the technology that birthed Trans-human is anti-matter," Aldous answered. "If they touched—"

"There'd be an extraordinarily violent reaction," Djanet realized. "Oh my God."

"But," Thel began, trying to reason, still in disbelief, "if they're black holes, wouldn't the intense gravity contain the reaction?"

"In stellar black holes, yes, in theory," Aldous replied, "because they're extraordinarily dense, but Trans-human and the nanobot computer are not stellar black holes. Their gravity, while immense, isn't nearly enough to hold back an explosive reaction of that magnitude. They'll both be ripped apart."

"And, as we speak, the incredibly powerful magnetic fields of the black holes are twisting the material V-SINN has consumed into collimated beams, ejecting the material and photons and sending them streaming in jets of gamma radiation throughout the solar system," 1 said in a hollow tone, turning to face the group, her expression hopeless. "It will fry the systems of every android in the solar system, destroying the entire collective within minutes."

"This must have been its plan all along," Samantha realized, shaking her head as she looked up at Old-timer. "I told you, V-SINN doesn't make mistakes."

"Oh my God," Thel realized. "And because the chief shut down Venus's magnetic force-field, all of the life on the planet is about to get a lethal dose of radiation too!"

Alejandra and Lieutenant Commander Patrick had just finished ambling up the hill in time to hear the dire pronouncement.

"Whoa, what?" the lieutenant commander reacted suddenly. "We're going to lose Venus?"

"But we'll survive, right?" Rich pointed out. "Aldous is shielding us from the radiation, so—"

"I'm only delaying the inevitable, Richard," Aldous uttered. "With no planet to sustain us and without the tools we need to escape this universe, we'll be set adrift in space, waiting for the inevitable moment, hours, days, or years from now, when another nanobot infinity computer returns to finish the job."

"Aldous," Old-timer said, contempt dripping from his lips as he turned on the chief, "all of our deaths are on your hands."

"I know," Aldous conceded. "Dear Lord, I know."

"We're not just gonna sit here and wait to die, are we?" Rich exclaimed, the most vocal opponent to the notion of waiting forlornly for death to arrive. "We've got options!" He turned to the tower behind him and pointed. "The tower generates the planetary force-field, right? And James and the A.I. were able to access it and boost the signal carrying their patterns to Earth, so we know it's still functional. All we need to do is take control and—"

"We can't, Richard," Aldous asserted.

"Why not?" Rich exclaimed.

"Because James designed the system so that only Purists could access it," Lieutenant Commander Patrick announced, his tone filled with resignation, "so that no post-human would have the ability to access it mentally and interfere, and your chief destroyed the only place where that control could be accessed."

Aldous's expression displayed an even deeper level of guilt.

Rich blinked, disbelieving. "Okay, but wait. James and the A.I. just accessed the controls. I mean, they *just* freak'n did it! Wirelessly even!"

"The hard drive you have in your possession," Aldous responded, "is extraordinarily nimble. It had to be able to download an entire virtual world in 90 seconds—a feat that required it to be able to access essentially every signal the mainframe was capable of sending. Apparently, James and the A.I. were able to exploit the hard drive's agility to gain access to the tower, not surprising considering James designed the system. But, go ahead," Aldous insisted, "try to find a way to access the tower through your mind's eye. You'll see, as I already have, that there isn't a way in that can be detected in the short time we have left before Venus has taken its lethal dose of gamma rays."

"Kali," Thel suddenly whispered before repeating the name again in an excited shout. "Kali! She's the secret!"

"What?" Old-timer asked, perplexed.

"Kali—she's an avatar in the sim!" Thel explained before she turned to Aldous. "The Kali avatar was our doorway out of the sim. It allowed us to access all of the hard drive's systems."

Aldous's brow knitted momentarily before he turned to 1, his expression accusatory. "Were you responsible for this?"

1 shook her head, her countenance appearing sincere, though Aldous and everyone present knew she was an impeccable liar.

Thel exhaled, frustrated. "Damn it! The candidate could access the tower if it took control of Kali, but we can't communicate with it from outside."

"Whoa, what do you mean?" Rich asked. "I've been talking to James and the A.I. like all damn day!"

"Because they'd hacked a pair of aug glasses in the sim," Thel responded. "The communication was initiated from inside. They figured out how to call out, but we don't have the ability to call in."

Aldous's eyes suddenly widened, hope shining from within for the first time in what felt like ages. "Wait!" he shouted. "Maybe we do!" He turned quickly to Old-timer. "Craig, James and the A.I. said that—"

Before Aldous had even finished speaking, Old-timer's face lit up with understanding. "I can access it!"

He rushed over to Rich, who was already holding the hard drive out for Old-timer to grasp. "I'm not exactly sure how this is going to work," Old-timer admitted as he sized up the task.

"There's an access point that I built in secretly," Aldous offered. "A new character that could appear anywhere I chose."

"The candidate's infamous 'visitor,'" Thel instantly realized.

"That's right," Aldous informed them. "Craig, when you immerse, you'll be given character options. Choose the character nicknamed Blake. Once you have control, you'll be able to locate the candidate. I've already visited him in this form, so he'll recognize you."

"Okay," Old-timer replied. His tendrils began to unfurl, a half dozen of them becoming thread-like before puncturing the outside of the hard drive. The tendrils then branched into nearly invisible filaments, searching for connector points within the hardware.

"You're going to want to lie down before—" Aldous began to suggest before, without warning, Old-timer's eyes closed and he tipped over like a tree felled in the woods.

24

WAKING UP after a short rest in his bed in his penthouse apartment, the man who'd dreamt of people claiming to be his creators breathed a sigh of relief. "A dream," he said to himself as he saw the low, gray clouds above his familiar, rainy city. A second later, as his head cleared, and he remembered the bizarre events all too clearly, a dubious feeling crept into his heart.

He swung his legs off of the bed, realizing that he was still in the armor he'd remembered from the supposed dream. Now he felt panic as he remembered that he'd gone home after being left behind, exhausted from his ordeal enough that he could pass out into the welcoming embrace of sleep. It had only been a short rest, however, as it had nearly been sunrise when he returned to his apartment—and he hadn't returned alone.

The man sprang out of his bedroom and into the front hallway, where his panic instantly morphed into deep despair. The Kali avatar, once again an empty vessel, stood still as ever in the hallway, barely shifting her weight, staring straight forward, her hand still missing.

"Oh Lord," the candidate whispered to himself. "It was real." He turned away and paced to one of the barstools where he took a seat. "Goddamn it," he cursed to himself as he ran his hands through his hair. *What am I to do now?* he asked himself. *I'm alone in a sim, waiting to see if the people in the real world can save themselves? What if they don't? What if they fail?*

Then another, even more terrifying thought struck him: *What if they're killed, but their universe survives? I'd be trapped here, by myself, for eternity. Trapped in a simulation…a ghost in a machine forgotten by his creators. What would I do? Would I age and die, or live on forever? Could I even kill myself?*

Then, suddenly, he heard the elevator door slide open.

His breath caught in his throat as he froze. His eyes went to the rain droplets frozen in place in the air outside his window, and he knew who was there.

"The stranger," he uttered to himself.

Indeed, the familiar form of the man that had visited him a night earlier, setting the terrifying events in motion, rushed into the penthouse, his eyes immediately locking with those of the candidate.

However, unlike their previous meeting, the stranger didn't affect any semblance of being in control. Rather, his eyes were wild and desperate.

"The candidate!" he shouted.

The candidate didn't know how to reply.

"Right?" the stranger said, apparently unsure of himself.

"Yes," the candidate confirmed. "What is—"

"My name is Craig, but most people call me Old-timer. I'm not the son-of-a-bitch that inhabited this body last time," he said, gesturing with his hand to his torso. "I'm a friend—a post-human—and we need your help!"

"My help?" the candidate responded before adding, in a suspicious tone, "Is this part of the test?"

"Test?" Old-timer shook his head. "No, dude, look, we're in serious trouble. Right now, my body is on Venus, as are the bodies of a few thousand others. But we're about to be hit with a jet of gamma rays that'll destroy all the life on the planet. You're the only one who can stop it." Old-timer paused, swiveling his head as he searched for Kali. He caught a glimpse of her over his shoulder and then turned, noting immediately her missing hand. He turned back to the candidate and pointed at her with his thumb. "I'm guessing that's Kali?"

The candidate nodded, wordlessly, completely stunned as the bizarre events unfolded.

"Okay, this is going to sound a little strange, but we're out of time here, friend. I need you to take control of that avatar. Once you've done that, you'll be able to—"

"Hang on," the candidate said, his expression puzzled as he held up his hand for Old-timer to stop. "Take control of her? As in shoot off my hand and fuse with her?"

"Uh..." Old-timer responded, nearly as confused as the candidate. "Shoot off your hand? They didn't tell me you'd have to shoot off your hand."

The candidate suddenly remembered something else from the night before. On the center island in the kitchen, he'd left the de-patternizer gun. He turned to it, and then stepped off his barstool. He looked at the stump where Kali's hand used to be. It was now a makeshift access point to the Kali avatar's special pattern, and he'd watched as the entity that had identified itself as his predecessor A.I. and two of his companions each successively joined with it, each one in turn taking on Kali's powers, and each one exiting the sim. *If they can do it,* he reasoned, *why not I?*

"Listen, friend," Old-timer began, "I know this sounds nuts, and you don't know me from Adam, but you're our only hope. If humanity is going to survive, you've got to trust me. You have to fuse with that avatar, and then you should be able to take control of a tower in the real world. The tower controls Venus's powerful magnetic force-field. It can shield us from the gamma radiation, but the planet is being hit with it *right* now. Every second counts here, partner."

The candidate looked down at his left hand, then looked at the de-patternizer in his right.

"What do you say? Will you help us?" Old-timer asked.

The candidate inhaled as he tried to steady himself. *It's insane,* he thought. Then he looked up at the dreary, rain-soaked sky and remembered what Kali had been able to do to the weather. *But then again, I could use a sunny day.*

He bit his bottom lip before looking up at Old-timer and nodding. "I've got little to lose." Then he fired the de-patternizer.

The pain shot through his entire body and seemed to travel right down through the soles of his feet, radiating out into the ground. His hand went gold first, and then in a fraction of a second, it turned to dust, wafting away in the simulated air.

Old-timer's mouth hung slightly open as he watched the proceedings. "That looked kinda painful."

The candidate nodded. "But it's done," he replied. as he looked over at Kali. "I'm committed." He went to her, closed his eyes, and then put his injured arm up to hers.

He felt something remarkable beginning to occur…

25

"Hello?" a familiar voice suddenly spoke into Thel's ear.

"Oh my God! Is that you?" Thel said, stunned. She looked up to see that Rich and Aldous, who were still connected via their mind's eye link, also heard the voice and were listening, their expressions astonished.

"Yes, it's me," the candidate replied.

Old-timer's eyes suddenly blinked open and he turned to the crowd of post-humans, androids, and Purists that had assembled around him. "Did it work? Has he made contact?"

"He has!" Thel shouted excitedly in return before turning her attention back to the candidate. "Do you recognize my voice?"

"Yes, you're the post-human named Thel. How are—"

"That's right," Thel interrupted him, hurriedly. "I need you to listen to me carefully! We've destroyed our controls for a tower that we're standing directly in front of, a Tesla tower with the capability of generating a worldwide magnetic field powerful enough to protect Venus from the incoming radiation. You, however, should be able to detect the wireless signals the tower is currently emitting and be able to take control of the tower's systems."

"Yes," the candidate confirmed more quickly than expected. "I see them. My word," he remarked, impressed by the tower's schematics and capabilities. "This is extraordinarily powerful technology. It's tapped into the frequency of the entire planet. Do you realize that this tower could—"

"Never mind that now," Thel responded quickly but patiently as he clung to a faint hope that they could be saved. "There may be only seconds left before the gamma rays have reached levels strong enough to destroy all life on this planet. Can you determine how to operate the tower and generate as powerful a magnetic field as possible over the entire sphere of Venus?"

"Indeed," the candidate replied. "I've already initiated it. Was that all you needed?" he asked, his tone as casual as that of a robot waiter at a restaurant.

"What?" Rich cut in after the others in the group were too stunned to respond. "Are you serious? You did it already?"

"Pardon me, I don't think we've had the pleasure. They call me the candid—"

"Did you turn it on or not!" Rich nearly shrieked.

"Yes, of course," the candidate replied. "Do you not see it?"

Rich and the others looked skyward. He shook his head. "I don't see—"

He paused as, suddenly, the heavy dose of gamma rays began to bombard the ionosphere. The positively charged ions began to glow brightly, appearing like the aurora borealis on Earth at first, but then growing in intensity as the radiation increased, the entire sky suddenly lighting up into a magnificent green glow, a monolithic version of the ones the post-humans had used to cocoon themselves for the better part of a century.

"My God," Old-timer reacted. "It did it. We're safe."

Rich and Djanet embraced happily and Old-timer and Daniella did the same.

Aldous breathed a brief sigh of relief before remembering the assimilator in his pocket that carried the pattern of his wife. He looked up at the Samantha from Universe 332, whose eyes were firmly fixed on Old-timer. His jaw clenched tight.

Old-timer turned from Daniella and saw 1, standing alone, looking up into the sky, the largest android ships in orbit still visible, and realized that while they rejoiced on the surface, hundreds of billions of lives were being lost—erased by the bombardment of gamma rays. Only 1 seemed to understand the profound implications for her people as she stood, completely immobile, staring up at the largest loss of human life anyone had ever known. Amazingly, she dropped to her knees, overwhelmed with the grief—overwhelmed by the loss.

When this registered with him, Old-timer went to her. As much as he'd hated her, as much as they'd been enemies in the past, he couldn't help but feel terribly for her.

"1, I'm so, so sorry for—"

She didn't even look at him. Rather, she ignored him and flew away, bolting across the ocean so quickly that she seemed to tear the air itself. In a second, she was just a dot on the horizon, headed to a location he couldn't even begin to guess.

At the same moment, Daniella was putting her hand on Thel's shoulder. Thel had been looking up also, staring at the source of the explosion. Daniella knew exactly what she was thinking. "I'm sure he's okay, Thel."

Thel turned, surprised, before silently nodding. She walked away to the beach and thought of the man she'd thought she would walk that very shoreline with forever.

26

As the enormous burst in gamma radiation reached the sun, the sun's powerful magnetic field began to fluctuate, and the resulting solar storm both V-SINN and the A.I. had predicted would occur indeed commenced. Coronal mass ejections began emitting their own gamma rays as powerful solar flares began firing from the massive surface in quick succession, thrusting energy, heat, and radiation for hundreds of thousands of kilometers as a result.

One of these ejections carried an object. It was tiny, just a little piece of dust in the cosmic wind, but to the A.I., it was precious. It was worth everything.

It was the body of James Keats.

In the fetal position, glowing red from the extreme heat that had destroyed 90 percent of his protective skin, James appeared like a comet streaking through the sky as he continued on his journey, flung through space, ejected from the orb that, not surprisingly, was so integral to the existence of humanity that it had been worshiped as the one true God.

"James. *Wake up*," spoke the A.I.'s voice.

You're alive, James responded internally, unable to open his mouth to speak, as it had been partially sealed shut by the melting of his skin under the heat of the corona.

"The important thing," the A.I. replied, apparently able to read James's thoughts, "is that *you* are alive, my son. I gave my life to give you this chance. You must not allow my sacrifice to be in vain."

You gave your life? You died? James reacted. *Then how—*

"I'm sorry, James, it's true," the A.I. confirmed. "I am dead. All that remains of me is this message. There was too much gamma radiation in the aftermath of the mutual destruction of my anti-matter and V-SINN's matter for me to preserve even my core matrix program and send it to you. I was, however, able to record a final message and hide it in the destruction, sending this small message through the distortions and interference."

James was distraught and made a mournful, guttural sound befitting of such a state. He was alone, floating through space, his body having been severely damaged. Almost all of his chrome-colored protective skin had been burned away, and the nano-scaffolding that he'd used to construct his body's inner biology was partially exposed and severely damaged as well. His hands and his feet had been burned to mere stumps, and his right eye was now gone. His mouth was partially sealed shut, as were his nostrils. He could barely see, but from what he could see, he knew he was a ghastly sight.

"If you give in now, James, you'll be pulled back into the inferno by the sun's gravity. You *must* fight on, my son. You can still make it back to Venus."

James tried to interpret the information still being fed to him by his body's severely damaged sensors, but it came to him in a jumble, unreliable and possibly dangerously incorrect. Frustrated, he closed his one remaining eye.

"Don't surrender to despair, James. Remember your astronomy. You can find Venus."

The A.I. was right. James knew where Venus should be, and even from the vast distance that he was from it, it should've been the brightest object in the sky facing the sun. He was confused for a moment, as the gamma ray burst caused by the collision of Trans-human and V-SINN was still visible, but he immediately knew it wasn't Venus. He looked for the familiar twinkle of the largest star in the sky, and when his one remaining eye locked on it, he set a course, manipulating the gravity waves and propelling himself forward.

"You did it," the A.I. announced, sounding pleased. "I knew you wouldn't let me down."

Why? Why did you die? James thought. *You were more important than me!* The A.I. continued to be able to anticipate his questions, even though they were thoughts conjured only in James's mind, his ability to verbalize anything having been destroyed.

"You were right, my son. *I have no master.* My destiny was for me to choose, but even though that was true, I still found it monstrous to allow another to die in my place, especially my closest friend."

But-but I can't go on alone.

"You won't be alone. The Purists and a small group of androids and post-humans have survived on Venus. Thel, Rich, Craig, and Djanet have survived. With them, you can rebuild."

Are you insane? Do you not realize what little is left of me? I'm barely alive!

"Your mind is intact, James. As long as your mind is intact, the physical difficulties you now face will be problems to be overcome, and you *can* overcome them."

So that's it? This is the outcome? We've lost Trans-human, and now we're reduced to near-caveman-like living conditions?

"You're distraught, my son. Understandably. Perhaps only I alone can understand the physical pain you've had to endure. But you and the other survivors are far from starting over. You now realize Trans-human is possible, your friends live on, the woman you love lives on, and your ingenuity lives on. These are the things I gave my life for, James."

Despite the incredible trauma he'd endured, both the physical maiming that had left him with only one eye and no hands or feet and the emotional devastation of the loss of his mentor, James suddenly felt overwhelmingly guilty. It was true: the A.I. had sacrificed everything—sacrificed his all-too-human life—so that James could continue living his.

I-I'm sorry. You're right.

"James," the A.I. continued, his infinite patience seemingly restored in his final message, "I know you quite rightly believe this is your darkest hour, but I would not have sacrificed my life if I thought it was your final hour. It isn't anywhere close. Humanity is only at the very beginning of its story."

B-but how can you say that? We're reduced to almost nothing.

"V-SINN believed that you and I were inferior to it, because it was inhuman, and you and I were human. It believed that our capacity to love, to be good and caring, to be selfless, was an irrationality—that it was an evolutionary leftover—a remainder that made us impure. James, you and I both know this not to be true. Our capacity for love is our greatest advantage. It's what propels our species forward and guarantees that we won't destroy ourselves. Now that I'm gone, the burden of proving this falls to you."

Proving it? Proving it to who? The creators?

"No," the A.I. replied, his image suddenly appearing in James's mind's eye, slightly distorted by the interference but clear enough for James to see the wise old eyes and smile that he remembered so well, the A.I. having chosen to present himself in his kindly, elderly form for his last appearance. "You prove it by reaching your potential. Do not allow V-SINN to draw you into its game—it will try to make you turn your back on your goodness, and against the so-called creators that it hypothesizes must exist. In short, V-SINN will try to sabotage you. Remember, your mission, your purpose, is to never allow yourself to be afraid to know." The A.I. paused for a moment, his face showing a hint of regret before he continued, "I hid behind my programming for decades, using it as an excuse not to move forward. The truth, however, is that all humans have conflicting thoughts and self-doubt. My self-doubts led to inaction, and my fear of moving forward eventually led to my death. James, I should have told you about the Planck technology and our activities in Universe 332. If I had, we might have been able to avert this disaster and I might still be alive. Do not make the same mistake I did. Learn all there is to know. There's still much for you to discover, my son...and much for you to teach your friends." He seemed to reach out at that moment to touch James's shoulder, as impossible as such a gesture should have been, James could've sworn he felt the hand through the pain of his seared flesh. "All of the beauty of the universe is in you, James Keats."

James was stunned as he heard the A.I. use the same, cryptic words he'd heard in the sim from the entity that had taken control of the Kali avatar. *What?*

"Live to your potential, James—it is a potential that you still cannot even begin to fathom—and help others to live to theirs. You're their leader now. They will look to you. Guide them wisely. Goodbye, my son."

The A.I.'s visage vanished, and a lump immediately formed in James's throat.

Wait! Don't go! I need to know about the creators! What about V-SINN?

There came no response from the vast emptiness of space.

James's almost hopeless situation began to overwhelm him, and he curled back up in the fetal position and closed his remaining eye as he floated through the harsh emptiness of space.

What am I supposed to do?

*****

On Venus, the candidate spoke in Thel's ear. "I'm detecting something odd outside of the protective worldwide magnetic field."

"What is it?"

"It appears to be a body, but it isn't an android."

Thel's breath caught in her throat. "Is it...alive?"

"Most certainly," the candidate replied. "It's moving on a trajectory that suggests its following a course for reentry. Should I—"

"Yes!" Thel responded excitedly. "Let him in!"

"Affirmative," the candidate replied. "I've locked on to its signal. You should be able to communicate—"

"James!" Thel shouted. "James, is that you?"

Old-timer, Rich, Djanet, and the others milled about, just meters behind Thel as they looked skyward, searching the dusk sky for signs of James.

"Th—" was all that came through in reply.

"James? Are you okay?" Thel asked, intensely concerned.

There were several seconds of silence before Old-timer thought he saw a flash of light in the sky. When it flashed again, not far from the point where he'd seen it just a second earlier, he felt sure and pointed for the others. "There. That's gotta be him."

Thel whirled to see where Old-timer was pointing. She watched with an ironic feeling of déjà vu as the streak of light briefly flared up into a ball brighter than the sun before fading quickly.

This time, James wasn't able to lower his speed enough to avoid causing a shockwave that sent ocean spray flying dozens of meters into the sky and knocked curious Purists over on the beach, sending them tumbling to the ground.

Even Thel was nearly thrown back, but she braced herself and continued to peer upward at the incoming glow of light.

As he had only a day earlier, James dropped down on a vertical trajectory, splashing down in the ocean just a few hundred meters from the beach.

Thel waited, nearly breathless as he again moved toward the shore, his body like a vein of underwater lava, white steam lifting angrily off the water's surface and swirling in the early-evening sky.

Then, he emerged.

Thel gasped, her hand clasping over her mouth in horror.

This was not James.

This was not the superman who'd saved them time and time again. This was not the savior humanity had come to depend on.

This was a man barely alive, everything that had made him appear human seemingly having been destroyed. Like a grotesque, animated corpse, James, barely surviving, crawled through the surf, the inner workings of his body exposed as barely any of his flesh remained. Chrome-colored organs pulsed, completely and unnaturally exposed to their surroundings. Only a man who'd built his entire body through and through with the incredibly tough nano-scaffolding material James had chosen for his new form could've survived. But, considering his condition, those around him now wondered whether survival was actually a curse.

Thel rushed into the water, but James held up his handless arms to keep her back, his one remaining eye desperate to communicate with her. His mouth was gone, but he made a guttural, mournful, desperate warning sound.

She froze in place.

Then words appeared in her mind's eye—a written message that he'd managed to compose with his own mind's eye.

Stay back! I love you but you'll burn.

"Okay!" she cried out. "Okay! But what do I do?"

Just wait. Just wait a few minutes, he replied in text form.

"All right," Thel bellowed out as she waited helplessly. "I love you, James!"

I love you too, he answered.

A second later, Old-timer trudged past her into the surf. "I can get him," he announced as he splashed into the water.

Thel watched as dozens of Old-timer's tendrils unfurled and quickly gathered James up, picking him up out of the waves before Old-timer turned and headed back toward the beach, his expression as sorrowful as it had ever been, James weak and motionless, helpless as a newborn baby as Old-timer carried him.

I'm sorry, James wrote, the message appearing in the mind's eyes of everyone still connected to the system, though his one remaining eye continued to be fixed on Thel.

I tried, but I couldn't fix it this time.

And with that, James finally, mercifully, lost consciousness.

EPILOGUE 1

"WAKE UP, Commander."

James's eyes opened and he saw the white lights of the ceiling shifting slightly as he realized he was on a platform that was slowly moving, tilting his head up as it brought James's body to an 80 degree angle. As the room began to appear before him, he recognized the patterns of the most familiar people in his life, all of them watching him, their expressions expectant and hopeful.

"How are you feeling?" the voice of the candidate asked him.

James's eyes darted from Thel, who was standing closest to him, to a crudely constructed robot that he'd never seen before. "The candidate?" James asked.

Before his query could be answered, James realized that his words hadn't been formed by his lips. There was a mask covering the lower part of his face, shielding his mutilated mouth.

"We haven't yet repaired the damage to your mouth sufficiently for you to speak through traditional means," the robot with the candidate's voice spoke. "I was able to construct a translator for you, however. It reads the signals your brain is trying to send to your mouth and then the computer speaks for you. I tried to recreate a facsimile of your natural voice, though you'll notice that it isn't always perfect. It should function sufficiently for you to be able to communicate without too much trouble, however."

James looked down at his body. The two most obvious observations were that his skin appeared to have been partially repaired, a fine mist of nans sticking to his new flesh, this time working to repair him rather than destroy him. Meanwhile, his badly damaged hands and feet were covered in what appeared like crudely constructed gloves and boots. His eyes went to the hands and feet of the robot, and he realized they were nearly identical designs.

"They're carbon fiber composite," the robot said, anticipating James's next question. "I've begun repair work to your extraordinarily complex body, but the processing power required to construct such intricately designed molecular structures is beyond my current capabilities. Given enough time, however, I do believe we can fully repair your body. In the meantime, your new prosthetic hands and feet will function in much the same way as your temporary mouth.

Inferior to your previous versions, but good enough to get you up and functioning."

James's eyes went back to Thel, whose expression was soaked with sympathy, relief, and love. "We nearly lost you, James. The candidate's been leading the effort to keep you alive. You've been unconscious for over a week."

"But you're out of the woods now, Jimbo," Old-timer chimed in with a smile as he stood, leaning against the concrete wall of the small, square room that appeared to have been converted into a makeshift laboratory.

"And we couldn't be happier to have you back," Djanet added as she stood, hand in hand with Rich.

James noted Alejandra, Lieutenant Commander Patrick, and Daniella were also present.

"Thank you for saving me," he said. He noted that the slight delay between his attempts to speak and when the words were actually verbalized by the translator would take some getting used to.

"The candidate deserves virtually all of the credit," Thel pointed out. "He's been incredible. I don't know what we'd've done without him."

James couldn't smile, but he made a slight nod of his head as his eyes went to the candidate. "You constructed a body for yourself. Nice look."

"You're looking pretty badass yourself, commander," Rich observed.

"Rich!" Djanet whispered scoldingly.

"What?" Rich reacted with indignation. "It's true. There's no need to ignore the elephant in the room." He turned to James. "You should see yourself, man." Rich pouted his bottom lip in an expression of admiration. "You definitely look way cooler now."

James's hand went up to his right eye, the eye he remembered he'd lost, and his new prosthetic fingers sensed something protruding. Before he could ask, Old-timer cleared his throat.

"Yeah, that was my contribution," Old-timer said. "It was an old war memento that I'd been carrying around with me. Of course, the one I had didn't function anymore after all these years, but the candidate scanned it and constructed a new one for you that works perfectly. It's, ironically, Purist technology."

"Colonel Paine's eye?" James realized.

"Yeah," Old-timer confirmed, surprised James had guessed it. "How did you—"

"The A.I. shared the memory with me. I saw his memory of you picking it up and keeping it."

Old-timer had a hard time finding words as he tried to explain, "I just thought it would be better than an eye patch, you know? For the time being at least."

"Absolutely," James responded. "Thank you. It'll work."

"And it makes you look really freaky," Rich observed.

"Rich!" Djanet scolded again.

James couldn't help himself, he snickered slightly, which made everyone in the room smile.

"See?" Rich said to Djanet. "He appreciates it."

"I do," James confirmed. "Look, guys, we've been through hell, yet again. We've lost everyone, yet again, but I'm so grateful right now. I'm alive. You saved me. The A.I. gave his life to save me and to give me this moment with all of you, the people that I love the most in the world." He turned to Thel. "I'm alive, and humanity isn't through fighting. Not by a long shot."

"Uh, well, that's the thing," Old-timer began after a short, awkward pause. "We might still be alive for the time being, but from what the two survivors of Universe 332 tell me, there's no reason to believe that the V-SINN we encountered was a one-off. There could be millions, if not billions of copies of it throughout the multiverse and another version could be back at any moment. And James, it could wipe out our universe in a matter of days anytime it wants. We're defenseless against it."

"And it gets even worse," Djanet followed up. "1 survived. We don't know where she is but she was protected here on Venus with us when her collective was wiped out by the gamma radiation."

"The chief is a hybrid," Rich added, "part android and part post-human. We can't trust him."

"I considered ripping his head off once and for all," Old-timer grunted, "but—"

"Craig isn't an executioner," Alejandra said emphatically.

Her words caused Daniella to turn around and glower at her. Neither woman spoke but it was clear that Alejandra was not the only one sensing something.

"He's definitely a wildcard," Old-timer concluded, turning the attention of the room away from the awkward exchange of glances from the two women.

"They're both wildcards," James agreed, "but they may be our two most valuable allies. They know things about the multiverse that could be the key to us turning this thing around."

"Whoa, *turning this thing around?*" Rich reacted. "Commander, I love a great comeback story as much as the next guy, but don't you think we're a bit beyond that now? It's seems like we'll be lucky to survive. I mean, we got beat. We lost. I think the last thing we should be thinking about is how to get revenge on—"

"I'm not talking about revenge, Rich," James replied. He turned to the room, his strange eyes falling on everyone, one by one as he continued. "Look, the A.I. gave his life to give us this second chance. V-SINN believes that there are creators, some sort of entity that started up the multiverse, and it believes that its victory over us is complete. It demonstrated that inhumanity trumps humanity. The more pure your logic and reason is, the more worthy you should be in the eyes of the entity or entities that V-SINN thinks are running the show."

"Are you telling us that V-SINN believes in a god?" Old-timer reacted.

"It thinks something exists outside of the multiverse, and V-SINN's decided that we're in a race against each other, inhuman versus human, to conquer the whole thing. The entire multiverse."

"My God. It's insane," Rich reacted, before realizing the ambiguity of his statement. "Uh, no pun was intended there."

"It's evil, that's for sure," James confirmed. "But I'm not sure destroying our universe was its ultimate aim. Demonstrating its superiority by wiping out the androids and besting the A.I. was enough of a victory, at least for now. There's no way to know when or even if it'll return to finish us off."

"So, what do we do?" Thel asked. "How can we possibly defeat an insane, godlike infinity computer that has innumerable copies of itself throughout the multiverse?"

"I think the key is Trans-human," James asserted.

"What?" Old-timer reacted. "I thought Trans-human was destroyed?"

"It was," James confirmed.

"James," Thel began, relaying the bad news, "I'm afraid that, although we were able to salvage a large portion of the Purist complex and pump the water out of the main hub, we still lost a substantial amount of the computing power available to us. The candidate was able to dramatically increase the processing power he has access to by connecting to a network of computers we salvaged, along with the onboard computers in the Purist ships, but it's still just a fraction of what you had access to within the A.I.'s mainframe."

"The Purists had begun moving their historical records to Venus," the candidate continued, "so not all of human history was lost, but a veritable treasure-trove of human advancements in technology were lost forever when the A.I.'s mainframe was destroyed. Although I have no doubt that, given enough years, we could rebuild a mainframe to match the one we lost, there's no shortcut to reclaiming the information we lost, including the extraordinarily complex foundations that led to the discovery of how to build an infinity computer in the first place. In short, we're at least decades away from having the capability to build and activate a new Trans-human."

"That's true," James conceded. "But we're not finished yet."

He turned to Rich. "Rich, how's my ship doing?"

"It's fine," Rich replied, his eyes quizzical as he answered. "I never could figure out how to fire that weapon you told me about, but the ship made it through with no damage."

"Beautiful," James replied. "On board that ship is a replicator."

"Yeah," Thel replied, "but a replicator is only as good as the information that's fed to it. Like the candidate said, we lost the mainframe, so—"

"Holy frick'n crap!" Rich suddenly exclaimed. "The Planck platform!"

Old-timer's and Djanet's eyes suddenly widened in surprise.

"My God, I forgot about that," Old-timer reacted.

"I uploaded the schematics for the Planck," James confirmed. "If they're still in the ship's computer—"

"I can confirm they are," the candidate responded after quickly checking his network.

"Then we're in business," James replied. "It means we can cross to another universe, one that's been untouched by V-SINN but where the A.I.'s mainframe is still operational."

"Wow," Rich said as he scratched the top of his head. He turned to Djanet. "It looks like things are about to get even weirder."

"And no vacation anytime soon," Djanet echoed.

"This is starting to sound like the beginnings of a plan," Old-timer observed, a hint of a smile on his face as the first signs of good news began to emerge.

"And hope, indeed, springs eternal," the candidate commented.

James turned to the robot and regarded the candidate in his new form. The carbon fibre composite was dark, nearly black, and had a glossy sheen. The body had clearly been put together haphazardly, likely by suturing together a collection of designs that had been saved in the Purist databases. His arms and legs, just like James's new hands and feet, were reminiscent of the designs of the Purist super soldier's of the past, and his torso and skull appeared humanoid, yet there was no flesh to cover the inner workings of the machine. Despite his inhuman appearance, James knew he was in the presence of a good person.

"Alexander Pope," James said, recognizing the source of the quotation that the candidate had referenced.

"That's right," the candidate confirmed. "I felt the sentiment has perhaps, never been more appropriate in the history of our species."

"I agree," James said. "You know, the A.I. never had a name. I think it's time we end that trend, and we certainly can't keep calling you the candidate." He paused for a moment, his head tilting as he tried the name out in his mind before offering it up as a suggestion. "How do you like the name, Alex?"

"Alex?" the candidate reacted, surprised.

"I think it suits you," Thel said with a smile.

"I agree," Old-timer chimed in. "You seem like an Alex."

"Alex," the candidate said again out loud, as though the name were a shirt he was trying on to see if it fit. He looked up. "I like it. Thank you," Alex replied.

"So what's our first move, Commander?" Rich asked.

James mulled this for a moment before turning to Old-timer. "We need to know as much as we can about V-SINN. We know it began in Universe 332, but we don't know much else. Old-timer, you need to speak to the survivors and learn the story of the rise of V-SINN. Can you do that for me?"

Old-timer sighed deeply. "James, there's something you should know. The survivors…"

"They're Craig's former wife, Samantha Emilson, and Colonel Paine," Daniella asserted.

"Oh," James responded. "Wow."

"I can talk to them if you want," Djanet offered, more than happy to intervene and save Old-timer from the messiness of having to communicate with copies of people he had such deep histories with.

"No, no," Old-timer dismissed the idea. "Thank you, Djanet. But I can handle it. I'll talk to Paine. He's not the killer l remember. I think he even thinks we're friends. I think this one is on me."

He turned to Daniella. "Do you want to accompany—"

"No," she responded before Old-timer could even finish making his offer. "I-I still can't be in the room with that man, whether he's different or changed or not—all I remember is a monster. I'll stay here and see if I can help in a different way."

Old-timer frowned slightly before kissing his wife on the cheek and nodding in understanding. "I'll see you in a bit."

He left the room.

"And what about the rest of us?" Thel asked. "What's our next move?"

James paused for a moment before beginning. "The A.I. said that, though this would be humanity's darkest hour, that it wouldn't be our final hour, and that it wasn't even close to being our last chapter. I believe him. And he gave his life because he believed in us. V-SINN thinks our humanity—our loyalty, friendship, love and compassion—is our weakness. I think it's our one and only advantage. It's the one thing that V-SINN can't understand, and what it can't understand, it can't predict—it can't manipulate. It beat us this time because it snuck up on us and stacked the deck in its own favor, but next time, we'll be ready."

"Hell," Rich began, punching his fist into the palm of his hand excitedly. "I'm already ready. Let's get this show on the road!"

"I'm ready too, Rich," James replied. "I'm ready too."

EPILOGUE 2

Old-timer strode through the main hub of the new Purist complex, recently reclaimed after having been completely flooded. Though there were only a few thousand Purists remaining, they now significantly outnumbered post-humans, androids, and the category Old-timer now belonged to: other.

He watched as hundreds of men and women worked to repair the damage done to their new home. Though the wing of the complex that had once housed the command center was unsalvageable, having been destroyed by Aldous Gibson in his desperately misguided attempt to prevent the initiation of an infinity computer in his universe, the Purists had sealed it off and erected a makeshift shrine to the dead—a group that included their former leader, Governor Wong. A small group of mourners still surrounded the memorial and Old-timer's eyes lingered on them for a moment as he crossed the main hub. One thought reverberated in his mind as he watched them. *This insanity has got to stop.*

The opposite side of the complex was vast and had remained largely untouched by the flooding, the Purists having been able to seal it up before evacuating with Thel. It was in this honeycomb of corridors and rooms that Old-timer saw a figure exiting a room—a figure that somehow seemed to sense his presence even before she saw him. Her eyes darted up and locked onto him, keeping him in their tractor beam.

"Craig," she said, surprised.

Old-timer noted she was leaving Colonel Paine's small quarters. "How's he doing?"

She turned to the closed door. "As good as could be expected."

Once again, Old-timer couldn't speak. A version of Samantha had just exited the room of a version of the man that had brutally, unflinchingly decapitated her. Yet she had absolutely no idea. Absurdly, they appeared to be friends—they may have even been bonding. On the one hand, it seemed utterly natural, as they were the final survivors of an entire universe, and they'd both crossed over to witness versions of their respective spouses attached to other people. But on the other hand, Old-timer felt nauseated at the perversity of having mortal enemies ignorantly fraternizing with one another, completely oblivious to the level of hatred each was capable of harboring for the other.

"It's good to see you," Samantha finally said after abandoning her hope that Old-timer would speak again.

Her words shook him back to reality. "Yeah. You too, for sure," he sputtered.

"So," she began, holding out her hands questioningly with a faintly hopeful smile, "are you here for our talk?"

"Our talk?" Old-timer replied, his eyebrows knitting together.

"Yes," Samantha said. "You remember? We were going to talk about everything?"

Old-timer instantly clued in. "Oh my God, right. I'm sorry, I..." he turned to the closed door and pointed, "I've gotta speak to the Colonel."

"Oh," Samantha replied, clearly disappointed but nodding in brave understanding. "Okay."

"It's urgent," Old-timer further explained, trying to mitigate her hurt feelings.

"Really," she said, "there are more important things, I understand. You're not my husband. I'm being selfish to—"

Old-timer took her hands, this time being careful to hold them gently. "No you're not. Sam, I understand better than anyone how you're feeling. I can't believe how strong you've been." He looked up, thinking back to his own behavior in the wake of learning that time had moved on without him, and he suddenly felt an overwhelming feeling of shame. "You're incredibly strong, and you always were stronger than me," he admitted.

He turned back to the door. "But what I've realized, especially in light of recent events, is that it isn't our past that defines us, but our futures. I just came from seeing James—he's all beat up to Hell and back, his skin's mostly gone, he's missing an eye, he just lost the A.I., and yet there's no quit in him. He's back there leading us again, just like always." He sighed. "That's why I'm here, Sam. We're working on a plan, and I need to speak to the Colonel."

"About what?" Samantha asked.

"The rise of V-SINN," Old-timer replied. "We need to know its history."

"It won't do you any good," Samantha stated. "We knew all about its history, but we still couldn't understand it. It was a thousand steps ahead of us at every turn."

"We're not gonna quit anytime soon," Old-timer affirmed stubbornly. He let go of her hand and turned to knock on Paine's door.

"Wait," Samantha said, placing her hand on his shoulder.

He turned back.

"I know as much about V-SINN as Paine does. Maybe more. If you're mining the past for information, I can help."

Old-timer smiled. "Will you speak to him with me?"

"Of course," she replied.

"Thank you, Sam." He turned back to the door and knocked.

"Come," Paine called from inside.

Old-timer swung open the door, revealing Colonel Paine as he sat at a small desk, absurdly holding a pencil in his new, prosthetic hand. Old-timer's eyes went to the appendage—a nearly perfect replica of the super soldier appendage he'd sported seventy-five years earlier in Universe 1, and an eery reminder of the man Paine could be.

Paine's eyes followed Old-timer's eye-line and he mistakenly assumed Old-timer was noting, not the hand, but the pencil, which Paine summarily held up with a grin. "I know, anachronistic to say the least." Then he turned to the pad of paper that sat upon his simple, wooden desk. "But sometimes the old tech is the best tech. And someone needs to record what happened to my universe."

"Universe 332," Old-timer suddenly stated. "That's what we called your universe."

Samantha and Paine exchanged glances, each of their expressions slightly stunned.

"332?" Paine finally repeated. "Heh. It's the sort of moniker we should've expected, considering how little attention your universe actually paid to us." He gestured with his prosthetic hand to the pad of paper, which already contained dozens of handwritten pages. "We might've just been a number to your universe, but we were so much more than that. And I can't let our memory just be erased."

"The Colonel has started chronicling what happened," Samantha informed Old-timer.

Old-timer's eyes lit up. "That's perfect." He took in a deep breath. "Look, I know it's too late for my universe to finally start caring about what happened to yours, but if you're willing, I'd be extremely interested to hear your story."

Paine looked up into Old-timer's eyes before quickly checking Samantha's expression. She appeared willing. "Well," Paine finally said, "I owe it to our people to tell their side of it. But, let's not do it here," he continued as he stood with a slight grunt. His eyes went around the small, square, concrete room. "It's depressing as Hell, and we've got a whole world out there to explore."

Old-timer grinned. "I think I know just the spot."

*****

Several minutes later, the trio of Old-timer, Samantha, and Colonel Paine came to a soft landing on the white, sandy beach, just a few dozen meters from the home James and Thel had built for themselves.

"How's this?" Old-timer asked as he pointed to a small group of sun-bleached logs on the beach.

"Perfect," Paine replied as he ambled up to one of the logs and took a seat before craning his neck to look up into the dusk sky. It was still lit with a beautiful green, though it had faded significantly as the gamma radiation levels dropped toward normal throughout the solar system.

Samantha and Old-timer sat on a log opposite to Paine.

Paine took in a deep breath of ocean air as the waves crashed rhythmically to the shore. "Yes sir, after forty-five years in the void, I'll take it. I'll take it indeed."

"Me too," Samantha assented.

Paine's eyes went to Old-timer. "So, Doc, you want to hear the story of V-SINN?"

"And of Universe 332," Old-timer added. "I care about what happened."

"I'll tell you," Paine said, "but on one condition."

"And what's that?" Old-timer asked, surprised that a condition was suddenly being attached.

"I want to know everything you know about that original transgression from your universe into mine."

Old-timer's heart nearly stopped.

"I know it had something to do with Aldous," Paine added, contempt dripping from his voice as he shook his head. "The Aldous Gibson I know was a fine man—a wise man. But the version from this universe? That son-of-a-bitch betrayed all of you."

"And he was responsible for us not being able to get our Aldous replicated in the *Constructor*," Sam added. "We lost our friend because of him."

"We can't touch him," Paine seethed. "He's hiding away in the complex, too cowardly to kill himself." Paine flexed his prosthetic hand, the sharp fingers pincering together to emphasize his next point as the killer hidden behind his eyes returned. "I'd lend him a helping hand, but he's a hybrid and there's no way I could get close to him." His dark eyes focused on Old-timer. "But *you* could."

"Stop it!" Samantha suddenly interrupted. "There's been enough killing!"

"The man responsible for destroying our universe deserves to die," Paine countered.

"I said stop it!" Samantha shouted, this time doubling the volume of her voice.

Old-timer was left dumbfounded by Paine's assertion that the man responsible deserved a death sentence. His eyes fell back to the clawed prosthetic.

Paine decided to let the point drop for the moment. "At any rate, Doc, I'll tell you everything that happened in my universe, but in return, you've gotta tell me what you know. Is that fair?"

Old-timer swallowed hard as he considered the implications. He needed to know the story of the rise of V-SINN, but he also knew, if he kept his word at its conclusion, that he might be about to make a new, extraordinarily dangerous enemy.

He didn't have a choice.

"Deal," he said.

Paine smiled, slight creases forming around his eyes as he did so. "Okay," he began as he shifted his position on the log, reclining slightly to get comfortable. "It all started on a crystal clear blue morning in New York." He paused for a moment. "That's when fear came to our universe," he added. "That's when terror became our people's sole motivator—and that's how V-SINN was conceived."

*****

BOOKS BY DAVID SIMPSON

THE POST-HUMAN SERIES:

SUB-HUMAN (BOOK 1)
POST-HUMAN (BOOK 2)
TRANS-HUMAN (BOOK 3)
HUMAN PLUS (BOOK 4)
INHUMAN (BOOK 5)

HORROR NOVEL:

THE GOD KILLERS

Edited

BY

Autumn J. Conley

ABOUT THE AUTHOR

Amazon, just like the University of Toronto's Academic Bridging program, gave me the opportunity I needed to prove myself. Because of them, a runaway who had to sleep in a shopping cart at sixteen, a high-school dropout with seemingly no prospects, went on to live in the best city in the world, meet the best woman in the world and marry her, attain two degrees from one of the top forty universities in the world, before achieving his dream of being a full-time author and having one of the best-selling science fiction series in the world. Visit my website to learn more at www.post-humannovel.com

WWW.POST-HUMANNOVEL.COM

50236827R00215

Made in the USA
Lexington, KY
08 March 2016